GILLIAN E. HAMER
SACRED LAKE

THE GOLD DETECTIVES III

TRISKELE BOOKS

First Edition, 2017.

Sacred Lake Copyright © 2017 by Gillian E. Hamer.

The moral rights of the author has been asserted. All rights reserved. No part of this publication may be reproduced, distributed or transmitted in any form or by any means (including photocopying, recording or other electronic or mechanical methods) without the prior written permission of both the copyright owner and the publisher, except in the case of brief quotations embodied in critical reviews and certain non-commercial uses permitted by copyright law. For permission requests, write to the publisher, addressed "Attention: Permissions Coordinator," at the email address below.

Cover design: www.jdsmith-design.com
Printed in the UK by Lightning Source.
Published by G E Hamer.
All enquiries to contact@gillianhamer.com.

ISBN KINDLE - 978-0-9934377-3-7
PAPERBACK - 978-0-9934388-4-4

Acknowledgements

Another year, another book, and one I've really enjoyed writing. With each new book in the series, I seem to get inside the character's heads a little more - until it's hard to leave!

As ever, I have to give huge thanks to my Triskele colleagues, who despite having their own troubles, have supported me as much with this book as with my first, and I know how far my writing has come because of their invaluable help. So, thank you, I couldn't do it without you – Jane Dixon-Smith, Jill Marsh, Liza Perrat and Catriona Troth.

And to my mum and Maysie and my lovely little island of Anglesey - you all, in your own way, help give me the freedom to write and I appreciate it so much.

Thanks to every single person who reads my books, your kind words and reviews make the hard work worthwhile. I look forward to your thoughts on this one. Enjoy!

PROLOGUE

JANUARY 1st 1977

I jump the gate and run for my life. Lungs on fire, legs pounding, I zig-zag through a misty tunnel of high hedgerows and out onto a road. I stumble along the centre white line, unbalanced and disorientated, one way, then the other, praying to see a car. The road is an empty black strip disappearing into the distance. Which way? I stop, hands on knees, panting, head turning, back and forth. Come on, which way!

A muffled cough spurs me onwards. The road leaves me too exposed. I leap a ditch, heading for the cover of trees, and the distant lights of houses beyond. Willing my legs to move, not to fail me now. Breath swirls around me as I stumble like a blind man, crashing into unseen obstacles but not daring to slow my pace. Slipping, sliding, arms wind-milling.

My toe snags a tree root and I hit the frozen ground. Air escapes with a whoosh, and I bite back a cry, the tang of rusted iron filling my mouth. My eyes flood with tears that bring a little warmth to my cheeks, and I strain to see and hear in the dark silence.

I need a second to catch my breath and refocus. I cannot believe this has happened. My life has turned on its head, and

SACRED LAKE

I've looked death in the face, all since the chimes of midnight brought in the new year a few short hours ago. But we both knew. All our plans for a bright, new future were ripped into shreds, scattered to the four corners, the second we heard his voice and knew he'd found our secret place.

Footsteps thud to a halt and I'm alert again. Close. He is close. Heavy breathing and the acrid scent of him on the wind. A dog barks, excited and keen. A man's angry retort as he struggles to control the beast. On hands and knees I crawl, belly flat to the ground. Slimy leaves heed my progress, smooth and glistening like a slug's trail as I slip silently across the forest floor. Pine needles pluck at my clothes, animals scurry from my path.

And then I am in a clearing. I gasp. A sparkling expanse, like a ballroom of crystal, a dance floor of diamonds, spreads before me. On the furthest side, a high bank of stones edges the silver oasis, and beyond that the spray and crash of the ocean.

I step forwards, arms outstretched to keep my balance. Ice. A huge sheet of ice. I take a tentative step, then another, sliding my feet across the surface in tiny, baby steps, a novice ice-skater among a more confident crowd.

A twig snaps behind me and I come to my senses. I can hear, almost feel, his breath on the back of my neck. I try to run but lose traction with each stride, a picture of Bambi, on ice, my sister's favourite cartoon, spirals into my brain. Torch beams glitter and dance between my feet. He is closer. A man's voice penetrates the darkness, words snatched away with the breeze.

Then a cracking noise. Hard and sharp, like a pencil snapped in two.

I look down to see dirty trainers, once, in another life, expensive silver Nikes, half-covered in murky water, as a jagged crack widens under the surface of the ice, splintering forward like an arrow pointing the way. Beneath my feet, the hard, smooth surface begins to buckle, and water creeps higher to lap against my ankles.

Fear pulls me forward, but as the water rises, a gunshot cracks the air. For one second I wish it were a real gunshot, and then I'm plunging down. Icy water engulfs me, surging into my nose, ears, mouth. I press my lips tight, swallow, gag and choke, all the time whirling in a vortex of arms and legs and fear and coldness.

Finally, I stop spinning. My head makes contact with a hard surface, and I use my hands to roll myself onto my back. My lungs are screaming, and, as I exhale a tiny stream of air, I realise I've hit the underside of the ice. Blood pounds in my ears, as through the frosted surface, I make out torchlight flashing back and forth. I hear the muffled bark of a dog. I pound my fists against the ice and open my mouth to scream, expelling the last of the air, lungs and brain roaring so loud it blocks out every other sense.

Black pads cross my face, the underside of dog's paws. A man shouts, then as my body surrenders to the dark grip of death, a human shadow passes above me. The tip of a walking stick comes down right between my eyes. He can see me. I open my mouth, but cannot be certain real words come out.

"H-help. P-please …"

The shadow shifts and fades. The tapping of the dog's paws retreats.

My family's faces run through my mind as I say each goodbye.

It's over. He has won. I surrender to the lake and close my eyes.

JANUARY 1st 2017

Janine Taylor trembled with anticipation as her husband ushered her out of the noisy warmth of the hotel reception, the last chords of Auld Lang Syne still reverberating around its walls, and down the front steps out into the frosty darkness. Andrew winked and squeezed her hand, tugging her along, whilst attempting to conceal two glasses and a half-empty champagne bottle which chinked together in his other hand. Giggling like naughty children, they hurried across the car park, ice crunching underfoot.

"Andrew, stop! It's freezing! Where are we going?" Janine was aware her words were slurred and slow. She giggled again. God, she loved champagne. She loved parties. She loved New Year's Eve. She loved Andrew. She loved her bloody life full stop.

Her husband responded with a gentle tug. "Come on, not far. Want to show you something."

"But I'm cold. I want to go back to the hotel." She halted, yanking her arm back hard so the momentum swung Andrew round in an arc to face her. She hooked her hands around his neck and pulled his face down to hers. "I want to go to bed, baby. And I'm not tired." She kissed him deeply, feeling the warmth of his tongue on her own.

Andrew groaned and pulled away. "Come on. Do this for me." He kissed her again. "I'll warm you up soon, I promise."

Janine smiled, a fizz of electricity shooting from her stomach, radiating outwards. She loved this sense of adventure about her husband. Married four and a half years and she still felt like a newly-wed, still couldn't keep her hands off Andrew, still couldn't imagine life before his solid presence.

They paused at the road, checking the deserted tarmac both ways, then hurried across, taking care to negotiate the piled snow on the kerb. The moon was high and bright, a few random firework explosions rumbled away in the darkness. New Year at the hotel had been Andrew's idea. Their first New Year alone as her parents were away on a cruise, and he'd wanted to spoil her. And he'd certainly done that. She couldn't wait to show him her gratitude.

Andrew stopped in front of her, swaying slightly as he deposited the bottle and glasses on a picnic table that had appeared out of thin air. He bent and slid out a box from beneath the bench seat, then turned, and pushed her down into a sitting position.

"Stay there," he whispered. "Two minutes."

Before she could respond, he'd disappeared behind a gorse bush, box in hand. Janine clapped her hands together, before burying them deep in the pockets of her fur-lined coat, trying to ignore the creeping coldness through the delicate silky fabric of her trousers.

"Andrew!"

He was back, settling on the bench beside her, grinning as he pulled the cork from the bottle, pouring both glasses until the champagne fizzed and spilled over the table.

"Happy New Year, darling!"

Andrew held the glass aloft, and, as the crystal clinked, the sky exploded into a huge fountain of silver and gold that lit up the hotel grounds, the golf course, right across to village of Rhosneigr. As the flaming stars began to fall to the ground, Janine sipped her fizz and drew in a sharp breath. Behind them, a frozen lake appeared, illuminated like the set of a Disney Ice Spectacular.

She sat open-mouthed, aware of Andrew moving beside her, feeling his hands slip inside the warmth of her coat, inside her blouse, inside her bra …

"Oh, Andrew," she murmured into his ear. "It's so beautiful."

"I wanted something special for you to remember this New Year. I wanted to show you how much you mean to me."

"So that's where you disappeared to earlier on your supposed jog!" She giggled again, swallowed the last of the champagne, pushing herself harder against her husband's exploring fingers. "How can I show you how much you mean to me too?"

Andrew leaned in closer until his tongue probed the delicate skin of her ear lobe. She shivered and moaned. "I think you know exactly what I want."

With a sigh, she pulled his face to hers, kissed him, moved her hands lower to his trousers, tugging at his belt.

He groaned. "Not here. Come on. In the trees."

She hurried to keep up, skirting the edge of the lake and

disappearing into the copse. Moonlight reflected off the lake, but under the canopy of fir trees she could barely make out Andrew's face.

"Turn around," he breathed into her hair.

Janine twisted in his embrace, rubbing herself against the hardness of his body. She loved the buzz of outdoor sex. Andrew knew how it excited her. She got off on imagining some old guy, or a peeping tom pervert type, off across the lake, watching them. The image made her suck in her breath. Her feet were almost at the edge of the frozen surface now, and she felt like she could step out onto the ice and disappear into the sparkling whiteness of it.

Andrew moaned and shifted position. His fingers worked on her zip, before slipping inside, teasing her. She bit her lip, wanting to beg him for more, but holding back.Icy air tickled her naked backside as he slipped her trousers lower. She breathed hard and stared down at the ice, bracing herself to take his weight, frowning as she picked out a dark smudge in the pure white expanse of the ice. What was it? She squinted and bent lower. Her mind went to the image of the old pervert, spying on them. Open eyes stared back at her, mouth gaping.

Janine dropped to the forest floor, trousers and panties tangling around her knees, opened her mouth, and screamed.

A face. A face beneath the ice

CHAPTER ONE

"For Auld Lang Syne, my dear. For Auld Lang Syne. We'll take a cup of kindness, yet ..."

Amanda Gold winced, gripping Kelly Morgan's fingers a little tighter with her right hand, as an over-exuberant WPC, whose name eluded Amanda's alcohol-fogged brain, swung her left arm so enthusiastically back and forth it threatened to dislodge from its socket.

"For the sake of Auld Lang Syne!"

Cheers and whistles, laughter and party poppers filled the air. Outside, the night sky exploded in a shower of multi-coloured fireworks, followed by echoing booms. Amanda hugged and air-kissed the cheeks of those around her, before retreating to her seat beside the window and reaching for her wine glass. In the chill of the bay window she shivered, glancing at the intricate ice crystals forming along the outer edges of the glass. She settled back with a sigh, content to let the party carry on around her without the desire to get involved. This was one year Amanda would not be sad to see the back of and it felt hypocritical to be celebrating.

More fireworks burst into showers of gold and red sparks reflecting in the inky waters of the Menai Strait. Beyond Bangor pier, showers of red and silver stars cascaded from displays in the Anglesey town of Beaumaris. It was a spectacular sight, and, like many times in the past few years, Amanda's spirits were lifted by the stunning surroundings in which she was lucky enough to live.

"Happy New Year, ma'am."

Amanda looked up; a shimmer of red sparks reflected in the glasses of DS Gethin Jones.

"And Happy New Year to you too, Geth." She got to her feet and leant across the table to kiss his cheek. "Hope it's a good one."

"Yeah, me too. Can I sit here a minute? I'm keeping my eye out for a cab," he said, glancing through the window.

"Of course." Amanda slid along to make room. "I'll share it when you get one, if you don't mind. My head is telling me I've had enough, even if Kelly is insisting I haven't."

Gethin laughed and followed Amanda's gaze. DS Kelly Morgan was barefoot, bouncing up and down on the dance floor in time with Slade; her sequinned black dress revealed a pale expanse of thigh and cleavage with each bounce. One hand clutched a half-full glass of red wine and the other waved a huge artificial daffodil.

Amanda smiled. "It's been a good night. I'm glad I came."

Gethin nodded. "So am I. I'm not a fan of New Year. There's something about forced jollity really raises my hackles. I don't like being told I have to go out and have a good time and get drunk." He laughed at Amanda's open-mouthed expression. "Not saying I don't do any of that, ma'am. I just like to do it on my own terms."

Amanda took a sip of wine. "I know exactly what you mean. And call me Amanda at least for tonight, Geth, for god's sake. I feel about eighty when you call me ma'am off duty."

"Sorry. Just comes natural." He leaned across Amanda to rub a clear patch on the window as the music ended; she inhaled the subtle aftershave and clean, minty smell she associated with her DS.

"No sign of any cabs." Gethin sat back with a sly smile. "Wonder if it would be rubbing too much salt into the wound to ring Fletch and cadge a lift home?"

Amanda grinned. "I think I'd rather walk home than face Fletch tonight. I thought I could sulk, but he's taken it to a new level."

"Take no notice, it won't kill him. It's the first New Year I remember Fletcher drawing the short straw. It's usually Dara who puts his hand up, but I'm glad he's had chance to visit the family in Ireland this year."

"Me too."

"How's your new place by the way?" asked Gethin, taking a sip from his bottled beer.

"Bijou. It's fine, actually, quaint and big enough for the two of us, and I'm so glad to be out of the hotel at last. But I see no point paying a fortune in rent for a bigger place. Six months will suit us fine, hopefully the flat will sell and I can look to put a deposit down on a new place."

"You'll not go back to the flat when the work's finished?"

Amanda shook her head, recalling the sad remains of her once beloved apartment. "Emily doesn't want to and I won't force her."

"How is your daughter? I don't like to ask at work …"

"She's doing okay, Geth. Thanks. She's spending New Year with her father."

Amanda frowned and sipped her wine, recalling the heated telephone call with her ex-husband, Simon, the night before. He was reluctant to send Emily back to North Wales, insisting she would be better transferring to Warwick University and move in with him 'at least for a while, at least until you can be fully honest with her. I don't like these false pretences…'

Amanda shook the memory away as the music started up again. Another Seventies classic that only seemed to air over the festive period. She kept an eye on Kelly, now propping up the bar, drinking a multi-coloured concoction with a straw. Kelly held her own secrets and heartaches, and no doubt tonight was her attempt at burying her troubles. What was it about New Year that was so bloody depressing?

Gethin was watching Kelly too. "She does nothing by halves, does she?"

"Who can blame her," said Amanda. "We only have one life. May as well live it. She's determined to meet the man of her dreams this year – or so she tells me."

"Well, good luck with that," said Gethin, meeting his boss's eye with a knowing look.

"And how about you, young Geth? What are your resolutions for the coming year?"

"I don't make them, ma'am … Amanda. No point. I never keep them past the first week."

"No young lady on the horizon? You'd make someone a perfect house husband, you know? I've never known a bloke who can iron shirts the way you do …"

Amanda trailed off, reading the awkwardness in Gethin's expression and the flush of his cheeks. Damn. Alcohol-fuelled tongue again.

"Although," she added, lifting her glass. "I will raise a glass to never having to iron a bloody shirt again in my life. Men and me are finished." She swallowed the last of her wine. "Finito. Done. Over. I am hereby a fully signed-up member of the spinsterhood."

Gethin finished his own drink. "I'm sure you don't mean that. You know, everyone has their soul mate out there somewhere -"

"Well, I'm done with trying to find mine. I do mean it. You can hold me to it. You and me, Geth, we shall stay sober, sensible and single. That will be our New Year's resolution."

Amanda pushed the table away, and, with a wobble, got to her feet and fumbled with her jacket.

"Not so sure about the sober, even if we pull off the other two," said Gethin, taking her arm as she tugged at the zip of her coat.

"Ma'am."

"Bloody hell, Geth, I've told you, off duty do not call me-"

"Ma'am!"

DS Duncan Fletcher stared at her across the table.

"You rang him then?" Amanda looked from Fletcher to Gethin, who was shaking his head with a puzzled expression.

"Sorry, ma'am. Was passing on my way."

"Way …. where?"

"Llyn Maelog Hotel, Rhosneigr. One of the guests has made a gruesome discovery in the lake. Wasn't sure if you'd want to attend?"

"Oh, God." Amanda reached for her bag, feeling the alcohol seep from her system. "I'd better. Gethin, stay with Kelly will you, make sure she gets back to the B&B in one piece and tell her I may be needing her in the office tomorrow. I'll call."

Gethin acknowledged with a wave and melted into the crowd.

"Right, Happy New Year to you too, Fletcher." Amanda exhaled and caught hold of his arm. "Lead on."

Amanda rummaged in her handbag as Fletcher covered the deserted Anglesey roads at top speed, eventually finding the packet of extra strong mints and popping two into her mouth. Thank goodness she decided to stay relatively sober this new year, almost like her sixth sense knew something she didn't.

"Tell me what we know so far," said Amanda, pulling down the sun visor to check the state of her eyes.

"Two of the guests took themselves and a bottle of champagne down to the lake to bring in the New Year in style. Bit bloody cold for that kind of shenanigans I'd have thought, but there you go." Fletcher indicated to take the turnoff from the A55 dual-carriageway towards Rhosneigr. "Must have put a bit of a dampener on any thoughts of a romantic romp when they saw a naked bloke trapped under the ice gazing back up at them."

Amanda glanced at Fletch's profile. "Bloody hell. The lake is frozen?"

"Yeah, apparently so. Has been for a week or more."

"And we've been called in because …?"

"It's a locum pathologist, not a name I know. I've jotted it down, Simpkins, Simpson, something like that. Anyway, Holyhead station called the locum guy out and he's pretty certain it's murder. Strangulation to be exact. He's plays by the rules by all accounts, refusing to let anyone move the body or disturb the crime scene until CID turn up."

"I like the sound of this Simpson already. Any ID?"

"No. But apparently the chef from the hotel went missing before Christmas, caused quite a bit of local intrigue, according to uniform. So, first assumption is it's him, but obviously nothing confirmed as yet."

"And the hotel … what do we know?"

Fletcher shrugged. "I know it's out of my price range but that's about it. I went to a wedding there a few years back, stunning place, but not for the likes of you and I."

"Speak for yourself, DS Fletcher." Amanda rummaged in her bag again. "I shall consult my trusty Google."

"Best of luck, I can't imagine they have 3G out here." Fletch heaved the wheel to the right. "They've certainly not invested much in the way of rock salt, these roads are atrocious. Thank god for four-wheel drive."

Amanda gritted her teeth with frustration as the web search opened at snail-pace speed, finally revealing a sophisticated website full of stunning photographs of a gothic-styled building that looked more like an Oxford college than an Anglesey hostelry. Miles of rolling beaches and dunes bordered its rear, with many aerial shots of the wide blue expanse of Llyn Maelog in the foreground. Amanda clicked the tag 'About Us.'

"Right, so apparently the hotel was opened in 1900 by the Glenowen family to cater for wealthy Victorian families attracted to the island because of its rich history and wealth of archaeological finds which were booming at the time. Sort of like the Tutankhamun effect in Wales, I suppose," added Amanda, looking up as the sturdy Mitsubishi Shogun jigged across the icy road surface.

She consulted the website again. "Built between the rolling dunes at the edge of Traeth Llydan, a spectacular ocean landscape popular with surfers, and the stunning remoteness of Llyn Maelog, a sixty-five-acre freshwater lake, today popular with fishermen, but once the base of a thriving shipbuilding industry that started on the site as early as 1787."

"Blimey. Didn't know that. You can't take a step on this island without tumbling over the past, can you?"

Amanda looked up, surprised. "Remarkably deep for you, Detective."

"Why's that?"

Amanda shrugged. "Don't know really. Didn't imagine you were interested in the past so much as the present."

"Ah, well, you see. Never judge a book. I can often be seen wandering remote beauty spots with my ordnance survey map and a book of lost ancient Roman settlements."

Amanda's jaw dropped and she found herself at a loss for words.

Fletcher snorted. "You look like someone side-swiped you with a plank, ma'am. No, I don't spend my Sundays roaming farmer's fields with a metal detector, true, I'm not that sad. But I'm island born and bred, remember. A local lad. We had our history rammed down our throats at school. Anglesey is a proud place, and rightly so. Right, looks like we're here."

CHAPTER TWO

Frost crunched beneath their feet as they left the warmth of the Shogun and headed towards a cluster of vehicles beneath two large arc lamps illuminating the nearest bank of Llyn Maelog. Uniformed officers were busy cordoning off the area with police tape, and setting up a common approach path with numbered tiles. Amanda headed towards a blue tarpaulin, folded neatly across a human-shaped form, wincing as her new pair of red kitten heels pierced the frosted turf and sunk into the soft earth below. Shoes were her nemesis, and despite best intentions, her recently acquired Wellington boots were in her own car boot, many miles away, serving no purpose whatsoever.

The lake spread before them like a giant ice-skating rink, sparkling under the stark whiteness of the lamps, spoiled only by dark water lapping against a narrow gash near the bank, where brute force must have been used to crack open the ice and retrieve the body beneath. As she picked her way gingerly in Fletch's wake, a tall man wearing a paper over-suit, with hair the colour of brushed-steel and the clean-cut features of a modern-day politician, got to his feet and greeted them with a nod and smile.

"Detective Inspector Gold, I assume?" he pulled off a latex glove and held out his hand.

"That's right." She shook the strong grip. "Dr Simpson, is it?"

His expression slipped into a slight frown. "No. Sixsmith. Dr Stafford Sixsmith."

The name matched the public-school accent. Amanda flashed a scowl at her DS. "Apologies. Breakdown in communication channels. Nice to meet you, doctor. Thanks for ensuring the scene is preserved, what can you tell us?"

"Well, I'm not one for clichés so I won't bore you with any. Initial findings are pointing to suspicious death. There are marks around the neck consistent with strangulation, or possibly hanging, although I would lean towards the former. I'm pretty certain we'll find the hyoid bone broken when we open him up." He paused to consult his notes. "Also, anti-mortem bruising around the wrists consistent with restraint by a chain or similar, and nothing in the airways in terms of foam or residue to point towards drowning."

"He was dead before he entered the water?" Fletch asked.

"Most probably, though I can't be one hundred percent certain yet."

"So, it's unlikely he took himself out for a late night naked stroll and fell in is what you're saying?" said Amanda, steeling herself as she approached the blue sheet. "May I?"

"It's what I'm surmising at this point, yes," said the doctor as he lifted the plastic. "Although as you can see the rest of the body is blemish-free."

Naked flesh shone in a pale blue, almost transparent, patina beneath the brilliant white light, illuminating the labyrinth of purple veins and arteries beneath the skin's surface. Despite the gruesomeness of the scene, there was something almost beautiful and ethereal in the image.

Male, Caucasian, aged thirty to forty. Tall, around six foot. Slender build, but well defined legs and arms, perhaps a sportsman. Full beard and full head of hair, brown in its current damp state, but perhaps a light brown or dark blond. Tanned skin, lightly scattered with hairs on the legs and chest. One visible tattoo on the left side of his chest, above the heart, a Celtic design. Something about surfing sprung into her mind, probably the locality to a popular surfing beach, but this guy had the look and build of a surfer.

"Almost too clean …"

Amanda tuned back into the conversation between Fletch and Dr Sixsmith.

"Yes. I suspect he's been cleaned down, evidence destroyed."

"Could be why he's naked. Time of death?"

The pathologist shook his head. "I couldn't even hazard a clue at *day* of death, let alone time. You know your stuff I'm sure, but the temperature of this water …"

Fletcher nodded. "Slows everything down, sure. But on the table, will you be able to tell?"

"It won't be as accurate as I'd prefer but I will narrow down as much as I can. Might be one reason for disposing of the corpse here. Just a thought."

Amanda nodded. "Yes, wouldn't be the first time. Conceals the body and muddies the waters too, so to speak. Whatever you can tell us and as soon as you can. You'll be doing the post-mortem, doctor?"

"Yes, I'm around for a few weeks, so you're saddled with me for a bit longer I'm afraid." He chuckled and Amanda noticed for the first time the vivid blue of his eyes, which sparkled when he laughed.

She met his eye and smiled. "I'm sure I'll cope."

Fletch cleared his throat.

The doctor re-covered the corpse and added. "One final nugget of good news I can't claim credit for … the hotel sent one of the managers along with flasks of coffee. He got a brief glimpse at the body and confirmed a resemblance to their missing chef. Wasn't keen on getting too close so it's certainly not definitive."

"It's a start. The witnesses who found him …"

"A WPC is with them at the hotel. The lady is pretty shaken as you can imagine."

"I'm sure … not the best way to bring in a new year."

Fletch closed his notebook as the doctor returned to his tasks. "Any instructions for SOCO, ma'am?" He signalled towards a white van parking up on the road. "The cavalry has arrived."

Amanda looked around. The chances of finding anything out here in such a public spot were remote.

"Probably best to concentrate on entry and exit points. How was the body transported here? Tyre tracks. Footprints. The usual. I'd keep it brief tonight, ensure the scene is preserved, let's do a full search in daylight."

"Should we call in the dive team?"

"Tomorrow. For now, let's pay a visit to Llyn Maelog Hotel."

Amanda yawned as they took the steps into the grandness of the hotel lobby. Despite the flashing blue police lights out on the main road, hotel staff had clearly tried to stop the unsavoury news reaching guests who had no doubt shelled out a fair few hundreds of pounds each for the opportunity to celebrate New Years' Eve at Llyn Maelog.

Men in black tie, and women in a colourful array of floor-length evening dresses, passed to and fro, and the tinkling of a grand piano from the bar added to an atmosphere of 1930s grandeur. The centre-piece of the lobby was a huge Christmas tree, decorated in sparkling red, filling the air with the heady scent of pine, mingling with wood smoke from the open fire that blazed away to their left. A few members of staff, wearing worried frowns and pasted smiles, flitted back and forth in smart, grey uniforms.

Fletch touched her sleeve and pointed to a desk marked 'Reception' next to a smaller one labelled 'Concierge.'

"Never seen so many penguin suits in my entire life," whispered Fletch as they crossed the polished marble floor.

"You need to go to the Commissioners' Annual Ball more often."

"Never been invited. I'd have to hire the get up anyway. It's like something out of an Agatha Christie novel."

Amanda found herself open-mouthed again. "You read Agatha Christie?"

Fletched looked down with a grin and winked. "Told you, hidden depths, ma'am."

"I can more easily picture you out roaming the fields of Anglesey with your metal detector, than spending your evenings with your nose buried in *Murder on the Orient Express*."

They approached the desk and waited to be noticed.

Fletch whispered into her ear. "I dated a fit Russian graduate who was a Christie fanatic, think that was the main reason she chose to study in the UK. Had to do a bit of research and play the part, you know, ma'am …"

"May I help you?"

A blonde-haired girl smiled at them brightly. Her shiny oval badge announced her name was Sarah. Amanda felt Fletch straighten to his full height as he reached into his jacket to retrieve his identification.

"Police. We're looking for the guests who –"

"Yes. Yes. One moment please."

Her nose wrinkled as if she had caught a particularly noxious small; she picked up a telephone. A brief, hushed conversation followed which ended with a sharp nod.

"My manager has settled Mr and Mrs Taylor in the South Stack meeting room." Sarah leaned forward, an ample cleavage straining the white blouse. She spoke in a hushed whisper. "Follow the corridor in the corner right to the end, you'll see the signs. He asked me to ask for discretion …"

"Of course. But you have a hotel full of several hundred potential witnesses, maybe even suspects, and at some point, my officers will need a full guest list. It would also be convenient to have a room we could use for interviews, so I'm going to need to speak to your manager too at some point. Can you pass that on?"

Sarah's face whitened. "Yes, of course. I believe Mr Glenowen has been contacted."

Amanda was surprised to hear the hotel was still in the original family ownership. "Good. Well, you know where we'll be. South Stack, right?"

Sarah nodded and pointed the way for a second time.

"One last thing. Tomorrow we'll need to interview all staff who were on duty tonight. Can you ask your manager to organise that for us too? Set up a rota."

Sarah made a note on a hidden pad. "Yes."

"And his name?"

"Sorry?"

"Your manager?"

"Oh, the general manager. Mr Jones. Terence Jones."

"Thank you."

Amanda turned to leave as Fletch leaned across the reception desk. "I know it's a bit cheeky, but any chance of getting some coffee, you reckon? It's freezing out there."

He was rewarded with a return of the toothy smile and the flicker of interest in her pale blue eyes. "I'll see what I can do."

"You're an angel," said Fletch, his eyes roaming her body. "Seriously."

He winked at the blushing receptionist and hurried to join Amanda.

"You amaze me, DS Fletcher. Or should that be appal me?"

"What?"

"Ever heard the phrase 'a time and place?'"

"Just being friendly, ma'am. You never know when it might pay dividends." He gave her his cheekiest smile. "Besides, she has a cracking …"

Amanda pretended to cover her ears.

"… smile."

Amanda released a pent-up sigh and leaned back in her chair as the door of the South Stack meeting room closed behind Mr and Mrs Andrew Taylor.

Fletch got to his feet and crossed to a side table where a tray containing two cafetieres and various cups had been left by a young waiter. "Waste of time," he said. "Knew it would be from the minute I clapped eyes on them. Poor buggers."

Amanda nodded, recalling the young couple; the man's pale, frozen features and his wife's red, streaming eyes. Both had been unable to stop shaking and barely able to string together a coherent sentence between them. No, they hadn't seen anyone else on their excursion or recognised the man under the ice. Yes, they had both rushed back to the hotel together and dialled 999 on Andrew's mobile on the way. No, they hadn't heard about a missing chef. Yes, they were happy to make a full statement. And when could they head back home to Cheshire?

"I sometimes think we are too unaffected by death," Amanda said, accepting a steaming cup from Fletch. "I see the shock in other people's faces and it concerns me I don't get it."

Fletch frowned and stirred his own coffee. "Don't get what?"

"Don't get their reaction. It makes me suspicious, like they must be putting it on or covering up something. But that couple were seriously traumatised, they weren't faking."

"Well, I don't know about you, ma'am, but every dead body I come face to face with leaves something in my head too."

"Really?"

"Yeah. I agree the Taylors were incapable of lying. There's nothing more they can tell us …"

Fletch trailed off as a sharp rap sounded through the room and the door inched open. A white-haired man, mid-fifties, with a pleasant round face, wearing a smart dark grey suit took a tentative step into the room.

"Hello. I saw the Taylors leave and thought I should introduce myself. Terence. Terence Jones. Anything you need, please ask. Our MD, Stephen Glenowen, is on the way but until then I'm your point of contact." He spoke with a strong Welsh accent and from the tone was clearly a man used to giving orders.

Amanda nodded, recognising the name of the General Manager. "Yes, please, come in Mr Jones. Take a seat. We do have questions, of course. And we appreciate the use of the room and your hospitality."

He smiled, a practised gesture, and puffed out his chest.

"Well, if we can't offer that then we would rather be failing at our job, wouldn't you say."

He crossed the room and Amanda noted the trace of a limp. "Yes, but I can't imagine tonight has gone down as one of the better New Year celebrations in the history of the hotel."

A frown clouded his features as he pulled out a chair and settled across the long table from them. "Well, no. Absolutely awful. Do you know who ...?"

"We don't have a positive ID yet. That was one area I hoped you may be able to assist?"

He frowned again. "Assist?"

"I thought you may have heard the news. I understand one of your managers saw the body as it was recovered from the lake and reported a likeness to your chef –"

A hand went to his mouth. "Greg? You're joking. Greg?"

Fletch retrieved his notebook and flicked it open. "Could I take the full name, please, sir?"

Terence Jones swallowed. "Yes, yes. Gregory Chapman. But, oh god, no, I can't believe ..."

"So, that news hadn't filtered through to you?" asked Fletch.

The man shook his head, face still dazed. "I've not left the shop floor. Erm, that means I've been with the guests. Overseeing the restaurant, then the ballroom. I heard of course ... knew Anthony, he's our restaurant manager, had gone out there ... but no. God. You're sure it's Greg?"

Amanda shook her head. "No. We will need an official identification. Do you have details of his family?"

"Yes. He was Australian, from Perth, I'll find the details, of course."

"Anyone locally?"

The man paused, then shook his head. "No family. Could a fellow staff member do it? Greg lived in-house most of the time, travelled a bit when he wasn't working. But his career was his life."

"And he's worked here, how long?" asked Fletch, jotting notes.

"Goodness. Must be four years now. He was our find of the decade, a truly gifted, inspirational chef. He took our food, and our reputation, to another level."

"And he's been missing …?" Amanda left the question hanging as she picked up her cup.

"A couple of weeks." Terence paused, licked his lips. "Nightmare. Christmas and all that. He's always been volatile. What chef isn't?" He pulled a face. "I think the general consensus was he'd took off back home for Christmas. We hoped he'd cool down and reappear in the new year."

"Cool down?" asked Amanda. "There'd been an altercation before he disappeared?"

Terence shrugged. "Nothing more than usual. Wrong mushrooms. Scallops delivery late. Customer who didn't appreciate his new terrine. Could have been anything."

"Did you try to contact him?"

"Of course. Numerous times. His mobile was off and he seemed to have just disappeared. He was known for his moods, so I for one wasn't overly concerned. I had plenty more important things to worry about, like getting food on the table in his absence. I guess I thought he'd be back when he was ready and I'd deal with him them. It wasn't the first time. He jetted off to Thailand without notice about two years back."

Fletch snorted. "Blimey. You're one flexible employer. I can't imagine my bosses putting up with that kind of behaviour."

Terence shrugged. "Like I say, he was a special talent, on the way to his first Michelin star, which would have been huge kudos for the hotel. It was worth a few bumps in the road to have him here. We were very lucky, we knew that. Anglesey isn't known as the foodie capital of the world, doesn't attract the big names, but it's changing, slowly for sure, in part due to Greg." Terence sighed and folded his arms. "We put up with him because it made business sense and paid dividends, not because I'm a soft touch. I just do as I'm told. The highs of having him here outweighed the lows. While that were still the case, we covered up his absence, people still got the same food. He was training up a local lad as his sous chef and he's doing a good job reaching Greg's high standards."

Fletch hurried to keep up with his note taking. "We will need to speak to his understudy. Is he around?"

"Dewi? Yes. He's clearing down in the kitchens. But are you sure, I mean ... Greg. It doesn't seem real."

The door opened again, without a knock this time, and a bearded, black-haired man strode into the room. Late thirties, handsome and tall, he moved with the confident gait of someone who owned the place. Amanda suspected he did.

Terence Jones was on his feet, hand outstretched to guide the new arrival to his vacated chair.

"Stephen, I'm so sorry ..." He cleared his throat. "Sorry to drag you out here. Have you heard ...?"

Stephen Glenowen's face was a mix of shock and confusion. "Anthony called me. Is it true? Is it Greg?"

Terence put a hand on his employer's shoulder and guided him down into a sitting position. "We aren't sure yet. These are the police, Stephen. CID. They've recovered a body from the lake. We were discussing identification ... what with Greg's family being –"

"I'll do it." Stephen Glenowen sat up straighter, seeming to notice the other people in the room for the first time. "Apologies, I'm Stephen Glenowen, owner of Llyn Maelog Hotel. Please accept apologies for my ignorance. I'll identify the body. I need to do it for my own sake, it doesn't seem possible it could be Greg."

"Thank you," said Amanda. "We'll make the arrangements."

Stephen glanced around the room, his gaze finally returning to his general manager. "I knew I should have stayed here tonight. The poor people who found ... him ... the body ... must be distraught. Make sure they are well looked after and compensated. But what on earth was Greg doing down at the lake in the first place?"

Fletch cleared his throat. "He didn't fall in today, sir, if that's what you're thinking. There's no way he could have done, the lake is frozen over."

"Really?" He glanced at Terence who nodded. "Then what …?"

"We'll know more after the post-mortem," said Amanda. "I understand the chef has been absent for a period of time, so it's not beyond the realms of possibility his body could have been in the lake for what, as long as a fortnight?"

Stephen clasped his hands together on the table in front of him. Pale, slender fingers, twisting around each other. "That's impossible."

Amanda sat forward. "Is it? Why?"

Terence Jones cleared his throat. "I think Mr Glenowen was in the same mind set as everyone else. Greg had gone home for the holidays. That's what you mean, isn't it, Stephen?"

The two men glanced at each other for the briefest moment before Stephen nodded and dropped his gaze to the table. "I can't believe it."

"None of us can," said Terence.

"Then we should do something about it. This grief could all be all for nothing if it's not Greg." Stephen pushed his chair back and was on his feet. "Can I see the body now?"

"I'm not sure pathology will be ready for us yet, sir," said Fletch. "I'll put a call in."

"I want to go now. Please. See what can be done." He turned his back and headed to the door. "I'll be in reception in half an hour."

And with that he was gone.

Terence clasped his hands together and retreated one step at a time. "If you don't need me for now, is it okay …" He gestured with a nod towards the door.

Amanda nodded.

When the door closed behind Terence Jones, Fletch met Amanda's gaze. "Shall I call the morgue?"

"Please."

"What are you thinking, ma'am?" said Fletch as he pushed buttons on his mobile.

"I'm not sure. But Terence Jones seemed very on edge once his boss appeared. I don't think it was my imagination. Did you get that too?"

"Absolutely. He acted more like his father than his general manager, total change in personality and he clearly wanted him silenced too. Why?" He adjusted the phone next to his ear. "Ah, pathology? Can I speak to Dr Sixsmith please?"

CHAPTER THREE

Amanda ran her fingers around the edge of her mobile, constructing and deconstructing the message in her head. Finally, she typed out the text, read it, shook her head, and deleted all but the first word. She sighed and tried again. 'Emily, sweetie, Happy New Year. Sorry I didn't call you back last night, something came up and I was working. Didn't want to disturb your beauty sleep this early! Haha. Call me when you can. Mum xx.'

She paused for a moment, then deleted Mum and added 'Miss you. Love you, Mum xxxx.' Happy this time, she pressed send. She scrolled through her Inbox, cursor hovering over the message headed 'Richard'. She took another second, pressed delete, then went into her phonebook, selected the contact also called 'Richard' and deleted that too. True, it had only been a simple HNY message that arrived in a bundle with half a dozen others in the early hours, but at least now the temptation to reply had been erased. Satisfied, Amanda slid the phone into the top drawer of her desk.

The ceiling lights in her office were bright, and she rubbed her eyes and yawned. Part of her wanted to go home and curl up under her duvet, the other half knew her brain was far too wired for sleep, even if her body craved rest. Outside her window, the orange glow of the car park lights glittered off the icy surface of the window pane. On the building opposite, a central heating pipe shot plumes of white steam up into a dark sky betraying not even the slightest hint of the dawn to come. Which, she checked her watch, could only be an hour away at most.

Outside in the main office, Gethin was already at his desk, head bent over his computer. Fletch was yet to return from his trip to the morgue with Stephen Glenowen, and, until they had official identification, Amanda felt at stalemate. At least it had given her time to change out of her scarlet party frock and the ruined red satin heels, into the sombre black trouser suit and blouse she always kept in her office for emergencies.

She yawned, rolled her neck, and got to her feet. She needed something to keep her awake. Outside in the main office, she headed for the Espresso machine – a Christmas present from her to the rest of the team – one she knew she would benefit from too.

"Coffee, Geth?"

Gethin looked up. "Please. I think I've become a convert since I'm not forced to drink sludge."

Amanda smiled. "I figure we deserve it. We spend enough time here …"

The outer office door opened and Amanda turned, expectant, hoping to see Fletch. Instead, Kelly Morgan eased herself around the door, as if its weight was too much of a challenge. Make-up free, chestnut curls scraped back into a harsh pony tail, eyes bloodshot in a face the colour of porridge, wearing a baggy grey jumper, black jeans and boots. Amanda recognised a 'hide me' outfit when she saw one.

"Morning. Coffee, Kelly?" Amanda said brightly.

Her DS replied with a grunt that could have gone either way.

Amanda bit down on a smile. "I'll take it that's a no."

Kelly held a litre bottle of water aloft and headed for her seat, while Amanda crossed the office with Gethin's coffee and exchanged knowing winks with him.

"Good night was it, after I left?" said Amanda.

Kelly lowered herself into her seat and began to rifle through her handbag. "Dunno. Can't remember much. Just remember him …" she flashed a look of animosity towards Gethin, "… ringing me about twenty times at five am."

"It was three times," said Gethin. "And it was six am. I did warn you last night when I dropped you off at the B&B."

Kelly looked up from the strip of foil between her fingers that seemed to be resolutely hanging onto to the Paracetamol inside. "You did?"

Gethin nodded. "I told you the boss had left to attend a possible murder and we'd be called in if it was confirmed."

Kelly shook her head and continued to twist at the plastic. "Don't remember that. But my head feels like it's going to explode if I can't get these sodding things open!"

Amanda stopped at Kelly's desk and held out a hand. "Here." She deftly popped out two tablets and held them out. "If you're seriously not up to it, Kelly, then perhaps you should head home, we can manage here."

Kelly unscrewed her water bottle. "I'll be fine. Give me a few minutes. With Dara down too, I'll have to sort myself out." She swallowed the tablets with a grimace and gulped down some water, then wiped a hand across her mouth. "What's the story then?"

As Amanda opened her mouth, the office door banged open, and Fletcher burst into the room, a look of nervous excitement lighting up his handsome features.

"Hold the front page. Whoever our dead guy is, it's not Gregory Chapman!"

"So, there's no doubt?" said Amanda a short time later, balancing against the edge of Kelly's desk as Fletch related his visit to the morgue.

"Absolutely none. The relief on Glenowen's face was palpable. If good old Terence hadn't been there to support him, I think he'd have been in a heap on the floor."

Amanda raised her eyebrows. "Really?"

Fletch took a gulp of coffee from his Batman mug. "Yes. They were both steeled for the worst, you could tell that. I kept my eyes on their faces, obviously expecting the same, but when they saw it wasn't him they seemed both relieved and confused."

"Did they have any idea who the guy was?" asked Gethin from his desk.

"None. Terence admitted there was a likeness. The beard and physique."

Gethin stood and crossed the room, handing out A4 photographs as he passed Kelly's desk. "I downloaded these off the internet. There's quite a lot of stuff about Gregory Chapman. Awards he's won, reviews and interviews. He's building quite a reputation and not a bad-looking fella, either."

Amanda took a photo and turned it towards her. Blond hair, blue eyes, white smile in a tanned face. He was wearing an open-necked white collarless shirt, with an unfastened bow tie hanging loose down the front, staring into the camera lens with a glassy-eyed post-wine expression she recognised. Someone at ease in front of the camera, who knew his looks would do him justice from any angle. Confident. That's what she took from the photograph. A man at home in his own skin.

"Well, I can confirm it too now I've seen this. That's not our bloke." Fletch flicked the photo with his nail. "Similarities for sure, but this bloke is younger. Better looking too. Bet you'd not kick him out of bed if he came round offering you a taste of his pastrami, would you, Kelly darlin'?" He grinned at his hungover colleague, purposely intimidating her with his fake, put-on Cockney banter voice, tensing himself for the blows to come.

Instead, Kelly dropped the photo and reached for her bottled water. "Grow up, Fletcher."

Fletch pulled a face at Amanda and headed for his desk. "So, where does this leave us?"

Amanda slid down from the edge of Kelly's desk and approached the white board, formulating her thoughts as she fixed Gregory Chapman's photo to the top right corner. She picked up a pen and tapped her bottom lip several times.

"I'd say it leaves us with not one, but two possible investigations. We still have a suspected murder victim. And we also have the disappearance of Gregory Chapman."

"Could they be linked?" asked Fletcher.

Amanda paused. "They could be. We need to do background on Chapman. If he's sat at home in Perth with his family, we need to know, so we can close down that line of enquiry. Kelly … can you handle that? If he's not at home, let's not alarm the family. But do an all ports as a next step."

Kelly gave a thumbs-up, looking relieved she could stay at her desk for the time being.

"For the rest of us our priority needs to be the dead man. Identification. Fletcher, can you take that? Trawl the missing person files. Get a photo sent up from pathology and start sending it out. We need fingerprints and DNA. If it comes down to dentals that will delay us with the holiday period."

Fletch nodded. "Sixsmith was about to start the post-mortem when I left."

"Good. I'm going to head over there next. Right, Gethin, can you get back out to the crime scene? The dive team are due first thing. Check with SOCO if they have anything to report, and then use a couple of uniforms to set up interviews with hotel staff and any guests who have something to tell us. I want a full guest list too, so we have our work cut out. I'll head there after the morgue. See how Kelly gets on with the Gregory Chapman angle and I may ask her to join us later."

Amanda faced her team. "We have far too many questions and almost no answers. Let's see what progress we can make in this critical first twenty-four hours. I appreciate you all coming in today. Back here for six pm debrief if nothing else has turned up by then."

Rivulets of rose petal pink greeted Amanda as she stepped into the pathology department. Stafford Sixsmith gave one final spray with the hose and switched off the gushing water, watching as the pink swirls turned clear and disappeared into the long thin drains that traversed the room.

"Morning, DI Gold," he said with a tired smile. "My body feels like my watch is part of a conspiracy. But … needs must." He wiped his hands, picked up a blue clipboard, and headed back to the covered gurney in the middle of the room.

"I appreciate your commitment, doctor," Amanda said, picking her way between puddles in her awkward overshoes.

"Part of the job. Never a huge fan of New Year celebrations … especially since the divorce. It's sleep I crave, that's all."

Amanda smiled in mutual sympathy. "Amen to all of that. I'll try not to keep you. What can you tell me?"

He drew back the sheet to reveal the corpse below. "I apologise in advance as holiday hours are in force. I'm waiting for the lab assistant to arrive to stitch him back together and tidy up the body, but I am quite sure this is nothing new to you, so I won't make the mistake of patronising you either."

Amanda gave a weak smile and let her eyes move quickly over the dismembered remains.

Dr Sixsmith pointed out livid purple bruising under the chin, above a gaping flap of skin that revealed the white gleam of bone beneath. "My first suspicion was correct. Death by strangulation. We have massive blunt force injury to the tissues of the neck, further confirmed by a broken hyoid bone. Evidence of asphyxiation, recognised as pinpoint haemorrhages called petechiae, small bleeds, on various sections of the skin. Substantial damage to the trachea, which indicates it was crushed by something of strength, and from the markings around the neck, I have a couple of suggestions."

Amanda reached into her pocket and pressed the Voice Memo button on her mobile. "Go ahead."

"We have evidence of sexual activity. The strangulation

may have been sexually motivated. There was anal penetration shortly before death and lesions across the back of the corpse that indicate flagellation with a whip or something similar. It's my belief the victim was strangled from behind, by an assailant of considerable strength, perhaps during the act of penetration. There are no signs of defensive wounds on the body. I've run toxicology tests and will feed back if he was drugged prior to death once I have results."

Amanda cleared her throat. "Rough sex? BDSM? Was it a one off or was he gay?"

Sixsmith shrugged. "Hard to determine and I've no physical evidence to back up either option. But there's one other interesting point. See here." He pointed with his pen to a ring of bruising at the edge of the victim's beard, almost invisible in the stubble. "I shaved the beard away and these are marks left by a chain, a thick, chunky one, you can clearly see from the bruises left by individual links. These marks are anti-mortem, but the bruises have stretched pointing to skin slippage." He glanced up, reading Amanda's question in her eyes. "I mean the chain was tightened around his skin while he was alive, but left in place after he was dead for some considerable time."

Amanda paused, let the information settle. "Planned then."

Sixsmith nodded. "And the corpse was definitely cleaned. There are traces of chemicals all over the body, even inside the mouth, consistent with a bleached anti-bacterial detergent. I've taken samples but don't have results yet. But sprayed with cleaner and hosed down is my guess, then moved to the lake."

"Any DNA traces from the killer?"

The pathologist shook his head. "I've taken nail clipping and scrapings, that's our only hope."

"Damn." Amanda sighed. "Time-frame?"

Sixsmith clicked his tongue. "I was dreading this question. I really can't be accurate which bothers me. He could have been dead anything up to three weeks to a month, decomposition has been slowed so much by the temperature of the water. The cold snap has lasted over two weeks, I checked back on the Internet, and I would hazard an opinion he'd been in the water around that length of time from the extent of bloating. What I can say with a fair amount of accuracy is he was dead a maximum of three to four days before he entered the water, at which point every process slowed. I've got a number of tests still to run, but I feel fairly confident with that. When, and if, I can give you more, of course I will."

"Thank you," Amanda looked down at the pale skin. "One final thing, to be clear, this is murder, doctor? Not some weird kind of self-harm or …"

The doctor shook his head. "One hundred percent murder. I know there are all kinds of exploits people get themselves into nowadays, but there's no way these wounds were self-inflicted. No way."

CHAPTER FOUR

Gethin shivered and stamped his feet, wishing he'd thought of thermals when he dashed out of his house at god-knows-o'clock. But despite the severe cold, he couldn't help admiring the beauty of the frozen dawn. Shafts of pale sunlight pierced a thick mist which hung in the dip of Llyn Maelog, reducing visibility down to a hundred metres at most, whilst behind him across the dunes, the rising sun lit the sky with an apricot glow that shimmered across the surface of the ocean. It was one hell of a greeting for the new year to come.

"Sarge?"

Gethin turned at the voice of the uniformed officer. "Dive team have arrived. It's no quick or easy task with the ice, can I give them the thumbs up to get started?"

"Sure. Have SOC finished?"

"Yeah. They were optimistic about finding tyre tracks, but it's such a huge area and so much activity." He shrugged. "They're not holding out much hope."

Gethin shoved his hands in the pocket of his overcoat. "Not surprised. I'm going to head back to the hotel, start interviews, can you take over here? Call if you need me."

The PC nodded and headed towards a group of men near the water's edge.

Gethin turned his back on the lake, crossed the road, and followed the drive to the hotel. He was forced up onto the verge half a dozen times as an expensive procession of vehicles passed. Last night's guests, he pondered, watching a silver Bentley sweep past with barely a hum from its engine. Maybe making an earlier than planned homeward journey, not impressed with police activity and dead bodies spoiling their festive celebrations. The rich, in his experience, were not the most tolerant of types.

As he passed through ornate gates into the car park, he noticed a woman, standing on the rise of the dunes, ethereal almost in the rays of sunshine behind her, one hand raised to shield her eyes, focused on the activity on the other side of the road. There was something about her features, her body language, that drew Gethin, and rather than take the direct route across the car park to the hotel main entrance, he skirted snow-topped low yew hedges out onto the open dunes.

As he approached, he noticed a black spaniel-type dog, bounding back and forth through the marram grass, unnoticed by its owner, whose gaze never faltered from the lakeside activity.

Gethin had no idea what had attracted his initial attention, but up close he was aware of the sad eyes and fragile beauty of the woman. Late twenties or early thirties, long black hair, and the palest skin he'd seen. Tight denim jeans, cream padded jacket, Ugg boots. She was tall, 'thin as a rake' as his mother often said, when bemoaning the current fashion for skeletal supermodels.

"Hello there," said Gethin, bending to pat the excitable dog.

"You came from the lake."

It was a statement, not a question, and an odd greeting in the circumstances.

"Yes."

"You're police."

"Yes. CID."

"They found a body my brother said. Whose body?"

Gethin frowned, puzzled by the randomness of the encounter. "We don't know yet. And you are ...?"

"Our sacred lake giving up her secrets." The woman's eyes still refused to meet his. "Just one body?"

Gethin, floored for a second, turned towards the lake as if to convince himself he'd not missed anything. No. The dive team were kitted out and testing equipment, voices muffled as they bantered between themselves. Fluorescent-jacketed officers were positioned at regular intervals, one chatting to a couple with a Labrador on a lead. Another in conversation with a cyclist at the roadside. A few cars slowed as they passed in and out of Rhosneigr.

When he turned back, the woman was gone.

Gethin was still puzzling the odd encounter as he waited in the hotel reception minutes later. There was a queue of people, suitcases at their feet, waiting to check out at reception, and the general buzz around the ornate foyer seemed to be one of unease and frustration. Gethin searched for a staff member, but everyone was caught up with their duties or listening patiently with painted-on smiles as guests bent their ears. Eventually, he caught the eye of a harassed-looking man, who came hurrying through the main doors, car keys in hand.

Gethin pulled his identification from his pocket and sidestepped the man. "Hello, Bangor CID, I'm looking for Mr Terence Jones. I'm here to interview staff about the body in the lake."

The man's smile faded as he took hold of Gethin's arm and guided them into the shadow of a gigantic Christmas tree. "Yes, yes, of course. I'm Matt Craig, duty manager." He spoke in a hushed whisper. "Thing is, it's turning into a nightmare. I've just taken a minibus full of guests to the train station, none of whom were due to check out today. As you can see we're more than a bit stretched right now, and could do without more disruption. It's been a hell of an inconvenience, all the hassle over the road. Not what our guests pay for, they're making all sorts of demands, and that's those staying on. It's the very last thing we need at one of our busiest times of the year …"

Gethin pulled his arm away from the man's lingering grip. "Well, I'm sure the victim didn't plan on spoiling your festivities, sir."

Matt Craig stopped fidgeting, the annoyance in Gethin's tone hitting its target. "No, of course. I'm sure that sounded quite stupid to you. But it's turned into a huge problem for us. We could lose thousands of pounds. Not your fault, of course, I know."

"No, sir, it's not our fault. But we do have an unexplained death on our hands, and a legal obligation to investigate. I am going to have to demand a little assistance. We can do it the easy way, where we will be as discreet as possible, or the hard way and I shut the hotel down and keep the visitors here. Your choice."

"What? Like … murder? But I thought …"

"We have more evidence now it may not have been accidental. And I really need to get on and do my job, sir."

"What can I do?"

"I believe we have a room made available?"

"Yes."

"To start I need a list of your current employees, and then I want to speak to the staff, one by one. Starting with people who either worked directly with your chef, Gregory Chapman or who were on duty over the past forty-eight hours. Can you arrange that?" The man nodded as Gethin checked the notes on his phone. "First off … I'd like to speak to the sous chef, Dewi Thomas. Okay?"

Dewi Thomas was twenty-three years old according to his employment records, but with his lanky frame and acne-marked face had the look of someone five years younger. His blotchy skin was smooth and greasy, and his hands were red and rough, not the graceful touch Gethin expected from a chef. The chef's whites, however, along with a checked bandana that held back what appeared to be equally greasy black hair, were pristine.

Everything about the man screamed discomfort, and it took a lot of cajoling from Gethin, and nervous throat-clearing from Dewi, to get the young chef to relax.

"What was Gregory like to work for?" said Gethin, swallowing a gulp of excellent Earl Grey tea and replacing the cup on the saucer.

Dewi shrugged. "Fine, I suppose."

"Fine. That doesn't give me much, does it? Come on, you won't get in trouble. I bet he was a tyrant in the kitchen?"

Dewi frowned and shook his head. "Who said that?"

Gethin laughed. "No one. But I watch those cooking shows on telly. Chefs are a nightmare, right?"

"They're entertainment. A lot of it is put on. Greg was nothing like that."

"No?" Gethin leaned forward across the table in the bright, airy meeting room. "What was he like?"

"He was a genius. With food, like."

Gethin waited.

Dewi rubbed a face across his hand. "An' he was a perfectionist, like. If you didn't understand food the way he did, he'd get frustrated. But that was the worst of him. You either clicked with him or you didn't."

"And you clicked?"

Dewi nodded.

"How long had you worked with him here?" Gethin said, knowing from the records supplied by the hotel, but wanting to build more trust with the young man.

"Three years. Since I left college. Got on an apprenticeship. Couldn't believe my luck to be honest."

"And you understand food …"

"Yeah, Greg could see a passion in me from day one, he said." Dewi's eyes brightened for the first time. "I'd been planning dishes and menus ever since I was a kid. But I come from Maes Gwyn, you know?" He paused and Gethin nodded. He could imagine how a love of cuisine went down on that notorious

Holyhead estate. "Well, cooking was soft so they said, for girls, like. My folks wanted me to be a mechanic like me dad."

"But you did your own thing anyway? Went to college?"

"Yeah. But the folks made it clear if I didn't get a job after, there was no way I was going on benefits and I'd have to take an apprenticeship in the garage. Lucky for me I met Greg and everything changed."

Talking of changes, the difference in the young man was remarkable. Gethin had no doubt Greg Chapman had seen that same spark of desire in his young protégé.

"And you've excelled here, so I've heard?" said Gethin.

"Yeah. Got certificates comin' out of me ears now."

"Your parents must be very proud?"

Dewi shrugged as the barriers came back down.

"And when Gregory disappeared …"

Dewi cleared his throat, the nervous habit back. "No one thought that. He'd been talkin' 'bout going home. So that's what we all thought."

"Bit odd though? Right before your busiest period of the year to go off like that?"

Dewi shrugged. "Suppose he reckoned we could cope." He checked his watch. "Anyway, I have to finish the prep for lunch, it's a big one today. Is that all? I mean it's not been confirmed it is Greg in the lake, has it?"

Gethin paused. "I can confirm it's not."

Dewi's eyes widened with relief. "Really? I thought …"

"There was a likeness. But your boss, Mr Glenowen, has positively confirmed it's not Gregory."

Dewi's face clouded at the mention of his boss. "So, what's with all the questions about Greg then?"

"He's still a missing person. We're looking at every angle."

Dewi pushed back his chair, a melting pot of emotions seeming to struggle across his features. "I told you he was making plans. He'll be in Australia. Sorry … I gotta go."

Gethin watched the chef leave, his gait more of a shuffle than a stride. He sighed and looked at his list. The receptionist who'd been on duty the previous day was next. He drained his tea cup, lifted the telephone and called reception. This was not going to be a quick job.

Sarah Shaw was the polar opposite of Dewi Thomas. Blonde, bright, bubbly, and with her designer spectacles and bright crimson lipstick, she looked a good deal older than her twenty years. The pale grey uniform and red cravat gave her the look of an air hostess, polished and professional. The air around her was heavy with a concoction of fragrances; a light, flowery perfume, a strong essence of coconut Gethin assumed came from the liberally applied fake tan, and a smell that took him back to many hours sat bored, waiting for his mother in the local hairdressers. Sarah also talked at an alarming rate, and had a habit of letting her mouth run away with her inner thoughts.

"Really? It's not Greg's body?" she said at receiving the news. "I mean that's good, right, of course it is, but who is it then?"

Gethin shook his head, opened his mouth to respond.

Sarah got in first. "I know a few people who'll be glad about that, more than a few, what with all that hassle before Greg left. I wonder if there's a connection then –"

"What hassle before Mr Chapman left?"

"Ooooh. Right kicked off. Lucky I was on duty or I wouldn't have known. Great for covering up things here you know. Like those thefts from the guests' rooms. We all knew about it, and had a fair idea who was behind it, I tell you. But Mr Jones, he's not one –"

"These thefts were connected to Greg Chapman?"

Sarah threw back her head, and laughed with a loud snort. "No! Of course not."

Gethin sighed. "Okay, let's recap. The trouble before Mr Chapman left?"

Sarah rolled her eyes. "Oh, yes. A family put in a complaint about the food, claimed two of the children and the old grandmother came down with food poisoning after eating Greg's 'Mona Seafood Supreme.' Thing was they didn't report it until the day they checked out, had a doctor's note and everything, threatened bad press, crap reviews and were demanding a full refund for the whole stay … the lot. No way I could sort that one out, had to get Mr Jones involved. And it didn't go down well. They were …" Sarah leaned forward and lowered her voice, "… a large Indian family. I got the feeling Mr Jones weren't right keen."

"But the matter was resolved?"

Sarah shook her head, blonde curls bounced. "No. Mr Jones refunded the food part of their bill, but said they had to pay accommodation. Fair enough, I thought. Like Mr Jones said no one else had problems with the 'Seafood Supreme' that night and our produce is all caught local, supplied fresh. But I mean you do hear about these seafood allergies, don't you? Who's to say –"

"So, how was it left?" Gethin tried to hide his impatience.

"Well, they paid the balance, grudging, like. But this Mr Patel said his uncle was a solicitor and it wasn't the last we'd be hearing. Mr Jones went storming down to the kitchens, and there was a right bust up according to Sian. She's my mate. Pastry chef." Sarah concluded with a smile.

Gethin made a note and consulted his list. "Sian Owen?"

Sarah nodded.

"How long was this before Mr Chapman left?"

Sarah wrinkled her nose, then counted off on bright crimson fingertips. "About five days. Less than a week anyway."

Gethin made another note. "And your relationship with Mr Chapman –"

Sarah's face darkened, the first hint of a frown. "We weren't in a relationship. Who said that?"

"No. I mean your interaction. How did you get on with him?"

Sarah shrugged, a blush creeping under the scowl. "He was okay. Bit mardy but that's chefs for you. A lot of the girls thought he was a bit stuck up. Didn't mix with the riff raff."

"Really? I thought from what I'd heard he was pretty popular. Award-winning chef, good looking guy, sexy Aussie accent ... he had a lot going for him. Bet he got his share of attention, no?"

Sarah crossed her arms and leaned back in her chair. "You'd have thought so. But he was strictly off limits in terms of socialising. Never mixed with any of the staff ... unless you count the Glenowens of course. Was proper in their pockets all right."

"Can you tell me about the Glenowens? How do you get on with Stephen?"

"Okay. He's kind enough, pleasant when he meets you. Remembers your name, or maybe has a way of checking your name badge without you seeing. Has this kind of aura though, like everything is for show, like he hides behind a big smoke screen." She shrugged. "His sister though, she's right potty."

Gethin jotted a note. "How'd you mean?"

"Eliza is strange. Don't know how else to explain it. She kind of drifts around like she's on another planet. One of the cleaners told me she was some kind of Druid, don't know how true it is, but she's single and I've never seen her with a bloke so maybe it is fact. But when she meets you, she kind of smiles and looks right through you. Gives me the creeps. Only thing she has any time for is that bloody daft dog, she lets it run riot in the hotel, paw prints and slobber all over the furniture, and I've told Mr Craig before it's not in my job description to mind dogs, nor clean up after them. But of course, no one listens."

Gethin paused, pen mid-air. "Black spaniel?"

Sarah nodded. "Braint. Bloody funny name for a dog if you ask me."

So now he knew who ethereal woman was he'd met out on the dunes.

"Okay, and last thing. You've been on reception over the past few days. Any gossip you can tell me while all the activity has been going on down at the lake?"

"It's been a nightmare, I can tell you." Sarah spread her palms and gave a dramatic sigh. "I should get entry to that actors' guild, whatever it's called, what with the false platitudes and fake smiles I have to keep up. There's no training prepares you for a both-barrels assault in front of a queue of guests. And of course, once one gets a refund, it's like a domino effect. Stretched Mr Craig to breaking point, and of course, no sign of Mr Jones. The amount of moaning I've listened to, you would not believe, honest, and it's cost the hotel a pretty penny, I can tell you. Mr Glenowen had a face like thunder when he arrived, bet he's terrified the news he's lost his star chef will ruin the place."

"But it's not Mr Chapman's body. Any idea who it might be? Any gossip?"

Sarah shook her head. "No, we're all in shock. Suppose we all assumed it was Greg and it was a terrible accident. There's no one else gone missing sudden, not that I know of, and I'd probably know being on the front desk."

Gethin checked his notes. "Okay, thanks for your time. If you think of anything else, here's my card. Always call me, however small a thing."

Sarah took the business card and studied the details, before slipping off her spectacles and leaning forward to make eye contact. "I might just do that, you know. I think you're the first real life detective I've met, and I bet your life is a lot more exciting than mine. Maybe we could meet up in the Menai Bar later, they have a half-price cocktail hour at seven, and you can fill me in on all the gory details?"

Gethin was aware of heat rising in his cheeks, and hoped it wasn't visible. A tingling itch started at the nape of his neck and he fought the urge to scratch it. "Sorry, things are a bit manic, I have a de-brief later."

Sarah gave a sexy chuckle. "A de-brief, eh? Sounds interesting."

Gethin forced a grin. "It's not. No doubt I'll see you around the hotel though."

Sarah sat back with a sigh. "Shame. What you said about Greg being a popular guy. You're not too shabby yourself. Bet you get lots of attention, right?"

"Beating them off with a stick. Now, could you do me a favour and ask Sian Owen to pop in next please?"

Sian Owen. Age twenty-four, assistant pastry chef. Welsh, plump, and very astute. Just the kind of witness he liked. Told it like it was, neither too much detail or too little. Sensible, straight and normal. Gethin sighed with relief.

"So, this confrontation, you were there?"

Sian nodded. "Yeah, was no biggie. Least I didn't think so. Greg and Mr Jones rarely saw eye to eye, different personalities, is all. Seemed to me it was another point scoring exercise, and when Greg brushed it off, Mr Jones started yelling like the world was coming to an end. Stupid, really."

"Point scoring?"

"The top chef getting taken down a peg or two, you know. Lots of jealousy in this place and it boils over from time to time. Way I see it, anyway."

Gethin made a note, no doubt Sian was right. "Did you speak to Mr Chapman about it?"

Sian shook her head. "No, it weren't my department so I stayed out of it. I heard him ask Dewi to contact the supplier in Valley just to be sure. He was angry, right enough, but he didn't retaliate, not while I was there."

"So, when he disappeared you didn't connect it to the row?"

"No, of course not. We'd all seen worse."

"He was a tough boss then?"

Sian frowned, chewed her thumb nail. "Mr Jones?"

"Sorry, no, Mr Chapman."

Sian shook her head. "Not at all. People get the wrong idea about him. He's a perfectionist, top chefs usually are. You want to swim with the big fish, you learn to cope. I get on with him fine, mutual respect, and you can't ask for more."

"How about socially? I heard he wasn't one to mix with other staff?"

Sian studied him for a moment. "Why are you talking past tense?"

"Before he left I mean," said Gethin, realising his error and liking Sian even more.

"No, he mixes fine with the other chefs. He just feels uncomfortable with people who aren't on the same wavelength, that's how I see it." Sian folded her arms and smiled. "You'll have been talking to Sarah, right?"

Gethin nodded.

"She's just bitter. Her charms didn't work on Greg."

Gethin looked up. "Go on."

"She's done everything to snare him bar strip naked and ambush him in his room – although she may even have tried that for all I know. She loves a bit of celebrity, does Sarah. Oh, don't get me wrong, she has a good heart and is honest as the day is long, but dangle fame in front of her nose and she's like a greyhound out of the traps as my grandad used to say."

"And Greg wasn't interested, I take it?"

"Never even remembered her name which wound her up rotten."

"Did he ever date any of the staff that you know about?"

Sian paused, went back to worrying at her thumb nail. "He was a very private person."

"What does that mean?"

Sian shrugged. "I never saw him with anyone."

"Okay." Gethin shuffled the papers on the desk. "Tell me about you?"

Sian looked up, surprised. "Me? What about me? I don't drown people for a hobby if that's what you mean."

Gethin laughed. "I didn't think for a minute you did. No, I was looking at my notes, you've been here since you left school at sixteen."

"Yeah. It was written in the stars. My mother and grandmother both worked here, so I was destined to carry on the family tradition. The Glenowens have treated my family well over the years. I'm content enough, I get married next year, so it suits me."

"Your mother still works here?"

"Yes, she's a manager now. Head of Housekeeping, though she started as a chambermaid. She's seen it all, I tell you, anything you want to know about the Glenowens then my mum is the one to ask."

Gethin jotted a note. "Thanks, I'll bear it in mind. One last thing, now the body in the lake is confirmed not to be Gregory Chapman ... have you had any ideas?"

Sian paused, then shook her head. "No. And it's all anyone is talking about. Dewi was broken when he thought it was Greg. But if it's not him, who is it? And is that why Greg's disappeared? It makes no sense, things like this don't happen round here, it's crazy."

Gethin opened his mouth to respond, but was interrupted by a loud rap on the door. It opened to reveal a uniformed WPC whose name Gethin couldn't recall.

"Yes?" he said.

"Sorry to interrupt, sir, I've been sent to fetch you. You're needed down at the lake. Urgent."

CHAPTER FIVE

Amanda tried to ignore the rumbling in her stomach as she drove away from the hospital, but the thought of hot coffee and something sweet drew her with magnetic force towards the small supermarket and café in Menai Bridge.

Ten minutes later, a takeaway Café au Lait and an almond Danish pastry in hand, she settled back behind the wheel of her car with a sigh. One bite in and her mobile rang. She groaned, swallowed, and accepted the call.

"Kelly. Okay?"

"Yes, ma'am. Couple of updates for you."

"Go on." Amanda took another bite of pastry and brushed crumbs from her blouse.

"Gregory Chapman isn't in Perth, I'm afraid, or any other bit of Australia for that matter. I've spoken to his father and his sister, and neither has heard from him since before Christmas. They can't remember exact dates but both seemed to think early December."

Amanda reached for the cardboard cup. "Not the news we wanted."

"No. And I could tell from their voices more than their words they're worried and have been for some time. Not hearing from Gregory over Christmas is obviously out of character. The sister's voice was really shaky when she said Gregory always rang on Christmas Day so her kids could talk to their uncle and thank him for their presents." Kelly cleared her throat. "Apparently, the gifts he posted arrived mid-December."

Amanda took a pull of coffee through the small slot in the lid, then wiped her lips. "Have they done anything about finding him?"

"Alice, the sister, rang the hotel on Boxing Day but had no joy. She wasn't more specific. She didn't get the name of the person she spoke to either which is a pain."

"Friends? Other family?"

"I asked. No one came to mind. Alice said his career was his life. All the friends she knew are still in Australia."

"Damn."

"Exactly. The father was talking about flying over but I've tried to calm the situation, played it down a bit. I've not mentioned the body in the lake, didn't think it wise. I made out the hotel staff were concerned and left it at that."

Amanda chewed and considered for a moment. "I think you did right. There's a chance Gregory isn't a victim here. He could be a killer. We don't want to be telling that to his family until we know more. Shit, I wish he'd been fine and happy, cooking shrimps on his family barbie with a cold lager in hand."

"Amen to that. But it was never going to be that simple, was it, ma'am?"

Amanda sighed, sipped her coffee. "No, I guess not. What's the second thing?"

"Oh yeah. Gethin called while I was on the phone to Australia, left a voicemail. You're needed back out at the crime scene."

"Okay. I've got one quick stop off. Tell him I'll be there in an hour."

Amanda climbed out of the car and paused to breathe in the frosty morning air, feeling alive with the tingle of icy cold that flooded her body. Across iron-grey waters of the Menai Strait, the snow-capped mountains of Snowdonia rose against a sky the colour of marmalade. The reflected beams of watery sunshine against the brilliant frosted whiteness was nothing short of stunning. A landscape painter's paradise.

The croak of a pheasant, invisible in the mist-covered fields, was the only sound to break the silence. Another thing Amanda had come to love about Anglesey was the remoteness of the place, especially in winter. You really could stand in awe at the beauty of the island, and yet feel like the only living soul who inhabited it. No wonder it had millennia of history around these shores, the most sacred of all places to the Druid order for thousands of years. On a morning like this it wasn't hard to see why.

She pushed the buzzer, stamping her feet as she waited. She checked her watch. Everyone at Plas Coch was more than accommodating with visiting times, but she was earlier than usual.

Janice, one of the regular staff, let her in with raised eyebrows and warm smile. "Well, good morning, Mrs Gold. Happy New Year."

"And to you, Janice. Apologies for the early visit. I hope it's not too inconvenient?"

Janice gestured Amanda inside. "I shouldn't think so. We were expecting you later, you do know we're putting on a teatime spread for relatives?"

"Yes, I was looking forward to it." She swallowed the lie, hoping it wasn't too apparent. "But I've been called into work on a new case, and you know how it is, I've no idea when I'll next come up for air. I wanted to wish Mother 'Happy New Year' while I had chance. It's a flying visit."

Janice nodded as Amanda bent over the reception desk and signed the visitor's book. "It's also one less lump of guilt you'll have to carry around with you all day, taking up space in your brain you really can't spare. I understand."

"Sounds awful when you put it into words."

Janice shook her head. "Not at all. We're all human. Outside of these walls, life goes on as normal. It's not an easy thing to balance, but we're here to help you try."

"And you do an amazing job."

"Bless you. Now, like I say, Mrs Walsh is generally an early riser, I'm sure she'll be at breakfast. We can check and if not I'll take you up to her room."

"Thank you."

Instead of heading straight for the lift as usual, Amanda followed Janice along a corridor away to the right. Bunches of fresh flowers in large cream jugs on half-moon tables, lined the hallway, the heady scent sweet and welcoming, as was the morning sunshine filtering through each open door.

Janice halted, causing Amanda to bump into her.

"Sorry," said Amanda.

"It's okay. One second."

Amanda became aware of a faint mewling sound, like a trapped kitten or an injured fox. Janice had clearly heard it too. The door on their right opened into a moderate-sized television room. A children's cartoon flickered silently on the screen to a horseshoe of empty chairs. In the furthest corner, tucked between the television and a floor-length curtain was what looked like a bundle of blue and grey rags.

Janice tutted and stepped into the room, Amanda following on instinct.

"Now, now, now. What is this all about?" Janice made her way around the chairs. "Diana, sweetheart, what on earth are you doing down there?"

The rags unravelled, white hair and a pale face appeared. Scared eyes shimmered with tears. Amanda's stomach turned somersaults. Relieved on one hand it wasn't her own mother, but bursting with compassion for the poor woman. She followed Janice who was already on her hands and knees, crawling carefully through the labyrinth of wires, finally wrapping the old woman's shaking body in her arms.

Amanda stood helplessly, fighting back tears as the two women rocked in each other's arms. Finally, with a sniff of impatience, she began to push chairs aside, and worked loose the plugs to free both women from the tangle of wires. Janice looked up and gave a smile of gratitude.

"Now, see, that's better. Thank you, Mrs Gold. Shall we get ourselves out of here now Mrs Gold has made some space? Come on, Diana. Don't know about you but my knees are killing me."

Slowly, one careful inch at a time, Janice coaxed the woman out of the corner. Her long navy blue nightdress was streaked with dust. As Janice settled her into one of the armchairs, she whispered to Amanda.

"Could you stay with her one minute whilst I go and fetch Pat? So sorry."

Amanda waved away the apology, forced a smile and settled into the chair beside the window. The old woman sniffed and looked up, appearing to see Amanda for the first time.

"I couldn't find him."

Amanda smiled. "Who were you looking for?"

"Stephen."

"Stephen?"

The woman stared down at her hands. "My son, of course. Stephen."

"Ah, I see."

"He was here. There was fireworks and cake. Then he was gone and he never said goodbye. He always says goodbye."

Amanda gave a wide smile. "Perhaps you were asleep by then?"

"He was on television you know. Won an award." The old woman continued and began rubbing her hands together, sand paper on wood. "I thought that's where he'd gone."

Amanda nodded, swallowing hard. "Ah. Inside the TV? You went to find him?"

A toothy smile broke out on the pale face; she tugged down the sleeves on her grey crocheted cardigan. "Yes. He wasn't there though. Too much colour."

"I know. I've turned it off. No more colour."

"Thank you."

They fell into silence. Amanda glanced out at the frosted lawns, mist whirling and rising as the ground warmed. She reflected on the irony and cruelness of life. How could it be easier to find a connection with this distressed stranger, to calm her even, when it was something she seemed incapable of achieving with her own mother?

"Eliza?"

The woman was looking at her now, studying her for the first time, head cocked to one side like an inquisitive puppy.

"No. Amanda. I'm Amanda."

"Where is Eliza?"

Amanda was saved the task of answering by the return of Janice and a small round woman, with a blonde bob and vivid pink spectacles.

"Well, look at you, lady. Turn my back for five minutes to make your porridge and there you're off gallivanting." Her voice was warm with a strong lilt of Irish. Amanda thought of her DS, Dara Brennan, accompanied by a sharp pang of emptiness. She missed him more than she cared to admit. "You're trying to get me the sack, so you are, Diana."

Pat settled into the chair beside Diana and took both of her fragile hands in her own. Pat looked up and mouthed 'thank you' to Amanda. Janice touched her elbow and indicated they should leave.

Amanda stood, and hovered a moment, before leaning down to squeeze Diana's bony wrist. "Lovely to meet you, Diana. I'll see you again. Keep giving them hell, you hear?"

Amanda winked and was rewarded with one of the toothy smiles.

"I'm sorry about that," said Janice, back in the corridor. "She keeps Pat on her toes."

"What's her story? Sorry, that sounds terribly nosy, blame the job. And ignore me, I know all about patient confidentiality."

Janice smiled and pushed open a door at the far end of the

corridor. "She's another of our Alzheimer's patients, from a very close family, lived with her children until a few months ago. She's suffering badly from separation anxiety. This disease has many faces, I'm sure I don't have to tell you that."

"Poor woman," said Amanda. "I hate this bloody disease, it seems the cruellest thing ever. Robbing you of someone you love and know so well while they're still breathing."

Janice squeezed her arm as they entered the restaurant, clusters of tables scattered around a large brightly lit room, whose central feature was a large bay window affording a superb view of the Menai Strait and the mountains beyond.

"Your mother is with Gloria, over by the window, tucking into toast by the looks of it. Can I get you anything to eat or drink while you're here, Mrs Gold?"

Amanda shook her head. "I'm fine, thank you. I'm not here to inconvenience you even more. I'll have five minutes with mother and be on my way. Thank you anyway."

Her mother was sitting in her wheelchair, wrapped in one her favourite tartan shawls, her gaze far off outside the window. Amanda hoped, as she had countless times, the views afforded her mother some release, allowed some part of her mind to wander free among the heather and gorse, taking footpaths she'd once trod with Amanda's father. Both keen walkers, they'd reached Snowdon's summit more than once, something Amanda was certain she'd never replicate.

Gloria spotted her as she threaded her way between tables, and raised a hand in greeting, leaning close to wipe her mother's mouth with a napkin, and talk into her ear at the same time. The encroaching deafness was the least of her mother's problems, but still seemed to present yet another barrier to scale. Gloria, however, a shiny-faced Filipino woman with a penchant for costume jewellery and bright fuchsia lipstick, seemed to sail over any obstacle like a bird on a thermal. There weren't many things in life Amanda envied in others, but she wished more than anything she had a quarter of Gloria's skill and patience where her mother was concerned.

"What a lovely surprise!" said Gloria, vacating her seat, so Amanda could sit beside her mother. "Look who it is, Mrs Walsh, it's Amanda. Say hello."

Her mother's head turned slowly, vacant eyes behind her spectacles. "I don't know anyone called Amanda,"

"Ah, there's your memory playing tricks again. Amanda is your daughter, remember?"

Her mother responded with an icy stare.

"Happy New Year, Gloria," said Amanda, pulling the chair into the table. "Happy New Year, Mother." She leaned across and kissed the smooth cheek, breathing in the smell of soap and talcum powder, but eliciting no more than a frown from her mother's features.

"We weren't expecting you yet, Mrs Gold," said Gloria, beginning to clear away the half-eaten cereal and toast. "We thought you may come along for the party later. Your mother is quite fussy about wearing her purple party dress tonight, aren't you, Mrs Walsh?"

"Yes, sorry. Work, I'm afraid. But I wanted to come and wish you all the best for the new year from me and Emily," she said, turning to address her mother. There was the slightest reaction in her mother's gaze at the mention of Emily. "She's staying with her father but sends all her love. She'll be visiting soon."

Amanda spoke slowly, her cheeks aching from the fixed smile, a hive of bees dancing a tango in her stomach.

"Ah, that's nice. Isn't that nice, Mrs Walsh?" Gloria leaned closer, brushed her mother's cheek with an intimacy Amanda couldn't dig out from even her deepest depths. "It's a shame you'll miss the party, your mother is so looking forward to it."

The pale blue eyes were empty again. Amanda wondered, not for the first time, if the interaction Gloria regularly described wasn't a figment of her imagination. There was nothing here to indicate her mother knew what day it was let alone there was a party planned for later.

"Can I get you some breakfast, Mrs Gold?"

"No, thank you, I'm fine. It's a flying visit. I'll be back on Sunday as usual." Amanda forced herself to cover her mother's age-spotted hand, resting on the festive tablecloth, with her own. "Did you watch the fireworks over in Beaumaris, last night, Mother?"

Her mother frowned again, dropped her chin to stare over the top of her spectacles. She wrinkled her nose and slid her hand from under Amanda's.

After a pause, it was Gloria who answered. "We did, didn't we? The fireworks, remember? You kept asking when we'd get the all clear?" She laughed. "And two glasses of sherry to see in the New Year too!"

Amanda smiled, trying to ignore the pain of yet another rejection.

Her mother's voice was low and quiet. "I have to get changed for the party. Gloria? Take me to my room."

Gloria patted her shoulder. "We have plenty of time, Mrs Walsh. Hours yet."

"No, I want to go now. I don't like interruptions to my breakfast."

"It's only Amanda come to join us," Gloria reasoned. "She's made a big effort to come and see you today."

Her mother's hands left the table, sliding down the sides of her wheelchair, bony fingers groping for the brake levers. "Well, she shouldn't have bothered. I don't know anyone called Amanda anyway."

Gloria was at her side as the chair began to roll backwards. "Five more minutes, yes? Then we'll go and see the hairdresser."

There was an edge of desperation in Gloria's voice that sent ants marching across Amanda's skin. She got to her feet.

"Don't worry, Gloria, it's fine. I need to make a move."

Gloria couldn't hide the relief. "Ah, you are sure?"

"Positive. I don't know why I thought it was a good idea coming today." She shrugged, forced an ironic smile. "It's never gone down well in the past, breaking her routine, I should have learnt my lesson by now."

"Well, if you're sure it's not a problem," said Gloria, patiently untwisting her mother's fingers from the brakes. "I'll go and get her settled."

Amanda paused, leaning down to hug her mother's stiff shoulders. "I'll see you on Sunday. Enjoy your party."

There was no response. Gloria patted Amanda's arm as they passed, and approaching the door, she heard her mother's voice. "Who was she, spoiling my breakfast?"

Gloria hushed her mother and glanced round. Amanda raised a hand in parting and hurried back along the flower-scented corridor, not even taking time to glance into the television room, yearning for the privacy of her car before the tears came.

CHAPTER SIX

Half an hour later Amanda was back at Llyn Maelog. She parked behind a black Range Rover that looked like Dr Sixsmith's vehicle. Amanda's heartbeat quickened. That could only mean one thing. She hurried from her car to the group of men standing at the edge of the lake. Amanda recognised Gethin with Dr Sixsmith gazing out across the lake to where the dive team were still working. The ice was shattered in several places, jagged black gashes zig-zagging the surface, looking cruel and harsh somehow against the perfection of Mother Nature. As she approached, she glanced from one man to another.

"What is it?" she asked. "Another body? I'd have got here sooner."

Gethin shook his head. "No rush, ma'am."

"What do you mean?"

It was the pathologist who answered with a warm smile. "Hello, again, Detective Gold. We must stop meeting like this. I got the call just after you left the lab but this one isn't my jurisdiction, I'm afraid. Come and see."

Amanda flashed a questioning glance at Gethin and followed Dr Sixsmith to a green tarpaulin. As he lifted the plastic sheet to reveal a pile of glistening bones, he added. "I can confirm they're human. But that's about all. There's about fifty percent of the skeleton intact from what I can see, and we're missing a skull. The rest is probably disturbed and scattered. The divers are back in having another look."

Amanda gazed down at the jumbled assortment of bones, some brown, some green and slimy. "I don't understand."

"Simple enough. It's another body but this one has been in the water a lot longer than a month."

"How long?"

The pathologist shrugged and recovered the remains. "Impossible to say at this stage. A hundred years maybe, decades certainly. I've put a call into the Coroner's office, this is his headache. He'll need to attend before we remove anything. And then there are specialists who'll be able to give more accurate dates, decide if it's a crime scene or a piece of archaeological evidence, but it's not my field of speciality I'm afraid."

Amanda sighed and turned to Gethin. "This is bizarre. Anything else turned up?"

"No. I've been interviewing hotel staff. Got the call and came down here. The divers found this quite near the shore, not too far from where our corpse was first seen at the edge of the woods on the eastern bank. But once I'd spoken to Dr Sixsmith, I realised it's clearly not connected to our investigation."

Amanda looked across the lake to where an orange inflatable raft was balanced on the ice, lines leading down beneath the shattered surface. Raised voices carried across, as the men moved methodically in a grid pattern, assisting the divers down in the murk below. Rather them than her. She watched as a red-suited man lay flat on his belly and pulled a rope to the surface, retrieving a bag from the end and transferring the contents to the inflatable raft.

Amanda shivered. "Or is it ..."

"Ma'am?"

"Sorry, Geth. Thinking aloud. I'm not a big believer in coincidence. I'm wondering if there could be a connection."

Gethin shrugged and rubbed his hands together. "Corpses decades apart, can't see it."

"You think it's normal? Every lake in the country might be a dumping ground for human bodies? Can't see that either, can you?"

"No, of course not, but we could be looking at a drowning for the skeleton. Or suicide. This lake was used for shipbuilding hundreds of years ago, could be an accident to do with that. Loads of explanations make more sense to me."

Amanda sighed. "You're probably right. I'm seeing intrigue and connections where there may be none. Can we leave this one with you, Doc? We need to focus on our original body and our missing chef."

Dr Sixsmith nodded. "The Coroner is on his way. I'll sign this one over to him. Although … I'm with you, DI Gold, I wouldn't discount anything. I'm not a believer in coincidences either."

Glenys Owen knocked on the door of their makeshift interview room, pushing it open with her hip, she deposited a huge tray onto the table, crammed with coffee pot and two plates piled high with triangular dainty sandwiches on one, and an assortment of pastries and finger-sized cakes on the other.

Gethin groaned. "Oh, my days. Come in, Mrs Owen. You're one welcome sight."

Glenys Owen smiled, wide brown eyes behind gold spectacles. She was stout and solid, with her warm smile and sensible bobbed haircut, streaked with strands of grey amongst the dark blonde. She had a matronly look of someone who oozed kindness but also had a hidden streak of metal when called upon. "I spoke to Sian. Always playing mother, that's my trouble, but I figured it would be welcome."

Gethin reached for a plate and began shovelling sandwiches and miniature sausage rolls onto it. "You're not wrong. I'm starving."

"Thank you," said Amanda. "I'm the mother-figure on this team … the one with the manners."

Glenys smiled as Gethin mumbled his thanks through a mouthful of flaky pastry.

Amanda waited while delicious smelling coffee was poured and distributed, then scanned through Gethin's notes.

"We won't keep you from your duties for too long, Mrs Owen …"

"It's Glenys, please."

Amanda smiled. "Glenys, my DS here, who is very choosy with his food, so clearly knows the classy stuff when he sees it," she flashed a look at Gethin's puffed cheeks, "tells me he was impressed with his interview with your daughter. And Sian suggested for general background information, you were the perfect candidate. That's why we've called you in."

Glenys wrinkled her nose. "I'll be thanking Sian for that later."

"There's nothing to worry about, Glenys. Anything you say here is in strictest confidence. We need an insider's point of view. It's impossible for us, walking in quite literally from the cold, to know important details about an establishment like this."

"Oh, don't get me wrong. I'm happy to help." She paused, looked at her hands. "I guess it feels like betrayal. I've kept a lot of secrets over the years, well, maybe confidences more than secrets. The Glenowens have been good to me. Me and my family. I don't want to betray their trust due to them getting dragged into something that's really nothing to do with them. Do you understand?"

Amanda stirred her coffee. "Of course, believe me I could write a book on loyalty. But we have a missing person enquiry and a murder enquiry here. And the hotel seems smack bang in the middle of certainly one, possibly both. We really need your help."

Gethin wiped his lips with a lemon-coloured napkin. "Your daughter is a credit to you, Mrs Owen. She was a perfect witness. I hoped you could do the same with filling in some background details. I doubt anything we ask would count as real betrayal."

Glenys Owen took a couple of moments to consider, then straightened her back and gave a determined nod. "Yes. I do understand. I'm shocked at all this going on right on our doorstep. I mean out here, this kind of thing doesn't happen in Rhosneigr ... it's beyond bizarre. And to think young Gregory could be involved in some way ... well, that's even more bizarre if you ask me."

Gethin slid his notebook across the table and brushed crumbs from the tablecloth. "You liked Mr Chapman?"

Glenys shrugged. "Nothing not to like. He treated my Sian well. All the chefs had nothing but good to say about him. And he had a talent with food, that's for sure." She paused, looked up, cheeks flushed. "Has a talent, I mean. Let's not talk about him as if he's not coming back. I couldn't stand to do that."

Amanda sipped her coffee as Gethin got back into his stride. "Your daughter confirmed something, I admit, surprises me. No one seemed too bothered when Gregory disappeared. Did you feel the same?"

Glenys shrugged. "I don't work in the kitchens, and I don't always know what's been agreed. I suppose I took Sian's view he'd gone back to Australia. Looking back though, I can see that would seem odd to have been given time off at short notice at this time of year. But maybe he had family problems ... I don't know. Sorry, in hindsight maybe we should have worried more. But he had done similar before and got away with it, if you know what I mean."

Gethin nodded. "Yes, I heard about that."

"Gregory was a little arrogant, came with the territory. Knew he had the talent to get away with things most of us wouldn't dare. And he could always rely on Stephen's support if he needed it. It gave him a bit of an edge, made some of the staff a bit wary of him."

Amanda frowned and watched the woman's round face, the pinkness of her cheeks crept down her neck, flushing the skin against the whiteness of her blouse. Glenys fiddled with the bronze badge. Head of Housekeeping. Amanda cleared her throat. "This special relationship he had with Stephen Glenowen …"

Glenys looked up, relief in her eyes. Words left unsaid to fill the gaps. "I wouldn't say relationship. But … friends, good friends. They were close. Are close … damn. It comes too natural to speak of someone in the past tense, doesn't it?"

Amanda smiled. "So, this friendship. You think this is the main reason none of the staff were alarmed when Gregory didn't turn in for work."

"Yes. No one questioned it as they might have done with someone else. And my view is that was because of perceived special treatment due to his friendship with Mr Glenowen. I'm not saying that's right, but …" She opened her hands, like opening the pages of a book, laying the evidence on display for the detectives.

"I see that," said Amanda. "Thanks for your honesty."

"I'm supposing you have checked with his family?"

"He hasn't been home," said Gethin.

"I wish he had." Glenys sighed. "I refuse to believe he's anything to do with this dead body business. Shocking, that's what it is. Shocking. Gregory wasn't like that."

"Like what?" said Amanda.

"Well, like these stupid rumours. Like he's a killer on the run. Gregory was always seeking peace and quiet, loved spending time out on the dunes, alone, watching birds or writing poetry. He spent hours over on the beach, kayaking, reckoned it got him closer to nature. He was nothing like your stereotypical Aussie, once you cut through the arrogant edge he was a wonderful human being. He's the last person would take any form of life. It's ridiculous." Glenys paused for breath. "Sorry, it's just … sorry."

"It's okay. Go on."

Glenys shook her head, the smile back in place. "He brought out the mothering instinct in me I suppose. Lioness defending one of her cubs."

"Oh, I know that feeling," said Amanda. "But we have no evidence Gregory has any connection with the body. Anything you've heard to the contrary is gossip, nothing more."

"And no news about who it is you've found?"

Gethin shook his head. "We're working on photo-fits. When we have them we'll show them round the staff. But nothing yet." He glanced at his notes. "Can you tell me a bit about the Glenowens. It's Stephen and Eliza who run the hotel now, is it?"

Glenys nodded, straightening her name badge for the umpteenth time. "Stephen really. Eliza's touch can be found everywhere in the hotel, she's a very talented interior designer you see … but I wouldn't say she has much involvement in the running of the place. Have you spoken to Eliza yet?"

Amanda shook her head and Gethin added. "I think I ran into her in the car park. She seemed quite vague … not sure that's the right word."

Glenys smiled. "It probably is. She's a gentle soul. Had a promising career with one of the big designers after she finished Uni. Flat in Mayfair, drove a Porsche, the family were brimming with pride. Then one day she appeared back here, heavily pregnant, no mention of a father. Anyway, there were complications with the birth … the boy died before his second birthday, spent most of his short life in and out of hospital. And it changed Eliza. She never went back to London." Glenys sighed, folded her hands in her lap. "She's joined the island's Druid community. I'm not one to judge on such things, but it seems to have given her some inner peace. But yes, vague is about the right word I'd say."

"So, the responsibility of the business is left to Stephen?"

"Well, yes. Him and Terry. Terence Jones, the general manager. He's like a father to Stephen since Oliver, Stephen's father, died. Terry has given his life to the Glenowens. He was married to Stephen's eldest sister, Clara, but she passed away in her forties, breast cancer." Glenys paused for breath, memories clearly coming thick and fast. "Oh, they've always had the wealth and status, the Glenowens, but they've had their share of bad luck, that's for sure."

"And Stephen's not married, no children to inherit?" Amanda asked.

Glenys glanced down, more nervous name badge fiddling. "No, he's far too career focused. I think that's another worry. One of the last things I had a sensible talk to Diana about. What was to happen to Maelog in the future?"

Amanda frowned, aware of the scratch of Gethin's pen. "Diana?"

"Oh, sorry. Stephen's mother. Diana Glenowen, bless her soul. Another family tragedy. Held the family together after Oliver's passing and then suddenly, from nowhere went downhill with dementia. Less than two years and barely knew her own name, pushed poor Eliza over the edge, and Stephen had no choice but to find a place in a care facility for her a few weeks back. Terrible."

Amanda's head was filled with memories of Plas Coch that morning, the bundle of blue rags, colourful cartoons flickering to an empty room, and the sad, empty eyes of Diana Glenowen.

CHAPTER SEVEN

Gethin waited for the lift doors to open, then followed Glenys Owen along the anonymous cream corridor, identical to so many other corridors in so many hotels worldwide. He wondered if that's how hospitality staff saw their accommodation and if it built resentment being constantly surrounded by the unglamorous side of life. Whether it be top hotels, luxury cruise liners or first-class air travel, there was still the same mundane underbelly, the cream or grey painted internal workings, that kept the glitzy exterior alive.

He'd experienced a taste of it himself, growing up in a small flat above his parent's restaurant in Beaumaris. Retired now, back then their whole lives revolved around the business, and Gethin had always felt like an afterthought. Kept out of sight from the bustling tourists, most nights eating leftovers from the previous day's menu, resenting the strain the long hours and lack of free time put on his family. He'd hated the restaurant with its noises and smells, a constant back-drop to his life right up to the time he left for Uni.

Glenys stopped in front of a brown door and swiped a key card across the lock. Green lights flashed and, with an electronic hum, the door swung open at Glenys's touch.

"Thanks for bringing me down here, Mrs Owen. Let's hope we can find something in Greg's room that points us in the right direction."

Glenys slid the card into the light switch inside the door. "I hope so."

"Has the room been searched, do you know?"

"I came down here with Terry on the first day Greg didn't turn up for work, in case he'd taken ill or the like. But nothing has been touched since so far as I know."

"DI Gold wants us to have a look for a mobile or laptop and take it into the station for the experts to examine, so if you wouldn't mind hanging around to sign a release form that would be great."

"Sure, no problem."

"Not the biggest of rooms, are they?" said Gethin, his gaze following the oddly-shaped narrow room, from the small walk-in shower room, across the neatly-made single bed to a corner desk and wardrobe.

Glenys laughed. "Nope. Basic and functional. The more room for paying guests the better. I reckon all hotel bosses try to discourage live-in staff by making the rooms as poky as possible."

"Even for top chefs, it seems," commented Gethin as he opened the wardrobe door, moving the desk stool out of the way to allow the door to swing open.

Three sets of chef's whites hung in a neat row. Pushed into the shadows was a rubber wet-suit alongside a white dress shirt and a smart, navy-blue suit Gethin had seen in the prize-giving photo in the local press. He crouched to pull open one of two drawers at the bottom of the wardrobe, folded t-shirts, socks and boxers in the top one, two pairs of smart shoes and a pair of brand new trainers in the other.

He looked up at Glenys Owen. "Some clothes are here but it feels to me like there's stuff missing too. Casual stuff he'd be wearing in the winter. You know, jeans and jumpers. Boots. Coat. Any idea if he'd store stuff anywhere else?"

Glenys shook her head. "No, all his belongings would be in here. There are lockers in the cloakroom but only for coats and the like for staff who don't live in. He was an Aussie though, maybe he didn't have many winter clothes."

"As an Aussie I'd think he'd suffer from the cold even more than us. This all looks like summer gear he's packed away."

Gethin stood up, brushed his hands. A multi-coloured surfboard was wedged in the gap behind the wardrobe, a large yellow oar balanced upright in the alcove behind the door. He stepped up onto the stool to check the top of the wardrobe. Layers of undisturbed dust.

"How about suitcases?"

"They're kept in the storeroom off the staff cloakroom. Not exactly room for one in here. Although …" Glenys paused and looked round.

"What?"

"Greg did carry a rucksack with him a lot of the time, especially if he was off exploring the island. Grey and purple, if I recall right. Big chunky thing, looked heavy." She crouched to look under the bed. "Can't see it here."

Gethin made a mental note. "Maybe we could check this cloakroom on the way out? Now, let's see about a laptop."

"I've seen Greg using a tablet down in the canteen. He'd Facetime his family on it quite often. I always assumed he carried it with him in the rucksack. And he certainly had an iPhone. I heard him and young Dewi debating the benefits of Apple products one day."

"That's useful information. You wouldn't have his mobile number, would you?"

"No, but our Sian would, I'm sure. Shall I nip and get it for you?"

"Please."

Gethin waited until the door closed and began to rifle through the desk drawers. There was little of consequence. A folder of payslips, dentist appointment cards, which he made a note of name and number, plus receipts and bills. In the bottom drawer, there was a pile of birthday cards, most jokey or rude. One with Brother, another with 'World's Greatest Uncle.' Scrawled messages from staff in others, Dewi and Sian amongst them. The largest card showed a glossy black and white view of the Manhattan skyline. Inside, the message was brief. 'One day, my love, we will celebrate your birthday here. S x'

Gethin paused with the card in his hand for a moment. So, there was a love interest somewhere. Here or Australia? How long ago was Greg's birthday? Who was 'S'? Were they still together, or could she be married? Could it explain his love of privacy and solitary trips? And why would she not have come forward by now? Unless that explained the chefs' sudden disappearance and they'd ran off together.

Head buzzing with questions, Gethin did a quick sweep of the rest of the room. There were no electronic devices of any kind, which maybe pointed to him having taken off somewhere. One thing the search did reveal was that Greg Chapman was as clean and organised in his personal life as he was in his professional.

Gethin put his head inside the bathroom, scanning the shelves for anything female. Cosmetics or perfume, girly shower gel or deodorant. Nothing. The bathroom was sparkling clean with an electric beard trimmer plugged in at the power point and a small wash bag hanging from a hook beside the sink, containing toothpaste, toothbrush, facial scrub and shave balm. Greg certainly liked to travel light, which was unsurprising as he was living on the other side of the world, but still … Gethin gave one last look around the room. It almost felt as if there was nothing of Gregory Chapman here because he spent hardly any time here.

He waited at the door for Glenys Owen to return from the kitchens, and took the number from her with a smile, texting the information across to Kelly, who he knew was still busy trying to search any tangible sign of the chef's final known movements.

"Right, let's take a look at this storage room for a suitcase, and I'll be out of your hair. Thanks again for your help."

Glenys nodded and led the way back along the corridor. "It's a pleasure. We all want Greg back. I keep thinking about his rucksack, it could mean he's taken off somewhere, couldn't it? It gives me a bit of hope."

Gethin kept his face blank and decided not to reply. It could, of course, suggest an innocent trip. But it could also just as easily point to guilt.

Gethin glanced out of the window next to his desk. Just gone five pm and already pitch black. He hated the long, dark nights this time of year. Hated everything about the month of January in fact. It was almost like being in hibernation. Dark when you got up in a morning, dark when you made it home at night. So cold you didn't linger outside during the few short hours of daylight, and quite often sunshine was nothing more than a distant memory of summer.

He shivered as he remembered the icy rawness out on the lake earlier. The members of the dive team were certainly much hardier souls than he was. No way could he cope with those sorts of conditions. And the thought of plunging himself down into that water sent chills thorough his body even here in the central-heated warmth of the station. It was his greatest fear. Drowning. Something subconscious from his childhood, and yet he'd never himself been in any difficulty in water. He was a competent swimmer, enjoyed hours spent in the pool at the local gym. No, it was outdoor swimming that freaked him. Any water with waves or currents, weed or wildlife, cold and unpredictable.

He'd been twelve when Ash died. Ashley Griffiths. Short and strong, blonde and sun-tanned from hours spent out on their boat with his father, emptying the lobster pots they kept along the Menai Strait. Ash had been his best friend since nursery. His confidante, his protector, his guardian angel was how he thought of him now. He'd loved Ash as the brother he'd never had.

There had been a storm. 17th January. He'd never forget the date, and another reason he hated the first month of the year. Ash had pushed to go out as the weather had kept them on land and the pots needed emptying or they'd be wasted. His father relied on the forecasts, wanted to let the storm pass, but this time Ash got his way. They got in trouble in the currents of the Swellies, between the bridges, like many sailors before them. Ashley's father managed to make it to shore, clung on to rocks until the Coastguard arrived. His son's body was carried away, found days later out on Caernarfon Bar, left for his mother to identify while his father clawed his way back to life. No, there was no way Gethin would ever put himself at that kind of risk. He knew the pain it left behind.

The office door opened and the DI entered. From the lines across her forehead and the pinched expression on her face, he could tell she was displeased. When DCI Idris Parry appeared seconds later, he understood the cause of her distress. Amanda headed to the front of the room and used a tiny coloured magnet to fix a close up facial shot of their first body to the whiteboard, shooting sideways glances at the DCI who took the empty seat at Dara's desk and crossed his arms with a grunt.

"Right, team, let's get this done as quick as possible. What a day. Just scratching the surface of the investigation into one murder and we have another corpse on our hands."

Fletch looked up. "It is murder then?"

"The pathologist has no doubts. Full report should be with us in the morning. Strangulation. Possibly sexually motivated, unable to say whether consensual or not. Time frame is a nightmare – death anything up to a month ago. Finally, the body was left chained up somewhere after death, but prior to being dumped in the lake, skin slippage around chain marks on the neck prove this fact. This is the best evidence the corpse is giving us so far and we should try and run with it."

Gethin cleared his throat, while scrawling notes on his pad. "You're thinking we should focus on finding the crime scene, or at least where the body was kept?"

"Yes." Amanda tapped a pen against her chin. "We need to start a search from the lake outwards. I know the body could have been transported there by car, but we have to start somewhere."

The DCI cleared his throat with a phlegmy cough. "Seems to me we're clutching at straws here."

Amanda turned towards him, her face fixed in a blank expression. Gethin could almost feel the tension emanating in waves from her body outwards.

"You have another suggestion, sir?" she asked.

"Well, two things seem obvious to me. Identification. And finding a link between the body and this missing chef chappie. No one thinks it's coincidence, do they? This chef could well be our killer. Find him, solve the crime. That's the way a logical brain would be working at this point, surely?"

Amanda acknowledged his words with a dip of her head and gave no indication she'd picked up on the insult. "I was coming onto identification. Now we have the PM stills, I assume you'd suggest going public and take it you'll be happy to arrange a press conference, sir?"

"If that's what you think, Gold, then of course I'll be happy to help."

Gethin stole a sideways glance at Kelly, whose expression of distaste was clear.

"I think we've all been focusing on the chef connection," said Kelly. "It's the only tangible lead we have, but unfortunately if he's gone to ground he's done a bloody good job. I've spoken to his mobile phone provider. The number hasn't been in use since the 19th December – the day he went missing – and there's no pinging or triangulation information to trace the handset either so the phone must be turned off or the SIM has been removed."

Gethin cleared his throat. "And I've searched his room at the hotel. No computer or mobile there. Very little to let us into his life, apart from some birthday cards from his last birthday in August. I checked the date with payroll before I left. Seems he did have a love interest, though I'm not sure if that's relevant or not."

Gethin explained briefly about the New York birthday card and ended with the mystery of the missing rucksack.

"The mobile usage and missing tablet are concerns," said Amanda.

"Why? If he's a killer it makes perfect sense," said Idris Parry.

Amanda winced. "Yes, of course. I see that too, sir. Back to our body … I think we should push on with the public appeal as soon as possible."

Idris Parry got to his feet with a dramatic sigh. "Glad you've finally come round to my way of thinking. I'll go and get the ball rolling, see if we can get something on the breakfast news."

The whole team waited until the door closed behind the DCI and then gave a collective sigh as the atmosphere in the room relaxed.

"Anything to get you out of the way," Amanda muttered, giving Gethin a wink. "Much else in the room search, Geth?"

He shook his head, thinking of the compact, orderly personal space. "Nothing. If he had a woman, no sign she was ever there. Which made me think about staff comments he liked his privacy – maybe she's married?"

Fletcher turned to face Gethin. "Ah, found himself a MILF, you think."

"Fletch!" Kelly looked up, eyes ablaze.

Fletcher grinned. "You are so easy to rile. Pipe down."

"When you learn to treat women with a bit of respect, I'll happily pipe down."

Amanda gave a loud tut. "Pack it in, both of you. Fletch, grow up. It's a serious consideration, Gethin. Explains the secrecy and why he's not interested in attention from girls at the hotel. You have a way with the ladies, Geth, so let's see if that line of enquiry leads us anywhere, will you?"

Gethin nodded, heat flooding his cheeks as he scribbled a note onto his pad.

Amanda drummed her fingers against the edge of Gethin's desk as she passed, taking her time to continue. All eyes studied her as she paced the room.

"I think we have to split the investigation into two distinct channels in order to keep both sides moving forward. At the moment, it feels too blurred. We may be making connections where there on none or missing vital evidence by discarding it. Kelly and Fletch, let's have you two concentrate on the identification of the corpse. Kelly, now we have a photo, let's hit every missing person's website and run it through the national police database too. Hopefully we will get public responses following the DCI's press release, I'd like to you handle that too." Kelly made a thumbs-up gesture and turned back to her computer.

Amanda looked across the office. "Fletcher, I think we should give due consideration to the pathologist's findings there may be a homosexual connection. He couldn't rule out this being a sexually motivated murder. How about spending a few hours this evening showing the dead man's photo around the gay bars in town. It's a fairly tight crowd. I'm sure they'll talk if he's known."

Fletcher gave a dramatic groan. "Ma'am, really? I have plans for tonight. Can't Gethin take that on?"

"Hang on, why me?" said Gethin. "Maybe I've got plans."

"Oh, go on, mate, please. I'll owe you. You know how I feel about bloody –"

"Save your breath, Fletch," interrupted Amanda. "I have plans for Gethin too. Besides, it won't take you all night. I'm sure your date will think you're well worth waiting for. Keep 'em keen, isn't that your motto?"

Fletch turned back to his computer with a scowl and hammered the keys with more force than necessary, grumbling to himself under his breath.

Amanda gave a soft smile and got to her feet. "Gethin, as you've done most of the work at the hotel, I'd like you to concentrate on the disappearance of Gregory Chapman. Go have your tea out at Llyn Maelog Hotel tonight, on expenses of course, spend a bit more time there. Maybe try and get talking to some of the younger staff when they're off-duty and alcohol has loosened their tongues. Then tomorrow, let's start sending out Chapman's photo to other forces, see if it rattles any memories. Whatever the reason he's gone to ground, we need to find him, if only to clear him from the investigation."

Gethin nodded and reached across to power down his computer.

"And I'm off to Bangor Uni to see what our collection of human bones can tell us," said Amanda with a sigh. "See you all in the morning, people."

CHAPTER EIGHT

Gethin pushed away his plate and patted his stomach in satisfaction. The sirloin steak and cooked-three-times chips were a million miles removed from the spaghetti on toast he had been planning. Even his added special ingredient of grated Parmesan wouldn't have topped the lusciousness of the juicy steak. Growing up in a restaurant environment, he'd learned to appreciate good quality food, but his childhood had also left him with an aversion to cooking. And it was a bit of a trek out to his parents' cottage near Conwy every night to get a decent meal. In an ideal world, where his wages were at least treble his current salary, he'd choose to dine out every single night somewhere akin to Llyn Maelog.

So far the small cocktail bar area had been quiet. A large family group, on vacation from the London area judging by the accents, spilled across two tables in the middle of the room. A couple chatting intimately in the corner, holding hands around the glow of a candle, were the only other customers. The quiet after the storm of New Year, he surmised, with most people back at work the following morning.

He was pondering on his choice of pudding when a presence at his table forced his attention away from the menu. Expecting the waiter-come-barman to have arrived to clear his plate, he looked up with a smile. His jaw dropped when he saw Eliza Glenowen looking down at him with a quizzical expression, like a curious art student studying a piece of work in detail. He squirmed and hoped he didn't look as uncomfortable as he felt, but there was something about Eliza that disconcerted him in a way he couldn't quite fathom.

"Hello," she said. "Can I join you?"

Gethin nodded, shuffling around the booth to make room, and clearing his plate to the furthest side of the table.

Eliza slid onto the bench seat, looking elegant in a simple black jumpsuit that clung to all the right places, and a chunky matching necklace and bracelet of shimmering crystals. Gethin knew little about fashion, but knew what he liked. And he liked the fact Eliza had taste.

She called across to the bar before settling down. "Can you get me my usual, Tim, please?" She looked at Gethin's glass. "And yours is a pint of Old Speckled Hen if I'm not mistaken?"

Gethin nodded and blushed, wishing he had cooler, more expensive, tastes.

Eliza relayed the information to the barman and then sat down with a sigh.

"I wouldn't have put you down as a real ale connoisseur." Gethin was relieved to have found his tongue.

Eliza gave a lazy smile. "I wouldn't touch the stuff. But I've done my share of bar work, especially during my Uni days, and it's the only real ale we sell. Doesn't take a detective, really, does it?"

Gethin laughed. "Ah, so I've been busted already."

"If you like." Eliza twisted the bracelet around her wrist. "If you were planning to cross examine me covertly that is?"

Gethin shrugged, wide-eyed. "Me? I'm just out to enjoy a quiet meal. That's not a crime surely?"

"No, and I'm delighted you'd choose our humble establishment, of course. Call me a cynic."

Gethin was saved a response by the arrival of drinks. The bartender cleared the dirty plate. "Can I get you anything from the dessert menu?" he asked.

Gethin paused. It would be rude to get stuck into his favourite pudding in front of his guest. He shook his head but his expression must have given him away.

"Of course, go ahead and order," said Eliza. "And while you're at it could you get the kitchen to make me up a turkey club sandwich. I've not eaten since breakfast."

"And apple pie and custard for me, please."

Gethin finished off the dregs of his first pint and swapped glasses, while Eliza mixed her drink with a cocktail stirrer. He closed his eyes for a moment, breathing in the delicate floral perfume, mentally planning how he'd like the conversation to go - but he was equally aware with Eliza Glenowen he may not have much say in the matter.

Gethin cleared his throat and gestured to her glass. "So, your regular drink is …?"

"Whisky and soda."

"Really? I'd have put you down as more of a Prosecco or Bellini type."

Eliza mixed her drink and looked at him steadily. "Then that's a lesson why one should never judge a book by its cover." She took a small sip. "And not just any whisky. Has to be Famous Grouse because it reminds me of my father. He said any other whisky, even the most expensive ones, gave him heartburn … but he loved a drop of Grouse. We even smuggled a tiny bottle into the hospital for him in his final days. Odd how these things stay with you and shape your life, isn't it?"

Gethin sipped his pint, wishing he had something sage and sympathetic to say in response. Eliza was a curious individual and he really couldn't fathom her. Remote and detached, and yet more than happy to share intimate comments about the death of her father. He'd never met anyone like her before. He decided his best bet was to let her take the lead and let the conversation run its own course.

"So, other than our reputation for the best steaks on Anglesey, what other motivation did you have for dining alone here tonight?" she asked, propping her chin on the back of her hand and studying Gethin.

He shrugged, deciding to change gear and try the honesty policy. "Suppose I'm trying to find out what secrets there are hidden under the glossy, professional surface of Llyn Maelog Hotel."

Eliza threw her head back and laughed, then took a sip of her drink. "Well, I knew that was the real answer but I wasn't expecting you to give it. Aren't policemen supposed to be as shifty as politicians when it comes to the truth?"

"Maybe that's yet another lesson why one should never judge a person by their drink of choice?"

Eliza grinned, raised her glass, waited for Gethin to clink his own against it, then added, "Touché!"

They both sipped their drinks in silence as Tim arrived with a large tray containing a steaming plate of golden-topped pie and custard, and another holding a high tower of brown bread layers oozing meat and salad, held in place by a wooden skewer.

Gethin stuck in, wincing as the hot custard scalded his mouth. He took another sip of his pint and studied Eliza over the top of his glass, picking pieces of lettuce from the stack and chewing with a disinterested expression.

He cleared his throat. "So, are you going to tell me?"
Eliza looked up. "Tell you what?"
Gethin smiled, willing to carry on entertaining Eliza with this game of cat and mouse if it ended in something worthwhile.
"Skeletons, closets. That kind of thing."
She fixed his gaze. "Surely we all have those, don't we?"
Gethin felt heat rise, and looked down at his pie.
"What makes you think anything in our past will help you find a missing chef?"

Gethin blew on a spoonful of custard. It was a valid question. But did he detect a sense of unease or dislike in her tone? Was Gregory Chapman no more than a 'missing chef' to Eliza Glenowen, when her brother's reaction had been so much more?

"Because people tend to go missing for a reason," he said. "Whether it's missing by accident or design, or even something more serious, there's always a series of events that leads to that decision, or critical moment. In which case someone, somewhere will know something, or have seen or heard something important, whether they realise it or not. And more times than not it's events of the past that shape our future."

Eliza paused. "I like that ... very deep."

"Not really. It's my job."

Gethin slid the spoon into his mouth, swallowed another mouthful of rich creamy dessert and closed his eyes. This was excellent custard, with the hint of vanilla pod he loved, as good as his mother used to make back in the restaurant days, when his favourite season had been autumn, hot afternoons of fruit-picking, apples, plums, blackberries, damsons ... and the smells of his mother's baking.

"Enjoying that?"

He opened his eyes, aware of Eliza's amused gaze.

"What gave you that idea?"

"Looked like you were about to do your orgasm face."

Gethin snorted. "I like food a lot, but not quite that much, don't worry."

"Glad to hear." Eliza pulled apart two slices of bread, removed a thin strip of bacon and popped it into her mouth. "So, what else do you like apart from food?"

Gethin swallowed, dabbed his lips with his napkin. "I thought we were talking about the hotel?"

Eliza rolled her eyes. "Boring. I'd much rather talk about you ..."

"And you want to avoid boring? I'd much rather talk about Gregory Chapman."

Eliza sighed. "So, the bit about policemen never being off duty is true then?"

Gethin smiled. "Afraid so."

Eliza took her time chewing a mouthful of sandwich, all the

time keeping her gaze on Gethin, who felt the hairs on his arms and back of his neck tingle. There was something about Eliza that sent his senses into overdrive. Not unpleasant exactly but maybe a little unnerving.

Eliza swallowed and wiped her fingers on her napkin. "Gregory Chapman was a typical chef in a lot of ways: passionate, driven, focused. He had ambition. I always felt we were but a stepping stone on a strategic career plan. He wasn't loud though, wasn't one of those Sergeant Major types who feel the need to shout at everyone around them, thank God. He was polite, well-spoken and knew how to bring the best out of his ingredients. Certainly the people he worked with held him in the highest regard." She paused. Gethin felt she'd been on the brink of saying more, but instead gave a brief shrug "Not sure what more I can say."

"But you didn't like him personally?"

"I didn't say that."

"You didn't have to."

Eliza smiled. "Ah, the detective-therapist. I didn't dislike him. I just didn't connect, I suppose. We had little in common. And connecting with people is so important, don't you think?"

Gethin avoided the weight of her gaze. "You're talking past tense I notice … you don't think he's coming back?" Eliza shrugged and remained silent. "So, what did you think when he disappeared?" added Gethin.

"I felt bad for Stephen, that's all to be honest. I didn't worry at first about his whereabouts, if that's what you mean. Everyone thought he was a typically selfish bloke doing what typically selfish blokes do day in, day out."

"You say you felt bad for Stephen?"

Eliza darted a quick glance across the room and reached for her drink. "Well, the timing was pretty rotten. We had a big corporate dinner on the very day he left. Luckily it was a set menu and much of the prep had been done … but still … I was surprised he up and left."

"I heard there was some kind of argument before he left. Do you think that was connected?"

"No, not at all. The amount of egos within any hotel environment make it inevitable." Eliza rolled the glass between her fingers. "If you want my take on it, I don't think like the others, I don't think he left voluntarily. As much as I didn't gel with him, I don't think he was the type." She paused, sipped her whisky. "He had commitments here, reasons to stay. I worry it's all tied up with the business at the lake. I've tried saying the same to Stephen, but of course, he just tuts and rolls his eyes like I'm some kind of mad woman."

Eliza broke off and Gethin heard the hurt in her voice. She drained her glass and held it aloft, gesturing towards the bar for a refill.

"Can I get you another, sir?" the barman asked Gethin as he arrived with a new whisky and soda.

"No, thanks. My limit. I have to drive home."

"Oh, go on. Don't be a spoilsport," said Eliza as Tim cleared their empty plates. "Stay. Book a room."

There was a pretend flirtatiousness in her tone, but Gethin sensed another edge in her words. Loneliness, maybe?

"I don't think my boss would stretch to that on expenses. And my wages definitely wouldn't stretch …"

"My treat. Go on, please. I don't often get to talk to interesting people."

Gethin pondered the ethics of accepting material gifts from someone involved in the case, while Tim hovered. Finally, Gethin shrugged, drained his glass, and held it toward the waiter. He could talk his way out of it if necessary.

"Okay, I'm sold."

Eliza smiled. "Great. Bring another Grouse too, Tim. I'll educate you," she added to Gethin.

They sat in a comfortable silence for a while, watching the noisy departure of the large family. The ensuing silence was broken only by the hiss and pop of flames in the open fire away to their left. Outside the blackness of the windows, the wind whined around the eaves, and the sparkle of snow across the frozen lawns reflected in the arc lamps that lit up the building.

"It's a hell of a place to live," said Gethin.

"Oh, we don't live here now," Eliza replied, following Gethin's gaze. "We used to when Stephen and I were kids, but after the extension, paying rooms were a priority and our wing was converted. We have a lodge house on the Bodorgan Estate. It's nice actually to lock yourself away from the world. It helped my mother having some peace and solitude. You know about my mother, I take it?"

Gethin nodded.

"Yes, of course you do. I suppose we're all part of your investigation." She sipped her drink. "Tell me what you've discovered about me in the course of your enquiries then, detective?"

"Ah, we never reveal our sources."

"Okay." Eliza's vivid blue eyes searched his face. "Then let me guess."

Gethin shrugged.

"You've been told I'm some kind of mad witch."

He laughed aloud. "No! What do you mean?"

"Oh, come on. I can't believe not one member of staff has called me a crackpot? It's what they all think."

"Apparently not."

Gethin was careful to protect what he'd learned, but he remembered Glenys Owen's summary of Eliza's life changes after the death of her son, and how she'd now become part of the local Druid community.

He cleared his throat. "The first time I met you, out in the car park, you seemed interested in the discovery at Llyn Maelog. Why?"

"Is this you tactfully changing the subject?"

Gethin shook his head. "No, it seemed an odd response."

Eliza sipped her drink, twisting the crystal bracelet back and forth. "I'm certain you already know this and you're either being a perfect gentleman or a wily cop ... but I'm a practising member of the local Druidic order." She waited and Gethin kept his face blank. "Anglesey, or if you want to use the old Druid name *Mon Mam Cymru*, is the most sacred place on the planet to us. It's been the seat of learning for our beliefs for thousands of years. And some of the most sacred places for us are the lakes, our steps into the underworld, places where all of life and death has been celebrated for thousands of years, quite often in ceremony, worship and offerings. Llyn Maelog is to us a sacred lake. It has many generations of ritualistic offerings buried deep in its waters. Seeing divers there ... it threw me. I didn't know if I should inform the Chief Druid. I didn't know if it was breaking any of our ancient laws. It really upset me." She smiled. "But I'm okay now. I have my moments but I'm not mad, I promise."

Gethin frowned. "Offerings. Human offerings, is that what you mean?"

Eliza shrugged. "We don't have all the answers of our ancestors."

"But it is possible there may have been human sacrifices?" Gethin thought back to the pile of aged green bones the divers had brought to the surface, piece after piece of skeleton of indeterminate age. Could that be their answer? He made a mental note to inform the DI.

"It's not part of our ceremony now of course. And despite the propaganda of history, there's no actual proof it ever was. But there have been battles over time here, invaders who came to steal our special island away from us, and much blood has been spilled. Have you not heard of the famous clash between Romans and Druids during the invasion in 60AD?" Gethin shook his head, feeling he should have heard of it. "Well, you can still read the words of Tacitus today of the violence of the attack, how the local Celts and Druids combined to ward off the invasion. It took the might of the Roman army three attempts to succeed. And if people were killed in the course of these clashes, it's my belief they would have been given back to the gods in these sacred lakes. That's what I meant. That Llyn Maelog may have many secrets hidden in its depths."

"So, there's no chance the body we found was some kind of modern sacrifice, is that what you're saying?"

"What I'm saying is that I'm not part of some secret cult that goes around sacrificing chefs to our ancestral gods before you ask!" She laughed and Gethin liked how her face came alive in the glow of candlelight. "You want my advice?"

"Advice?"

"If you want answers, try to ask the right questions. Do as I do. Go out to the lake at sunrise as the sun breaks above Snowdonia, and watch the changing light on the water, feel the awe that emanates from its depths. Connect with the sacred beating heart of our island, and tell me you don't feel the urge to bend a knee or bow to the power of the gods and goddesses that rule over our land. They know all truths and you may learn a lot." She sighed. "It sickens me such a sacred lake has been sullied in this way. I'm trying to do all I can to maintain the natural balance of things. And it's not easy. Especially when most people think I'm just a mad witch!"

Gethin shifted in his seat, feeling the warmth of the whisky envelop him. The conversation had shifted. Eliza had changed. He could imagine his colleagues' reaction to her Druidic beliefs and questioned why he didn't feel the urge to laugh. But he didn't.

"So, will you meet me there at sunrise?" Eliza asked quietly.

"I rarely see any sunrise and after a few whiskies …"

"I'll put in an alarm call for you. It's midwinter. Eight am is hardly early. Please?"

He met her gaze and nodded slowly.

Eliza's smile was wide. "Thank you."

"Are you scaring off the guests again, dear sister?"

The connection was broken.

Eliza looked up and stretched her arms out to hug Stephen Glenowen. "No, I am educating our guests, darling brother. Join us?"

Stephen nodded a greeting to Gethin as he disentangled his sister's arms from around his neck. "I'm heading home. You sound tipsy. Want a lift?"

Eliza shook her head. "No, I'm staying here tonight. Don't worry I have police protection."

Stephen shot a glance at Gethin. "Oh, I see …"

Gethin was certain he didn't see at all. He also couldn't work out why Eliza seemed to have changed her personality so much in the presence of her brother. Was that what women did? Her voice was far more slurred than it had been previously, and he'd hazard a guess it would take more than a couple of whiskies to get Eliza drunk. No, it felt like an act. A kind of roleplay between brother and sister he wanted no part of. It hadn't felt like Eliza was lining him up as her bed fellow at all, so why give that impression to her brother?

Gethin cleared his throat. "It was a suggestion. But I can easily get a cab."

Eliza put a hand on his arm. "You're going nowhere. We have a date at the lake, remember?" She gave him a wink as if sensing his unease. "So, you can leave me here, dear brother, safe in the knowledge I'll still be here in the morning. I'm not planning to be our next murder victim."

Stephen sighed and straightened. "You are such a drama queen, Eliza Glenowen. But I do love you. If you're sure you're okay, I'll see you tomorrow." He looked at Gethin. "Good luck and don't let her bully you into doing anything you don't want to."

Before Gethin could open his mouth to respond, Stephen grinned and strode away, tall and lean in what looked like casual, but designer, golf attire in a striking navy blue and white design with a nautical air. He looked much younger than he had in a business suit, much better looking too with his stylish beard and those deep, dark eyes. No wonder the young receptionist had such a crush. Gethin wondered how he could get the conversation onto Stephen Glenowen's love life without it being too obvious. Stephen raised a hand and had a brief exchange with Tim as he passed, their words ending in laughter. There was a similarity between brother and sister, and a likeability about Stephen Glenowen he'd not picked up before.

"Ignore him," Eliza said as she watched Gethin across the top of her glass. Her voice was normal again now, measured and calm. "He's just jealous."

Gethin looked at her. "What ...?"

Eliza winked. "Tim. Another round over here please!"

CHAPTER NINE

Amanda tucked her feet under her, pulled the pile of paperwork onto her lap, pushed her glasses up her nose, and reached for the large gin and tonic on the coffee table. The meeting with the Coroner and the osteology and palaeontology experts from Bangor University had been extremely interesting and impressive. They had done a brilliant job narrowing down the date of their latest human remains.

Unfortunately, Amanda's hope that the bones were pre-historical relics or remains from an eighteenth-century shipbuilding era were dashed when both experts gave a date no older than fifty years. From the seventy-one percent of the skeleton discovered so far, they could also deduce it was the remains of a young male, with a height of approximately five foot, nine inches. The skull had not yet been recovered and from the bones under analysis no cause of death could be recorded.

Amanda scan read the rest of the report, pleased with the professionalism and speed the bones had been examined, but disappointed the dates meant yet another investigation had to be opened. She sipped her drink and relished the fizz of tonic in the back of her throat. This case was becoming increasingly difficult. She couldn't even use the singular term with any confidence, with this latest discovery, they now had three different investigations running, all significantly based in and around Llyn Maelog. But were they connected, and if so, how? A fifty-year-old skeleton. A murder victim. And a missing chef.

She closed her eyes and rubbed her temples. So many of their usual investigatory techniques were useless here. No eye witnesses, no CCTV, no motive, and most crucially, no identification of the first corpse from IDENT1, the national fingerprint database.

Amanda tutted and sipped her drink. She shivered and pulled the tartan blanket off the back of the sofa and wrapped it around her legs, not for the first time bemoaning the inadequate heating. Amanda had rented this small terraced cottage in the back streets of Beaumaris following a major fire at her own apartment. The picturesque views from its elevated position across the medieval castle walls, out to the Snowdonia skyline had been its best feature, and in those warm, heady August nights she hadn't given a second thought to the size of the tiny electric storage heaters, or the pile of chopped wood in the back yard.

Now, with one of the coldest, prolonged spells she could remember, the constant need to stock up the wood burning stove, in the vague hope of achieving a decent supply of heat and hot water, was a chore she resented. Since Emily left to visit her father on Boxing Day, Amanda hadn't even bothered to buy more wood, instead taking to wearing thermal pyjamas and bed socks around the house.

She drained her glass. More gin. That was the answer to most of life's problems. She untangled herself and got to her feet as her mobile began to ring. She saw Emily's name on the display and grabbed the phone, dropping back down onto the sofa.

"Hey, honey! I was just thinking about you, you must be psychic."

"How sweet, I'm touched."

Amanda's growled and put down the glass, before a temptation to throw it at the nearest wall might overcome her. Her ex-husband's voice still sent a shudder through her body, and had the capacity to bring a whole deluge of unwanted memories back with one keyword. If time was a healer, it was a slow burn.

"Is Emily okay? Why are you using her phone?"

Simon Gold gave a loud sigh. "Calm down, she's fine, no need to get hysterical."

Amanda bit down hard on her bottom lip. The arrogant bastard never changed. She wasn't being hysterical, didn't sound remotely hysterical, but if she started yelling back at him now it only offered more ammunition.

"So, how can I help you?"

"You sound like you're on the job. I'm not a suspect, you know. We can be polite without this forced formality you adhere too. It's rather childish."

"Can we? Good. I'll ask again, why are you ringing?"

"What's the rush? Am I disturbing you?"

She could see the lazy sneer from here. Something she'd once thought sexy and engaging, a look she'd once craved from him, now fired up a simmering pit of anger in her gut and it took all her willpower to keep it under control.

"I'm not sure that's relevant. We're not exactly known for our chit-chat of late, so can we cut to the chase?"

"See, formal. There you go again."

Amanda's voice tightened. "Simon, this is getting boring. Either start talking or I'm hanging up. Is that informal enough for you?"

A pause. "Blimey. I can see what Emily means."

"Simon …"

There was an underlying warning tone in Amanda's voice. You didn't mess with her head where her daughter was concerned, and even Simon Gold had the sense to know that.

"Okay. But I warn you you're not going to like this." He paused. "Amanda, I've spent a lot of time with Emily over the past week, and we've done a lot of talking –"

"Isn't that rather the point of the visit? That's what *most* fathers do with their daughters."

She regretted the interruption as soon as the words passed her lips, but she couldn't help herself. Why couldn't she hold her tongue?

"Yeah, well, *most* fathers probably have decent access to their children. *Most* fathers live within a sensible distance. *Most* fathers don't have to put up with the shit I've had to since god-knows-when or spent the last six months worrying about the mental welfare of my only daughter."

"You do remember it was you who walked out and never looked back?" Amanda spat back. "Never regretted it for a single moment I remember you telling me once."

"I never walked away from Emily. If I could have taken her with me that day I would have … and never had a reason to look back."

Tears sprung from nowhere and her vision blurred. "You bastard," she whispered.

"You started it. As it ever was."

There was silence. He'd always been able to hurt her and what was worse, he knew it. Even now, he could sense it. If she persisted it would only descend into further name calling, resulting in Simon's gloating that she really had to learn to control her bitterness and jealousy. She wasn't bitter. She wasn't jealous. She was simply furious.

Amanda sniffed and rubbed a hand across her face. "So, this talk you've been having …"

"Ah, so you are interested?"

"Enough, Simon."

"Emily's not coming back to Anglesey."

Amanda's pulse was suddenly loud in her ears, distorting those six words into a meaningless jumble of noise. "What do you mean?"

"What I said. She doesn't want to come back to that horrible little backwater. She can't face it. And after what she's been through, who can seriously blame her."

It wasn't a question and Amanda couldn't supply an answer anyway. But she couldn't lose Emily. She wouldn't lose her daughter as well as her mother. No, it wasn't going to happen, she would not let Simon ruin her life for a second time.

"Put Emily on the phone, Simon. Right now."

"Even if I could, I wouldn't. But she's not here."

"So, if all this is true and it's what she really wants, why couldn't she tell me herself?"

There was amusement in Simon's response. "You really have to ask?"

"What do you mean?"

"Do you think our daughter is mentally strong enough right now to cope with your reaction?" Simon paused. "Christ, I'm more than a match for anyone across a courtroom, but you wear me down. Emily's mind is made up and it's nothing to do with me, before you start. I've sensed her unhappiness on the phone every single time we've spoken in the past few months, and if you haven't picked up on that, perhaps you're not the super-mother you think you are."

Amanda concentrated on her breathing for a moment, in and out, slow and steady, keeping the anger under control. Had she noticed? Or had she been trying so hard to make everything okay again she hadn't had time to notice. Or was Emily being typically Emily and doing everything she could to spare Amanda's feelings? She remembered her daughter's quietness on Christmas Day and recalled a conversation where Emily admitted she was finding it tough getting back into university life after the events of the previous summer.

Amanda closed her eyes. She didn't want to relive that period and had the strength to control that. But she knew Emily hadn't yet found that strength, every time she closed her eyes all she saw was a towering inferno all around her, and all she heard was breaking glass and screams. Amanda had recognised a change in her daughter, but she'd thought it temporary, thought she could help her erase the memories given time.

She swallowed. "How long?"

"What?"

"She wants a break. I get that. A holiday would be good for her –"

"It's not a holiday, Amanda. It's permanent."

His voice was serious and she sensed no triumphalism in his tone.

"No!"

"I'm sorry it's come to this. But I'm not surprised. And if Emily knew the truth … if she had any idea *he* might be out there somewhere, watching and waiting. I never liked the dishonesty, I went along with it to protect my daughter, but I've woke up every morning worrying today might be the day he returns."

"He won't. I told you …"

"You don't know that."

"But Emily was making progress, I don't understand …"

"No, she wasn't, we both know she's an expert at putting on an act to make us happy. There are too many negative memories for her there. She sees *him* everywhere … and it's wearing her down. She's tried, mostly for you, and feels she's given it her best go. But it's not getting any easier for her, in fact it's getting worse, every day is getting harder. She's really struggling … those are her words, not mine." Simon sighed. "I know you won't believe me but this is giving me no pleasure. Our feelings aside, it kills me to see my daughter in such a bad way. She needs help and a fresh start. I can offer both."

"But what about her studies, her degree …"

"She doesn't want to continue. I think what happened was the final nail in the coffin. We have to accept that. She doesn't see her future in law. I've put in a call to Warwick Uni and set up a meeting, she wants to transfer to an archaeology course."

Amanda swallowed, glancing at her empty glass, wishing it was full. This couldn't be happening. Had she really not seen this coming? Was she such a bad mother?

"Down there?"

"Yes."

"Fine, then I'll get a transfer. Warwickshire or Worcestershire. I have contacts."

"Amanda, I get it. I do." His was voice was gentler now, calm but firm. "But the last thing Emily needs is you piling more guilt on her shoulders. The best we can do is support her and help get her life back on track. When that happens, and it will, then is the time to think about your own plans. Not now."

There was common sense in his words and she knew them to be true. Much as she'd spent a decade hating him, he was still an intelligent human being who, she knew, had the interests of his daughter paramount. He'd been a good father, despite her insults, someone Emily had always known as a solid and reassuring presence in her life. It didn't surprise her really that in her hour of need Emily had run to her father to put things right.

"This will break my heart," she whispered, more to herself.

"I know. I really do understand. I've been there, remember?" He paused. "But this isn't about you. Or me. It's about Emily recovering and rebuilding her life. And you need to support her, Amanda. You have to be there for her and let her know it's all going to be okay."

Amanda gulped. "I know. I will. If it's what she really needs."

"It is. But even so she's going to take a few months out and really think about her future. I'm going to book us a nice holiday, we've not decided where yet. Jamaica, perhaps. She needs time to heal. I'm worried about her."

"Tell her to ring me."

"Fine. She will. She just couldn't do this bit, she couldn't tell you. It's been stressing her out so much. I sent her to the cinema with Kat."

Amanda bridled at the mention of his fiancée's name. Again, she reminded herself this wasn't about her. This was about Emily. And Emily got on well with Kat, they were nearer in age, shared fashion and beauty tips, liked the same music, went to festivals together. No wonder Emily wanted to escape from, what had he called it, this horrible little backwater with its horrible memories.

"Are you okay?"

Simon's voice cut through her thoughts. What did he think, seriously? He'd dismantled her life as effectively as he had the day he left a note and disappeared off to a conference in Zurich from which he never returned.

"What do you think?"

"I know how you feel. Emily won't forget you, you'll always be her mum. Just like she never forgot me."

Tears were streaming down Amanda's face now and she let them. She'd heard enough. It felt as if he was twisting the knife.

"Tell Emily to ring me as soon as she gets in, whatever the time. Tell her I'm not angry. Tell her I need to hear her voice." She gulped. "Thanks. Bye."

She disconnected the call and threw the phone across the room, hearing a loud crack as it hit the far wall, not caring if it broke, not caring if an earthquake were to hit and everything came crashing down around her head. She'd lost her daughter. She'd lost Emily. And what was worse she'd lost her to the man she most hated.

They'd made the move to Bangor so they could stay together while Emily studied for her law degree. They'd clung together from the day her father abandoned them. Now, Amanda felt more alone than at any other moment in her life, like a lone shipwreck survivor clinging to a piece of driftwood, lost and adrift in a huge expanse of ocean.

Blindly, she groped for her glass and stumbled through to the kitchen, retrieving the bottle from the counter and half filling the tumbler with gin. She took a long drink of the neat alcohol and held it in her mouth, feeling the burn in her throat as tears stung her eyes. This wasn't the answer, she knew that. But all she needed right now was oblivion. Somewhere to hide until the pain went away. Once she could breathe again, then she could surface.

She took another sip before unscrewing the top of the bottle of tonic water and splashing a measure into the glass. How much until she passed out and slept? Emily. Her darling sweet Emily. All she wanted to do was hug her tight and never let her go. God, she hated that man, and what he'd done to her daughter, so much. If he ever turned up again, and it was a big if despite his veiled threats, she'd wipe him out the first chance she got and worry about the consequences later.

As she headed back into the lounge, she remembered her phone. Emily would be calling. She'd thrown it somewhere, what if it was broken, what if Emily was trying right this second and couldn't get through? She dropped to her knees and crawled behind the sofa, running her fingers across the tiled floor. Suddenly, she heard her phone's ring tone from somewhere behind her, and her heart picked up speed. Thank the Lord! She reversed out on her knees and slid her hand under the corner unit and touched the vibrating phone, sliding it out and accepting the call all in one fluid movement, before settling back on her haunches against the door frame.

"Oh, Emily. Thanks for calling, honey ..."

"Sorry, DI Gold ... is that you?"

Amanda blinked. A man's voice. Not Emily. "Yes?"

"Ah, sorry to interrupt you at such an unsociable hour. This is Dr Sixsmith."

Amanda shook her head. "What?"

"Dr Sixsmith." He paused. "The pathologist."

"Yes, yes." She had to get him off the phone, Emily was due to call. "What is it?"

"We've had confirmation of a positive identification from dental records for the corpse from Llyn Maelog. The delay was due to location, a match with records from a surgery up in the Shetland Isles. Your man is named as a Peter McDonald, age twenty-nine. That's all I have right now, but I'll email full contact details over to you once I have them."

Amanda swallowed as her head cleared. "Thank you. At last the breakthrough we so badly need."

"Like I say, I thought you'd want to know the second I did. I'm sorry if I disturbed you."

Amanda realised she must have sounded at best ... confused. At worst ... drunk. Another wave of fresh emotion rose and threatened to spill.

"It's fine," she muttered through a throat as tight as elastic.

He cleared his throat. "Can I ask … I mean, tell me to mind my own business, of course. But are you okay, Amanda?"

Don't be nice, don't be nice, she pleaded silently. Touched the pathologist took time to ask, there was no way at the moment she could answer truthfully.

"Oh, yes. Fine. I'm fine. Thanks again. Speak to you tomorrow."

She ended the call and held her head in her hands. It would all be fine tomorrow.

CHAPTER TEN

Amanda reversed her car into her parking spot, turned off the ignition, and retrieved her phone from her bag. She'd heard the ping of an incoming text moments earlier and smiled as she read the message. "Feeling better this morning, Mum? XXX" Yes, she was, but she could hardly have felt much worse than she had the previous night. She still felt nauseous and teary when she imagined a home without Emily, when she saw the powerfully clear image of spending the rest of her life alone. But overpowering all those fears was the urge to see her daughter happy and fulfilled and enjoying life again.

She wanted to grab hold of Emily's face between her palms and cover her pale skin with kisses, anything to reassure her daughter she was fine. That Emily was the only important thing in her life worth worrying about, and she would make any sacrifice she had to in order to help her daughter find happiness again. But she couldn't do that, or say that, right now. So instead, she clicked reply and typed: "I'm fine. Sober. Fed. Off to work. You're in my thoughts every second. Call me anytime. I love you! XXX"

The phone conversation the previous night had been long and emotional. Both of them had spent a lot of time crying, but Amanda ended the call understanding the struggle her daughter had been going through in secret … and totally committed to making sure that struggle stopped right then. At the end of the call, after submerging her face in a basin of cold water, Amanda had slept soundly. And other than a tenderness around her eyes, she'd woken re-charged and ready for the day ahead. She had more motivation now, was determined to put aside any lingering self-pity and concentrate on working towards a bright future for her daughter and herself.

Her phone pinged. "Love you too! XXX"

With lighter footsteps, she hurried through reception, fumbling with the key code as she got to the CID corridor, and pausing outside the main office door. Her heartbeat quickened as she heard laughter and the low rumble of voices. How could she have forgotten?

She pushed open the door, eyes scanning the room, finding the face she wanted near the new espresso machine. "Dara!"

"Howdy, ma'am. Hear you've missed me, eh?"

"You've no idea. No idea at all. Hope it was a good trip?"

Dara's eyes darkened for a split second, recovering quickly. "Ah, it was grand. You've not lived until you've experienced New Year in Dublin. My brother will be detoxing for a month, he's such a sad lightweight, but I've bounced back already."

"Am very glad to hear. Well, we need you back for sure. And …" she turned to Fletcher and Kelly who were both lingering near the coffee machine. "I have news. Finally, late last night, an ID on our corpse. I'll check my emails for the full info. In the meantime, Fletch, can you get Dara up to speed, please."

Minutes later, Amanda reappeared with a printed copy of Dr Sixsmith's email. "So, we have work to do, guys. The dental match has named a Peter James McDonald, age twenty-nine from a place called Sandwick, near Lerwick. However, the telephone number listed for him at the surgery is no longer recognised, so their records may not be up to date." She glanced at the detail of the email. "Apparently, McDonald wasn't a regular patient but had a six-week course of treatment for a root canal procedure four years ago. So, whilst he may not be born and bred in the town, he was clearly resident for some time."

"And this Lerwick is where exactly, ma'am?" said Dara. "It doesn't sound local."

"It's not." Kelly replied, looking up from her computer screen, before Amanda could answer. "It's the biggest town, the capital in fact, of the Shetland Isles."

"Shetland Isles?" echoed Fletch. "Christ alive, no wonder no one recognised him last night. He's not exactly local."

"Nothing around the bars at all?" said Amanda.

Fletch shook his head. "Had a few offers that made me hair stand on end … but nothing to assist the enquiry."

Dara snorted and Kelly giggled.

"So, what's a guy from some remote Scottish island doing dead in a lake in our neck of the woods?" said Dara.

"And that's only the first question I need answering," said Amanda, taking a marker pen and writing Peter James McDonald's name up on the white board. "Let's split the workload and start the usual searches – friends, family, occupation. Let's hope the address is current even if the phone number isn't. By the end of today, I want to know everything there is to know about Mr McDonald – including who killed him if at all possible!"

Dara cleared his throat. "And this other man, this chef. I know Gethin is following that lead. From where I'm standing surely he's our number one suspect – in fact he's our only suspect."

Amanda wrinkled her nose and shook her head. "It's not that simple. Location is our only link and it's not enough. We have no proof the men knew each other at all, and the timings are all wrong, so that's a line we can now follow-up, Dara. When we have more information to work on about McDonald, let's get out to the hotel and see if he's known. Now you're back you can assist Gethin."

"Talking of Gethin, where is he this morning?" asked Fletch. "Wonder if he pulled last night and stayed over at the hotel?"

Kelly tutted. "You know, only you could think that. Honestly!"

"Let's check up on him to be on the safe side," said Amanda. "I'm sure he'll be working on a lead or something, but we need to update him on the ID anyway."

"On it," said Kelly, picking up the phone. "I bet the DCI will be annoyed you stole his thunder."

"What's that?" said Amanda.

"His press conference at 11am," said Fletch. "He was hoping for a spot on the lunchtime news, but there's no need now."

Amanda glanced at her watch. "Damn. I should update him. He should still appeal for anyone who knew McDonald to come forward with information. We have more questions than answers but I hope by the end of the day that will be turned round." She sighed and fastened the single button on her jacket. "I'll go see the DCI now. Wish me luck!"

Amanda pushed open the heavy glass door and stepped out into the car park, feet crunching through handfuls of scattered rock salt, as she headed for the smoking shelter all the time mumbling obscenities under her breath. Despite her protestation that New Year resolutions weren't worth the time of day, she had secretly managed to abstain from cigarettes so far this year, a fact she had been bursting with pride to reveal. However, the past half hour in the presence of Idris Parry, on top of last night's explosion of emotion, had pushed her over the edge and her nerves were screaming so loudly for nicotine, she could hardly hear the sounds of real life above the din. In fact, she was sure she'd ignored Dara's voice calling her on the stairs. He'd understand. He was a smoker too.

As soon as she reached the sanctity of the smoking area, she dug the packet of cigarettes from the side pocket of her handbag and lit up with a shaking hand. Hating herself and her complete lack of willpower, but also right at that moment, not caring about anything but the blessed calm relief to come. She inhaled as hard as she could, ignoring the tears, and holding the smoke in long and deep. God, that was so good … and yet so bad at the same time. Images of Emily's disappointed face, her mother's blank stare, Simon's acerbic smile, Idris Parry's jowly anger …

mixed and swirled behind her closed lids. She didn't care about any of them right at that moment. All she cared about was her craving and if that made her a bad person ... then what the hell.

She exhaled and opened her eyes.

"Good god!"

"I've had a few reactions in my time, but that's a new one on me," said Assistant Chief Constable Richard Wills with raised eyebrows and the hint of a smile.

Amanda took a deep breath, fighting the instinct to hide the cigarette behind her back. What did it matter now if he saw her smoking? He was the fitness guru, not her, and seeking his approval was a thing of the past.

"You surprised me ... sir," Amanda faltered, not sure how appropriate protocol was in the circumstances.

"Clearly." He frowned. "I've been meaning to catch up with you. Sounds like an intriguing case out at Rhosneigr?"

Amanda wrapped her coat around her, aware of the icy chill creeping upwards through the soles of her boots. She would not have chosen to have a conversation with Richard Wills under any condition, but out here, with a cold wind blowing, and slushy snow beneath her feet, it was even more hideous. She flicked ash from her cigarette, watching as it burned away, an ache in the pit of her stomach not yet satisfied. She couldn't take another drag without blowing smoke in his face, and despite it feeling like a good idea, it was a step too far.

Up close, Richard Wills could still send chills through her body that had nothing to do with the weather. Amanda had worked hard over the past months to distance herself from the tanned skin, salt and pepper hair, tall, muscular frame and the secret sexiness behind a smile that at one time had set her body aflame with desire. Today, he wore the same spicy aftershave he'd always favoured, and Amanda could sense the hardness of his muscles beneath the tailored uniform. Unspoken, they both knew it wouldn't take much for their mutual attraction to re-ignite with the slightest hint of encouragement from either of them.

But despite the fact Richard's name had flickered through her consciousness in the early hours of the morning, he wasn't the answer. She'd turned the final page of that chapter a while ago. Why turn back the clock and make the same mistakes again?

She sighed and dropped the half-smoked cigarette to the floor, grinding it underfoot. "It's complicated, that's for sure, sir. But we've had our first positive ID this morning, so at least we have something fresh to work on."

"Good."

They both stood, facing each other in silence. Amanda's cheeks were beginning to turn numb from the cold.

She indicated towards the office. "I should make a move before my feet turn to ice."

Richard glanced down as if checking her footwear and mumbled something Amanda failed to catch.

"Sorry, sir?"

He looked up, anger blazing in his gaze. "For fuck's sake, Amanda, what's with the *sir*?"

Amanda took a step back. "Sorry. I don't know how ... I don't know what's appropriate. No offence. I wasn't being sarcastic." She glanced around, checking the area was still deserted. "It's a bit awkward ... for both of us."

Richard sighed, his eyes fixed on her. "I actually said ... I've missed you, Amanda."

"Oh. I – I don't know what to say."

"Then don't say anything. Just listen. If you'd responded to my messages, talked to me when I asked, I wouldn't have to be saying this here. Now." He checked over his shoulder. "Hardly the time or place ..."

She remained silent.

He ran a hand through his hair, a gesture she remembered. "Thing is ... it's not getting easier, it's getting harder. Seeing you from a distance, how cold you are ... but knowing the real you, all those memories ... it's killing me." He swallowed. "You know me, I keep everything bottled up, that's how I deal with stuff ...

but over Christmas, I couldn't stop thinking about you. Wanting to be with you, in fact, needing any form of contact with you. I texted you and when you didn't reply ... well, it's caused problems at home. I'm distracted and restless. Lily has ..." He stopped. "Too much?"

Amanda shook her head. "I won't faint at the sound of your wife's name, Richard. Not anymore. But the whole thing is too much."

"What do you mean?"

"Well, it's all a bit out of the blue, isn't it? This ..." She struggled for words and instead held her arms wide. "It's over. We're over. You can't turn to me when you're down and use me as an excuse for your unhappiness. You've been moaning about your marriage for as long as I've known you." She glanced around, lowering her voice, feeling anger uncoil inside her. "I gave myself to you, every part of me, and you could have been brave enough to choose me over your wife back then. I would have done anything for you, gone through anything to be with you. Christ, I even begged you!"

"It wasn't Lily, it was the kids. You always knew the score. Then we had her family problems, it was such a bad time. You know ..."

Amanda put a hand on the middle of his chest, shiny buttons cold beneath her palm, and gently pushed him backwards. "What I know is ... that was then, this is now. I won't let you screw my life up again." She brushed past him. "Sorry ... I have to go."

Feet slipping and sliding in her rush to put distance between them, she blinked away tears at the injustice of timing in her life. If only she and Richard had worked out back then, he could have been her support now at a time when she needed it. But instead, he'd left it months and months ...

She collided with a large form as she dragged the heavy door open and rushed through. Strong hands steadied her at the elbows. Dara's voice cut through her thoughts.

"Oomph. Whoa, ma'am. You'll do one of us an injury."

"Sorry," she muttered. "Sorry, Dara ... I didn't see you."

"You okay, ma'am? You seem a bit shook up."

"Yes, yes, I'm f-fine." She hiccupped. "No, Dara ... actually I'm not at all fine."

"Ah ..."

As she looked up, she saw Dara's gaze as he followed the back of the Assistant Chief Constable across the car park towards his Volvo.

His grip slackened as his voice spoke warm in her ear. "Fancy a coffee in the canteen, ma'am?"

She took a sip of hot chocolate and closed her eyes. Okay, chocolate wasn't quite the antidote for her that nicotine or alcohol was in times of stress, but it came a close third. She took another gulp and squeezed the bridge of her nose, feeling the build-up of a headache behind her eyes.

"Everything is such a mess, Dara. I seem to lurch from one crisis to the next, never learning a damn thing on the way. Why can't real life be more like an investigation? You know, a process, an order, the ability to make choices that affect the outcome. I can do that. I can process anything work related, and trust myself my decisions are spot on. Why can't I carry that over into my personal life?"

Dara took a sip from his mug of tea and wiped his lips. "Ah, you've probably asked the very worst person inside this building for advice there, ma'am."

She smiled. "But it's a serious question. What's the matter with me? Why can I handle work with relative ease, and yet go to pieces when I have to cope with personal stuff?"

"Is that rhetorical? I mean, do you really need an answer?"

"I think I do, Dara."

He sat back and crossed muscled forearms across his chest. "I suppose I should ask what's bothering you so much right now? But if you don't want to tell me, I'll understand."

She met his gaze and smiled. "Oddly, it's not what you're thinking. That's a side show to the main event."

Amanda took another gulp of her hot chocolate and related her call with Emily. Dara sipped his tea and listened, taking his time to respond.

"I think you've been brave to put Emily's feelings first. It's the right thing to do, of course, but certainly not the easiest." He paused as if deciding how to continue, then met her eye. "Besides, there's surely a part of you thinks putting distance between Emily and Anglesey can only be a good thing, just now?"

Amanda looked down, flustered. "He's not here, Dara, and he's not coming back. I have to tell myself that on a daily basis."

"Yes, but Emily –"

"Emily doesn't know, she doesn't need to know … and that's the way it's staying." Amanda swallowed, recalling her ex-husband's words, but refusing to let guilt dictate her choices. Emily was her daughter and she was trained in these matters, no one was going to tell her what was right and wrong.

"Fair dos." Dara took another sip of tea. "Then give yourself a break, ma'am, give yourself time to adjust. I can see you're panicky because now you're thinking of how you'll cope. But you will, because that's what life throws at us – cause and effect isn't it? And I think we humans are programmed to deal with change, with a kind of 'life goes on' mentality – even if we hate the idea of change in the first place."

Amanda looked up, surprised. "You've really thought about it, haven't you?"

Dara shrugged. "I've always felt my life will be a series of chapters. I've joked I'm the proverbial cat with nine lives. Each time one scene comes to an end, I'm always thinking the worst, how will I cope, how can I possibly recover. But I do. And so will you. It's part of the human spirit."

Amanda pondered his words, swirling the thick brown liquid around her mug. "Do you never worry about being lonely?

Growing old alone? Do you ever worry about what you'll do when you retire?"

Dara shook his head. "No, because none of us can see into the future. Why worry about a future that might never come and miss the chance to live for today." He sighed, ran a hand across his shaven scalp. "I think I made a conscious decision when I parted from the former Mrs Brennan, I'd never try to plot my life out again. I'd spent best part of a decade making plans, choosing baby names, building a future … that suddenly disappeared. It's taught me one thing more than anything … I'll never put myself in anyone's hands ever again. Whether love or lust or commitment or whatever … from now on I'm going to be in control of my own life because this isn't a rehearsal … this is it, the only life I'm getting."

"Wise words."

"And if I meet that special person who wants to share the journey with me, then bonus. If not …" He shrugged again. "… then so be it. I'm going with fate from now on."

"My first instinct was to follow Emily. If she was going to stay down in the Midlands, then that's where I wanted to be too. However, even though my ex-husband might make my toes curl, he does speak sense, and running after Emily now and making her feel more pressured isn't the right thing. So, you've got me here, I'm afraid, at least for the time being."

"Well, I'll not pretend I'm not glad. And you won't be alone. You'll always have me and Kelly, Gethin and Fletch. We're not family exactly, but probably just as problematic at times."

Amanda laughed aloud. "You can say that, again. Although all seems quiet on the love-life front at the moment?"

Dara grinned. "Me? I'm as celibate as Father O'Neal to be sure."

"But not by choice, I'll wager?"

"What'll be, will be."

"Have you spoken to Kelly about any of these new life principles you've put in place. Is she up for sharing your journey?"

Dara shook his head. "We talk, but don't talk, if you know what I mean. I'm a way from seeing the divorce sorted, and my money is still tied up. I'm in no position to be making demands on anyone. Kelly is young and beautiful and could meet the man of her dreams any day now. I don't want to get in her way."

"But, Dara –"

"And there's another thing, ma'am. I'd like to speak about this in confidence for now." He paused, leaned forward and gripped the blue mug with both hands. "I may be needing time off at short notice. I've things back in Ireland I need to sort." He let out a long breath. "My mother told us all before we left that she's got cancer. It's terminal. They've given her nine months or so."

Amanda reached across the table and took one of Dara's huge hands between her own. "Oh, no. Dara, I'm so sorry and there I was wittering on about my problems and you with all this to cope with. It's so unfair."

"I'm not the one having to cope with it, though, that's the thing. It's me ma who's going through it, and according to my sister she's determined to go through it alone. She doesn't want any of us around her and I don't understand it."

"Is there nothing they can do?"

"She's had two courses of chemo already. I knew nothing about any of this, she's a fine actress, I'll say that for her. Nothing came across on the phone at all over the past few months." He sniffed and sighed. "Started in her bowel, but it's spread to her liver and lungs. And the chemo has had no effect at all other than making her feel so ill she said she already wished she was dead. So, she's refused further treatment." His voice caught and he paused. "I so bloody admire the strength of her … but still, it's me ma, and well, you know if anyone would know …"

Amanda sniffed back tears and squeezed his hand tighter between her own. "Yes, I know. But like I had to accept Emily's decision, you have to accept your mother's decision. Even if it breaks your heart in the process."

Dara sniffed and rubbed his nose. "Oh, I know that, ma'am.

She's not a woman you've any hope of changing anyway. But … it's the waiting for someone you love to die. God only knows how she copes with it, to see her, you'd not believe it. Honestly, cooked full Christmas dinner for all the family, though thinking back she only picked at her own food … and out walking Tilly, her dog, at the crack of dawn every day. Made our last Christmas together perfect, I suppose." He shook his head. "Me … I'd be rolled up in a ball under my duvet feeling sorry for myself."

Amanda squeezed his hand. "No, you wouldn't. You've got your mother's spirit, I've no doubt about that. You'd want to grab life and live every single day while you could. I get that. She sounds a remarkable woman, Dara, and you should be very proud."

He looked down. "Ah, that's fer sure. The thought she'll soon be gone though … it's killing me …"

He broke off and Amanda knew he was struggling to hold back tears. She stayed silent and gave him time. There was no easy fix or placating words.

In time, he brushed his cheeks with the back of his hand, sniffed and stood up. "You'll keep it to yourself, ma'am? I'm clinging onto normality at the moment, it's all that's keepin' me going."

"Dara, you don't even have to ask, you know that."

CHAPTER ELEVEN

"Gethin. Are you okay with that?"

Gethin jerked as he recognised his name amid the noise of the office. "Ma'am?"

Amanda bent low across his desk to study him at eye level. "Ground control to DS Evans. Are you with us?"

Gethin looked down, embarrassed. "Of course, ma'am. I was running through the latest information in my head, trying to find any connections."

"More likely reliving last night's adventures, you ask me," said Fletch from the next desk. "We'll nag you into submission, fella, you will tell us, you do know that?"

Gethin blushed. He *had* been thinking about Eliza Glenowen. Fletcher was spot on. But that was something he was not going to admit now, in a busy incident room, especially in the presence of heathens like Dara and Fletch. He needed more time to privately revisit the morning sunrise out at Llyn Maelog, and the intensity and spirituality of the feelings he'd experienced. He couldn't focus his mind on anything else. But he had to try … and fast.

He scowled at Fletch and turned away. "Sorry, ma'am. I'm all ears."

"You and Dara. You're okay to take on McDonald's home visit?"

Gethin frowned. "Sorry, have I missed something, have we

found his address in the area? I thought last we had was an address in the Shetland Isles?"

Dara clicked his tongue. "Gethin, man, have you been on the magic mushrooms, again? You've not been listening to a bloody word I've said for the past half hour."

"I have!"

"No, you haven't."

"Yes –"

Amanda stepped forward. "Boys!"

"I missed the bit about the Shetland Isles, that's all," said Gethin.

"Well, switch yer brain back on then, little man," said Dara in an amused tone, "because you an' I have an early start. I've booked us on a 7.40am flight from Manchester to Glasgow. And from there a mid-day flight to Sumburgh Airport. Which …" he consulted his computer, "is twenty-five miles south of Lerwick on the main island, and around a dozen miles from McDonald's last known address in Sandwick."

"And I've booked two rooms at the only B&B in Sandwick and sorted car hire at the airport." Kelly called across the office. "You're ready to go."

"Crackin', thanks, Kel, I'll put a call into the local police at Lerwick, let them know we'll be on their patch." Dara stretched and rolled his neck. "Hope it's worth the hassle and expense, but there's so little else to go on. Address matches with DVLA records, so we know it's right. But other than that the guy's an enigma."

"Well, I wouldn't be signing off a trip to the Shetland islands on expenses if I didn't think it was absolutely necessary," said Amanda. "Idris Parry is going to bust a nut, but hey, we've got to know everything there is to know about Peter James McDonald because he's the solitary link we have to our killer. And if you could find our missing chef on your travels … that would be mighty appreciated too."

"Wake up, sleeping beauty. We're about to land and the view is worth a look."

Gethin grunted as Dara's elbow buried itself in his ribs. He yawned and rubbed his eyes, squinting against the blinding glare through the small cabin window. The pitch of the aeroplane's engines dropped an octave, and beneath his feet the floor juddered as the wheels lowered. He twisted his face towards the window and gasped. Dara had, in typical Dara-understatement, failed to describe the vista beneath them.

Foamy-topped waves crashed a jade-coloured sea jagged rocks. And in front of them, spread out like an iced Christmas cake, the rolling hills of the main island sparkled under pale winter sunshine. As the plane buffeted in the breeze, a strip of black tarmac cut into the expanse of whiteness, and the snow-topped airport terminal appeared at alarming speed. Seconds later, they landed with a thud and a rumble.

"Always glad to feel the bump of terra firm." Dara leaned forward to retrieve the book that had slid from Gethin's lap as he dozed. "What's this you're reading? Who's Tacitus –?"

Gethin grabbed the book and shoved it into the bag between his feet. "Nothing."

Dara raised his dark eyebrows. "Touchy. Is it a bit of Fifty Shades, eh?"

Gethin zipped up his bag with more force than necessary, determined to avoid two days of piss-take if Dara discovered his latest interest in Druids. "Tacitus is an historian from the Roman period if you must know … just a bit of local history I've been reading up on as background to the case. Some of us take our jobs seriously."

"Ooooh, meow, that's me told. Of course, you keep your little secrets. I wouldn't want to get in the way of the class favourite."

Gethin stared forward in silence, ignoring the provocation, glad to see the line of exiting travellers begin to shuffle forward along the aisle, relaxing as Dara manoeuvred himself out of the tight space to join them.

Half an hour later, still dazed and yawning, Gethin settled back into the seat as Dara expertly handled the hired 4X4 across the ice-packed car park surface and out onto the main road.

Dara blinked against the white light and flicked down the sun visor. "Wish I'd brought me sunglasses. Who'dve thought midwinter in the remotest part of Britain would be so stunning?"

"Reminds me of North Wales to be honest."

"Ach, you're biased."

Gethin shrugged. "Maybe. But give me Anglesey any day."

"Have you checked the map?" said Dara. "There'll be no phone signal here."

"Yes," said Gethin, pulling a paper map from the bag between his feet. "Turn right onto the A970 towards Lerwick and it takes us straight through Sandwick. We can ask once we're there."

"Can't imagine it'll be a big place."

Dara was right. Small in size, but blessed with the most stunning views, Sandwick was a hamlet of around a two dozen houses, a church and a pub - right on the coast road. Dara pulled to the side of the road, and they took in the view across the straits of deep blue choppy water Gethin hated to admit reminded him of the Menai Strait. And in the distance, on the far side of the water, was, according to the map, the Isle of Mousa. He showed the page to Dara.

"And what's that black tower?" said Dara, lowering his window to squint through the misty sunshine.

Gethin consulted the map. "It's marked as 'Broch of Mousa'. Dunno what that means."

"Ah, I know about brochs, similar Celtic history to Ireland. They're Iron Age towers, thousands of years old. Shame we're not here on a sight-seeing visit, I'd have liked to have a close-up look."

"Well, we're not and we've twenty-four hours to build up a history of Peter James McDonald. I reckon we've about two hours of daylight left at best, so we better get a move on," said Gethin, checking his watch. "Let's check if there's a Post Office for a start, see what info we can get there, then find the quickest route to his address. What you say?"

Dara started the engine. "I say you sound almost like a detective, Detective."

The village-stores-cum-Post-Office was like something out of a television documentary about war-time Britain. None of the remotest villages of North Wales could boast such a relic. Much of the stock, with sun-faded labels, looked well past their sell-by-dates, and the bent old chap who shuffled into view from the dimness of a doorway behind the counter, looked as if he could have been here at the shop's opening. Bushy white hair and sideburns surrounded his face in a halo of candyfloss. He squinted at their identification badges with National Health spectacles, Gethin had last seen in the 1980s, and wore a hand-knitted beige cardigan with buttons the size of half-walnuts, a style he recalled his own grandfather wearing at his allotment.

He listened with intensity as Dara explained the purpose of their visit.

"Ach, that'll be Grace's lad. Ah yes, God rest her soul. What are you wanting with wee Peter?"

Gethin glanced at Dara to see if he'd picked up the remark. Clearly he had.

"Grace McDonald has passed away?" Dara asked.

"Oh, aye, was the cancer took her, few months back. God rest her soul."

"And how about the rest of the family – are they still in Sandwick?"

"Who's that then?" the man frowned. "You'll have to speak up, see, I'm not the best at hearing and you're not local, are ye?"

Dara sighed, spoke slower and louder. "The rest of the McDonald family. Where can we find them?"

The man shrugged. "Not round here if there are any. Peter is the last of the McDonalds in this village. Crying shame, but there you are."

"Can you give us directions to Peter's address, please, sir?" said Gethin, over-enunciating his words in case Welsh accents caused the man similar problems.

"Oh, aye." He scribbled something on a piece of paper, out of sight behind the counter. "It's a mile or so out, on the Lerwick Road. Look for the first crossroads and tek the turn off away on the left, quite a steep climb to a white cottage, you can't miss it. But you won't find him there."

Gethin knew that, sadly. "No?"

The man shook his head as he passed the piece of notepaper to Dara. "Ach, no, he found it hard out on his own at the croft after Grace passed. Mebbe if he finds a lass and wants a family of his own he'll come back one day." He shook his head slowly. "But I can't see that happenin'. Shame, but there you are, that's life for you."

Dara cleared his throat. "Any idea where Peter has been staying?"

The man shook his head. "We don't have a forwarding address. He used to come back for a weekend, every couple of months. Pay the bills and see things right. Then he'd be off again. With his job, I assume."

"Which was …?"

"What was?"

"His job?" Dara almost growled. Where was he working?"

The man waved his hand in an extravagant gesture. "Ach, all over, wasn't he? One of them eco-friendlies, went round saving the planet. Always was one who wanted to change the way of things. Refused to let his mam keep any pigs or chickens after his dad died, way back. Wouldn't have anyone killing animals for food, one of those vegan types, you know?" The old man winked as if he'd announced Peter was some kind of pervert. "Not going to survive so easy out here in the Isles if you've got yourself them kind of fancy ideas. But there you go …"

Gethin thanked the man as Dara headed for the door, then turned back.

"We might need to take a look round the property. Does anyone keep a key?"

The man laughed. "It won't be locked. Not round here, it's not the way of things. And anyway, you didn't say what it is you want with Peter ..."

The lane from the main road up to the McDonald cottage tested the 4X4's suspension to the limits. Gethin staggered from the car feeling like he'd been on fast spin cycle in a washing machine. If the house was as neglected as the drive, he wasn't hopeful it would hold many clues. The black-painted front door, and small square windows, peered at him from freshly white-washed stone walls that bulged in irregular angles as if the weight of the roof was crushing the structure slowly into the ground. Snow covered the surrounding area in a pristine white blanket, their footsteps the first to tarnish its smoothness.

Dara turned the handle and pushed the door with his shoulder, taking a step back as it swung inwards. Gethin followed him inside, aware at once of the silence as they stepped out of the constant howl of the wind. He spotted an ancient-looking Bakelite light switch, and was delighted when a single bare bulb in the middle of the room flickered into life. They were in an open-plan room; one side an alcoved lounge with a huge fireplace taking up one gable wall of the cottage, and to their right extended an old-fashioned kitchen, deep butler sink and coal-burning range its central features. Most of the rest of the floor space was clear, furniture either already removed, or pushed to the far end of the sitting room area and covered with white dust sheets. There was the smell of fresh paint and disinfectant.

Dara stooped to miss the thick central beam that ran from one end of the cottage to the other and did a three-hundred-and-sixty-degree rotation. "Well, it's not exactly abandoned, is it? Someone's been working here quite recent I'd say. These walls are not long painted and the floor tiles have been re-treated too."

Gethin nodded. "Someone has plans for this place. But it doesn't have a lived in feel, does it? Looks more like he was packing up. Let's check out the other rooms, bedrooms especially, see if there's any personal stuff."

Two doors led off the kitchen, the first revealed a tiny bathroom with an original roll top bath, and the second led to a narrow flight of stairs, barely shoulder-width and again illuminated with a single bulb. Floorboards creaked as Gethin turned left at the top and explored the first bedroom, which had clearly belonged to Grace McDonald. All clothes and personal possessions were removed, leaving an iron bed frame, single wardrobe and under the window, a small dressing table with an ornately-carved mirror. Every drawer and cupboard was empty, save for a wooden sea chest full of mildew-spotted towels and bed linen.

Hearing the creak of floorboards behind him, he headed back to the tiny landing and met Dara coming out of the second bedroom.

"Anything?"

Dara shook his head, standing on a tilt to match the slope of the ceiling. "Not much, everything left is already in packing cases. Two boxes of clothes and one box of knick-knacks – old videos, computer games and the like. One thing though, there was a hefty selection of pretty hard-core gay porn magazines, so I think our guy was homosexual. Not sure whether he was out or not but it's one thing we didn't know that's worth noting. Didn't the boss mention something after the post-mortem about that?"

Gethin turned and headed towards the stairs. "Did she?"

"Yeah," Dara's voice followed Gethin. "I'll check but sure she did. It might explain why he didn't stick around the village – being the only gay an' all. Poor fella. Couldn't be easy in a place like this."

Gethin paused, reaching out to steady himself as he negotiated the steep stairs. "Slightly judgemental, no?"

"What's that?" Dara grunted. "Christ these cottages weren't made for Irish Adonises, were they?"

Gethin waited at the bottom of the stairs. "Nor tubby middle-age Irish coppers it would seem. I simply meant this is the twenty-first century, detective, being gay isn't illegal anymore and for all you know Sandwick might be as popular as Brighton for the gay community."

Dara snorted as he appeared, brushing plaster dust from the shoulders of his leather jacket. "Don't ya be kidding yourself, take it from someone who was raised in a place a lot like this – albeit with an even larger dollop of hypocrisy over on our side of the Irish Sea. Ach, face it … it'd be hard enough coming out back on Anglesey, even today, let alone announcing in a village pub full of family friends and relatives in a tiny place like this that you can't marry young Jessie as presumed as you actually fancy her brother a sight more." Dara drew breath and shook his head. "No, he'd not have fitted in, fer sure, and explains why he took off as soon as he could, if you ask me."

Gethin gave a mock salute. "Fine, whatever you say, I bow to your superior knowledge. Where else then?"

"We can take a look round the back, see if there's a shed or something, but my hunch is Peter McDonald was making his move permanent and was in the process of doing up and selling the place. Let's hope we're in luck tonight in the pub and the locals are a chatty – and a nosy – bunch."

CHAPTER TWELVE

"So, it's one pint of dark and one of light, you're wanting, aye?"

The landlord looked at Gethin expectantly.

"Er … thanks."

Gethin shrugged. They'd have to drink it, whatever. Dara had gone off investigating the back room, where a game of darts was reaching a noisy climax. If he made a fuss about his drink, he could order the next round.

Low-ceilings with smoke darkened beams, and garnet-coloured upholstery, flickered in the light from the real fires at both ends of the lounge. The air was tangy with the smell of mulled wine and wood smoke. Strands of fairy lights bobbed along the beams, and the handful of regulars dotted at a couple of tables were all rosy-cheeked and vociferous. It was the kind of place that made you sigh with pleasure and relax into its warm, beery embrace as you stepped across its threshold.

The landlord was tall and heavyset with a thick, dark beard, wearing a navy-blue Scotland rugby shirt. He stole a glance at Gethin and pumped a hand-held beer pull, smiling when he met Gethin's eye.

"You're a new face in here?" he said, his voice booming above the background noise as he pushed a brimming glass of what looked like dark stout across the bar. "First drink's always on the house fer strangers."

Gethin glanced at the glass and hoped for something a little more palatable next time as the man moved to another pump.

"That's very kind of you, thanks so much. Yes, it's my first time on Shetland."

"Ach, yer welcome, we like to treat tourists well, so we do, we rely on them now round these parts. The name's Malcolm Hyde. You can call me Malkie, everyone does. I run the wee place here with my wife, Carol. Hope you have a nice time here on Shetland."

He placed a glass of pale real ale on the bar and Gethin heaved a sigh of relief. "Cheers! I'm sure it won't be the last of the night and we'll be eating here too." He took a sip of the beer and wiped froth from his top lip. "God, that's a nice pint and more than welcome. It's been quite a journey."

Malkie smiled, pride shining in his eyes. "Thank you. Give me mo, I'll fetch you a menu."

Gethin looked round as his sipped his drink. A burst of laughter erupted from a table in the corner, the rattle of coins and a cheer from two youths playing on a fruit machine over by the door. He thought back to Dara's summary of Peter McDonald being an outcast because of his sexuality. Would that have been the case? Or was it impossible, not to mention wrong, to categorise everyone based purely on their background?

His thoughts were interrupted by the return of Malkie, menu in hand. "So, you can tell me to butt out and mind me own … but you'll be one of the fellas asking about Peter James in the Post Office earlier I don't wonder?"

Gethin swallowed his mouthful of beer and smiled. Perhaps this place wasn't so unlike Anglesey after all.

"That's right." He pulled his identification wallet from his pocket. "DS Gethin Evans from North Wales CID. We're hoping we might get to speak to anyone who knew Peter McDonald. Can you help at all?"

Dara appeared at that moment, face flushed, stooping to dodge the low ceiling and fairy lights. "Man, I could sieve sand with me throat, where's me drink, Geth?"

Gethin nodded towards the dark concoction. "On the house. Thank the Landlord, Malkie."

Dara held out a hand across the bar and both men shook. He took a long pull of the dark beer and sighed with satisfaction. "Ach, that's a real pint, so it is. I've somehow got enrolled in the next game of darts, so I'll catch you later, Geth, okay?"

Gethin saw a knowing look he recognised in Dara's gaze. He'd made contact with someone who could be useful and was going 'under cover'.

"Sure. Maybe pick what you want from the menu before you disappear. I've told Malkie we're looking for information on Peter McDonald."

"Ah." Dara glanced behind him, noting the bar area was clear. "I'm about to break that snippet of news to the lads next door. Any tips?"

Malkie leaned forward on his elbows. "John and Laurie Stewart are your best bet of those rabble in there. I'll go and fetch my other half, she was close to Peter at one time. School buddies as wee ones and she tended to Grace on and off before she passed." He paused, gaze switching between the two men. "You used the past tense, talking about him, I mean. I'm assuming it might not be good news?"

Gethin shook his head. "We have a body that's been identified by dental records as Peter. We're hoping to get a positive ID and find out what we can about him. Would your wife be able to help?"

"Oh, Lord. I'm sure she'd assist. She's a nurse, made of strong stuff. Choose your dinner gentlemen and I'll fetch her down."

Carol Hyde was the polar opposite of her husband – petite, blonde and quietly-spoken. When Malkie appeared with Carol, dwarfing her slight frame, Gethin had first thought it was a teenager by his side, not his wife. Her blue eyes, pale skin and exquisite features were doll-like. Gethin had to fight the urge to reach out to touch her to convince himself she was real. Even dressed in double denim, which Gethin knew even with his limited knowledge of female fashion was a complete no-no ... she still looked elegant and fragile. *'Made of strong stuff'* was not the first thought that came to mind on meeting the woman, but once pleasantries and introductions had been dealt with, it was soon clear who wore the trousers in this marriage.

"I'm one of three district nurses here on the island. That's my real job when I'm not washing dishes and generally skivvying for Malkie Hyde, that is." Carol smiled, knowing her husband was in ear shot.

"Yes, dear," said Malkie as he pulled a second pint for Gethin.

"Mine's a Chardonnay," said Carol. "Bring them over."

"Yes, dear."

Settled at a table by the window, Gethin outlined the case and upon agreement removed a post-mortem facial shot of Peter McDonald from his inside pocket. Opening his notebook, he slid the photograph towards her.

Carol closed her eyes for a moment, seeming to steel herself, then picked up the photo, taking a while to study the features before placing it back on the table, face down. She took a long breath and nodded. "Aye. So sad. That's Peter James. What on earth happened?"

"We're not sure, that's why we're here. I'll not lie, we need all the help we can get with this unexplained death. So ... Peter James ... that's what he was called locally, is it?"

"Aye, his father's name was James. Bit of a family tradition to use both." Carol shook her head and smiled. "He had a phase in his teens of calling himself P.J. but Grace soon put a stop to that. She was a tiger, old Grace McDonald."

"You knew her well?"

"All my life. She was one of my ma's best friends, almost like an auntie to me growing up. So, I suppose Peter James was as close as a cousin. It's the way with crofter families, even today. We were all so reliant on each other back then, for pretty much everything. Even when I was a bairn, visits to the mainland were rare, so in our parent's generation they'd have been unheard of." She sipped her wine and sighed. "And then I cared for Grace towards the end. She was fiercely independent, so she managed on her own for as long as she could ... but the last few months were difficult. Peter James came home but she made it clear she didn't want him nursing her. Proud to her final breath, she was."

"When did she die?"

"Last February. She took to her bed before Christmas. I'd known for a while she was ill and doing her best to ignore the fact. She'd been diagnosed with bowel cancer the previous spring but refused treatment, couldn't put up with pointless trips to mainland, she said. Personally, I think the idea of chemo terrified her. Who knows, perhaps she made the right choice."

"Peter was working away before his mother's illness, you say," said Gethin. "Do you know where?"

"He worked all over the place. He was a marine biologist for a company based in Aberdeen. He worked on testing sea samples all around the British Isles, last time we spoke he told me he was based in Anglesey, North Wales. Something to do with water pollution and the effect on the dolphin population in the Irish Sea. He was so passionate about his work, you should understand that, detective. It was his life."

Gethin scribbled a note. Marine biologist, not a chef. "And family? Was he married? Kids?"

Carol's eyes darted to the door, where a noisy bunch of men had entered, an icy wind in their wake. She looked back to her wine, tracing the edge of her glass with a slender finger.

"No, a confirmed bachelor, he liked to say. Married to the job. And he wasn't one for the bairns. No brothers or sisters either, the line ends with him."

Gethin took a sip of beer and pondered how, or if, to ask the next question. Before he had chance, Carol continued.

"Our families both had us down as the next generation of crofters, probably had us wed to each other before we were out of nappies. But I always knew, right from a very early age, I wasn't Pete's type." Carol looked up, met his gaze. "I think you know what I mean, detective?"

Gethin nodded but stayed silent, sensing there was more.

Carol exhaled and shook her head, memories coming thick and fast. "Oh, I adored Peter James. It was impossible not to. He was as cute as a button as a child, blond curls and a smile to die for ... then wise and intelligent as he matured, never lost his looks either. But he was modest and kind, a perfect gent. I used to tell Malkie he should be more like Peter James, and that went down well as you can imagine." She took another sip of wine. "Funny but we looked like twins as bairns ... and I will admit to the wee occasional daydream about a happy-ever-after future together, but I knew it would never be. Oh, and it wasn't easy for him, I'll tell you. It took a strong person to stand up to Grace McDonald, but he did, he lived his own life, in his own way, and once he left the island for University, he never really came back. I was proud of him. Jealous sometimes, too."

Gethin watched as Carol sniffed back tears. "And the croft ... we've been up there, it's far from derelict," he said. "What were Peter's plans, do you know?"

"I think your man in the snug might find out more. Pete had plans to sell the croft on to Laurie Stewart once the permissions had gone through from the Scottish Crofting Federation who rule the roost round here. Laurie was only in here moaning last week about the time it was taking, how the solicitors were dragging it out. I guess now we know why."

"Peter wasn't planning on moving back then?"

Carol shook her head. "No, last time I spoke to him ... would have been August time I think ... he said he was really happy in North Wales. He was into water sports in a big way, had joined some local kite surfing club ... and he was content. I could see it in him. Despite the loss of his ma, I could tell he was settled. I thought he might have met someone special but he was as tight-lipped as ever. We promised him a big send off when he finally left ... so sad that never happened and I'll never get chance to say goodbye."

Silent tears welled and slid down her cheeks. She wiped them away with the cuff of her denim shirt. Malkie appeared at the table with two fresh drinks, which he deposited quickly as he saw his wife's tears. Gethin looked away as the couple embraced.

"Is that enough for now, detective?" said Malkie as they broke apart and he rubbed the tears from his wife's cheeks with two huge thumbs. "Seems our Carol ain't as tough as she likes us to think."

"I'm fine, stop yer fussing," Carol said, shooing the big man away. "Just hit me I'd never see Pete again, is all."

Gethin drained his pint. "I think we're done for now, Mrs Hyde. Thank you for your time. One last thing ... do you know the name of the company Peter worked for?"

Carol frowned, wiping her nose with a tissue. "Let me think. It had marine in the title, something about marine services, but definitely in Aberdeen. Does that help?"

"I'm sure I can Google it. Thanks again." He handed over his card. "If you think of anything else, my mobile number is on there. Give me a call."

"Aye, I will. Whoever killed him, you make sure and catch the bastard. He was a good man ..."

Her voice broke and she picked up her wine without another word and disappeared through an alcove behind the bar. Malkie hovered at the table.

"Surprised at the tears, she's not one to show emotion is our Carol," he said. "But I always reckoned he was her first love, you know. Did she tell you? Hard act to follow he was ... Pete this, Pete that ... but I do my best."

"She'll be fine."

"Was it murder?"

Gethin nodded.

"Aye, well, can't say I'm surprised."

"No? Why's that?"

Malkie leaned lower, face level with Gethin's and whispered through the side of his mouth. "The lifestyle. He was a queer. Did she tell you?"

"I'm sorry, sir, but I fail to see the connection."

Malkie straightened, cleared his throat and looked at Gethin with a puzzled expression. "Well, no one will be shocked he's been killed, that's all I'm saying." He picked up the empty glasses and headed to the bar. "Dinner will be served in five minutes. I'll give your pal a call."

The steak was tender and juicy and cooked to perfection ... but still it stuck in Gethin's throat. He chewed and chewed but each slice tasted like shoe leather. He popped a couple of chips into his mouth, pushed the plate away and reached for his fifth pint.

"... as if I have all the fecking answers. Phone the solicitor in the morning, I said. Nothing I can do."

Gethin looked up as Dara's voice cut through the maelstrom of thoughts buzzing around his brain. A hammer drill thumped away in the back of his skull, pain blurring his vision.

"Yeah," he mumbled.

Dara put down his knife and fork. "Have you been listening to a single word?"

"Course. Call the solicitor in the morning. Good advice."

Dara chewed in silence, studying Gethin. "Yeah, well." He picked up his cutlery and carried on where he left off. "I'm here to try an' find out who killed the fella, right, not issue his last will and testament."

Gethin glanced across to the bar. Malkie Hyde was in close conversation with another bearded local, worn sage green dungarees giving him the look of a farmer. From the quick glances that kept shooting his way, there was no prizes for guessing the topic under discussion. And there'd be no doubt either this chap agreed with the Landlord's views that Peter James McDonald was one hundred percent to blame for his own death. However, uninformed they were, however irrelevant the actual facts of the case ...

Gethin jumped as Dara slammed down his pint glass. "What is the matter with you? It's like talking to my ex-wife trying to get sense outta you. Who's rattled your cage?"

"No one. Eat your chips."

Dara scowled and discreetly slid Gethin's uneaten chips onto his own plate. "Seems to me Peter-Bloody-James wasn't too popular with folk round here. No one seems to miss him. Seems I was right, eh?"

Gethin's throat tightened. "You're always right, Dara. We all know that."

"An' what you mean by that?"

"Well, like you said, you were raised to hate *the queers* too, weren't you?"

Dara stopped chewing. He swallowed hard, reached for his pint and took a long gulp, his eyes never leaving Gethin's face.

"Where the hell did that come from?" he growled.

Gethin waved the remark away and lifted his glass.

"I'm serious," Dara said. "You're angry at me, fair dos, at least do me the honour of telling me why."

Gethin could feel the effects of the alcohol loosening his emotions – and his tongue. The pain in his head made it difficult to reply. "I need a slash."

"No, you don't. Sit down."

Gethin stood up as Dara's big hand reached out and grabbed him, crushing his wrist. "Ow. You're hurting."

"Then sit down an' save yourself a scene."

Glancing across to a line of blurred faces at the bar, he sat.

"Explain," said Dara, pushing his plate away. "Not much gets to spoil my tea."

Gethin sighed and rubbed his eyes, wishing he could dissolve the pain in his head as easily as he had to dissolve this confrontation. He had no choice. And in truth he didn't want an argument with Dara, not here, not ever. He had to stop the rising tide inside himself, threatening to turn into a tsunami and flood his whole life. Christ, it wasn't as if he hadn't had to do it a thousand times in the past. Why was it harder here, now, today?

He held up his hands in surrender. "It's the ale talking. It's strong stuff. Ignore me. I'm sorry."

Dara sipped his pint and shook his head. "You'll need to do better than that."

Gethin shrugged. "I have nothing else to offer in my defence, m'lord. I'm pished and exhausted and the best thing for me would be to take my bad manners and put them to bed." He gave a sheepish grin. "I'm sorry. You've done nothing."

Dara's gaze wandered across to the men at the bar and back again. Gethin's eyes followed, drawn magnet-like by the intensity of the stares. There were four of them now, hairy and huge, like a breed of Shetlanders.

Dara leaned forward, spoke quietly. "You should know the mentality of people out in these remote places, Gethin. Has a lifetime living on Anglesey really taught you nothing?"

Gethin snorted. "You make island folk sound like Neanderthals. Anglesey blokes ain't nowhere near as bad as the ones I've met today. Trust me, I'd know."

Dara shrugged. "Okay, I bow to your superior knowledge." He studied him for silent moments. "But whatever it is that's bothering you, Geth, you can talk to me. You do know that? About anything? I'll never judge you –"

Gethin got to his feet, feeling his legs tremble as he gripped the edge of the table. "Sorry, Dara, mate. I seriously gotta take that leak right now ... then I'm hitting the sack. See you bright and early."

Dara's eyes burned into Gethin's back all the way across the pub. When he finally managed to force open the heavy door and stagger out into the sting of the wind, he was stunned to feel tears trickling down his cheeks.

CHAPTER THIRTEEN

Amanda took a final pull on her cigarette, ground the stub into the slushy pavement, and pushed open the reception doors, sighing with relief to leave the icy wind behind. The morning was barely light, despite being almost eight am, dawn was still a tantalising shimmer of orange above the Snowdonia peaks shadowing the town.

She'd been awake for hours, the emptiness of the cottage seeming to press in on her like a physical force. Every night-time creak of the old building pushed her to the edge of tears. If Emily was staying with her father, and Amanda had no choice but to accept she was, then her next move was finding a permanent house, somewhere light and airy where she could put her stamp on the surroundings and make it a home. She made a vow this would be the only winter she spent in the Beaumaris cottage.

Trying to remember the name of the Estate Agents in Castle Street, Amanda turned left and headed for the stairs. She stopped short when she met a more-angry-looking-than-usual Idris Parry on his way down.

"I'd not bother taking off your coat, you're on your way out again."

Amanda cleared her throat. "Morning to you, too, sir. What's that?"

"Control had a call from a couple of uniforms in Rhosneigr. Your famous lake has thrown up yet another surprise."

Amanda's pulse thudded in her temples. "Another body?"

Idris Parry gave a curt nod. "Get yourself over there and find out what the hell is going on. This is beyond a joke. We are coming across as a bunch of clueless amateurs. No clues, no victim info, no suspects. This is going to be the last body on my patch, do you understand?" He brushed past her. "I want this case solved and I want it solved fast – or I'll get someone else as SIO who is capable of doing the job. I'll expect a full report in my office at six pm."

Amanda watched, open-mouthed, as Parry disappeared down the corridor, heading towards the custody cells. She swallowed down the hot ball of indignation, turned on her heel, re-buttoned her coat, and headed back out into the wintry chill.

Amanda pulled her car onto the grass verge, skidding across the packed ice stopping inches from the rear bumper of Kelly's Peugeot. Anger hummed in every nerve ending, sharpened by her own senses of both frustration and dread. Her stomach had been doing somersaults since the run in with Idris Parry, and despite the unfairness of his allegations, they only added weight to her own anxieties they were getting nowhere fast. With Dara and Gethin en route from Scotland, she could only pray they would bring good news back with them.

Amanda levered herself out of the car, trying not to wince as her boots sunk into a bog of slushy snow and mud. Kelly appeared and took her arm as they trudged towards the lake.

"Good morning, ma'am."

"Nothing good so far and I need another visit to this place like a hole in the head," said Amanda, searching the deep zippered pockets of her wax overcoat for the latex gloves she always kept there – but coming out empty-handed.

"I think it's rather a beautiful spot …" Kelly began, cutting short as she caught the expression on her DI's face. In silence, she handed over a spare pair of gloves, which Amanda accepted with a tight smile. "Not that it's a particularly pretty sight at the moment. Watch your step and follow me through this rough bit, careful as there's brambles under the snow."

"Great," grumbled Amanda as the bottom of her coat snagged on hidden thorns. "Who found him? I take it it's a him?"

"Dog walker, lives on the other side of the lake. She's over in the police car giving a statement. A nice old biddy, made of stern stuff, so she says, but it's clearly shook her up."

"No doubt. Any ideas why it was missed by the dive team?"

"Yes, a very good reason, actually, according to the doc –"

"Ah, DI Gold. We really must stop meeting like this."

Amanda came to a stop as a plastic blue-suited human form rose from its knees at the water's edge, where melting ice had retreated from the edges of the lake to reveal the murky brown water beneath. Tanned skin and pale blue eyes appeared from beneath the hood of the protective over-suit.

"Dr Sixsmith, that's you under there I assume?"

"The very same. I won't offer to shake your hand." He held aloft green-slimed fingertips. "As your colleague was about to explain, no blame on the part of the original search team. This chap has been in the water less than twenty-four hours, I'd say. I'm taking water temperature readings and samples so I can be more accurate once I get him back to the lab."

Amanda's spirits lifted an inch. "Thank god for that. At least that's one less bollocking to look forward to. Where is he?"

Kelly tugged her sleeve and pointed to a slope further along the lake. "Over here ma'am. There's a narrow shingle beach. Let me go first, it's really slippery."

"Anyone been across from the hotel?" asked Amanda. "I was thinking about the missing chef, and if it is him getting a prelim identification before we move the body."

"Great minds, ma'am. I've had a quick look and I think there's a good chance it's our man from what I recall of the photos back at the office." Kelly gripped Amanda's hand as they side stepped down the snow-covered embankment. "I've sent PC Jones to see if any of the managers are willing to come across and take a look. I'll radio him now and see how he's getting on."

Amanda jumped down onto the gravel and crossed to the black tarpaulin, lying as if in state, over the human form in the middle of the beach. She peeled back the sheet and unzipped the top of the body bag to reveal the grey, bearded face of a male of around thirty years of age, plum-coloured bruises haloed each closed eyelid, thin lips the same colour. The mouth was agape, revealing small, even teeth, stained brown by dirty water. The skin was pulled taut and shiny across prominent cheekbones and jawline, sallow cheeks sunken in death. Even without any sign of life, she was almost certain she was staring into the once attractive, vibrant face of Gregory Chapman.

She sensed movement beside her and Dr Sixsmith pulled the plastic aside to reveal more expanse of skin. Amanda noticed a dolphin tattoo on his chest, nestled in the soft curls of dark blond hair above the region of his heart.

"Naked again same as the first victim. There's no visual signs of sexual activity this time though."

"Different cause of death?"

The pathologist grimaced. "Possibly."

"If you had to guess …"

"Guessing isn't really my forte, detective. Sorry. Signs of strangulation are less prominent this time, but I can't rule it out. There's no sign on the skin of poisoning or tell-tale marks of drug addiction. I doubt he drowned, airways are clear. I would say he looks severely malnourished, so it could be that … or dehydration. Suffocation, maybe? See?" Dr Sixsmith smiled as he stood up. "I told you. I'm rubbish at guessing."

"Ma'am."

Amanda looked up to see Kelly at the top of the bank; a tall, slim woman stood beside her, visibly trembling, long dark hair buffeting around her face in the breeze. She wore green Wellington boots, denim jeans and a tartan poncho that went twice around her body secured with a wide leather belt. At her feet, an excitable spaniel with a huge lolling tongue tugged and whined against the hold of his leash.

"Can we keep everyone back, please, Kelly?" called Amanda, surprised at her DS.

"This is Eliza, ma'am. One of the owners of the hotel. She's asked if she can help."

"So that's *the* Eliza Glenowen," said Amanda as they prepared to leave the crime scene. "The one Fletch reckons our Geth has a thing for?"

Kelly nodded.

"Surprised. I wouldn't have thought her his type." Amanda paused as she reached her car, kicking each boot in turn against the front tyre to remove the caked-on snow. "What did you think of her?"

Amanda watched the retreating back of Eliza Glenowen as she picked her way across the snowy front lawn of the hotel, her dog, Braint, racing back and forth in her wake. Eliza had given them a positive identification – the body was that of Gregory Chapman. However, she had shown not the slightest hint of emotion at either the loss of the hotel's head chef or the sight of a dead body.

"Odd was the first thing that came to mind. Did you see her doing that prayer thing over the body?" said Kelly. "Bit freaky. And all that mumbo jumbo about sacred lakes and healing water. I thought she was going to be proper flaky, but in fact she was the complete opposite. No sign of emotion – not what I was expecting."

"That's what I thought. Unusual reaction. She seemed more concerned she be allowed to tell her brother. Wonder what that was about?"

Kelly shrugged. "Some of these posh families play by their own rules."

Amanda was relieved to see Dara already at his desk, telephone wedged between ear and shoulder, as he typed away at his computer in his usual ungainly style. As she kicked off her boots and slipped into comfortable wedges, Gethin appeared at her door with a steaming mug of coffee.

"Ah, you're a god's send, I need that. Give me two minutes and I'll join you for a catch up."

After pulling on a spare cardigan, and applying a coat of lip balm, she carried her drink across to Kelly's desk and waited for Dara to finish on the phone. It was a raw wind that blew across the dunes out at Rhosneigr, and not even the highest heater setting had thawed her bones on the drive back. Eliza Glenowen's reaction to the corpse played on a loop in her mind's eye. Something hadn't felt right, something she knew Kelly sensed too, but it wasn't anything she could put a finger on or put into words. Grief, she knew, affected people in different ways, but with Eliza it had felt more like … acceptance, validation, relief maybe?

She took a sip of coffee, relishing the smooth taste. Gethin sat across the desk from her and opened his notebook, as Dara closed his conversation with multiple thank yous and dropped the phone back on the receiver.

"An' how are you doing, ma'am? Seems we can't leave you for a day and you're not piling up the body count."

"Don't even joke, Dara. Idris Parry is well on the way to a coronary."

Dara grinned. "Ach, every cloud, eh, ma'am?"

Amanda smiled, despite herself. "I'm hoping you're going to brighten the mood. Who was that? Sounded as if they were being pretty obliging – either that or she was a sexy blonde."

Dara shook his head. "Not at all. That was a very nice Scottish chap by the name of Edward McKeown. He's the manager of the field team at Deeside Marine and Environmental Research Limited in Aberdeen to be exact."

"Ah," said Gethin, nodding as he scribbled notes.

"Ah … what?" said Amanda with a frown. "Who and what is Deeside Marine and … whatever you said."

"I'm guessing they're Peter McDonald's employers?" said Gethin.

Dara nodded. "Yeah. I spoke to HR first and they confirmed he was on the payroll and put me through to this McKeown guy. Eddie was ready to spill. McDonald was sent to Anglesey last April for twelve months to report on ... and I quote ... pollution levels and effects on migration patterns of Risso's and Bottlenose dolphins in the Irish Sea."

"Blimey," commented Gethin. "Never even heard of Risso's dolphins. And what did the guy say about McDonald?"

"That he went off the radar sometime in November, stopped contacting the office around 18th. They sent a guy out to Peter's flat, which is in Rhosneigr – I have the address – on the 2nd December but they couldn't get access or contact the landlord. Eddie actually reported McDonald missing with Aberdeen Police this week, after worrying about it all over the Christmas holidays. Said he'd made his mind up if McDonald didn't turn up for work in the new year he was going to do it. Shame he didn't do it sooner and maybe the poor guy might still be alive."

"We can't know that," said Amanda, gripping her mug between both hands. "We don't know enough of anything to reach that kind of conclusion. You told him, I assume?"

"Didn't see any reason not to as we have a positive ID and dental match."

"Bet he was gutted," commented Gethin. "Had McDonald worked there long?"

"About five years, he said, but mostly field work at various remote locations around the coast. He was a specialist marine biologist. Sure, Eddie was in shock but admitted he wasn't close to McDonald outside of the job. I get the feeling our guy was a loner and moving around the country for his work suited his lifestyle. Seems to me he wasn't one for putting down roots. An' everyone we've spoken to have all said the same thing ... McDonald was a bloke who kept himself to himself. If we have any hope of finding out any personal information, we have to hope it will be in his Rhosneigr flat as there was nothing of use in his place in Sandwich. Want us to go take a look round his place, ma'am?"

"Yes, I don't think he would have been kept there before his body turned up. But we need to check it out. What else did you find out up in Shetland in terms of friends or family?"

Gethin checked his notes, flicked through several pages. "Mother recently passed away and McDonald was selling the family croft to a local guy who's already working on the place. Seems he left for University in his late teens and hadn't spent a whole lot of time in Sandwich since then. No one had much of a bad word to say about him, though there's no family left and only a couple who knew him as friends. A quiet, private guy most reckoned, and as Dara said everyone reported he very much kept himself to himself."

Dara looked up from his computer. "An' we think we know why that might have been, ma'am. We're pretty sure from magazines and stuff at his cottage, plus remarks from the locals in the pub, that Peter McDonald was homosexual."

Amanda saw a glance pass between the two sergeants. "And …?"

"An' I was checking back on McDonald's post-mortem notes and there were comments about sexual injuries that might indicate he was homosexual."

"So, we've confirmed what we'd already guessed. What's the problem? Am I missing something?"

Gethin shut his notebook and got to his feet. "Nothing, ma'am. We had a difference of opinion as to whether that was relevant to the case, that's all."

"An' I said it might be," said Dara. "We shouldn't overlook it as irrelevant at this stage. We don't know who is behind this or why it's happening. An' it's as likely I suppose it's someone with a grudge against Risso's dolphins as it is a grudge against gay men … I get that. But I think it's relevant enough to mention." Dara held his hands up in a gesture of mock surrender. "I'm the least politically correct person around this desk, fair dos, but doesn't mean I'm wrong."

Amanda nodded, sensing an unrest between Dara and Gethin, usually the two least uptight members of her team. "I think that's valid. Not something to be blinkered by, but certainly it should go in the mix." She got to her feet and picked up her coffee mug, making an instinctive decision to give the men some time apart after forty-eight hours in each other's pockets. "Dara, maybe you could go out to McDonald's flat, take Fletch for a run out to stretch his legs. Gethin … you've got some strong connections developing at the Llyn Maelog Hotel. I met Eliza Glenowen this morning, and with the recovery of their chef's body, I'm becoming more certain we should be focusing our attention at the hotel. Can you go break the news to the staff and start re-interviewing as a murder enquiry rather than a missing person's?"

Both men got to their feet in silence, without making eye contact, and within seconds Gethin had left the room with little more than a grunt.

"What's happened?" said Amanda.

"Ma'am?" Dara looked up as he shrugged on his leather jacket.

"Don't '*ma'am*' me. The tension in here is worse than it was when you and Kelly were at each other's throats. What happened in Shetland?"

Dara shrugged. "Search me, ma'am. He had his arse in his hand whole time we were away. I put it down to time of the month. Any road, I'll go find Fletch and be off, then."

Amanda closed her eyes for a moment, bit down on the response that threatened to erupt from her lips. She knew Dara did it to provoke, but sometimes she wished he would at least try to be a little more diplomatic. And she didn't like to see tension between her team either. Perhaps she'd get more sense out of Gethin later, for now she had a report to write.

CHAPTER FOURTEEN

Gethin stood in the hotel lobby, watching as staff bustled about him, most engaged in the task of removing decorations, or the delicate operation of dismantling a ten-foot tall Christmas tree. Even the few remaining guests looked lost, wandering back and forth as the pomp and glitter of the festive celebrations were dismantled around them.

"Detective?"

Gethin jolted. "Sorry, yes."

He turned to face a middle-aged man in a smart grey suit, pleasant features, receding hair, plump face. But the blue eyes were tired and troubled, frown lines etched his forehead. Doubtless the news had filtered through about the latest discovery.

"Terence Jones?"

"Yes, sorry to have kept you. Follow me, my office is through here."

Gethin followed, back across the reception, down a plush-carpeted corridor and into an open door on the left. He noticed the man walked with a slight limp, an old man's gait to Gethin's mind, and he wondered if Terence Jones might be older than he looked.

Settled either side of a polished oak desk, Gethin removed his notebook.

"I'm sorry I've not had chance to speak to you before now, Mr Jones. I handled most of the staff interviews after the first body was recovered from the lake, but my boss had already spoken with you so I saw no reason to inconvenience you further at such a busy time."

The man ran a hand across his face as if brushing away any trace of exhaustion. "It's appreciated. Call me Terry, please. It's been quite a time. Worst festivities I can remember, for more than one reason. And now, this latest news, it's rocked me, I can tell you that. Totally knocked me for six."

"Eliza Glenowen told you, I assume …"

He nodded.

"So, you can guess why I'm here?"

"I suppose Greg's case is now a murder enquiry? It's totally unbelievable. I guess the questioning starts all over again. I don't envy you." He exhaled. "I don't know what I can tell you I didn't tell your DI though. Greg went missing early December. I thought he'd flounced back home, to Australia I mean. He had a reputation as a bit of a flouncer. I was more focused on the chaos his absence left behind. I regret that now, deeply regret it obviously."

"And you were angry I imagine?"

"Yes, I was. I don't mind admitting it. If you've got his mobile, you'll doubtless know I left more than a couple of stern messages on his voicemail." He rubbed his face again. "This is going to stay with me till my grave. To think all the time …" he trailed off, shaking his head.

"We were led to believe there may have been some kind of disagreement between Gregory Chapman and yourself in the days before he disappeared. Can you tell me about that?"

Terry frowned and leaned forward, a darkness snaked across his face as if he'd moved into shadow. A chill ran through Gethin. There was another side to this man. The thought popped into his head, and once there, clung on for dear life. Another side to the professional persona he wore on a daily basis, and not someone you would want as an enemy. Perhaps that came from his position, having to deal with both the guests and staff, juggling contrasting roles.

"Argument? I don't recall an argument at all. Who said that?"

Gethin looked down at his notebook, pretending to scan an earlier page. "I don't have the details to hand. It may have been something or nothing, a complaint if I remember, a problem with a meal?"

Terry sat back, exhaled, the shadow faded. "Ah. The Patels. I remember. It was nothing, truly. Greg was a typical chef in many ways, he despised any criticism about his food. We clashed often in that regard, never seriously though."

"What would you say your relationship was like in general with Mr Chapman?"

"Solid. He was professional and creative where food was concerned, we were lucky to have him and we appreciated his skills. I didn't really have any kind of relationship with him outside of work. I saw him down at the beach once or twice when he was surfing with Stephen."

"Mr Chapman and Mr Glenowen were friends outside of work?"

Terry cleared his throat. "I wouldn't call them friends really, they shared a love of water sports, and quite a few different clubs have their meetings here – kite surfing, paddle boarding, you name it. Stephen is always happy to get involved with local community projects." He glanced at his watch. "I've been waiting to hear from Stephen actually, he's on his way back from a meeting in Chester. I've put off contacting him because Eliza wanted to tell him in person. He'll be horrified. No one can understand what's happening. I mean, here, in Rhosneigr. It's such a quiet, beautiful, out of the way spot. Murder seems almost ludicrous."

"We've not released details of Mr Chapman's death as yet."

"But the first body was murder. So, you must assume …"

"We don't assume. First rule of our job." Gethin checked his own watch. "What time are you expecting Mr Glenowen?"

"Anytime now. But Eliza is on guard, she'll get to him first." Another hint of shadow, gone in seconds. "As is her way."

"While I have you here, I also wanted to ask if you could give me a quick summary of your movements yesterday?"

Terry looked up, surprised. "Yesterday? You mean …"

"We're waiting post-mortem results, but initial findings indicate the body may have been in the lake less than twenty-four hours."

"And you're asking my whereabouts because …?"

Gethin glanced up, working hard to control his facial features. "Because it's my job. I'll be asking the same to everyone who works at the hotel. Witnesses are rather short on the ground at the moment."

Terry sat back and crossed his arms. "I see. Well, I doubt I can help you. I was here all day from around 7.30am. I did leave a bit earlier than I often do, probably around 9pm. I was exhausted. But it was pretty much pitch dark when I arrived and left, I seem to see very little of the outside world at the moment, except by the glare of car headlights."

"And when you left?"

"I went home, I've a cottage on the headland out at Bodorgan. I'd already eaten here, so I had a shower and went straight to bed. Watched the ten o'clock news and remember nothing else until the alarm woke me at 6.30am this morning, and the routine began all over again."

"You live alone?"

"I do. Other than my cat. I'm rather surprised you don't already know that, with a team of detectives apparently on my trail."

"You've not been under investigation to the best of my knowledge," said Gethin, licking the end of his finger and flipping to a clean page. "But if you'd care to fill in the blanks it might save me some time. I'm led to believe you have a long history with the Glenowens, Mr Jones?"

"Terry. Yes, a lifetime's history you could say. My father worked here before me, my grandfather before him when this was still a country house and the Glenowens were Lord and Lady of the Manor so to speak. Grandad Joseph was head butler and Grandma Lillian was head housekeeper – can you believe?"

He shook his head. "My family have given lifetimes of loyalty for the best part of a century, not many people can say that."

"You're obviously proud?"

Terry tilted his head back and gave a hearty laugh. "I don't know about that. My dad would have been proud, that's for sure, he was the most devoted man I knew. Devoted to the Glenowens anyway." A frown replaced the mirth. "To be honest, I never thought I'd keep the tradition going. As a lad growing up I was determined to break away from the hotel, from Anglesey even, and travel the world. But then I fell in love."

He paused, looked at Gethin expectantly, but when the detective remained silent, he seemed happy to continue his story.

"You don't know? I married Clara Glenowen, Stephen's sister, the eldest of the three children. Overnight, I went from employee to one of the family, and I thought my father might well spontaneously combust with excitement and pride. My wedding day was the only day he ever told me he was proud of me." He cleared his throat. "Anyway, Clara had my heart good and proper, was everything I could have wanted in a wife. But it wasn't to last. We were trying for children for five years with no luck. She went for tests and they found cancer. She was dead within a year."

"I'm so sorry to hear that."

Terry lowered his gaze to his lap. "Have to say the Glenowens couldn't have treated me better. Made it clear I had a home and a job for life. If I ever truly understood the meaning of loyalty it was in the months following Clara's death. Oliver and Diana, Stephen's parents, were kindness itself. And then my father died to top off the year from hell. Without the family and the hotel to fall back on, I think I would have unravelled. As it is, they supported me, all of them. And I hope in the years since I've done the same for them."

"Stephen's father, Oliver, he's no longer with us?"

"Yes, that's right. He lost a long battle with lung disease about five years ago. And poor Diana is battling dementia. She's only recently gone in a care home and the main reason why I'm so protective of Stephen. He has so much weight on his shoulders at the moment. I remember how that feels. I'm worried the added stress of all this might crush him."

Gethin heard the catch of emotion as the older man fell silent.

The sound of raised voices out in the corridor broke through the hush of the room. Terry was on his feet, heading in that direction, as the door swung open and Stephen Glenowen strode into the room, closely followed by his sister. Eliza looked pale and tormented, a shadow of the vibrant personality Gethin had carried in his head for the past days.

"Is it true?" Stephen asked.

Terry reached out to embrace him. "Stephen, I'm so sorry …"

Stephen backed away, hands raised as if to defend himself. "Is it?"

Terry nodded.

The three of them stood in a silent triangle, awkward and unsure, unspoken words passing between them. Gethin got to his feet and cleared his throat, cutting into the tension like a knife through soft fruit. Stephen Glenowen focused and seemed to see him for the first time. He took a step forward, reaching out to grasp the back of the chair nearest him.

"I would like to see the body," said Stephen. "I mean it was a mistake last time, who's to say …"

Eliza stepped forward, tears gleaming on her cheeks. "Stephen, it was me. I saw the body when it was recovered from the lake. I identified him. It's Greg."

Her brother spun round, voice full of rage. "You! How dare you be the one! I need to see him." He coughed, covering a sob. When he spoke his voice was controlled. "Please sort it out, Terry. I'll be in my office."

With that he marched from the room, his sister following, trying and failing to grab his arm.

Terry's head slumped for a moment, and he spoke to the carpet. "I knew this would happen. Damn that woman," he whispered, before turning to Gethin. "Can you arrange it?"

Gethin nodded and got to his feet. "Thanks for your time today. I'll leave you to see to things here, looks like your loyalty is required yet again. I'll be in touch."

CHAPTER FIFTEEN

The room had an over-bearing smell of floral air freshener from a basket of silk lilies on the window sill, but despite best attempts it failed to completely mask the lingering odour of death. It took Gethin back to his very first post-mortem during his early days in CID. A homeless man, kicked to death by thugs, who'd thought it hilarious to use him as a human rugby ball, drop-kicking him against the glass windows of a department store as their finale, in an early hour's rampage of a shopping centre. Gethin remembered the initial shock as the body was opened, the gagging smell of the gases released from the intestine, the noise of the electric saw as the skull was carefully removed. He'd found the whole process curious, had bombarded the pathologist with questions, but afterwards the enormity of it had caused many sleepless nights.

True, none of the physical elements of the procedure had ever really affected him. It was the mental connotations of death that became a problem. The lifeless cadaver, now no more than a specimen in a laboratory had once been a living, breathing person with emotions, skills and intelligence. A person who had loved and been loved, and in most cases whose sudden passing would leave behind a wave of grief. The image of the poor homeless man, bruised and bloodied, inside and out, stayed with him for months and was the main reason Gethin was always the last to volunteer to attend a post-mortem.

He jumped as the door to the small waiting room opened. The pathologist, Dr Sixsmith stepped inside.

"Sorry to have kept you chaps waiting." He directed his smile to Stephen Glenowen and Terry Jones who both got to their feet. "We weren't expecting anyone today." He flashed a look at Gethin. "But we're ready for you now if you'd like to follow my assistant, Libby."

The two men stepped out into the corridor and followed the white coat and bobbing blonde ponytail. As Gethin made to follow, the pathologist touched his arm.

"I could have done with a little more notice, detective," he whispered.

"Apologies," muttered Gethin. "It came a bit out of the blue. Any shocks during the post-mortem?"

Dr Sixsmith shook his head. "Not really. Severe dehydration and malnutrition as I predicted. There were faded signs of attempted strangulation, bruising mostly healed, but I don't think it was the cause of death as the hyoid bone was still intact. No violence or sexual activity evident this time. I'd suggest the victim was locked away somewhere and left to die after a forceful capture. One bit of good news, though it's not official until I've run further tests, but I'm pretty sure the chain used to secure Chapman is the same as the previous victim. It will all be in the report."

Gethin mulled over the information as he hurried to the viewing room, wanting to be there when Glenowen saw the body. Thankfully, Libby was waiting, and nodded as he entered the room. Stephen stood with his head bowed, lips moving as if in silent prayer, hands clasped in front of him, fingers moving rhythmically, reminding Gethin of a nun with a rosary. Terry was close beside him, watching him with an expression of intense pain; his left hand resting on Stephen's right shoulder as if supporting the other man's weight. Gethin found the scene extremely touching and almost hoped for their sake it was another false alarm.

Libby turned down the pale green sheet, being careful not to dislodge the padded pillow masking the post-mortem scars on the skull. The face was ashen grey, puffy and empty with its closed eyelids and mouth slightly ajar. Gethin glanced at the two men. Terry's eyes were brimming with tears as his fingers buried deeper into the fabric of Stephen's jacket. Stephen himself stood as still and lifeless as a statue, the silent words had stopped, and his eyes were fixed on the face. He cleared his throat, took one step forward, and placed the back of his fingers against the bearded cheek, letting his hand rest there for several moments, until Libby gave a nervous cough and the mood was broken. Gethin tried to read the man's expression, but there was nothing in the stony gaze other than shock and confusion.

Terry sniffed and urged Stephen backwards with the same grip on his shoulder.

"Poor, poor, Greg. So awful," Terry muttered. "We've seen enough. Come on, now. Let's go, Stephen."

Stephen appeared not to hear as he studied Gregory's body, his hand moved upwards to his own face, the back of his fingers rested against his lips. Terry slid the hand from Stephen's shoulder, around his neck, and urged him backwards.

"We need to go, Stephen. It's a shock, I know, but we can't stay here, these people have a job to do. Come on now …"

He stepped backwards and Stephen pulled away from him, shrugging off Terry's grip. "Leave me. I want to be alone."

"Sorry, sir, we can't … we're still working on the body." Libby began to slide the sheet upwards. "You'll be able to arrange private viewings with the undertakers of course."

"Wait, please, don't. I'm not ready to say goodbye."

Libby flashed a desperate glance in Gethin's direction. He moved to the door, and held it open, encouraging the visitors from the room. Terry gave him an apologetic smile and made another attempt at embracing Stephen.

"Enough, now, Stephen. Please. We have to go."

This time the other man moved, stiffly, as if sleepwalking his way out of a dream. Terry held his arm, guiding him towards the door, while Stephen turned and looked over his shoulder. He stopped abruptly, tugging his arm free, and addressed Libby.

"You will look after him. Be gentle. He deserves that. He had such a gentle soul."

"Of course," said Libby. "Take as long as you need in the visitor's room. Can I get anyone tea? Coffee?"

Gethin shook his head, and both men followed suit as they re-entered the small room with the floral smell. Gethin was almost grateful of the aroma of lilies now, after the tension of the previous room. Stephen dropped into a chair, elbows on knees, he lowered his face into his hands. His shoulders moved in time with his breathing, and Gethin thought for a second he was crying.

Terry dropped to one knee beside him, clearly assuming the same, and slid an arm around his shoulder. "Hey, come on, now. Stephen, dear, Stephen. I can't stand to see you crying."

Gethin squirmed, wanting to disappear out of the door, and leave these men to grieve in private, but knowing it was his job to observe and report.

Stephen remained silent, shoulders heaving.

Terry looked up from his employer's side. "Do we know what happened yet?"

Gethin shook his head. "It's still very early stages of the enquiry."

"But it must be connected," said Terry, rubbing Stephen's back. "To the first body I mean. You must have some idea what's going on? Stephen's family have been through enough …"

Stephen muttered something incoherent.

Terry continued. "If you can't help, who can we speak to? Stephen knows your Chief Superintendent personally. I'm sure he would be devastated to know what effect all this is having on the family, never mind the hotel. It's really not good enough –"

This time Stephen looked up, his face a blank mask, and Gethin realised he hadn't been crying.

"I asked you to shut up Terry. For god's sake ... shut up."

Terry crouched lower, leaning against the chair to mutter into Stephen's ear. "I'm only standing up for you, Stephen, saying what needs to be said. We can all see how much this has disturbed you, I can't stand to see you upset."

Stephen brushed the other man away with such force, Terry landed on his backside on the carpet. "I don't need your protection. I am not a child. And if you can't stand seeing me upset, get the hell out of my face. In point of fact, I'm not upset ... I'm livid. Someone did this ... this unspeakable act ... to Greg, and I need to know why and I need to see justice done." He got to his feet, towering over his employee, who looked as if he were grovelling at his master's feet. "What I seriously do not need is you fussing over me and acting as if you're my goddamn father!"

"Stephen! That's hardly fair –"

"Fair! Fair? You want fair! What's fair about any of this? If you'd let me go after Greg weeks ago ... if you'd made any serious attempt to find him when I told you he wouldn't have left like that ... none of this would have happened. You ... you ... don't deserve fairness!"

He strode across the room, through the door, slamming it behind him. Embarrassed, Gethin held out a hand to assist Terry, who was still sprawled on the floor, open-mouthed with blazing cheeks. Gethin saw shock replaced by a shadow of fury as the man scrambled to his feet, brushing down the seat of his trousers. Gethin expected anger in the man's voice, but when he spoke it was in the same soothing, sympathetic tone.

"Poor Stephen. I knew something like this would happen. And unfortunately it's usually me that bears the brunt of his rage. Sorry you had to witness that little scene." He sighed and headed for the door. "If you'll excuse me, I'll have to go and catch up with him. I drove and I've got the car keys."

Gethin crossed to the window and stared out at the greyness of the car park, taking a moment to ponder what he'd learned. Terry seemed oblivious to his boss's feelings and didn't seem at all humiliated by the way he'd been treated. Other than the flash of anger, it almost seemed he expected to be kicked. And what of Stephen's reaction to Greg's body? There was a story, no doubt about it. A maelstrom of thoughts buzzed around Gethin's brain as he left the building and headed towards his car.

"Excuse me!"

Gethin turned and his breath caught in his throat as he saw Stephen Glenowen hidden in the shadows of the Victorian red-bricked building. Gethin approached, wondering what had happened, then realised Stephen was huddled under the metal frame of a smoking shelter.

"Would you mind giving me a lift back to the hotel?" Stephen asked, his face illuminated by an orange glow as he inhaled hard on his cigarette. "Terry's driven off at top speed, and anyway I don't think I can handle being trapped in a car with him right now."

"Sure," said Gethin. "He's probably gone looking for you, he's concerned."

Stephen shrugged and ground the cigarette into the slushy snow at his feet. "He'll get over it. And I'll text him before he reports me missing. Promise."

"Thank you," Stephen said as Gethin pulled on the handbrake outside the hotel forty minutes later. "And thank you for the peace and quiet too. I needed it."

It was an acknowledgment of doubtless questions to be answered, and yet the journey had passed in virtual silence. Gethin's current CD of choice was an old favourite, Faith by George Michael, and Stephen seemed to appreciate the music, closing his eyes and laying his head back against the headrest as they'd sped across the island. Gethin thought his passenger had nodded off, but the second he'd turned into the driveway of the hotel, Stephen sat upright, ready to depart.

"No problem," said Gethin. "Make sure you let Mr Jones know where you are."

"I will. Eventually." Stephen gave a slow smile. "Any chance you fancy joining me for a coffee? I suddenly don't feel all that keen to be left on my own at the mercy of kitchen staff who will doubtless have a million questions."

Gethin checked his watch. He hadn't promised he'd make it back to the office for debrief, and he only had a microwavable lasagne waiting for him at home. Maybe this was an agreement to answer those questions Gethin had allowed thus far to remain unasked.

"Sure. Why not."

Whilst the restaurant seemed to have at least a third of its tables occupied, the lounge was deserted. Stephen placed an order at the bar and settled into one of the arm chairs beside a roaring open fire. Gethin took the other, watching orange flames lick against the chimney, and breathed in the wonderful smell of wood smoke. Once the coffees, along with a plate of delicious looking sandwiches had been distributed, Stephen poured himself a drink and relaxed back into the chair, slipping off his shoes and lifting his feet towards the fire.

"What a day." He sipped his drink, replacing the cup onto the saucer. "If I'm honest it's a day I feared would come from the day Gregory went missing. Not that I ever dreamed his poor body would turn up in Llyn Maelog of course."

"What makes you say that?" Gethin stirred two sugars into his coffee and took a sip.

"The way he disappeared without a word to anyone. I didn't believe Gregory would do that. He was loyal. I was all for calling in the Police and reporting him missing, but both Terry and Eliza thought it was a bad idea. If only I had …"

"You were close to Mr Chapman?"

Stephen paused, took another sip of coffee. "I was his employer first and foremost. We shared some common interests and got involved in a fund-raising project last year that's taken on a life of its own. He was a good man and we got on well." His mouth set in a straight line and an almost physical shutter came down.

"You've no idea why this has happened or who may be involved?"

"I wish I had, believe me. Gregory wasn't a person to go around making enemies. One can only speculate it must have something to do with the first body you recovered, and there's a serial killer that needs to be caught." Stephen shivered and put his cup and saucer on the coffee table. "Eliza thinks there's a mad man out there using some pagan ritual associated with the sacred lake. I don't know if I believe her, she lets people talk a whole lot of nonsense to her and she takes it all in. But I have started questioning why the bodies ended up in the lake. All I want now is this sick bastard caught so we can all sleep easy in our beds. Will you be letting Gregory's family know in Australia?"

"We have a family liaison officer on the case who will take charge of notifying relatives. Did you know any of his family?"

"Not really. I met his youngest sister, Georgia, last year. She stayed for a week or so while over here backpacking on her gap year. I'd have loved to have seen Australia, don't suppose it will ever happen now though."

"I imagine the hotel takes up a lot of your time," said Gethin, helping himself to three dainty egg and cress sandwiches. He desperately wanted to keep the conversation centred on Chapman, but at the moment it felt like running uphill on soft sand, the harder he pushed, the less headway he made.

"You could say that. It's a lifestyle, certainly not a job," said Stephen, pouring more coffee and gesturing to the girl behind the bar for a refill. "Oh, don't get me wrong, I'm proud of everything we've achieved here. But I do feel I've missed out on life, whereas my father never wanted anything more, this was his dream. Sometimes it feels as if his legacy has become a ball and chain around my neck."

"You want more time away then you surely have staff who could run the place for you?"

"Short term, yes, I'm blessed. For all he infuriates me at times, Terry is an excellent manager. As are Matt and the others. It's not just the hotel, it's Eliza too ... and I'm not sure if you know about my mother?"

Gethin chewed and swallowed. "Eliza filled me in. I'm sorry. Terry is your brother-in-law, too? It must be nice to keep it in the family. Helps in terms of trust, I imagine?"

"Yeah." Stephen rolled his neck, unfastening his tie. "Although it can cause tension ... as you saw today. He can be too much. But his heart is in the right place. Terry wouldn't hurt a fly and I have nothing but respect for the way he treated my sister when she was ill. There wasn't a day he left her side, and she passed away knowing she was so loved. Everyone deserves that, don't you think?" He stopped and pinched the bridge of his nose. Moments passed until finally he exhaled and continued. "But Terry ... oh, sometimes I think he tries too hard to please and it comes across like he has to control every tiny detail about our lives. Sometimes he knows best, I get that, but I had my father tell me what to do for the first thirty years of my life, I really don't need someone else taking over now." Stephen smiled and held up a hand in a gesture of apology. "Sorry, sorry. I guess I'm feeling pretty raw today, but you don't need all of our dirty laundry rolled out on display."

"I don't have a big family, but I do know they come with as many negatives as positives. You're head of the family as well as the business now, it must come with its own pressures. It's to be expected they come to the boil at times like this."

Stephen studied Gethin, nodding in agreement. "What frustrates me most in truth is I know I'm using everyone else as an excuse, when in fact it's the way my father brought me up, coupled with my own loyalties, that are to blame for my dissatisfaction with life."

Gethin wiped his lips on a paper napkin and slid his empty plate onto the table. "Most would say they're excellent qualities to have."

"True. Still doesn't stop me feeling like a bird whose had its wings clipped and has never learned the joy of flight." He closed his eyes for a moment as a fresh pot of coffee arrived. "I suppose that's why I'll miss Gregory most of all."

"He allowed you to be yourself and taught you how to fly – is that what you mean?" Gethin's pulse drummed in his ears. It was a risk but a risk worth taking. If Stephen was ever going to open up, he had to lay the hint down he already knew.

Stephen turned his head and met Gethin's steady gaze. They studied each other, holding eye contact. A log popped in the fire, distant voices mumbled, cutlery chinked. Gethin held his breath. Come on … come on … tell me. He tried to read the other man's expression, but his eyes were cold, guarded … but questioning.

"Ah, I see, no one thought to invite *me* to your impromptu afternoon tea party?"

A voice came from behind Gethin's chair.

Stephen's gaze shifted upwards. He sighed. "Take a seat, Eliza."

"Don't mind if I do." She dragged another arm chair towards the fire. "But you need to ring Terry. He's about to call out the emergency services. He's been trawling the roads around Bangor for the past hour and he's not a happy chap. He thinks you're about to end it all and jump off the Menai Bridge."

"Oh, Christ. I forgot about him." Stephen got to his feet. "Excuse me, detective, and thanks for the lift. I'm sure my sister will keep you suitably entertained."

Gethin stood. "I should be making a move."

Eliza gripped his wrist and pulled him down as Stephen strode away, taking Gethin's unanswered question with him. He wanted to growl in frustration, but instead he smiled and complied.

"Half an hour, then I really have to go."

Eliza clapped her hands together. "Excellent! Beverley – can I get a fresh pot of a tea and some cakes please."

Gethin accelerated along the A55, glancing at the clock. 9:09pm. It had taken hours to finally escape from Eliza's clutches. Something told him she was using him as an excuse, a reason to stay away from the simmering tension between her brother and Terry Jones. Eliza was back on the Famous Grouse whisky by the time Gethin made his excuses, and had to work hard to ensure he wasn't lulled into alcohol and another expenses-paid night at the hotel. He could do without more office banter. And to be honest, he needed time to think.

He was beginning to think Eliza Glenowen was coming on to him. She became more flirtatious with each sip of whisky, and whilst if she was attracted to him, on one hand it was a massive confidence boost, on the other it became an unwanted distraction to his ability to do his job. Not to mention the ethical implications of getting involved with a person closely involved with the current enquiry. He had to be careful. Eliza had already wormed her way inside his brain once, her stories of Druids and sacred lakes and human sacrifices had turned his head, and he wasn't about to do it again.

And then the enigma that was Stephen Glenowen. Such an eloquent, intelligent man but Gethin knew he hadn't even begun to scratch the surface. But *that* look, the lengthy eye contact, he hadn't imagined that. A shiver ran up his spine as if someone had blown against the delicate skin at the back of his ear. He reached down and turned up the car heater. There was something there, something Stephen had been on the verge of confessing, when Eliza had arrived at the worst possible moment.

He glanced in his rear-view mirror as he turned off the dual-carriageway towards Bangor town centre. It must be a large 4X4 that had followed behind him most of the way across the island, it's high Xenon headlights particularly powerful against the glare of the snow. He scowled as the car followed him down the slipway, through the retail park, before he lost it at the island by the supermarket.

He'd have to tell the boss his suspicions about Stephen Glenowen's relationship with Gregory Chapman being more than that of an employer and employee. But it would have been so much better had he been able to supply tangible proof, rather than a gut instinct and a dollop of eye contact he might have misread. As he reversed into a parking spot outside his house, he decided that standing up and announcing the relevance of that look at the morning briefing was a complete no-no. He could already imagine Fletch's nudges and winks, along with Dara's sage expression, as he admitted he felt a connection not only with Eliza Glenowen ... but now her brother, Stephen, too.

Gethin folded himself out of the car, cursing and flattening himself against the door as an engine roared and bright headlights swept across him. A large dark-coloured SUV sped along the narrow street. He paused as he locked his Vauxhall. Increasing numbers of cars had powerful Xenon headlights, he knew that. But for a second, he could have sworn it was the same vehicle that followed him down the slipway after the Britannia Bridge.

He watched the tail-lights retreat, brake lights flashing as the driver slowed to take a tight left at the far end of his street. What was the matter with him? Why was he reading drama into everything? And was he also guilty of reading too much into both Eliza's full-on attention and her brother's enigmatic behaviour? He shook his head. He didn't know and right now he couldn't trust himself either. Maybe a microwave lasagne, a can of Carling and a good night's sleep would ground him.

CHAPTER SIXTEEN

Amanda dropped her coat and bag, placed a mug of steaming coffee onto her desk, and pressed her nose against the glass of her window. Nothing except misty blackness interspersed by the orange iridescence of street lights. She rather suspected she was fast becoming a victim of midwinter blues. Another night of tossing and turning, listening to the creak and rustle of the cottage timbers, wishing with all her heart she could hear the tinny noise of music or late night television coming from Emily's room. At six am she'd given up on sleep and, after a hot shower, headed into work.

Amanda settled into her seat, yawned, and clicked the mouse to wake the screen, taking her first sip of coffee. She accessed her email account and opened the top unread email, a report from Dara with a summary of the previous day's visit to Rhosneigr. Another dead end. Nothing found at Peter McDonald's flat relevant to the enquiry. By all accounts his passions were his career and his love of water sports, nothing dodgy that may have led to his death. Fletcher was following up one tenuous lead that both victims may have known each other through a regular kite-surfing meet, headed up by a local surfer, Alun Wyn Owens, but as the club had disbanded over the festive period until the following spring, the detectives were struggling to interview anyone involved. And even if they did, Amanda had her doubts they would discover anything relevant. These killings had all the hallmarks of random killings by an active psychopath ... and yet ...

Her eyes moved down to the next unread email, received late last night from forensic anthropologist, Dr Jenny George from Bangor University. Jenny was one of Dr Sixsmith's contacts and came highly recommended. Amanda double-clicked and waited for the email and attachments to open. Forensic anthropology was a fairly new research route for her team, luckily this was the first 'cold case' she'd encountered since her move to North Wales. But she'd read of many successful and high-profile court cases that relied on evidence from this scientific source. How much could they learn from a bunch of deteriorated old bones? On the phone, Jenny had been confident they would be able to supply a detailed analysis on the skeleton recovered from the lake – they could now call it a skeleton apparently, according to expert, as in total the divers had recovered over eighty percent of the bones plus a badly decomposed skull.

The report ran over four pages and firstly confirmed the remains were that of a male, over ninety percent chance of being Caucasian, aged between sixteen and twenty-four years of age. From combined measurements of the femur and metacarpals, height at death was recorded as five-foot-eight to five-foot-nine inches. Original body weight from bone wear and density was calculated at ten stone, nine pounds to eleven stone.

Dental examination suggested he came from a poor background, no sign of dental work despite tooth loss from an abscess on the right maxillary second premolar. He also had an orofacial cleft – or cleft palate – a small cavity in the soft tissue between the roof of the mouth and the nasal cavity, which in this case also extended to the front of the maxilla, the upper jawbone, which would have resulted in a cleft lip. This birth defect had been operated on in early life but meant he would most likely have spoken with a pronounced lisp. He ate a low-nutritional diet and was a heavy smoker of non-tipped cigarettes.

DNA data recovered from samples also taken from teeth

indicated the man had lived locally but had Irish lineage, specifically western coastal area around the counties of Galway or Mayo. She pulled the top off a biro with her teeth and reached across her desk for her notepad, scribbling a few notes before returning to the report.

Moving onto a study of the skeleton, the report revealed that despite a slender frame, pronounced muscle ligature ridges on the neck and upper torso, particularly the right arm, indicated he was of a muscular build, most likely a manual worker who was right-handed. The report suggested coal miner or farmer as job types. And fragments of fabric and rubber deposits around the feet bones show he was at least partially clothed when he entered the water. Cause of death impossible to distinguish, although no long term or degenerative illnesses were revealed from a study of the bones.

Dr George recorded the bones were not as ancient as the pathologist had first believed – no older than fifty years and no less than thirty. However, with the amalgamation of data recovered from the skeleton, particularly the repair to the cleft palate, associated fibres found on and around the bones, added to archived information about imported tobacco and cotton types, the computer system could give an amazing level of accuracy.

Although they made it clear this was a 'best guess' scenario, this was exactly the type of guesswork Amanda would appreciate in her job more often. Taking all factors into account, the system had generated a likelihood of the remains coming from a male aged 18-21 who had died in the winter months between 1975 and 1980 and had been deposited in the lake either at the point of death or within hours of death, and had remained submerged in the water since that time.

Amanda sat back and exhaled. Excellent! It narrowed down the field one hell of a lot. What it didn't offer was an indication of whether the skeleton was in any way connected with the latest crime scenes. Or why so many bodies were turning up in the same spot?

She opened the police database search engine, clicked on the relevant dates and categories until she was searching for unsolved cases including the correct person type in the correct period. She sipped her coffee as the tiny circle whirled around in the centre of her screen. With a ping a box flashed up – no results found. Damn. She stared at the screen and widened her target, pressed send and waited for the spinning circle. A second ping and the same message.

Three bodies in one lake, all murdered, all young men. If there was a start to all this then it had to start at the beginning … the body from the 1970s. If the murder hadn't been discovered for almost half a century, why would there be an unsolved crime file on the system? Of course, there wouldn't be. Changing tactics, she closed the local police database and opened her saved links, scrolling down to the National Crime Agency (NCA) link and then clicked through to the UK Missing Person's Bureau (MPB). She waited for the site to open and then added all known information into the search fields and waited. This time a thin blue line blinked across her screen. Amanda's palms were sweaty and she wiped them down the front of her trousers. This was why she loved this job, the thrill of the chase, the adrenaline rush when you knew you were onto something.

The screen went blank and Amanda groaned, but then in a blink of colour there in front of her were four separate files. Two with the blacked-out outlines of a human head and two with actual blurred photographs of real people peering out of the screen at her.

In the end, it was too easy. Three of the four open cases fitted little or none of the profile compiled by Jenny George, whereas one was a perfect match. Patrick Kavanagh, known as Paddy, age eighteen, height five-foot-eight to five-foot-ten inches tall, weight approximately eleven stone, disappeared over the Christmas period in 1976 reported missing in early January 1977 by his mother, Maud Kavanagh. Listed features were a Liverpool FC tattoo on his right arm … and a cleft lip scar and lisp. Amanda enlarged the photograph to study the blond-haired, tanned youth, leaning against a farmer's gate with a backdrop of hills and green fields. A tight white t-shirt and flared jeans revealed a lithe, muscular frame. His eyes were fixed on the camera, but his smile was awkward, no teeth on show, conscious perhaps of the missing tooth or the damaged upper jaw. Case unsolved.

Amanda leaned closer and tapped the screen with a fingernail. "Hello, you," she whispered.

Twenty minutes later, Amanda powered down her computer, pulled on her coat, and headed for the door, almost colliding with Kelly, first to arrive, on her way into the office, carrying a takeaway coffee and a collection of files wedged under her arm.

"Ah, perfect. Dump the papers, keep hold of your coffee, and follow me," Amanda called, holding open the door while a flustered Kelly deposited items on her desk.

"What's happening, ma'am?"

"We're off to Holyhead to interview a lady by the name of Ruby Kavanagh. I'll tell you on the way."

The narrow rows of terraced houses leading from the town centre down towards the harbour in Holyhead were quaint and well-tended nowadays, but echoes were everywhere to an earlier time when the docks would have been a bustling international trading port and busy fishing community. Many of the street names were evocative of the past. Mariners Row. Fish Market Street. Breakwater View. Amanda checked the Satnav screen for Hibernia Row and slowed the car, parking outside a white-painted end cottage in a terraced row overlooking allotments on one side, and the busy ferry port of Holyhead on the other.

Amanda had relayed her discoveries to Kelly on the drive across the island, not able to hide her joy with the accuracy of the anthropology report. She'd managed to track down Patrick

Kavanagh quite easily, finding him on the 1971 census, aged thirteen years, eldest child of Maud Kavanagh, listed as head of the house, with siblings George, Seamus, Eileen, and Ruby in this same little cottage at number one, Hibernia Row. Moving forward to the 1981 census, Patrick's name had been the only one missing from the list. And on the latest electoral roll, Amanda had discovered a Ms Ruby Kavanagh was now the sole occupant at that address.

Climbing from the car, Amanda breathed in the cold, salty air and imagined living so close to the docks in busier times. The view across the harbour to the mile-and-a-half long breakwater was something she'd never tire of waking up to if she lived here. This morning, a rolling sea fog blurred the view, bringing with it a slight increase in temperature. At last, she hoped, a thaw was on its way. She took her time negotiating the slushy pavements, through the small gate, knocking at the door, heart racing. Kelly rubbed her gloved hands together, and Amanda could tell she was buzzing with optimism too.

The door opened and Amanda knew she was looking at the middle-aged face of Patrick Kavanagh's youngest sister. Even with the advanced years, her features and dark blonde hair, looked so like the youth in the blurred 1970's photograph. Ruby Kavanagh was thin and smartly dressed, in grey trousers and cream jumper, her expression polite but curious. Amanda pulled her identification badge from her pocket and gave her warmest smile.

"Ms Kavanagh? Hello, I'm DI Gold and this is DS Morgan from North Wales CID. I wondered if we might take up a few minutes of your time. It's about your brother, Patrick."

The beginnings of a smile froze on the woman's face. "P-patrick? But he's ..." Her voice trailed off as if she was unsure how to continue.

Amanda leaned forward to touched her arm. "I know. Please ... can we come inside and I'll explain."

The woman took a step back, pulling the door wider and

gesturing them inside. The door opened directly onto a small, square sitting room, once no doubt a parlour, the best room of the house, but now a comfortable space with two small red sofas and a wood burner centre stage in the hearth, flickering orange shadows against the white walls, and filling the room with heat. Amanda loosened her scarf, and Kelly removed her gloves, as they sat on one of the two sofas facing each across the room.

Ruby balanced on the edge of the other, her face a mask of confusion. "Should I offer you a drink? I mean, tea or coffee, I'm not sure …"

Amanda shook her head. "We're fine, but thank you. I realise this must have come as a shock and I apologise for not calling in advance, but I couldn't find a number listed."

Ruby swallowed and gave a shrug. "I don't have a landline now, no point. I make most long-distance calls through Skype – and I have my mobile."

"I guessed as much. Sign of the times." She reached into her handbag and removed a printout of the NPB profile page. "Can I establish before we go on this is your brother, Patrick Kavanagh."

Ruby reached across and took the sheet from Amanda, it trembled in her hand as she held it closer to squint at the small photograph. A smile crept across her lips, but when she handed the paper back, there were tears in her eyes.

"Yes, that's our beautiful Paddy."

"Can you tell me about him, Ruby?"

The woman dug about in the sleeve of her jumper, produced a tissue, and wiped both eyes. "Well, as you obviously already know, he went missing over New Year in 1976 or 77." She paused. "I can't believe we're talking over forty years ago. I was eight at the time but it seems like only yesterday to me. Dearest Paddy. And my poor mother …" She looked up, fracturing the connection with the past, eyes clearing into a scared frown. "Why the questions? What's happened?"

"Obviously, I will tell you everything I know. But could I get your story first, without it being influenced by anything I might tell you?" said Amanda. "Believe me, it is important, and I'll answer any questions you have before I leave."

Ruby took a moment, dabbed her nose with the tissue, and replaced it inside her sleeve. "Okay. When I think back to that time, it's like time slowed down and I see it in a series of black and white stills inside my brain … it's hard to describe." She exhaled and sat up straighter. "That year, 1976, we'd spent Christmas here, all of us together. Mother and Paddy were like the grown-ups to me then, sorting out a turkey and the tree, no doubt worrying about money and the endless lists of presents each of us kids had … while the rest of us enjoyed ourselves. I was the youngest, then there was Eileen, who'd have been eleven. And the twins, Seamus and George, who'd have been fourteen. It was the last year I remember us as kids, acting like kids, without a care in the world and secure in the love and warmth of our family. All that changed when Paddy left."

Kelly cleared her throat and looked up from her notes. "Your father?"

Ruby shook her head. "He died when I was three … drowned when a fishing trawler he helped out on went down in a storm out past The Skerries. They never recovered his body."

"Goodness, your poor mother, bringing all five of you up alone."

Ruby nodded. "Hard times. Mother held down two jobs but money was still short, our clothes were charity shop or hand-me-downs. But we were happy. It was a close-knit community round here in the seventies, always someone to turn to in a crisis. My mother had our Paddy, that's what saw her through. He stepped up when he had to and became head of the house. And that's what made it so hard, like fate had dealt the same cruel hand a second time over when Paddy disappeared. No body to bury, no end to the grief. It broke my mother, that's for sure, I don't think she ever really recovered. Hope kept her going, and when it finally ran out, she gave up on life … or rather her heart did. Massive heart attack took her, over twenty years ago now."

"Can you tell me a little about your parents – were they from Ireland originally?" asked Amanda, remembering the DNA analysis in the report.

"They both came from a little village called Ballycastle in County Mayo, near Coleraine, out on the West Coast of Ireland. My brother George has moved back, actually, he lives in Coleraine now and I love it out there, whenever I visit I feel a real connection with the area."

Amanda leaned forward, resting her elbows on her knees. "I know this will be painful, but can you tell me what happened when Paddy disappeared?"

Ruby swallowed, studying the back of her hands for a moment. "We'd been to church on Christmas morning as usual, then out for dinner over at the Evans's place in Maes-y-Mawr … there must have been two dozen people being fed. Then in the afternoon, the boys all played dare jumping off the old quay by the Lifeboat Station into the water and seeing who could stick it the longest. My mother was sure one of the twins would die of hypothermia, they were so skinny. But we all ended up back here for hot rum punch and mince pies. It was wonderful."

She retrieved the tissue, and dabbed the corner of her eyes. "Paddy went back to work the next morning. He had a delivery job taking fresh shrimps and queenies off the boats coming into the fish dock, to fulfil orders round the hotels and restaurants in Holyhead. He had a little moped, noisy little thing, with an ice box front and rear. Paddy juggled loads of jobs – newspapers delivery, local gardening jobs, potato picking. We relied on the money he brought in and he knew it."

Ruby paused, took her time to gather her memories. "I don't remember anything out of the ordinary in the days after Christmas, then Paddy came in one evening and said a group of lads from the pub were getting a mini bus into Liverpool for New Year's Eve and staying over for the football match the following day. Our Paddy was a massive Liverpool fan and they were playing Tottenham Hotspur, that always stays with me for some reason, because there was some top player he said he couldn't wait to see play." She swallowed, stared into the dancing flames of the wood burner. "He wasn't asking permission as such, he was of age, and could do want he wanted. But he would never have gone against our mother. But she gave her blessing, he went off excited and pleased as punch that New Year's Eve morning … and that's the last we ever saw of him. I remember kneeling up on the sofa, waving until the noise of his moped died away."

"When did you realise there was a problem?"

"Not straight away. Mother wasn't too worried when he didn't come home the next day. It was a late afternoon match, she assumed he might have stopped over. But by the following day, people were out searching for him. Everyone knew our Paddy was the least likely runaway. His family – particularly our mother – meant the whole world to him. She went to the police the following day, filled in forms, and sat waiting for news. Nothing. I'm not saying the police didn't care, but he was eighteen, there was no crime. Mother even went to Liverpool, spoke to the local police there, walked the streets, asking anyone if they'd seen him. There was no sign he'd ever been there, and in the end, we found out there'd been no trip to Liverpool for New Year or the match, the lads in the pub knew nothing about it. Once the police found out his story had been a lie, they lost interest and closed the case."

"What did your mother think happened?" said Amanda.

Ruby shrugged. "We had not the faintest idea, none of us. If Paddy would have confided in anyone, it'd have been Seamus, they were always so close. But he knew nothing, thought the Liverpool story was real. We sat and waited, that's how it felt, for the rest of our lives. Certainly, that's how my mother felt. She said to me once, close to the end, she'd always imagined there could be nothing worse than losing a child to death … but god taught her the hard way there was something much worse … losing a child to life."

Amanda swallowed down a lump in her throat. "That's so sad."

Ruby blinked back tears. "Yes, it is. So many lives ruined. For such a devout Catholic, Paddy's disappearance rocked my mother's faith to the core, and for me it provided all the evidence I needed ... there was no religion to protect you, you were on your own. I turned my back on the church as a child, and I've never gone back."

"And what about friends or girlfriends? Did no one have any idea why he may have lied or where he might have gone?"

Ruby shook her head. "Paddy wasn't into girls, or at least he didn't tell us if he was. Mother spent countless evenings in every one of the pubs this side of Holyhead, questioning anyone who knew him, sure it was another set of friends who he'd gone with to Liverpool. She was ready for any news, even if it was unpleasant ... but she got nowhere, everyone was as shocked as us. People offered to help, but what could we do? After a while, I think my mother thought maybe it had been his own choice to leave us – the pressure of being head of the house pushed him away." Ruby paused and looked up, making eye contact with Amanda. "I never thought that, not for a single minute. Paddy wasn't like that. He didn't come home, because he couldn't come home. That's what you're here to tell me, isn't it, all these years later?"

Amanda nodded.

"I knew it. I only wish Mother was here to know it too."

"One last thing, did you notice any changes in Paddy in the weeks or months before he left?"

"I was only eight, if I had, I don't think I would have analysed it. I loved Paddy with all my heart. He could do no wrong in my eyes. I looked up to him, and he seemed so worldly-wise and mature. To be honest, he worked so many jobs, especially during the summer months, it was a special treat if he got to spend time with me."

Amanda sighed, feeling she knew so much about this missing boy from his sister's eloquent testimony ... yet discovered absolutely zero connection with the current murders. Back to square one.

"Do you know any of the places he worked?" asked Kelly. "You mentioned he laboured at farms and did gardening work in the summer?"

"Goodness." Ruby sniffed and rubbed her nose. "Seamus would probably know more than me. I know Paddy had seasonal jobs all over Anglesey - potato picking at a farm near Pentraeth, he took the twins there with him that last summer … and strawberry picking on a farm near Malltreath. Oh, and for the last few years, he used to work one day a week at a hotel over Rhosneigr way, cutting lawns and basic heavy outdoor tasks. The same family hired him to look after their garden too. I remember he was chuffed to bits about that. Can't remember the name of the place, though. I'll Skype Seamus later and ask him. Is it important?"

Amanda glanced at Kelly and saw from the open-mouthed expression, she'd made the connection too. "I think it might be. Was the hotel called the Llyn Maelog hotel, and the family the Glenowens, do you recall?"

"I've heard the names before, yes, it might have been. Why?" Ruby frowned and chewed her bottom lip. "Detective, I don't mean to be blunt, but all I've done is talk while you listen. If there's something I should know about my brother, I'd really appreciate you putting me out of my agony. Forty years is a long time to wait."

CHAPTER SEVENTEEN

Gethin blew out his cheeks and flipped up the collar of his overcoat. It was a raw westerly wind blowing in this morning, churning the incoming tide at Rhosneigr into foamy peaks that raced across the flat sands towards him. He tried to make himself smaller and shelter under the protection of the wall, but the wind seemed to change direction, squeezing itself into the smallest of spaces. He knew he should be out there, striding across the beach with Dara, tracking down their witness. But all he wanted to do was get indoors, out of the persistent wind, and have a hot drink. He was far from the adventurous type.

However, it seemed he was in the minority. Each crashing wave was peppered with an assortment of black dots – each rising first as a head, then a slick wet-suited body, as the swell peaked, either balancing on boards and racing shoreward, or grappling with multi-coloured sails or kites and shooting sideways across the ocean. It was an impressive sight. Clearly news travelled fast when conditions were right, and the narrow side road behind Gethin was rammed full with camper vans and cars, this Sunday morning. And even in his current frame of mind, he had to admit the view was breath-taking. The roaring spray of the ocean against the bluest of skies, and away to the left the hills of the Llyn Peninsular provided a snow-covered, sparkling backdrop to the scene.

Gethin squinted against the sun and wind, searching for Dara between the mix of dog walkers and squealing children. He'd refused to trudge across the sand, questioning every surfer who emerged from the water in the hope of finding the right one. Having received a call from the off-duty and otherwise occupied Fletch, telling them he'd received a text saying Alun Wyn Owens had been seen on the beach this morning, Dara had taken flight and dragged an unwilling Gethin along for the ride.

On the point of retreating in search of warmth, Gethin spotted Dara's heavyset form trudging towards him, face split into a smile.

"Good news. He's out there and willing to talk once he's put his gear away. We've arranged to meet in the café on the crossroads. Come on let's get something hot inside us, I need defrosting."

"That's the most sensible thing you've said all morning," mumbled Gethin as he hunched his shoulders against the wind and set off behind Dara.

The café was clean, bright, and most-importantly warm. Tacked onto the side of a busy fish and chip takeaway, the café itself was relatively quiet, only one other table in the window occupied. Gethin stirred a sugar lump into his black coffee and added a tiny drop of milk. He was fast becoming a coffee snob, he knew that, as he licked his lips with anticipation. He sipped and nodded. Not bad. Not as a good a blend as they served at Llyn Maelog Hotel, but at a quarter of the price, it was still a decent coffee.

Dara arrived at the table, drying his hands down the front of his jeans. "Ach, that's better. Thought my pipework had frozen solid but all is in fine shape you'll be pleased to know." He dropped three sugar lumps into his mug of tea with loud plops and stirred in half a jug of milk.

"I'm delighted," said Gethin, wrinkling his nose.

"Sure you don't want anything to eat? I've ordered haddock and chips."

Gethin shook his head. "I'm fine. And did I imagine it or weren't you putting away a full English in the canteen not a few hours back?"

Dara took a slurp of tea, then grinned as he checked his watch. "Ah, but that was a good five hours ago, so it was. An' a man has to keep up his strength when he's battling the elements."

"You strolled across a beach with a bunch of five-year-olds, Dara, it's hardly like you conquered the summit of Kilimanjaro."

"You say that ... but Christ, that wind took your breath away." He took another sip of his tea. "Besides, it's more than you did. Exercise not on your list of new year resolutions?"

The skin prickled on the back of Gethin's neck. "No more than dieting appears to be on yours."

Dara's cheeks reddened and he seemed on the point of retort, when the café door opened and a man headed towards their table. He was early thirties, dressed in cut-off jeans, sandals, and a black fleece top. His hair was a complicated style of short, damp dreadlocks that bounced as he walked. Colourful leather bands decorated both wrists, and his skin, even in midwinter, was a healthy golden colour.

"Hello, there. I'm Alun Wyn Owens." He held out a hand and shook both men's hands as Dara showed his identification badge and made their introductions.

"Can I get you a tea or coffee?" said Dara as the man pulled out the chair opposite.

"Ah, they do a great mango smoothie if you're offering?"

Dara made to get to his feet but the other man held up a hand, rocked back in his chair and called through the arched entrance that led into the takeaway.

"Trish! Can you bring us through a Mango and Banana Crush when you've got a minute, hon?"

"No problem," came the reply.

"It's an unusual way to order," said Dara, settling back in his seat. "But I like it."

"They know me here and do pretty well out of us guys. So,

you got me curious, have to admit, it's not every day CID come track you down on the beach. If I had a guilt complex, I'd be worried ... so, what can I do for you?"

Dara reached into the inner pocket of his leather jacket and removed two photographs, smoothing each flat on the surface of the table, then spinning them in Alun's direction.

"Jesus, are those guys dead?" Alun bent closer to study the images.

Gethin sensed heads turning at the window in the table.

"Afraid so," said Dara. "These are images taken at post-mortem. Both men had connections locally, and your name has come up in our investigations into their possible involvement in a water sports group here in Rhosneigr. We were curious if you knew either man or what you might be able to tell us about them?"

At that moment, a waitress arrived with a tall glass of yellow liquid and a plate piled high with fish, chips, mushy peas and two slices of buttered bread. Food distributed, Dara returned the photos to the table.

"Stocking up on your carbs, mate?" said Alun, nodding to the pile of food.

"It's to balance out the proteins and saturated fat he consumed at breakfast," said Gethin. "Shall I continue so your food doesn't go cold?"

Dara's face reddened. "Please do. And I'm right touched so many people are interested in my calorie intake."

Gethin shot Dara a look, but ignored the barbed comment. It was so unprofessional to question a potential witness with a mouth full of food, but then Dara made up the rules as he went, and no one was expected to challenge him.

"So, the photos, Alun," said Gethin, tapping the close-up facial shot of Gregory Chapman. "Can you help us with information?"

Alun nodded and reached for the straw in his smoothie, took a long pull, then wiped his lips. "I recognise both of them. I'm just taking it in they're dead. What on earth happened?"

"Both bodies were found in Llyn Maelog, not far from here…"

"I heard about that. Jesus. I thought it might have been a suicide pact or a drunk or something … I never dreamed … what a tragedy." He took another pull on the straw, then touched the nearest photo. "I knew him as P.J. Was it Peter? Peter McDonald? Scottish guy, worked for an environmental company, had a flat up in town. He'd only been a member since last spring."

"And the other?"

"That's Greg Chapman. He'd been a member for five years or so. I first met him at the sub aquatic club I also run and talked him into kiting lessons … and he took to it like a duck to water, if you excuse the pun. He's head chef up at the hotel … well, that is, he was … but I assume you know that already?" Dreadlocks bounced as he shook his head. "Jesus, dead, I can't take it in."

"You hadn't noticed their absence?"

"Not really. We don't have official meet-ups this time of year, it's only hardy souls who take to the water in winter. I hadn't given it a thought, but even if I had, I'd have assumed P.J was a fair-weather surfer. And Greg was often too busy this time of year, turned up when he could … which is totally cool." Alun rubbed his face. "Sorry, I'm so shocked. It doesn't seem real. Was it murder?"

"We believe so. That's why we're eager to talk to anyone who knew them."

"I'm not sure how much help I'll be. We weren't friends away from the water, other than socialising at club events. I got to know Greg a little more at a fund-raising thing last year." Alun looked up. "The Glenowens. How are they taking it?"

"Same as you, shocked. Were they close?"

"Well, he was their pride and joy, on his way to getting a Michelin star for the hotel so I heard. Stephen was a club member too, occasionally came to the meets, but he was more into paddle boarding and canoeing. I heard a rumour Greg was dating the sister, Eliza. She was usually to be found hanging around the beach whenever Greg was there. Odd creature … but the three of them were close. She must be gutted."

Gethin's palms began to itch and he rubbed them on his trousers. Eliza hadn't seemed half as cut up as her brother.

Dara swallowed and wiped his lips with a paper napkin. "Did P.J. ever come along with anyone? We're interested to find out if he was in a relationship?"

Alun frowned, took a moment to answer. "I can't think I ever saw him with anyone. He came across as a private type, not that he was rude or anything, just didn't open himself up to that kind of banter like some blokes do."

"You wouldn't have known if he might have been homosexual by any chance?" said Dara, spearing half a dozen chips onto his fork.

"Who? P.J.?" Alun looked surprised, then shook his head. "You know I have no idea. And considering I'm married to a guy myself, you'd maybe think I'd have picked up the vibes, wouldn't you?"

Dara coughed and swallowed hard.

"Don't worry," said Gethin, "we aren't the type of coppers who think all gay men should come with a health warning and a sign around their necks."

"No indeed," said Dara, taking a sip of tea, and nodding with vigour. "Take yourself, Alun, you'd have no idea, would you? Not that it has anything to do with anyone else, of course. But you didn't ever suspect P.J. might have been that way inclined?"

"You know the more I think about it, he may well have been." Alun grinned. "But if he was, then I clearly wasn't his type. Not sure how I feel about that … or the fact I never asked the question."

"We aren't sure ourselves, and even if he was, we don't know Peter's sexuality had any connection with his death. Most likely not, to be fair," said Gethin, focusing on keeping his gaze fixed straight ahead, ignoring the hostile vibes coming from Dara's direction. "It came up in our investigation as one line of enquiry.

I'm sure you find this too, Alun, but don't you think in this day and age, it's amazing how some people still make such a big thing about other folks' sexuality?"

He risked a look at Dara who was staring straight at him, chewing slowly, but remained silent.

"Doesn't interest me, one way or another," said Alun. "I fell in love with surfing, and fell in love with a bloke, when I was backpacking around the world when I was eighteen. In Thailand of all places, I ask you. Until I met him, I didn't know I was gay. And had I not met him, I could be married with kids by now. In fairness, my mother still lives in hope that might happen one day … even though she adores Carlos." He grinned and twisted the thin gold band around his wedding finger. "If you're thinking there was some closet gay ring that went bad, somehow tied up in our surfing club, then I'm sorry to disappoint. As far as I knew before today, I was the only gay in the village! And if there were any of those kinds of shenanigans going on in Rhosneigr, I'd be right in the heart of it, I promise you. Alas, there is none. So, I can't help thinking you could be barking up the wrong tree, detectives."

"We aren't barking up any kind of tree," said Dara, with a defensive edge Gethin didn't miss. "We're following leads and asking questions, which is kind of our job, fella. Whatever their preferences, we would be interested in our victim's love lives and their partners."

"Well, I don't know about any vengeful love triangle scenarios going on around here," said Alun. "And I can't tell you much about P.J. as I said, but if you want to know who or what floated Greg Chapman's boat, I'd strongly recommend Eliza Glenowen is the one with all the information."

They parted with Alun at the door of the café, leaving their contact details with him. Alun seemed to think he'd been roped in as some kind of undercover operative, and Gethin guessed it didn't hurt one way or the other.

What did confuse him was the sense of mounting tension between himself and Dara. It had started in Sandwich, and, without either man doing anything to fuel the antagonism, it was spiralling out of control. He knew Dara sensed it too. Despite the dense act, Dara liked to hide behind, he was one of the most intuitive men Gethin knew. It was hard to understand why he seemed to be going out of his way to wind Gethin up virtually every time he opened his mouth. The question was who would be the first to bring up the topic of the chasm opening between them, or whether they'd both take the typically male approach and ignore it completely.

In the end, Gethin didn't have to make the decision.

As they pulled off the dual-carriageway, towards Bangor town centre, Gethin sensed Dara giving him sideways glances.

"Problem?" asked Gethin, pulling down the visor and checking his reflection in the mirror. "Have I got spinach in my teeth or something?"

Dara cleared his throat. "No, I'm just fascinated by that massive chip on your shoulder."

Gethin twisted in his seat, noting Dara's left ear was glowing bright pink. "Excuse me?"

"Bit late to be apologising, you not think?"

"No idea. But something tells me I'm about to get the full benefit of your Irish wisdom."

"No," said Dara, his voice low and level. "But carry on like this much longer and you might get the full benefit of this Irish fist." He lifted his hand from the steering wheel for a second, and Gethin noticed the tremble in his colleague's fingers.

"You having a laugh?" said Gethin. "Are you seriously threatening me?"

Dara shook his head. "No, but I'm telling you, if you try one more pathetic attempt at humiliating me in front of a witness, then I'll take great pleasure in rearranging your pearly whites. I dunno what's eating you recently, or what exactly the problem is you have with me, but until you're ready to discuss it like an adult, I'd advise you stay as far away from me as possible."

Gethin exhaled with a whistle, determined to hide the pounding of his heart. "Touchy, touchy. I've really no idea what you're going on about – but let's pretend I'm shaking in my boots and consider me told. Okay?"

Dara flashed him a quick look as he negotiated a roundabout. "I used to really rate you, mate. As a bloke and a copper. But you've changed and not for the better. You know exactly why I'm pissed off, but let's pretend you don't, and I'll enlighten you - you went out of your way back there to make me look like a prick. Not for the first time. How bloody dare you! I ain't got time for that sort of bitchiness, this job is tough enough, so do me a favour and put in a request with the boss you get paired with Kelly or Fletch in future. Blame me, I don't care. But keep out of my way. You got that?"

Gethin swallowed as the smile slid from his lips. "Tell you what, if you've got so much of a problem with me, stop the car and I'll walk from here. I wouldn't want to contaminate your space one second more."

Dara slammed on the brakes, and Gethin gripped the seat belt, as the tyres squealed and the car bounced and skidded up onto the pavement, grinding to a shuddering halt.

"Don't let me stop you," growled Dara, staring straight ahead, knuckles white as he gripped the steering wheel.

Shaking his head with a forced grin, Gethin pushed open the door. "Safe trip."

Dara turned, looked at him sadly. "When you're ready to talk, come find me. I'll be here."

Gethin slammed the door and the car screeched out into the traffic, to a symphony of angry horn blasts from queuing motorists. He stood at the kerb, legs shaking, breathing hard. What just happened? Him and Dara ... they were mates, right? Or so he'd thought. They were part of a team. Why had Dara turned into some kind of monster ... or was the monster the one looking back at him in the mirror? He blinked and looked around, trying to work out the best way back to the station. In the end, he saw a bus stop a few hundred yards away, and after checking his pockets for change, headed in that direction.

CHAPTER EIGHTEEN

Amanda took deep gulps of cold sea air and fixed on her best smile, taking a moment to let the postcard views across the Menai Strait to the snow-capped mountains of Snowdonia beyond fill her heart with pleasure. It was a routine she carried out each time she visited her mother and she was too scared now to break the chain. It was with mixed emotions she entered the reception at Plas Coch. The staff were always so warm and welcoming, so positive and enthusiastic about her mother and what she'd been up to, that her stomach dropped in disappointment each time she arrived at her mother's room, to find the same scene that had greeted her for almost three years. Each time, she expected to see her mother sitting up in bed, spectacles balanced on the end of her nose, reading one of her favourite Catherine Cookson novels. Instead, she was greeted by the same cold, blank expression or the same volatile anger and denial.

How could the staff here see such positivity, even with all the training in the world, when all she could see was the shrivelled shell of the proud and glamourous woman her mother had once been? And how much of a traitorous bitch must she sound to even be having those kinds of thoughts about the woman who'd raised her with such affection. She shook the negativity away. No wonder her mother acted as if she hated her more with each visit, if only she could read her mind, she'd have every reason to do so.

As ever, the reception was bright and warm, multi-coloured furniture and paintings lifted the greyness of the day. Staff bustled back and forth, visitors chatted in small groups, telephones trilled and the low rumble of voices intermingled with outbreaks of laughter. It could have been the reception of a country hotel. But despite the jollity, forced or otherwise, there still seemed to be a lingering shadow and a hospital-type smell. This was not a place anyone wanted to be by choice, not the visitors, and certainly not the patients. And the staff did an amazing job taking that fact in their stride and making every single person feel welcome and important.

"Good afternoon, Mrs Gold," said Wendy, one of the local Women's Institute volunteers, who gave up their time freely to assist at the home. "Happy New Year to you. Here to see Mother?"

Amanda nodded and unwrapped the chunky scarf from round her neck. "Same to you, Wendy. Hope you had a good Christmas?"

"It was fine. Not what it was when the family were home and my Bill was still alive, but we make the best of it, don't we? I joined in with more parties here than I can remember in many a year. Shall I take you up to mother's room or are you planning to take tea in the dining room?"

"Whatever suits best. Is Gloria working today?"

"She is indeed. Shall I check with her?"

"Please."

"Hello, Mrs Gold. Look who's here."

Amanda looked up to see Gloria, as ever her wide smile rimmed with the brightest pink lipstick, steering her mother's wheelchair towards her. Her mother was upright, hair washed and brushed, in a cream roll-neck jumper, from the waist down covered by a tartan blanket.

"Mother is feeling up to tea in the dining room today, aren't you?" Gloria bent to her mother's height and ran her fingers through the soft white curls. "We've enjoyed a bath and a bit of pampering and we decided we might be up for a stroll in the garden. What do you think to a spot of fresh air, Mrs Gold?"

"It's pretty cold, will she be okay?" asked Amanda.

"She will be fine," replied her mother. "She is not deaf. Who are you anyway? The hairdresser? If so, you're not needed today, thank you. Gloria – fetch my hat and coat."

Amanda shrugged and smiled. And so it began.

The walk around the garden was pleasant enough. Amanda kept herself busy – and out of her mother's direct line of sight – by pushing the wheelchair and manoeuvring it around the muddier spots. Gloria kept up a running commentary about Christmas traditions in Wales compared to her home country, and her mother closed her eyes and appeared to fall asleep. Amanda's nerves were calmer by the time they returned to the house, and after a quick trip to the bathroom, she joined the group at her mother's table, looking forward to the traditional spread they served on a Sunday to encourage families to stay.

"Can't wait to try the scones," said Amanda, rubbing her hands together. "I had a passion for baking scones at one time. Remember, Mother? Cheese, currant, plain, jam. Anything as long it was a scone. Good job my father was such a fan of my baking, he'd never let anything go to waste."

Her mother studied her in stony silence, a frown creasing her brow.

"I am certain I have put on at least two stone in weight since I start working here," said Gloria, getting to her feet to reach across the table to retrieve the teapot. "I have never eaten so much cake in my life. But the ladies of the W.I. certainly make the best cake."

Amanda patted her stomach. "I've always had a sweet tooth. You weren't so into cakes or pastries, were you, Mother? Not like me and Father. And I never remember chocolate in the house. I used to sneak a bar on the way to school and eat it before I got home. Mother was always more health conscious than me."

Gloria smiled. "It is hard to get Mrs Walsh to eat her puddings even now. Although she's quite partial to Christmas pudding with a drop of brandy, and she polished off a fair few slices of Christmas cake. It is good to see her appetite back."

Amanda filled her plate with sandwiches, before accepting a cup of tea from Gloria. "You've done an amazing job. That flu-bug really pulled her down last month."

Her mother cleared her throat, and with an abrupt gesture, pushed her plate away, toppling her plastic mug of tea across the white table cloth.

"Ah, now, Mrs Walsh. Whatever is the matter?" said Gloria. "I'll go and get a cloth. Excuse me."

Amanda got to her feet, checking there was no danger of her mother pulling anything else over in a fit of temper or frustration.

Gloria returned seconds later, dabbing at the stain and tutting. "Now, let me see, there's none splashed on your lap, is there? What a mess. What was that all about?"

Her mother muttered something under her breath, shooting daggers across the table. Amanda's skin began to crawl and she put down the tea cup to hide the tremor in her hands. She'd seen that look many times before.

"What was that?" Gloria bent lower. "Who?"

Her mother spoke again, still in a whisper.

Gloria straightened, laughing. "No, no. It's Amanda. It is your daughter."

"No, it isn't. It's the new hairdresser!" The reply was louder this time. "I know exactly who it is, thank you very much, and I don't want to eat at the same table as the servants. It's common, I tell you, common." Huge tears welled and rolled down her cheeks. "Don't make me stay, please. I want to go back to my room. All these people staring and staring. Don't make me."

Gloria squatted to eye level and turned the wheelchair towards her. "Now, look. What is all these tears. Come now. This is Amanda. Your daughter. She comes every Sunday. It's not any hairdresser and no one is staring. Let's settle you down and get a fresh pot of tea. What do you say?"

"No. I don't want this woman. I hate strangers. I want Emily. Where is Emily? She should be here today. She always comes on Sunday and I won't have my tea with a stranger!"

Despite Gloria's best attempts at placating her mother, the scene escalated, her mother's voice got louder, Gloria's hand gestures became more effusive, and before long they were attracting looks from around the dining room. Gloria became increasingly red-cheeked and flustered, and finally admitted defeat, excusing them both and promising to let Amanda know once her mother was calmer.

Amanda got to her feet, grabbed her bag off the back of her chair, and followed Gloria and her mother out of the dining room. Her cheeks were on fire, and despite the sympathetic nods from staff and visitors, she still would have happily crawled under the table and cried.

"Don't worry about me, Gloria. I'll make a move. I think we've all had enough stress for one day."

Gloria couldn't hide her relief in her eyes. "You are sure?"

"Positive." Amanda bent down and kissed her mother's cheek. "Go and rest, Mother. I'll see you next week. Take care."

She turned along the corridor leading back to reception, while Gloria headed towards the lift. Amanda blew her nose on a tissue and hoped to make it outside before the tears came, annoyed at her own self-pity. It wasn't as if this was anything new. As she passed an open door on her left, David Attenborough's soothing tones slowed her stride. She put her head into the room and saw on the large television screen a white expanse of Arctic tundra, broken only by black dots of thousands of nesting penguins.

As she studied the flickering images, she recalled her last visit to the television room, and at the same time realised the room was occupied. A small, thin woman was huddled under a blanket, knees tucked under her chin, slippers protruding over the edge of the cushion of the arm chair, eyes wide, white flashes reflecting across her retinas, absorbed in the pictures. Amanda recognised the features, checked around her, then crossed the room and took a seat beside her.

"Diana?"

There was no sign the woman had heard her. Her sole focus was on the television. Amanda followed her gaze, a camera swooped high across snow-laden pine trees, across a frozen lake. The sight of the lake brought their crime scene out at Llyn Maelog back to mind. Amanda picked up the remote, lowered the volume so David's voice fell silent, then leaned closer to Diana, touching her arm and speaking close to her ear.

"Hello, Diana. How are you? Do you remember me?"

Diana's head turned an inch, eyes flicked sideways.

"I was here. You'd climbed into the corner under the TV. I untangled you. Remember? We sat and talked. You told me you were trying to find your son."

She blinked once. "Stephen."

"That's right. You were trying to find Stephen." Amanda held out her hand. "And I'm Amanda. Nice to meet you again."

Diana uncurled her arms and took Amanda's fingers, squeezing gently.

"Are you feeling better today?"

Diana nodded. "The colours. Too much colour."

"That's right. The colours were too bright."

"White." She pointed towards the snowy image on screen. "I like white."

"You're quite right. I love white too. Like the mountains, Snowdonia, do you like looking outside at the view?"

Diana glanced towards the dark window. "Snow. Snowdonia."

"Yes. It's a beautiful view from here, so calm and peaceful. Do you like watching natural history programmes. I do."

"David Attenborough."

Amanda smiled and stroked the back of the smooth hand. "He's great, isn't he?"

Diana turned her attention back to the screen. Amanda's mind was drawn back to Llyn Maelog, the frozen landscape, echoing the Artic scenes on television. Hiding its secrets. Secrets she was increasingly certain began forty odd years ago, and Diana was one of few people who may have been around back then to know the roots of the mystery.

Amanda pondered for a moment, then reached down into her handbag and removed a folded sheet of paper, keeping it tucked under the coat on her lap.

"Diana? Have you seen your son today?"

"Lunch-time. He loves roast beef and two veg."

"Oh, that's lovely. And Eliza?"

"Tomorrow. They take turns."

"They must be busy at the hotel."

Diana nodded once, eyes fixed on the screen.

"You remember the hotel?"

"I don't live there now. Oliver left me for another woman and now I have to live here."

"Really?"

Oliver Glenowen had passed away years ago, according to their research, but Amanda knew denial and abandonment were both symptoms of dementia.

"All alone now. Too much colour hurts my eyes."

"I know. But do you remember the hotel? The lake … Llyn Maelog?"

No response.

"Diana? Can I show you a photograph? It's from a long time ago."

Diana turned her head again. "Oliver?"

"No, not Oliver. I promise."

Amanda pulled out the hard copy she'd made from the missing person's website, enlarged so the blurred photograph was a few inches across.

"Do you know who this is? Have a think, Diana. This was taken around 1975."

Diana held the paper up in front of her face, tilting it so the screen lit the paper. She frowned in concentration, and Amanda noticed a thread of saliva, drip from the side of her mouth. She pulled a tissue out of the box on the coffee table and dabbed it dry. Her throat tightened. Such a natural reaction, but something she'd have struggled to do for her own mother.

Diana muttered something, almost as if talking to herself.

Amanda leaned closer. "What was that?"

"Is that Harry's boy?"

"Who's Harry?"

Diana frowned, nose almost touching the paper. "Not Harry?"

"No, I don't think so, have another look. He may have worked at the hotel."

She shook her head, threw the paper on the floor, and crossed her arms. "No."

"Oh. No problem."

"Take it away. Oliver left me too. Take it away."

"Okay, okay." Amanda paused. "Did this boy leave you too?"

"No."

"Diana, do you remember him? His name was Patrick Kavanagh but he may have been known as Paddy. He was a gardener at the hotel. Who else might have known him?"

"Oliver left me. Paddy left too."

"You remember Paddy?"

"He disappeared. Oliver disappeared. All men disappear." She stopped, turned. "Will Stephen disappear? Will he?" Her eyes widened. "Will he?"

Amanda reached for her hand, entwined their fingers. "No one else will disappear, don't worry. Stephen will visit soon. Eliza too."

"They will leave me here. I didn't want to come and I don't want to be alone."

"It's fine, Diana. This was all a long time ago. Do you remember when Paddy left?"

"Oliver left."

"Before that. The young boy, Paddy Kavanagh. Tell me about when he left. What happened?"

"Police came asking questions. Oliver explained. Big secret."

"What do you mean, Diana? Can you tell me the story?"

Diana shook her head. "Not our story to tell. That's what Oliver said. Not our secret to keep. Not our business."

"Who's story was it? Whose secret was Oliver keeping?"

Diana shook her head and put a bony forefinger across her lips. "Shush."

"It's important we talk about the story. Do you understand, Diana? Very important. Oliver would talk to us now if he could."

"Oliver doesn't love me anymore. He left me for another woman."

"No, he didn't. Oliver is dead."

Amanda realised the mistake the moment the words passed her lips. At the first scent of a breakthrough, she'd let her guard slip and allowed herself to get carried away.

Diana's head swung in her direction, eyes wide, teeth bared. "Dead?"

Amanda squeezed her hand. "No, I didn't mean to say that. I meant to say he still loves you."

"You said dead. You said dead! Is he dead? Is Paddy dead? Is Stephen dead?"

Amanda tried to wrap her arms around the thin shoulders, but the woman was shaking, loud wails filling the room. Amanda's heart raced and nausea swirled through her stomach. What had she done?

Diana opened her mouth and screamed, long and loud. Her eyes opened wide and she began to pant, fingers moving to claw at her throat as if she was being strangled. Then with a gasp, she slumped sideways, eyes closed.

"Diana?" Amanda shook the thin shoulder. No response. "Diana?"

Amanda checked for a pulse. It was there but little more than a flicker. Diana's left eye seemed to be pulling downwards, the left side of her mouth had dropped too, twisting her face into an ugly sneer. Amanda recalled the drooling from the same side of her mouth, angry at herself for ignoring the sign.

She jumped to her feet and ran out into the corridor, gesturing to a nurse who seemed to be heading towards the television room, perhaps attracted by the screams.

"Please, can you help! Diana Glenowen … she's in here. Hurry! It's an emergency."

CHAPTER NINETEEN

Gethin watched the bubble of carbon dioxide gas rise and fall, bouncing once, twice, then exploding with a pop and a fizz. He laughed. Cute. He took another pull of his pint, banged the glass down on the table and watched the same procedure over again. Bump. Glide. Bounce. Pop. Fizz. He chuckled to himself. Another drink. Bang. Bounce. Pop. Fizz. He liked it … it was hypo … hypno … what was the bloody word? Hypnotic. That's it. And wasn't there a saying about never looking at life through the bottom of a whisky glass? Shame no one thought to study life in a beer glass instead, it was a whole lot more entertaining than dull old whisky.

"You trying to smash my glasses there, mate?"

The deep Welsh voice made Gethin jump. He'd forgotten he wasn't alone, lost, as he was, in his world of bubbles.

"Sorry." He pointed to the glass. "Bubbles, see?" The bearded landlord was hovering above him, arms crossed and a mock scowl. Gethin gave his best grin. "Can I have another one?"

"Sure. If you treat the glasses with a bit more respect. But maybe it should be your last, eh?"

Gethin gave a mock salute. "Yes, sir."

"Good. I'll bring it over. Lager?"

Gethin nodded and handed over his last ten-pound note.

He turned his attention back to his drink, swirling the last dregs of the golden liquid around the glass, wishing he had enough money on him to get steaming drunk. But he knew he wouldn't, not on a Sunday night. There was something in his genes that prevented any kind of rebellious behaviour, not to mention the fact he loved his job too much to let himself down. Or his team.

Thinking of the team, turned his thoughts to a problem he'd spent the past three hours trying to lose in the bottom of a beer glass. Unfortunately, it wasn't working. He swallowed the last of his drink as the landlord arrived with a fresh pint, putting the glass and a pile of pound coins down on the table, retreating without comment. The landlord appeared to have enough experience to know when people needed their own company and were unlikely to become a nuisance to other customers. Besides, it was a quiet Sunday afternoon in the little back street pub; a table of elderly men played dominoes in the corner, and a noisy bunch of youths in the pool room next door. Gethin's spot in the window gave him a degree of solitude, but he enjoyed watching the passing traffic outside.

He'd made plans to visit his parents for Sunday dinner today, but had rung them earlier, using work as an excuse. His mother was fine, used to her son's last minute apologies, but still Gethin felt bad. He couldn't face polite conversation today, all he wanted to do was wallow in self-pity and drown his sorrows. The irony was the one person he might have chosen to talk through his problems with was the very person who a few hours earlier had brought an abrupt end to their friendship. When he thought about the conversation, Gethin could feel the press of tears at the back of his throat, choking him. How had things ever gotten this bad? It was like he was grieving. He was angry and upset and confused. Everything he and Dara had gone through together, this couldn't be the end. He wouldn't let it, if it was his fault, he could surely make it right.

Gethin took a long pull on the lager, careful not to slam the glass down on the table, still focused on the fizz and pop of the bubbles. Watching the tiny balls of gas bouncing back and forth, like a pinball machine, he couldn't help but compare the bubbles with how he felt about life. Pinging around between pillar and post, trying to please as many people as possible, trying to be everything to everyone, determined to prove himself and be a good person and a decent copper. And he'd succeeded, he believed, in ticking most of the boxes. Most people liked him, many respected him, colleagues rated him, friends trusted him. But in the end, was anything at all in his life making him happy? Or was all the confusion and complications pushing him headlong into a depression that would see him lose everyone in his life who was important to him.

The feeling was nothing new. This particular monkey on his back had visited him every single year of his life since the start of his teenage years. It was the same every January. A deep, painful bleakness that threatened to consume him. It built up till the seventeenth of the month, the anniversary of Ashley's death, then it burst like the bouncing bubbles in his lager – with his life gradually returning to normal. He'd often thought about Mr and Mrs Griffiths, Ashley's parents, whether he should contact them and let them know he still remembered, that someone else still cared. And say what? I loved your son and miss him so much. But how would that help?

And anyway, by spring the darkness would be a distant memory, packed away like Christmas decorations, for another year. This year things had been harder, more anxiety seemed to be tipping him nearer to his self-regulated edge. There was guilt and fear, stress and pressure, all piling down on him. Dara was right to say he'd changed. Every year he changed, but usually he managed to keep that change concealed. This year it had exploded into a life of its own.

He sipped his pint and heard his stomach rumble. His head ached and if he didn't get some food in his belly, he'd regret it in the morning. And he didn't need to feel any worse than he did right now, life was enough of a struggle without coping with a hangover. He scooped the pound coins from the table, drained his glass, and wobbled his way to the front door, raising a hand in general farewell as he pushed himself out into the night air. He stood on the threshold, gave a loud burp, and weighed up his options. He couldn't face a trek into town to a cash point, and he might just about have enough money for a taxi, or he could walk and call into the kebab shop on the way. As if in response, his stomach grumbled again, and shoving his hands into the deep pockets of his coat, he set off, already deciding what concoction to have on his kebab. Chicken tikka meat, chilli sauce and mint yoghurt, he decided. No salad.

The pavements were a hazardous mixture of solid compacted ice and sloppy melting snow, not something Gethin's alcohol infused brain found easy to negotiate. He kept one hand on the cold bricks of each building, risking going it alone only when he had no choice. As the welcoming lights of his favourite kebab shop beckoned, he felt the buzz of his mobile against his hip. On auto-pilot he retrieved it from his pocket, squinting at the unknown mobile number flashing on the screen, before accepting the call and holding it to his ear.

"Yo."

"Hello, is this Detective Sergeant Evans?"

Gethin cleared his throat. "Yes, who's this?"

"Sorry to bother you, it's Alun. We spoke earlier. Alun Wyn Owens."

"Yeah, yeah. At the café."

"Yes. As I say, apologies, but I've been chatting to a pal of mine and I've got a bit of info on P.J. McDonald for you."

Gethin leaned back against the doorway of a taxi firm, using the light from the office to dig out his notebook. "Okay, just a second. Finding a pen …." He wobbled and caught hold of the door frame, finally opening his notebook, and gripping his biro with fierce determination. "Go on."

"I texted a few mates this afternoon who'd known your dead guys via the club. I've had a call back from one of them. Aled Thomas. He's head barman at a club in Bangor. Place called Taboo – not sure if you know it?"

Gethin pictured flashing red lights, spiral stairs, and a heaving mass of bodies on the dance floor. "Heard of it, yeah."

"I thought you might know it. More likely you than your Irish mate, I thought."

"Yeah." Gethin kept his voice flat, non-committal.

"Well, there's the club downstairs, and upstairs there's a members' bar. It's a bit more select. According to Aled, P.J. was a regular visitor. And if you're interested in his relationships, I think that might be where you find your answers. I know they pride themselves on discretion, but I'm sure Aled would talk to you under the circumstances."

"Aled Thomas. Got it." Gethin mumbled, forming the letters with care. "Could I take his mobile number?" He copied down the digits, repeating them back one by one.

"Hope it helps. It's really shocked me. Anything I can do to help."

"This Aled guy. When's he next likely to be at work."

"That's the thing, detective, I thought I'd call you right away, he's there tonight till late."

Gethin thanked Alun and slid the phone back into his pocket. He stared across the road at the flashing neon sign outside the kebab shop. Two youths came out, open trays of chips in hand, laughing as they passed. Gethin caught the smell of doner meat on the breeze and stared through the window at the rotating stacks of meat, dripping with fat, and totally delicious. He groaned aloud and shook his head, retraced his steps, and pushed open the door of the cab company.

Gethin tapped his foot with increasing impatience. How long did it take to find a manager? The thump of the bass echoed through the floor, into his skull, aggravating the headache that was already making him edgy. He watched the mass movement of people on the dance floor, the strobing lights, the DJ booth on the raised stage – one man entertaining the crowd like demi-

God before his worshippers. This had been Gethin's scene for years. He'd loved having a secret lifestyle no one would expect of him, and he rarely missed a week. This hadn't been his club of choice, but he'd been inside before. For almost a decade, he'd adored the buzz and vibrancy of the club scene, but in recent years, that had turned to repulsion, and even now he couldn't wait to get back outside into the quiet night air.

The bouncer had been quite helpful as bouncers go. He'd hoped to get access to the upper floors, and the select member's area, without showing his ID but to no avail. Alun Wyn Owens said they prided themselves on discretion here, and he'd clearly not been joking. Gethin had the feeling he could more easily have accessed Fort Knox.

At least the wait, and the bumpy taxi journey, had given chance for the lager to dilute itself into his bloodstream to such an extent that walking and talking was no longer an issue. After wrinkling his nose in disgust earlier at Dara's consumption of fish and chips while interviewing a witness, he'd have choked on his own hypocrisy to be questioning someone while under the influence. The idea of contacting another member of the team to accompany him had briefly flashed across his brain in the cab, but what was the point in spoiling someone else's Sunday evening for no more than a confirmation of a sighting.

"DS Evans?"

Gethin turned, not seeing the approach of the man in the gloom of the club. "Yes?"

"I'm Aled Thomas. My boss asked me to come and meet you. I spoke to Alun earlier."

"Ah, right. I hope you can help me, we're compiling a background profile on Peter McDonald and we seem to be drawing a lot of blanks."

"I'm not surprised ..."

The music changed to a high-tempo retro version of a Bronski Beat classic Gethin recalled from his youth. A roar went through the crowd. Aled touched his arm and gestured Gethin to follow. He nodded. No way they'd be having a sensible conversation here.

Aled Thomas was a slim man, late twenties, floppy blond hair fell across one side of his face, dressed in the club uniform of black jeans and tight black t-shirt with a neon Taboo logo. He led Gethin into a small office at the end of the bar and pulled out a chair, removing unopened post as he did so.

"Can I get you a drink?" he said, closing the door, blocking out the noise.

Gethin sighed with relief. "If you have a bottle of sparkling mineral water it'd be appreciated."

"Sure thing. Two secs."

Aled was back with two bottles in a few moments, and settled himself on the far side of the desk. "I've worked here about ten years and I'm assistant manager now. I share this office with two other guys. But I spend most of my time upstairs. Find the noise hard to take the older I get." He grinned.

Gethin opened the water and smiled back. "Oddly, I was thinking the very same thing a few minutes ago."

"I've seen you here though, right? I'm sure I've served you in the past."

Gethin felt the surge of blood to his face. "Once or twice. With mates, you know?"

"Thought so. I never forget a face. Not one I like anyway."

Gethin swallowed his water and pretended he'd missed the final words. "So, you spoke to Alun about Peter McDonald. He was a member?"

"Yes. I signed him up only a few months back. I dug out the paperwork." He held across a yellow piece of paper. "Not that it will tell you anything you probably don't already know, his address and bank details for the direct debit are on there. I've got the top copy so you can take that if you like."

Gethin took the form and glanced at it. "I'm more interested in who Peter might have been with when he came here? Did he bring anyone along or meet up with anyone here?"

"I checked the guest register earlier. It seemed he always came alone. He never signed anyone in as a guest. But I do recall he left with a few guys on occasion."

Gethin let the thought settle. Damn, Dara. He could already imagine the gloating expression. "You think Peter used the club as a pick up joint?"

"I think that's almost certainly why he came."

"Did you ever see him with a woman?"

Aled laughed and brushed his hair away from his face. "Seriously? Here? I know women come here but they're rarely seen upstairs. I think we all know Taboo caters for the gay crowd, don't we? Even if it's unspoken, we all know what goes on here."

"Like I said, my clubbing days are behind me …"

"And like I said, I've seen you here a fair few times …"

The silence lengthened. Gethin wasn't about to be pulled into a conversation about his private life.

"Can you give me the names of anyone in particular you'd seen Peter McDonald with? Any dates you can recalling him leaving the club with anyone?"

Aled shook his head. "I don't know everyone by name, sorry. And if they're not members, I wouldn't even know their names. If nothing about them piques my interest, I probably wouldn't even recognise them in a crowd." Aled licked his lips and took a sip of water. "You should consider yourself highly honoured, see?"

"So, if you're not able to supply details, what information did you think might be relevant to our enquiry?"

Aled took his time replying. "This is in confidence, right? I know this is a murder enquiry and I'm not about to withhold information, but I have to think about my reputation, and, as my boss has just reiterated to me loud and clear, the reputation of the club. We promise our members confidentiality. Lots of them are married, or haven't come out, or are simply liars and cheats." He grinned the same toothy smile. "We could go bust if we go around spilling too many secrets."

"I understand. All I can promise is we can be discreet. If it has nothing to do with our enquiry, quite honestly, we're not interested. What people do in their own lives is no relevance. We're trying to find a killer."

"I hoped you'd say that." Aled took another swig from the bottle. "I got chatting to Pete one night, the night he signed up for membership actually. He had the sexiest Scottish accent and I suppose you could say he had the kind of face I'd recognise in a crowd."

Gethin nodded.

"I wouldn't go as far as to say we dated. I got the impression he was very much an anti-dating guy. Commitment wasn't on his radar, you know?"

Gethin removed his notebook from his inside pocket. "Go on."

"Okay, we're adults, right. So, there's little point me beating around the bush. We became sexual partners. When Alun rang, told me he was dead, I was stunned."

"How long did it last?" asked Gethin.

"Three months. Until he started ignoring my phone calls and texts, around end of October."

"Did you learn anything about Peter in the time you knew him that might be relevant to his death?"

Aled exhaled, small white teeth biting down on his lower lip. "I dunno if it's relevant. But I think it's something you should know. He was big into sex with strangers."

Gethin looked up. "Cottaging?"

"Cottaging. Dogging. All sorts of stuff I'd never even heard of. He showed me some of the websites he'd joined, a few were local, you know around North Wales, telling people where to go and when." He pushed hair away from his brow again. "Man, it was pretty sick. I knew he was trying to get me involved, but it made me feel physically ill. Just because we're gay, doesn't mean we all get turned on by the same stuff, does it?"

"Do you know names of any of the websites?"

"Not off hand. But they might be in my browser history. He used my laptop to show me. We used to go back to my place most times, I only live around the corner, and he showed me in bed one night. I could see how he was getting off on it." Aled shook his head, tapped the water bottle between his fingers. "To be honest, I thought that's why he'd started ignoring me, you know, unimpressed with my reaction. And I wasn't particularly bothered to be honest. Seems we were after different things."

"I'd be interested if you could send me the information if you have it. Here's my email address." Gethin dug into his jacket pocket. "What specifically started to put you off about him? Like you say we're both adults, and I can't imagine you're easily shocked."

"No, I wasn't shocked, it's just not my scene. Even in bed Pete liked to be submissive, he enjoyed pain, wanted to push boundaries. I became increasingly uncomfortable." Aled shrugged and shivered. "I think Pete had a deviant streak and needed some pretty radical things to satisfy him. I don't judge anyone but it's not for me."

"Did he mention anyone by name that also might have been involved in any of these websites or meets?"

Aled shook his head, a half-smile on his lips. "I think anonymity is kind of the point."

"How about places he frequented?"

"He talked about a few places. Behind the cathedral, five minutes up the road here in Bangor. The woods in Menai Bridge. He told me he'd been there a few times. A place near Aberffraw. Another spot at a car park at Llyn Alaw, the reservoir. He was into it in a big way." Aled exhaled. "When I heard he'd been murdered, first thing I did was thank my lucky stars I hadn't gotten involved. I mean I'm not pointing fingers at anyone, but in my head that kind of risky behaviour is asking for trouble. If there's a sicko out there looking to kill blokes, gay or not, then surely there's no better cover?"

Aled's words rolled round Gethin's head on a loop as he settled himself in the back of the taxi half an hour later. The summation was probably right. This revelation could prove be the how and where, if not the why, that led to the missing motive. He watched the passing headlights flash towards them and, as his guts cramped, remembered he needed food. He'd never get to sleep without settling his stomach. He glanced at his watch, pleased to see it was only half past nine. He'd been drinking since lunchtime, so it felt a lot later. He leaned forward, hoping the taxi driver could hear him as he had an ear-piece in one ear and seemed engrossed in a telephone conversation in his own Eastern European language.

"Excuse me, mate. Change of plan. Can you drop me at Trocadero Kebab House on Stanley Road instead?"

The driver nodded, gave a thumbs up, and continued his conversation without missing a beat.

Gethin slumped back into the seat and let his mind roam. This was a breakthrough. He could see that, despite his reluctance to accept it. It could mean they were looking at a random serial killer, and if so, their job had got one hell of a lot harder. He had a responsibility to pass on the information straight away, even if there was nothing he could physically do at this time of night.

He retrieved his mobile, scrolled through the contacts, and pressed dial. The call connected, then went to voicemail. A familiar voice filled his ear. 'This is DI Amanda Gold. Sorry I can't take the call right now. Please leave a message and I'll get back to you as soon as possible.' He cancelled the call, this wasn't the kind of conversation to have on tape.

He scrolled back through his contacts. His finger hovered over 'Dara' for several long seconds, then he shook his head, and thumbed down to 'Kelly.' She answered on the second ring.

"Geth. You okay?"

"Fine. You? I've not disturbed you?"

"I was half asleep watching some reality crap on telly. What's up?"

"I've received some information about the double murder case that could be important and I needed to run it past someone before morning. Just so I can sleep tonight. I tried the boss but she's not answering."

"Sure. Go ahead. What is it?"

Gethin gave a short summary of his tip off, the visit to Taboo, and the conversation with Aled Thomas. When he stopped for air, Kelly gave a low whistle.

"Makes sense, doesn't it? The thing that will clinch it is if we can find out if Greg Chapman was definitely homosexual, and if so, was he into cottaging too? Then we most certainly have a link. But it opens a whole ants' nest of problems, you must realise that, it points to this guy being either a gay serial killer or a total random psychopath." She paused. "I'm not sure which is worse."

"I know. I've had the same thoughts which is why I needed to get it off my chest. I thought if you could brief the team in the morning, I'd head straight to the hotel and re-interview some of the staff. Someone must know something. I have my eye on the sous chef, Dewi. He seemed close to his boss."

"Of course. Are you sure you don't want to be here to take the glory though?"

"It's the last thing on my mind, Kelly. It chills my blood to think where this could lead. The guy from the club, Aled Thomas, is coming into the station around mid-day, could you see to him if I'm not back. Get a full statement and a list of the places Peter McDonald told him he'd visited. When I've finished at the hotel, I'll take the scenic route back via Aberffraw and Menai Bridge. See if anyone might be there looking for action, though I have my doubts at that time on Monday morning."

"Be careful, you might see more than you expect," said Kelly. "Are you sure you want to go alone?"

"I'll be fine. Once we have details of the websites we can

research when the next meets are scheduled and turn up and spoil the fun. I'm sure people will be willing to talk if we promise confidentiality." He swapped the phone to his left hand. "My main concern I'd like you to run past the boss is whether we should be going public to warn the gay community. I didn't want to believe it was a gay killer, but it's looking increasingly likely, and it means there are a lot of men out there at potential risk."

"I know. But you're right, it needs to be the boss's call. No doubt Idris Parry will want to be in on the act. It's not our problem, but I'll make sure and be in work for when the DI arrives around seven and brief her straight away." Kelly paused. "Bloody good work, Geth."

"More luck than judgement. Ring me if there are any changes of plan. If not, I'll head back to the office once I've finished at the hotel and done a bit of cruising."

Kelly laughed. "Don't. It's not funny. Have you spoke to Dara?"

"Dara? No, I couldn't get him."

"He'll be equally as proud of you as he will be pissed off he didn't make the breakthrough. Want me to tell him?"

"Yeah, please." He paused. "And, Kelly, do me a favour?"

"Course."

"Tell Dara I'm a twat … and tell him I'm sorry, will you?"

"What? You two had a lover's tiff?"

"Something or nothing … but tell him, will you, promise?"

"Sure."

The taxi driver turned in his seat. "Trocadero, sir. We here."

"Where are you?" said Kelly. "Some sleazy strip club?"

"Ha! I wish. The local kebab shop." He handed across a ten pound note and climbed out the cab. "Thanks for listening, Kelly. See you tomorrow. I need food and sleep in that order."

"Night, Geth. See you tomorrow."

CHAPTER TWENTY

Gethin closed his eyes and wiped the grease from his lips with the back of his hand. There was something about eating a dirty kebab at a plastic-topped table, surrounded by semi-drunk strangers, in the middle of the night, that settled his soul. Food never tasted as good as it did after a few beers. And this kebab had been particularly splendid. Shame he only had a bottle of mineral water to wash it down, but his liver had taken enough of a battering for one weekend.

He bid a vague goodnight to the staff behind the counter, and headed out into the darkness, longing for his bed, and a chance for his brain to change down a gear and relax, even for a few short hours. His body ached he was so exhausted. The thaw had slowed to a stop as the temperature dropped, and the pavements were now transformed into glistening ice rinks. He negotiated the kerb and picked his way along the road, at least it had been gritted and he had a better chance of avoiding ending up on his arse.

He turned into his street, footsteps following the centre white line, keeping his ears open for approaching cars. He recalled the dark car he thought had followed him a few nights ago, the rumble of the engine as it had accelerated away, far too fast for the narrow side street. He realised he could hear the low rumble of an engine now, and grumbling, made his way back onto the pavement, skidding and grabbing hold of the nearest streetlamp. His heart pounded. Christ, it was lethal out here. He looked up.

Only another dozen or so houses and he'd be home.

Stepping like an army bomb disposal expert avoiding land mines, he arrived at his front door, and dug into his coat pocket for his keys. The engine sounded louder, closer. But no cars had passed and there was no sign of headlights. He stopped and turned, trying to seek out the source of the noise. The engine noise rumbled to a stop, a car door slammed, and a shadow moved between two parked cars three houses down. Gethin's pulse quickened. He jangled the keys, searching for the right one, annoyed as he saw the tremble in his fingers. "Hello, detective."

Gethin jumped. He'd been so focused on getting the key in the lock, he'd not heard the soft footsteps approach until they were behind his right shoulder.

"Who ...?" He turned, an angry retort on his lips. He frowned, focused. "Eliza?"

"How are you?"

"How am I? What sort of question is that? What on earth are you doing here?"

She held both hands aloft. One held a bottle of Famous Grouse whisky, the other a bottle of red wine. "I was hoping to convince you to have a drink with me. Don't be angry. I'm sure everyone has told you I'm as mad as a box of frogs. I like to live up to my reputation."

Despite himself, Gethin couldn't help but smile. "Eliza, it's getting on for midnight and I've got an early start. I'm not sure it's a good idea, as tempted as I might be. Or it's particularly appropriate come to that. Are you determined to get me the sack, there are rules about fraternising with witnesses you know?"

"Who will ever know, eh? As for appropriate? Oh, please. We're consenting adults. And you bloody owe me, anyway, I've been waiting here for hours and I'm frozen solid. And your watch is fast, it's not even eleven yet." She looked up and batted eyelids. "Please. I need a friend. I've come from the hospital and I don't want to go home alone."

"Hospital. What's happened?"

"My mother. She was taken ill at the care home. A suspected stroke. She's alive but it's not looking good. They've induced a coma so they can do tests." Her voice choked and she looked down. "I have to go back first thing to see the consultant and I know I need to prepare myself for bad news. Tonight, I want to drink and forget about it for a few hours. I won't be a hassle, I promise you. Don't turn me away."

Gethin felt trapped, he looked up and down the street. "You are really odd, reputation or no reputation. How did you find out where I live? It's not something I go around broadcasting."

Eliza spoke in a husky whisper. "Don't be angry. I have my sources. I called in a favour … lots of men like doing me favours."

He stared at her. "You've followed me, before, haven't you?"

She shook her head, puzzled. "No. Why'd you say that?"

He studied her, but her face gave nothing away, and he didn't fool himself he had any chance of reading a lie in that innocent gaze.

"Doesn't matter." He sighed. "One drink. Then I'm going to bed …" He held up a hand to stop her as she opened her mouth to interrupt. "… and you're going home."

One drink turned into two, then three, finally four. Eliza was good company, and, as much as he hated to admit it, he enjoyed having her around. Unwrapped from the huge cloak and Ugg boots, she looked groomed and sophisticated in a skin-tight pair of designer jeans and a simple black silk blouse. She settled herself down in one corner of the sofa, warming her toes in front of the gas fire, and questioned him on the progression of the case, fascinated by the news of the discovery of an earlier skeleton also recovered from her sacred lake.

It wasn't hard to bring up Gregory Chapman's name, and Eliza nodded with enthusiasm when he mentioned Alun Wyn Owens.

"Yes, I know Alun. He's a big name in Rhosneigr. Does a lot for charity. He's quite good friends with Stephen."

"He mentioned he'd seen you on the beach." Gethin took another sip from his bottle of mineral water, not allowing his thoughts to dwell on the excellent wine Eliza had brought with her. His liver was smiling with relief no doubt.

"Yeah. I enjoy chilling out on the beach in the summer. I was into paddle boarding for a while but then I grew up and left the boys to their toys. Now, I'm happy to cuddle Braint, watch the world go by, and enjoy the most fantastic sunsets."

Gethin watched her, but her expression stayed relaxed. "Alun gave us the impression there was something between you and Greg."

Eliza stopped mid drink and coughed. "No way! He said that … really?"

"To be exact, he suggested if we wanted to know what floated Greg Chapman's boat … then you'd be the best person to ask."

Eliza shook her head, pushing the sleeves of her blouse up to her elbows as if ready to land a punch, exposing a dozen or more slender silver bracelets on her left wrist. "Typical bloody bloke. Sees a man and woman together, checks they're not blood relatives, and concludes they must be shagging." She tutted. "And you'd expect better from him. He's gay … did he tell you?"

Gethin nodded. "Carlos."

"Yes, sexy Carlos. Now, that's a goddamn shame."

"What is?"

"Carlos being gay. He has a body to die for and I could enjoy myself there for days." She sighed. "Such a waste."

Gethin snorted. "If a bloke talked about a woman like that you'd be screaming sexist pig by now."

"I am only stating the truth. Wait till you meet him and then tell me I'm lying. He's stunning. But he's not for turning. I have tried."

"Eliza!"

"What?" She grinned. "I'm joking."

"So, he got it wrong, did he, Alun?"

"Put it this way, his taste in men is way better than his gut instinct. He was an employee who became a mate, no chemistry and nothing sexual. Why … are you jealous?"

Gethin threw a pillow at her and she caught it. "Don't flatter yourself. It came as a bit of a surprise when Alun mentioned it, and I wondered why you hadn't. I was curious is all."

"Whatever you say, detective."

Gethin laughed and excused himself, slipping into the kitchen to fetch another bottle of water from the fridge. Why would Alun lie? He pondered as he scanned the shelves to see what he had to put out as nibbles, and concluded a bag of Doritos and a chilli dip was better than nothing. Eliza could be right, of course, that Alun had the intuition of plank of wood … but could there be a more ominous reason? Alun was the only person who knew both victims in person. Could he be using diversion tactics?

Eliza's eyes lit up as he returned to the sitting room, and she held out her hands in glee.

"My favourite!"

"I can't claim any psychic powers, these are all I have." He decided to move from the chair opposite and lowered himself beside her on the sofa to share the dip. "Any more visits to Llyn Maelog since I was last there?"

"Most days. Dawn and dusk are my favourite times. It energizes me. And before you roll your eyes, I'm only repeating what generations of Druids have felt before me. I might be mad but I'm not delusional. There are powers beyond any of our understanding and I tap into that." She drained her glass and headed into the kitchen. "You could have filled mine."

"I can't keep up. I gave up counting after your second whisky."

She flicked two fingers up at him as her pert denim bottom disappeared around the door. Gethin grinned. He loved ballsy women, someone with substance, and Eliza fitted the bill. When she opened up and let her personality shine through, there was nothing remotely flaky about her as he'd suspected on first impressions. She was intelligent and articulate, witty and dry … and the more she talked about her decision to join the Anglesey Druidic Order, the more passionate she became.

"Why don't you come along next month?" Eliza said, appearing from the kitchen with her fifth double scotch and lemonade. "Meet Rhys, the Chief Druid, listen to him speak, and see how you feel?" She paused. "Can I be honest? It seems to me there's something missing in your life. I think joining the order could bring you the fulfilment you're searching for. It certainly filled a gap in my life."

Gethin raised his bottle of water and chinked it against her glass as she passed, watching as she curled up cat-like in the opposite corner of the sofa. She slipped off her shoes and the warmth of her toes burned against his thigh.

"I'm pleased for you. Serious, I am. But it's not for me. I don't hold any religious beliefs whatsoever."

Eliza slapped the cushion, her bangles clinked as if voicing her annoyance. "That's the whole point, you nutter. There's no priests or Popes or anyone recounting the voice of some invisible god. Druids came from a time way before Christianity, their beliefs are Pagan and Celtic. Druidry is as vibrant and alive today as it was in the days of the Iron Age. Our spirituality worships no god. We celebrate life, learning, tradition, heritage, and ancestry. We believe all answers can be found in the natural landscapes around us. Anglesey is our homeland. Admit it, that morning at Llyn Maelog you felt the power of the sacred lake, didn't you? I could see it in your face."

"That was hypothermia you could see …"

This time it was his thigh Eliza slapped. Her touch lingered.

"Be serious. This is important to me."

"As I said, I'm pleased for you. But I believe as much in Voldemort as I do in your Chief Druid. You're wasting your breath. I decided a long time ago the only person I ever want to answer to is myself. I trust myself. I know myself. And it suits me just fine."

Eliza look a long pull of whisky. "Ah, you say that. But I don't believe you."

"You don't know me!"

"You'd be surprised what I know."

"Oh … oh right." Gethin twisted to face her, tucking one leg beneath him, putting his bottle down on the coffee table. "Okay, then. You know me so well, let's hear it. Give me the wisdom your so-called faith endows on you."

"It's not my faith. And it doesn't give me any magic powers. But it allows me to use the gifts I have, we all have … to … see. Really see."

"So, come on them, I'm waiting. What do you see when you look at me?"

Eliza's smile faded and she shook her head. "I don't think so."

"Why?"

"Because we're having a pleasant evening."

Gethin frowned. "And?"

"And I don't want to do or say anything that might spoil it."

"Christ, that's ominous. You sound like a tarot card reader who's turned over the Death card."

Eliza laughed and sipped her drink.

"I can take it. Come on … spill. I'll give you marks out of ten."

Eliza studied him over the top of her glass. "Okay, I think you have a lot of attributes. You're intelligent, sensitive, empathetic, fearless and funny. You have all the talents you need to be a fantastic police man. You're able to be arrogant if necessary, but have the capacity to show humility as well. I like you … you should know that."

Gethin cleared his throat, reached for his water, unsure what to do with his hands. "I take it this is going to be the shit sandwich approach. A layer of soft, fluffy white bread before you tip the shitty filling over my head … and follow it up with a nice dose of sympathy."

Eliza threw back her head and laughed, exposing the pale

skin of her throat, and a beautiful jade pendant on a leather necklace. "You got me."

"So, what's the bad stuff ...?"

"You sure?"

"Unless you have got a tarot card up your sleeve and my days are numbered?"

She shook her head. "No, but I feel an innate sadness that emanates from you in waves. You manage it well. It's probably taken you a good chunk of your life to learn how to hide it, but when the darkness comes it threatens to drag you under. It threatens to hurt people you love ... and I think it scares and exhausts you. I don't know when it started, but I sense it's entrenched deep inside you so I'd guess it's from your childhood. Did you lose someone close, a parent or a sibling? Something rocked the foundations of your world and you've never felt sure-footed since."

Gethin stared at her, aware he was open-mouthed. Her face was so calm and peaceful, as if she was totally in tune with her words and had no doubt of their validity.

When he remained silent, Eliza sipped her drink, and continued. "Your life is hard, but it's hard because you choose to live that way. Smoke and mirrors. You hide much of the real person behind a charade, you spend far too much time worrying how other people judge you. All of that means by definition you're not only sad ... you're lonely, frustrated, scared and confused. And until you live your life openly, honestly and with abandon, you'll never lose the sadness. It's not your time yet, but it will come, just be sure you don't miss the chance to be who you really want to be."

Gethin closed his mouth and swallowed.

"And there endeth today's sermon." Eliza drained her glass. "One for the road!"

Speechless, Gethin watched her head back into the kitchen. What happened? How could Eliza have got so many things accurate about him? It wasn't possible. She didn't know him ... or did she?

As she reappeared, Gethin straightened his legs. "So, I assume you called in another of those favours, did you?"

"Sorry?" She frowned as the settled herself back on the sofa. "Who told you?"

"Told me what?"

"That potted life story. Where did you get your information?"

Eliza shrugged. "No idea. I can't exactly use Google. I told you. I use my sight. I also told you that you might not like it, so don't get shirty with me now. I'm only the messenger."

Maybe it was the day's excess alcohol playing with his mind, but he had to admit it felt as if Eliza had slipped a bangled wrist down his throat, into his gut, and kneaded his soul as if she were kneading bread. He felt sick, physically sick, as if he could vomit out all of the pain and loneliness. He had an urge to lay his life history out before her, fall into her arms and beg her to make everything right. But he knew he couldn't. Mr Reliable, Mr Conscientious, Mr Cautious … in the middle of a double murder enquiry he could not open his heart to a potential suspect. The idea of getting her drunk had appealed as an avenue to get her to open and talk and herself … not roles reversed.

"What marks do I get?" said Eliza, the cheeky smile back in place.

"Marks? I'm tempted to go cut my wrists and put us all out of our misery," said Gethin, forcing himself to wink. "I'll give you a six and half."

"No way!"

"Way. I did lose someone. And I do suffer from winter blues like lots of folks, but the smoke and mirrors mumbo-jumbo doesn't ring true."

Eliza raised her eyebrows. "Really?"

"Really. Your voodoo powers need fine-tuning."

Eliza studied him for a moment, then with the grace and speed of a cat pouncing on a mouse, she'd put her glass down on the carpet, and in one fluid move was on his lap, her lips pressed hard against his, tongue probing, hands roaming. Christ. Fingers reaching for his fly and …

Gethin took hold of her shoulders and eased her away. "Whoa! What the hell?"

Eliza licked her lips, held his gaze. "Come on, as I said we're consenting adults, let's go to bed. I am horny as hell for you, and unless I'm reading the signals wrong you're up for it too." She began to unbutton her blouse, the thin black silk glinted in the lamp light.

Gethin caught hold of her wrists as a black lacy bra came into view. He groaned as he felt her denim-clad knee between his legs, and knew he was responding to her touch, her smell, her closeness.

"No." His voice was husky, little more than a moan. "Stop, Eliza. We can't."

She leaned forward and kissed him hard on the lips again.

"Eliza, it's the drink talking." He mumbled, pulling away. "No, please, don't make me cry rape!"

She looked up and he grinned down at her.

Her voice was small. "Why?"

"Because it's not right. And because I respect you too much to use you as a one night stand …"

"Who said anything about one night? You know I fancy you. There's something between us. I know you feel it too."

"Even if I did, it's not the right time. I have to think about my job, this could get me thrown off the case." Gethin lifted her to one side and got to his feet. "Sorry."

She looked up at him with a curious expression, but remained silent.

Gethin checked his watch. "Christ, it's gone one am. I should get you home. You can't drive but I should be relatively sober with the amount of water I've downed. Come on, lady, on your feet …" He held out a hand. "… let's be having you."

She stretched like a contented feline. "Is that your best offer?"

Gethin smiled. "It's my only offer. Take it or leave it."

Eliza threw herself back against the cushions and held the back of her hand against her forehead in a dramatic swoon. "Rejected. How very dare you …."

"Sorry. It's nothing personal." He headed for the door. "I'll nip up to the bathroom while you get yourself sorted. I'm surprised you can stand with the amount of whisky you've necked. You'll have to get your car picked up tomorrow."

Eliza yawned and grinned. "You're a complete gentleman, detective. Has anyone ever told you?"

"I know."

"Gethin?"

He turned at the door. "Yeah?"

"I told you I was never wrong, didn't I?"

Gethin stared at her for a moment, pulse throbbing deep behind his left eye, tingles running across the skin at the nape of his neck … then left the room in silence.

CHAPTER TWENTY-ONE

Gethin slowed the car to a crawl as they left the village of Hermon, determined not to miss the entrance to the estate. Eliza had described the route to this point, before promptly falling asleep before they'd even crossed the Menai Bridge, snoring ever since. He saw the gates, as she'd described, took a sharp left, and recalled her saying to follow the drive for about half a mile before turning off the main drive to reach Pen Halen, the Glenowen's house. But even the main entrance caused him a headache as there seemed to be at least three separate drives and he'd no idea which to take. He had no choice but to wake sleeping beauty.

He braked and shook her shoulder. "Eliza, wake up. I've got us to Bodorgan but I don't know which way now."

"Hey. Wha'?" She rubbed her eyes, cute as a dozing puppy. "Where are we?"

"I turned left as we came through Hermon, through the main gate, but there's more roads here than the maze at Hampton Court ... and it's all black as sin. Which way?"

She yawned and eased forward in the seat to peer through the windscreen, waving her hand vaguely to the right. "That way."

Gethin revved the engine and turned the wheel. "You definitely never mentioned doing a right. It was all left, left, left ... and now it's right. I'll not get a wink of sleep tonight at this rate."

"Stop whining, it doesn't suit you." Eliza stretched and gave another loud yawn. "My head is banging. I need pain killers."

"I'm not surprised, you'll have one hell of a hangover in the morning."

She sat up and held her stomach. "I don't feel at all well."

Gethin shot her a look and pressed the accelerator. "Christ, don't get throwing up in here. It's a works car and I'll have to pay to get a hygiene valet …"

"Will you shut the hell up and get me home," said Eliza, resting her head against the window. "Or I might barf all over the upholstery just to annoy you. Next left."

Gethin bit back a smile and turned the wheel, braking as the car's headlights picked out a large wrought iron gate.

"How do we open the gate?"

Silence. He peered at Eliza, her eyes were closed, jaw slack, chin on her chest.

"Eliza! Wake up. For Christ sake …"

"Wha' now?"

"How do we open the sodding gate?"

"Press the buzzer."

Gethin peered out into the darkness. "Press the what …?"

"Drive closer. Open window. Press button."

"Ah, right."

He rolled the car forward, lowered the window, and pressed the button on the silver box mounted on the gate post. It buzzed. Then nothing. Eliza began to snore again. He selected first gear, ready to move. The gate stayed shut. This was becoming a nightmare, and sheer exhaustion was making him fractious. He pressed the button again, held his finger down … the buzzing grew louder, but still the gate didn't move.

"Eliza, nothing is happening. Don't you have a remote-control thingy?"

Silence.

"Eliza! I suppose even if you did, it would be in your own car, why didn't you think about it, you silly –"

"Hello."

Gethin jumped in his seat. The voice came from the silver box.

"Who is this?"

"H-hello." Gethin leaned on his elbow, speaking into the box. "Sorry about this. I've got Eliza with me. She's asleep and doesn't seem able to open the gate."

"Eliza? Oh, for Pete's sake. Hang on."

"I'm sorry. She said press the button. I assumed it would open the gate."

"Don't worry. I know Eliza. Drive straight on when the gate opens and you'll come to the house." The voice was tinny and echoed in the darkness. "Do you need paying?"

"What?" Gethin frowned. "Oh, no, no. I'm not a taxi. I'm a …" What exactly could he say to explain the position he found himself in. "I'm a friend and offered to drive her home, she was over the limit."

"Oh, right. Well, thanks."

There was a different kind of buzz, low-pitched like an electric motor, and with a jerk, the gates swung open. He drove through, wondering if he'd woke an angry butler who was going to give Eliza a piece of his mind for dragging him out of bed in the middle of the night. In fact, how did he know if the Glenowens had servants. This was their home, not the hotel, he remembered. Oh, well, he'd soon find out. The house loomed in front of him, white as a ghost in the moonlight, edged by a dark forest on one side, and landscaped gardens leading down to the estuary foreshore away to his left. The full moon glinted off the inky ocean and silver strip of sand, twisting away into the distance.

Parking next to a sleek black Range Rover Evoke with the Llyn Maelog Hotel motif emblazoned down the side, Gethin climbed out and went around to his passenger door. Hopefully the fresh air would do the trick and wake Eliza up enough for her to get herself into the house – and he could disappear before the angry butler arrived.

He pulled open the door and caught hold of Eliza as she toppled sideways and slid out of the car. With a groan, he took the full force of her weight, and wrapped his arms around her to stop her hitting the floor.

"Eliza. Come on. You need to wake up. You're home now."

He shook her body, struggling to keep her upright, hardly able to believe she weighed so much. This was what they meant by a dead weight, no way he'd be able to carry her into the house.

"Eliza!" He raised his voice. "Can you please wake up!"

Her body twitched, her eyes opened, followed by her mouth, and a stream of vomit launched itself skywards, and, as if in slow motion, hit him in the centre of his chest, and began to slide down the front of his jumper, heading for his jeans. He gagged, stumbled, and growled in frustration.

"Here, let me help. I'm so sorry." The voice appeared beside him like magic, and he almost cried in relief. He'd take any help now, even the angry butler. "My sister really knows how to make a scene."

"Stephen?"

"Yes."

The voice grunted as he lifted Eliza's feet from the ground, and Gethin took the upper body weight.

"Ah, I'm DS Evans."

"Of course." He grunted again. "I am sure there's a story behind how you come to be delivering my drunk and disorderly sister home in the middle of the night, but that can wait till we've got her inside."

"Couldn't agree more," said Gethin, side-stepping between the cars, up the steps of a porch and through the open front door.

"Do you mind taking her straight up to her room," said Stephen. "Then I'll show you the bathroom while I get her into bed. I'm pretty certain you'd like to get cleaned up before you leave."

Gethin wrinkled his nose, trying not to inhale too hard. "Please."

Gethin ran the jumper under the hot tap, trying not to gag as orange bile swirled down the plug hole. The smell made his stomach heave, and even as the water started to run clear, he knew there was no way he could pull the garment back over his head, it was sodden and stinking. Lucky for him he had his overcoat on the back seat of the car.

He opened the bathroom door and came face to face with Stephen Glenowen. Bare-chested, he attempted to protect his modesty, like a bashful bride. Then he smiled, aware how ridiculous he must look, cupping his non-existent breasts. At the same time, he noted Stephen was only wearing a white t-shirt and navy boxer shorts, and guessed he'd been in bed when the buzzer woke him.

"Sorry," Stephen said, taking a step backwards. "I was coming to see if you need a spare top. Don't imagine you fancy wearing that till it's been in the wash."

"I've got a coat in the car. I was on my way …"

Silence seemed to hover like fine mist between them, and Gethin cleared his throat, aware what on odd scene it must make.

"Where's Eliza?"

"In bed. Spark out. Little drama queen." Stephen smiled. "I'm sorry, let me fetch a jumper. You look frozen."

"No … I'm fine."

But the other man had disappeared through a door at the far end of the L-shaped landing. Gethin felt ridiculous, standing there in nothing but his jeans and a pair of socks. Stephen reappeared and handed across the most gorgeous grey John Smedley jumper still in its wrapping.

"Honestly, it's fine," Gethin repeated. "I don't want to ruin that if it's new."

"Think of it as compensation, it's the least I can do. I order half dozen at a time, it's not a problem, honestly."

Gethin shrugged and accepted the jumper, realising it might be a good idea if he put it on. Feeling increasingly more awkward, he snapped off the label, and wriggled into the jumper. It was quite tight, but it enhanced the muscles in his arms and chest, and it felt like silk against his skin. He was aware the other man was nodding in appreciation.

"You look better than me in that," said Stephen. "Wish I hadn't given it you now."

"I'll get it laundered and sent back to you."

Stephen put out a hand and gripped his bicep. "I was joking! It suits you. You're more than welcome." He paused. "Do you fancy a coffee before you leave ... I admit I'm quite curious how my sister came to get a police escort home."

By the time the two men had made it down the stairs, through the oak panelled hallway, and into the cream and slate farmhouse kitchen, Gethin had run through the events of the evening, right from the moment Eliza had surprised him on his own doorstep with her trademark bottle of Famous Grouse.

Stephen stood in front of a long counter that ran the length of one wall, dark windows behind him reflecting the brightness of the room. He pushed several buttons on a complicated looking coffee machine, and turned to face Gethin with a wide smile.

"I'm sorry. It's not funny. But that sounds so like my sister. Tact and diplomacy don't feature in her vocabulary. If she wants something, she goes out and gets it."

Gethin felt his cheeks redden and pulled out a stool next to the centre island. "She said she'd come from the hospital and needed company."

Stephen balanced a glass mug under the machine, and it came to life with a hiss. "That's very probably true. But it's you she chose to go to, not me. I'd say she's sharpening her talons as we speak. And you have no chance of escape."

Gethin cleared his throat. "I doubt that very much."

Stephen shrugged. "We'll see. I know my sister. Sugar?"

"Two, please. I'm sorry to hear about your mother."

"It's one thing after another. I was lying awake staring at the ceiling when you arrived. I can't remember the last time I slept more than an hour in one go. First Gregory … now Mother. I'm supposed to be picking Greg's parents up at Manchester airport in the morning, but I've had to ask Terry to go in my place, we have a meeting with the Consultant at the hospital at ten o'clock. I assume Eliza told you?"

Gethin nodded, accepting the mug in both hands. "Thank you."

Stephen returned to the machine and repeated the process. "I'm sure it's more normal for you. But death terrifies me and it's everywhere. It's like someone has taken a contract out against the Glenowen family. I'm scared to think what will happen next." His voice faltered and he busied himself reaching another mug down from the cupboard. "But anyway, thanks to you at least I have my errant sister back safe and sound."

"I'm glad she came to me to drown her sorrows rather than spending the night drinking alone in some back-street bar. I'm still no wiser how she knew where I lived though. And she's being typically enigmatic about it."

Stephen laughed, his face immediately ten years younger. "She'll tell you when she's ready. I suppose at this point, I should come across all stern and ask you what your intentions are, young man?"

"S-sorry?"

"Well, Eliza must reckon you feel the same as she does. She wouldn't have put herself up for a knock back, that's not her way. Are you serious about her? Sorry, that sounded very Edwardian. Are you an item?"

Gethin could almost feel the blood drain from his face. "I'm sorry, I don't know what Eliza has said, but there's nothing between us, our relationship is strictly professional."

The machine hissed and spurted as Stephen stirred in sugar. "Ah, my mistake. She was being all wistful about sharing a dawn experience with you, out at the lake, and I assumed you'd shared the night together as well. Sorry if I've caused offence, I didn't know you were involved. Your girlfriend must be very understanding if you make a habit of rescuing inebriated damsels in distress."

Gethin knew he was starting to blush again, could feel it creeping up his neck. He must look like someone was turning the light on and off inside his body. How bloody ridiculous.

"There's no wife, no girlfriend. No boyfriend either, come to that. No one to give me grief. I live alone, not even a cat for company, and it's how I like it."

Stephen took the seat on the other side of the island, blowing on his coffee before taking a tiny sip.

"Don't blame you," he said. "Love hurts."

Gethin's pulse quickened, and he felt his police brain click back into gear. "Tell me about it."

Stephen sighed and nodded.

Gethin leaned forward, resting his elbows on the smooth marble. "No, I mean … tell me about it."

Stephen looked up, meeting Gethin's eyes. "You know?"

"To be honest, I'm taking a punt. Or an educated guess. Call it what you will."

Stephen sipped his coffee. "I suppose I should be glad I don't have a flashing neon sign on my forehead announcing my homosexuality then. When did you suspect?"

"At the mortuary. Your reaction. I felt your pain. It didn't seem appropriate to question you then. I'll be blunt, it was on my radar though. Especially now."

"Especially now? Has something else happened?"

"Sort of, maybe. Could you tell me about you and Gregory first?"

Stephen exhaled a shaky breath. "I could. Of course, I could. But do I want to is more the question. I'd prefer you not to walk out of here, leaving me a sobbing wreck on the floor. I have a feeling once the dam bursts, that may well happen."

"I understand. But would you not prefer to help me catch whoever killed Gregory. Wouldn't that at least help ease your grief a little?"

"I don't know if anything will ease my grief. Ever. I've realised trying to hide the pain, not being able to grieve openly, almost makes it feel unreal. Eliza reckons if I don't let it out, I'll either spontaneously combust or turn into stone. Take your pick."

"Eliza knows you're gay?"

"Of course. She's my sister."

"Who else?"

"Most close friends and family."

"Not the staff?"

He shook his head. "It's not the kind of thing I've ever discussed at work. And when I met Greg … it seemed more appropriate to keep it to ourselves."

"And your relationship was serious?"

He sighed, lowered his head, and squeezed the bridge of his nose. "As serious as it gets. I loved him if that's what you mean, and believe he loved me. It wasn't a tawdry sex thing as most straight men imagine it must be." Stephen looked up. "Do you think that way?"

Gethin kept his face blank.

"No," Stephen whispered. "I don't think you do."

Gethin sipped his coffee and waited in silence.

Stephen spun the stool to look out through the long, dark window. "We were so happy. When he disappeared, I thought I'd die. But I had to carry on, believing he'd had a breakdown, or whatever I could do to get through each day. But deep down, I knew. I knew he was dead because if he was alive he would never, ever have left me."

Gethin could hear the tears start through a serious of hiccups.

"Don't think I'm rude, but I can't do this while I'm looking at you," said Stephen. "There's something in your eyes, it reminds me of him. He used to question me without words, like you do, without even knowing."

"Sorry …"

"No, it's okay. Anyway, we'd argued the night before he disappeared. So, whatever had happened, I knew it was my fault. Alive or dead. He'd gone because of me. And if the grief wasn't enough to cope with, I had a handy layer of guilt on top to add to the joy."

"Can I ask what you argued about?" said Gethin. "If the dam is still holding, can you tell me?"

Stephen cleared his throat and turned back to face Gethin. "Our plans. Nothing was going right. Mother had to go into care. I wanted to delay putting the hotel on the market –"

"You were selling up?"

"With both of my parents out of the business, I had no passion to spend the rest of my life on Anglesey. Eliza agreed. Greg and I were moving back to his hometown of Perth. We were planning on setting up our own restaurant there." He ran his hands through his hair. "God, it seems like another lifetime ago to me now. All the plans and excitement … just …." He spread his hands wide. "… gone!"

"Who knew about your plans?"

"Just me. Gregory and Eliza. Oh, and our legal team."

"You hadn't told the hotel staff?"

"Oh, Terry knew, but he wouldn't have told anyone else. He's been my rock for most of my life. I trust him more than anyone. And it hadn't gotten to the point where we needed to show people around the hotel and so start rumours. If we'd had talks with new buyers, we would have tried to do a deal so the staff were kept on. We would have told them then. But it was early days."

Gethin yawned and wished he had his notebook. He'd need to catch up on his notes as soon as he got home.

"Sorry to keep you up. You must be exhausted. Do you want to make a move?"

"I should. But I plan to return to the hotel in the morning. I've got a few more questions to ask about the new information that's come forward." He paused. "It was about Gregory …"

"Go on."

"Well, it's a bit sensitive …"

"Please. I'm beyond being shocked or hurt. Like you said, I want all the questions I have flying around my head to finally get answered."

"The other victim, the first body we recovered, has been identified as Peter McDonald. Someone you may have known through the surf club in Rhosneigr?"

Stephen shook his head. "Doesn't ring a bell. Have you spoken to Alun Wyn Owens?"

"I have. Thing is, Peter McDonald was also gay. And he was into sex with strangers in a big way via websites and local meets. I need to know if Gregory was involved with anything like that? It could be the missing link."

Stephen swallowed, held his face in his hands. "Just when you thought it couldn't get any worse … are you saying it could be some random gay killer out there?"

"We can't rule anything out. New evidence has come forward and we have to investigate."

"Greg wasn't into cruising or cottaging or whatever perversity this new evidence has brought to light. You have my word, he wasn't. Believe me, I'd have known. We shared everything. If I put my mind to it, I could probably name all of his sexual partners." Stephen smiled at some secret memory. "Gregory got more of a rush creating a new recipe. He was with me because he loved me. He'd had two serious boyfriends and two serious girlfriends before me. He was bi and he was proud and he was monogamous. He wasn't killed because of kinky sex with a stranger in a lay-by somewhere. I promise you that."

Gethin slid from the stool and got to his feet. "Thank you for your honesty. I had to ask."

"No problem. But you've had your answer, and it's the gospel truth, so is there any need to raise this at the hotel?"

"I'll do my best to avoid it. I can't say more than that."

Stephen waited for him in the hall, and reached out and squeezed his wrist again. "Thank you. And thank you for listening."

The hall was in darkness, light from the kitchen spreading shadows across the oak tiled floor. Stephen opened the front door and moved to one side to let him through.

"And I'll make sure Eliza gets the message in the morning to back off."

Gethin grinned. "Hey, it never hurts to have your ego stroked. I hope it's the best news possible about your mother in the morning. And good luck with Gregory's parents. Our family liaison officer will be involved too. We're here to help if you need us."

"Thank you."

Gethin realised Stephen was holding his wrist again. "Find his killer. Give me a chance to live again," he said.

"You have my word."

The grip on his wrist tightened. "My sister always did have the best taste in men."

Gethin laughed and held out his other hand. "Thanks for your time. No doubt I'll be in touch."

"I hope so. Very much."

They shook hands. Stephen's grip was warm and firm. And lingered.

Gethin looked at him, quizzically. Then the pressure on his hand increased, and Stephen pulled him into an embrace.

"Thank you," he whispered, lips brushing Gethin's ear as they hugged.

He shuddered as they held each other, both seeming to understand they each needed something from the embrace. Gethin could almost feel the tension and grief emanating from the other man's body. And he relished the closeness. Stephen's hair smelled sweet, slightly floral, like Eliza's, no doubt the same shampoo. They were siblings, who lived together, he reminded himself. Stop letting them screw with your brain. But there was something intoxicating ... about both of them. The thought sent another shiver through Gethin's body and he stepped back.

Stephen's eyes bored into his as they parted, and before Gethin realised what was happening, Stephen had taken a step forwards and their lips were pressing together, soft at first, explorative and wet, then hard and intense. Stephen's body weight pushed Gethin back against the door frame, strong hands slid around his back, fingers manipulating the thin fabric, as a naked, muscular thigh slid between his own, forcing his legs apart.

He opened his mouth to speak, but Stephen's tongue slipped inside, exploring hungrily. Gethin groaned, opened his mouth wider, slid his fingers into Stephen's silky hair and pulled him closer. He was so aroused, could feel Stephen was too, as the other man moaned and pressed against him, body to body, grinding together. He wanted to close his eyes and let go and never come down again.

He'd never been kissed like this before. Never. The solid warmth of this hard, male body. The scent of him overpowering. It was abandoned passion, an outpouring of emotion … and … and … it wasn't right.

He lowered his hands to Stephen's shoulders and eased him away, taking a lungful of air as he did so.

"We have to stop, Stephen. Please." His voice came in short bursts. "I'm not Greg. You're not ready for this. And your sister doesn't need to come downstairs and see it."

Stephen stepped back, a shell-shocked expression on his face, fresh tears on his cheeks. "I'm so s-sorry. I don't know … Christ, I'm sorry."

Gethin put the palm of his right hand against Stephen's left cheek, wiping the tears away with his thumb. "It's fine. I'm fine. No need to apologise. Just … not now."

"I'm such a mess. I know that … but you feel it. You do?"

Gethin planted a soft kiss in the middle of Stephen's forehead. "I do."

Gethin sat inside his car, motionless, waiting for his pulse to calm down and the giddiness to clear. He felt as if he'd climbed off the world's biggest, fastest, highest, rollercoaster and he needed time for his body to settle. He gripped the steering wheel hard and gulped in the cold night air. At times like this, he wished he smoked, wished he had something he could swallow or sniff or inhale to numb the volts of electricity flooding his body.

He glanced across to the driver's seat and remembered Eliza sleeping there little more than an hour ago. How she'd thrown herself at him, part in jest and part through alcohol, he assumed, and how he'd known, with very little encouragement, he could have yielded to her advances. And now, what had he done? Seriously, what had he allowed to happen back there?

Something in Stephen Glenowen – his vulnerability or pain maybe – had struck a nerve inside Gethin. A deeply buried desire. The man was attractive, no doubt, but that was rarely enough to provoke this kind of reaction. It had taken a long time for Gethin to accept what he was, who he was, and had been even longer since he'd succumbed to those feelings. There had been women, of course, so many he couldn't put a number on them or a name to most of them. But there had only ever been three men who he'd allowed to get close. Other than Ash and he was different.

Through the passenger door window he saw a light come on in one of the upstairs windows and decided to get moving. No point in him coming across as a stalker on top of everything else. He pressed his lips together, tender from the pressure of Stephen's mouth, and could still taste strong coffee. He knew, without a shadow of doubt, sleep would elude him for the remainder of the night, and he would be replaying the kiss, and inhaling the male smell on his skin, on a loop until it was time to get up for work. A tremor ran the length of his body as he soaked in the illicitness of the experience. For once he didn't care he might be breaking some unspoken protocol or getting too involved with a potential suspect. He felt alive. And that hadn't happened in a long, long time.

He started the car and reversed in three-point turn, heading back the way he'd come. The high hedgerows closed in on him the moment he passed the garages and left the parking area in front of the house, and he recalled the disorientation on the journey in, the feeling of being trapped inside an enormous maze with no end in sight. And, as little use as Eliza had been in the end, he'd have welcomed her presence beside him right now.

The headlights picked out the outline of six-foot-high curved wrought iron, and Gethin grumbled as he remembered the drama of the gate. Now what? It was a futile question to ask why he'd not thought of checking with Stephen how to exit the property – both had other things on their minds.

He urged the car forward, hoping there might be a pressure monitor that would react if he got close enough. Nothing. He lowered the window and searched for anything that looked like a button, but there were no pillars or gateposts on this side. However, he could see on the back of the gate itself, what looked like an emergency lever, he assumed was there for occasions, like this, when the exiting driver didn't have a remote-control device.

He sighed and yanked on the handbrake, levering himself out of the car. He'd taken two tentative steps, groping in the darkness, when he heard the crunch of gravel behind him. He turned, peering into the blackness, weak moonlight revealing nothing but hedges and shadows. A spidery fear rippled through his chest and he held his breath, listening. Silence.

He shook his head and slammed the car door, squeezing between the car's front wing and the hedgerow as he approached the gate. Another noise, a rustle, closer. Louder. A shadow passed across his own. As he turned, a heavy weight connected with the side of his head, knocking him backwards. He grunted as a wave of pain followed, stunning his brain. Instinctively, he put his arms out, hitting the gate with his shoulder as he fell.

Another blow struck the back of his head at the same moment his knees hit the gravelled drive. His ears rang for a second, smoke filled his vision, and he collapsed face-first onto the ground, landing in a slushy pool of melting snow and closing his eyes as pain consumed him.

CHAPTER TWENTY-TWO

"You cannot be serious?" Idris Parry's slack-jawed expression gave him the look of a confused toad.

As inappropriate as it might be, the look on his face, combined with the awkward use of John McEnroe's trademark line, almost sent Amanda into a fit of giggles. It was sheer exhaustion, she knew, playing with her brain. That or the fact her body was running on caffeine alone.

"It's not how it sounds," said Amanda. "I know it sounds awful but the doctors confirmed it had been a gradual build-up of pressure in her brain. Not an instantaneous thing. Nothing I said could have brought it on, in fact my being there may well have saved her life."

Idris Parry pushed back the chair and got to his feet, striding across her office and back again, as if unsure what to do with his feet. He threw up his hands, and waved them back and forth like an out of control jazz musician.

"Oh, that's okay then. That's dandy. When the Glenowen family and their expensive lawyers sue North Wales CID on the grounds their sick, elderly mother was questioned by the police, without permission or supervision, we'll lay it on thick they should be goddamn grateful we were there at all – and demand praise for saving their mother's life. If she survives, that is, and it's a mighty big IF!" He paused, took a deep breath. "Have I got that right?"

Amanda glanced through the window, out into the main CID office. Fletch had arrived and was removing his coat, but on hearing raised voices, turned to stare in her direction, eyes wide and questioning; while Kelly kept a determined focus as she studied her computer screen. This was nothing new. Idris Parry never missed an opportunity to use Amanda as a human punch bag, in fact she was sure he couldn't wait for the next occasion to roll round. Let's face it, she broke the odd rule when necessary, and he would always take advantage of the fact.

"It wasn't like that. I did explain … I was at Plas Coch to visit my mother. I'd come across Diana Glenowen on a previous visit, and while I wouldn't say she recognised me, it seemed a natural thing to stop by and say hello when I saw her yesterday."

Idris Parry nodded with enthusiasm. "Yes, yes, yes. All good so far. No problem with any of that. What I do have a problem with is you using the opportunity to question her, unaccompanied, about a possible murder victim. Showing her a photograph that clearly triggered something in the poor woman's brain. And by doing so, not only shocked her all over again with the news about her husband death, but also lead her to believe her son had died too. And you wonder why the poor woman had a stroke!"

Amanda sighed and bit down on her knuckles, the safest way to stop the torrent of abuse exploding from her mouth.

"Sir, she has dementia …"

"I bloody know she has dementia. Do not lecture me as if I am some kind of simpleton, DI Gold!"

"Sorry, sir, I didn't mean to do that. I have a lot of experience … and normal rules don't apply to dementia patients. My own mother can barely stand to be in the same room as me, but I can't take all the blame for that, much as I think I should sometimes."

Amanda looked down at her desk, shuffled papers, waiting for the surge of emotion to pass. She'd resign rather than ever shed a tear in front of Idris Parry.

He stopped pacing and dropped back into the chair opposite. "I know you have it tough, Gold. You know I sympathise."

She wanted to scream in his face that he had a stupendously odd way of showing it, but instead kept her gaze lowered and nodded.

"But putting all personal issues to one side, which we must," said Idris Parry, his voice now back to its normal deep gruffness. "You cannot continue to go through life breaking rules. Not on my watch, Gold. It's got to the point it seems almost intentional, as if the idea it will send my blood pressure soaring is one of the main reasons you are so irrational at times."

Amanda rubbed her face, hoping to pretend the gesture was to wipe away tears, when it was actually to hide her smile. Maybe Idris Parry was more perceptive than she'd ever given him credit for, because, she wouldn't lie, that thought had crossed her mind more than once. But not this time. Diana Glenowen had been a spur of the moment decision, and she wished to god it hadn't ended the way it did.

The long hours at the hospital had given her time to think, and she'd made the decision to talk to her DCI first thing, in case of repercussions. She'd watched the Glenowen family come and go, the brother and sister, taken through to the ICU department, and back again. The shocked white expressions and tear-filled eyes. She'd kept her distance, even though she was bursting with questions. And even though the doctors had urged her to go home, explaining the woman was stable, the induced coma giving her the best possible chance, Amanda had been unable to leave. Did guilt keep her there … as Idris Parry would have her believe? The slenderest hope Diana might wake and be well enough to question? Or the sickening feeling it could have been the same scenario but with her own mother … and the relief she was spared at least for now.

"It wasn't planned." Amanda finally looked up. "She seemed to be reacting to me, remembering details. And the discoveries about Patrick Kavanagh were fresh in my mind. It struck me Diana would be one of very few people who might have known him."

"So, why not clear it with the staff? Or the family? Or take someone in with you as witness? There are rules, Gold, there for your protection. Why not follow procedure?"

"I'm sorry. Like I said, it wasn't planned. In my defence, the staff have often encouraged me to bring in old photographs, diaries, scrapbooks … to show my own mother. It's part of the therapy to try to get patients to interact, and it seems to work. Because of that, I didn't think it would have such a profoundly negative effect on Diana."

Idris Parry shook his head, his breathing slowing to normal. "I hope and pray for your sake the family don't make a formal complaint. This could be a nightmare to handle if it goes to court, and it goes without saying it would end up in another IPCC investigation. And that's the very last thing you or I need."

Amanda nodded, accepting he was right. "I am sorry. It's only words I know. But it's the truth."

Idris Parry sighed, seemed on the point of blasting her again, then shut his mouth. "How are things looking at the hospital this morning?"

Amanda shook her head. "Not good. Machines are keeping her alive. They're giving her every chance but they're not hopeful she'll make it. The family are due back in around now. I guess decisions will be made then."

"Lord help us. Well, all we can do is pray." Idris Parry crossed his arms. "Putting all that aside, did you learn anything of value? Tell me again why you think a missing person from half a century ago can have any bearing on a double murder enquiry today?"

Amanda gave the DCI a succinct recount of her findings, her search through missing person's files following the accuracy of the report from the forensic anthropology department at Bangor Uni, pin-pointing dates and skeleton information, that made a match a relatively easy task.

"How sure are you?" asked Idris Parry.

"Personally, I'm ninety-nine percent certain. But we've traced the victim's sister, who has given a DNA sample, so we should be one hundred percent soon."

"And why so convinced there's a connection? Someone mentioned this lake was a sacred place, who's to say what's been thrown in there over the years. Like you said, there can't be many people around now who would have known this fella. Forty odd years is a hell of a long time. What are you thinking … retribution?"

Amanda wrinkled her nose. "I don't know. Not your normal revenge style killing that's for sure. Neither Peter McDonald nor Gregory Chapman could have had anything to do with Patrick Kavanagh's murder – neither of them were even born."

"Exactly my point …"

"But the connection has to be the hotel or the lake. Has to be." Amanda moved her mouse to bring the screen to life. "In fact, Kelly was briefing me on more information that's come in regarding the first victim, McDonald. We think our suspicions the murders might be related to homosexual activity are looking more likely. That was evidence first highlighted from the post-mortem and now validated by new eye witness testimony. Only verbal at the moment, but the chap is due in to give a statement later this morning." She turned the screen around. "Here, this is the email she sent me following a conversation with Gethin last night. He's gone back out to the hotel first thing … then he's going to look around some of these known hot spots."

She waited while Idris Parry scanned Kelly's summary.

He cleared his throat. "That could be relevant, could be how the killer is sourcing his victims. But there are still gaps. Unless I'm missing something, we don't have a link between McDonald and Llyn Maelog Hotel, unless it's a tenuous link to knowing the owner via their combined love of water sports. And from the other angle, we may have a link to the hotel with Gregory Chapman – but do we have any proof he was homosexual or involved in any of this cottaging business?"

Amanda shook her head. "You're right on both counts, sir.

That's exactly why DS Evans is heading back to the hotel as we speak. Hopefully we'll be able to tell you more by this afternoon's briefing."

"And then we're back to your skeleton. Diana Glenowen was scared, so you say, about some kind of secret. But you have no idea what it is or if it's linked to these deaths." He sighed, propped his hands on his knees and got to his feet. "Seems to me you're getting closer. You have all the pieces to the jigsaw, now you have to make them fit."

"That's exactly how I feel, sir. And we will."

"Well, do me a favour and make it quick. If we have a gay serial killer, we need it stopping before another body washes up or we end up having to go public which will terrify the gay community. Get it solved, Gold, and get it solved fast."

"Yes, sir."

"And keep me briefed about Mrs Glenowen. I hope she pulls through."

With that he was through the door, slamming it behind him. Amanda sat back and released a pent-up yawn. It could have gone worse, in fact, it almost definitely would have done had she not been able to show him progress had been made. Full marks to Gethin on that score.

She looked up at a knock on her door. It was Kelly. "Ma'am, just received a call from Dr George at Bangor University, she's emailing you the DNA analysis, but happy to confirm a genetic match between Ruby Kavanagh and the skeletal remains. She's definitely his sister."

Amanda realised she'd been holding her breath and let it out in a steady stream. "Okay, so now we have one more difficult question to ask, in light of Gethin's new evidence." She tapped her fingers together. "Kelly, can you contact Ruby and let her know about the DNA results, but could you also ask whether she knew if her brother was gay?

Bring it up in conversation, and see where it leads, will you?"

"I'll go and make the call." Kelly turned to leave. "And I came to remind you I'm leaving shortly to meet Gregory Chapman's parents at Manchester Airport."

"Ah, of course. Yes, off you go. And where are the others?"

"Fletcher has started a trace on any other missing gay men or gay related attacks in the area in the past five years. And Dara is meeting Peter McDonald's boss who has flown down from Aberdeen. Gethin you already know is on the tricky task of discovering Greg Chapman's sexuality, then he's going to snoop around some of the sites he found on the internet. He said he'd be back for this afternoon's briefing ... and I hope to be too, their flight lands at twelve o'clock." Kelly checked her watch. "In fact, I need to get a move on. Catch you later, ma'am."

Amanda took a deep breath and pushed open the door to the ICU. It was one of the last places on earth she'd have chosen to spend her lunchtime, but some invisible thread kept pulling her back. The waiting room was deserted, and the receptionist looked up with a smile as she approached.

"Can I help you?"

Amanda showed her identification. "I was hoping for an update on a patient, Diana Glenowen, and if there's a chance of seeing her for a few minutes?" She checked the wall clock. "I believe lunchtime visiting started at one pm?"

"If you'd like to take a seat, I'll find out for you."

Amanda chose to stand, pacing the room, making a concentrated effort to ignore the disinfectant smell. The walls were covered with leaflets and posters about smoking, obesity, diabetes. About flu injections and STDs. About hygiene rules and super bugs. It always amazed her that human beings managed to function daily, without giving much consideration to their general well-being, when in reality it was such a precarious job to stay healthy.

It was only when your life, or that of someone you loved, hit a brick wall, when a diagnosis including the terrible word – terminal – was given, you realised the remarkable gift you were about to lose. She'd seen that reality dawn in her mother's eyes not long after the initial diagnosis of Alzheimer's some six years earlier. The social care team had been doing their job, filling in forms, ensuring her mother got the level of care she'd need, and her mother had simply stopped mid-sentence and began to scream, shocking everyone in the busy office. The moment Amanda's life changed for ever …

"Mrs Gold?" The receptionist was back. "I've spoken to the nurse, she will page Dr Ashok to come down and speak to you. There are two visitors with Mrs Glenowen at the moment, so I can't take you through, but I've let them know you're here."

Amanda smiled. "Thank you."

The door opened and a white-coated Indian doctor approached, hand outstretched. Amanda had spoken to the same doctor in the early hours of the morning, and she briefly wondered at the length of his shift. His smile was still bright, his manner courteous, and his hair was a smooth, silky black, not a strand out of place. He looked as if he'd arrived at work fresh within the past hour, when Amanda knew he had not.

"Detective. Please take a seat."

Amanda followed him to the seating area.

"Mrs Glenowen's children are with her, and we have been looking at the initial test results. I am pleased to say there has been some improvement from last night, and we have taken the decision to keep her induced for another twenty-four hours."

"That's good news, isn't it? What are your predictions?"

The doctor shook his head. "It is still too early to judge. The part of the brain responsible for functional skills, everything from breathing to speaking, has been damaged, of that there is no doubt. But the tests we are doing now, will show us both the extent of the damage, and if the damage is irreparable. But it takes time, I'm afraid. Keeping her ventilated is the safest option for now, even though it is risky with her age and illness."

"I understand. And it's answered my query. Diana isn't going to be up for questioning any time soon?"

Dr Ashok shook his head. "Afraid not. Even if we take the decision to wake her tomorrow, we won't know her condition for some time. Patience is required as I have explained to the family."

The doctor got to his feet as a pager clipped to his pocket began to beep. "You will excuse me. Speak to you again." He hurried away, disappearing through the swing doors back into the ICU.

Amanda sighed and got to her feet. She had her answer.

"I'll make a move," Amanda said to the receptionist. "Please let Mrs Glenowen's family know I was here …"

Amanda broke off as the double doors opened and Eliza Glenowen appeared. Their eyes met and Eliza smiled. Amanda's felt a bubble of relief pop in her stomach. There was no anger in the woman's eyes even though she must have known Amanda was with her mother when she was admitted.

"Detective Inspector Gold. I heard you were here."

"I've spoken to Dr Ashok. The news is more positive today."

Eliza nodded, but there was a pained, distant look in her eyes. "Apparently so … though you wouldn't think it sitting in there. We are going with a rota, I'm leaving Stephen here while I get some fresh air, then I'll go back in while he heads to work. It's overwhelming after a while. Mother already looks like a corpse, I know that sounds awful, then there's the machines, and drugs, and noises … it's like a bad sci-fi movie."

Amanda reached out and squeezed Eliza's shoulder. "It's tough. How about we go down to the café and I'll buy you coffee?"

Eliza gave a sad smile. "If you could make it a green tea, that would be great."

The open-plan coffee shop took up a large area of the hotel lobby, decorated in bright colours, with comfy sofas, and long high-stooled bars, it had the look of one of the high-street coffee chains. Amanda carried the tray with the green tea, flat white coffee, and two flapjacks across to the quiet corner window seat where Eliza was examining her reflection in a pocket-sized mirror.

She looked up and grimaced. "I look like death warmed up. Which probably isn't the best analogy given the surroundings."

Amanda smiled. The expensive black silk blouse and tight jeans looked crumpled, as if they were the first thing she'd put her hands on, probably from the floor of her bedroom when she woke. Her face was make-up free, except a touch of lip gloss, hair scooped back into a tousled knot, but Amanda wished she could look half as refined with so little effort.

"Hardly. And I think you can be forgiven under the circumstances," she said, transferring the drinks and plates to the low table, and sliding the tray beneath.

"I'm afraid mine is somewhat self-inflicted. I have the habit of seeking solace in alcohol when life gets tough. And then regretting it for a long time afterwards." Eliza yawned and reached for the steaming cup of greyish liquid. "In fact …" She broke off and shook her head. "No matter. Thank you for the tea, let's hope its cleansing properties get to work fast."

Amanda stirred her own coffee … what had Eliza been about to say? Something to do with Plas Coch? It wasn't going to go away, better she got in first.

"I'm so pleased there's been an improvement in your mother's condition, things looked decidedly touch-and-go for a time last night."

Eliza bobbed the tea-bag in her cup. "I know. Total nightmare and so out of the blue. We were grateful you were there, detective. The staff do an excellent job, but they are stretched. Who knows, it might have been too late had you not been with her when it happened."

Amanda's stomach relaxed and she realised the tension she'd been holding inside for the past eighteen hours. "It was pure luck. I'd stopped in to say hello. It all happened very quickly."

"Your mother is at Plas Coch?"

"Almost three years now. They're brilliant. I'm so thankful they look after her so well. It appeases at least a fraction of the guilt I feel."

Eliza took a sip of her drink and closed her eyes for a second. "Ah, that's good. Don't talk to me about guilt. I never knew it could have such an effect on a person. From the day Stephen and I made the decision we couldn't care for mother on our own any more, it's felt like I'm dragging this huge weight around with me, all day, every day. And I know my brother feels the same."

"When was that?"

"November time. We looked at options, getting in a day nurse and caring for her ourselves at night, that sort of thing. Not looking at cost, but what would be the easiest for her to deal with. But the symptoms seemed to change each day, and the deterioration speeded up. And not knowing what we'd be faced with, we couldn't see how we could cope. We looked at a couple of places, but Plas Coch was the best by far. Still …" She waved her hands in a circle. "… the guilt doesn't go away, even though we know we've done the best thing possible in the circumstances."

Amanda sipped her coffee. "And now this."

Eliza sighed. "And now this. Although … and here's yet more guilt … there's a part of me, quite a big part of me in fact, thinks it might be for the best. Mother is in no pain, she could quietly slip away now, and save herself god knows how many years of further indignities and suffering." She paused, swallowed hard. "Does that make me sound like a bitch? I couldn't say that to Stephen, because he'd hate me, but you see, my beliefs teach us death is a natural part of living. It's part of the circle, part of the cycle. And knowing my mother as she was, she'd hate this. Absolutely hate it with every atom of her body. So, why prolong the suffering?" Eliza's eyes shone bluer than ever with fresh tears.

"I can't argue with any of that. You should say it to your brother though. You never know, he might agree with you."

Eliza sniffed and shook her head. "He wouldn't. It's all about the sanctity of life with him. Life is life no matter how crap the quality. It's the Catholic school upbringing in him."

"Well, then I think there's no guilt in saying it's left in the hand of whichever God you believe in to pray for the best outcome for your mother."

Eliza's face was pinched in anger when she looked up. "But what if that God is cruel and heartless and little more than a puppet-master? Don't we have the right to make our own choices?"

"There are things you can do. I take it your mother didn't make a living will?"

Eliza shook her head. "Death wasn't something we ever discussed in our family. I always had the feeling my father thought himself immortal, and would have been utterly shocked to discover he wasn't. And my mother did whatever my father told her to."

"Then maybe you could talk to Dr Ashok about a 'do not resuscitate' notice. He'd give you all the advice you need. It's one option. People are here to help you at these times, you know, you really aren't alone, even though that's often how it feels."

Eliza took another drink and broke off a tiny corner of her flapjack, popping it into her mouth and brushing her fingers. "Maybe a sugar rush will help clear my head. I can't remember when I last ate."

"You must look after yourself."

"I know. But there's calories in alcohol, right?"

Amanda smiled. "Most probably, but little in the way of vitamins. Eat your cake."

Eliza saluted with a gentle smile. "I can hardly believe on top of this drama, we still have Gregory's death to contend with, and all the stuff going on at Llyn Maelog. It's like a bad Stephen King novel, don't you think? How much more horror can we take?"

Amanda finished the flapjack and brushed crumbs from her skirt, washing it down with the last of the coffee. "I admit I was hoping in time your mother would recover enough for me to carry on a chat we were having about the hotel."

Eliza looked up, mid-chew, and gulped. "My mother was well enough to hold a conversation with you? Wow, you must possess some superpower I don't. What sort of chat?"

"About the past, actually. One thing I've learned from the staff at Plas Coch is many patients relate much better about the distant past than they do the present. I've taken old family holiday photos in, and my mother has happily recalled tales of camping trips to Devon and Cornwall. It's something to do with the particular areas of brain that are affected. Lord knows, I'm no expert, but it does work."

"I've been reading some of the leaflets they gave us at Plas Coch, but nothing I've tried has connected with my mother. She is obsessed with natural history programmes and can't bear my brother to be out of her sight. Me? She hardly notices if I'm there or not. Does a lot for your ego, doesn't it?"

"I'll say. Yesterday, my mother refused to eat tea at the same table as me because she thought I was a servant."

Eliza put a hand across her mouth. "Really? I'm so sorry, it's not funny, but if you didn't find some of it amusing, you'd spend every day sobbing. It's an unimaginably terrible disease, isn't it? As hard for those of us watching on, as it is for the poor souls suffering. What did mother say about the hotel, then? Was it all tales of her and daddy at their peak, entertaining the aristocracy of North Wales? Or her favourite story about when Edward VIII and Mrs Simpson came to stay in a top-secret visit?"

Amanda smiled. "That's another tragedy, isn't it? All the brilliant stories we lose to dementia." She looked down and cleared her throat. "No, actually, I showed her a photograph of someone who used to work at the hotel in the 1970's to see if she recognised them."

Eliza drained her tea. "Did she?"

Amanda shrugged. "I'm not entirely sure. She mentioned something about it looking like 'Harry's boy.' But that wasn't the name of the person's father, and his own name was Patrick Kavanagh, so I'm not sure what she meant. Unless Harry was a head gardener or something. Does the name mean anything to you?"

"Harry's boy? Sounds like the name of a horse to me, but my brain isn't wired like everyone else's, so I'm told. Did we have a gardener called Harry? It's not a name I recall." She shook her head, then her eyes widened. "Oh, hang on a mo. Daddy had an elder brother called Harold. Uncle Harold. He'd been injured in the Second World War, can't remember the details, shrapnel wounds and something with his spine, I think. I have a vague recollection of him coming to Pen Halen, sorry, that's our house, once … and he was in a wheelchair. But he died when I was, oh, seven or eight. I wonder if that's who she meant. But he was Harold, not Harry. And he never had a family because of his war wounds. Oh, you've got me thinking now!"

Amanda made a mental note to run a search on Harold Glenowen when she got back to the office, and chided herself for not having thought of it already.

"Anything you come up with will be gratefully received."

"Is it important?"

Amanda paused. "I think it could be."

"Well, I'm sorry I wasn't around in the seventies, though I've heard all the talk of those days. Stephen may know more about Uncle Harold, I could ask him, and I can look at the staff records if they go back that far. Do you have the photo, by the way?"

Amanda reached down to her bag and retrieved the computer print-out from the missing person's website.

Eliza took it from her and studied it in silence. "Nice looking chap. Sexy flares. I don't know him though, can't see any resemblance to anyone either, certainly not Uncle Harold." She peered at the photo. "It's a shame it's so blurred, but if I'm not mistaken, the photo is taken around South Stack lighthouse. I used to go climbing out that way, and that's definitely Holyhead Mountain in the background. As for who it is, I can't help. It's so curious you say my mother thought she knew him … you've got me intrigued now. Do you have a copy of this, I could ask around?"

"Take that one. Your mother also mentioned a story ... a secret, she said. Then she mentioned your father, Oliver. And something along the lines of it wasn't their story to tell, or it wasn't their secret to keep. The chap in the photo went missing you see, in 1976, and was never found. I had a feeling your mother knew about it. Or more likely your father told her. I could do with uncovering this secret." Amanda leaned across the gap and squeezed Eliza's wrist. "But no pressure. Goodness knows, you've more than enough to cope with now."

"Yes, but I also relish having a chance to switch off when I can. This will give me something to get my teeth into. I wonder if the secret was to do with Uncle Harold? How bizarre. Leave it with me. I'll ask around, some of the older staff have been with us years, maybe not forty though ... but they might know something." She frowned. "Harry's boy ... still say it sounds like a horse."

"Well, if you have any luck," Amanda fished in her handbag again, "here's my card. I'd appreciate you updating me about your mother too."

Eliza took the business card, slipped it into her jacket pocket, and checked her watch. "I should get back and take over from Stephen. He's keen to see Gregory's parents are settled in at the hotel, they're flying in today, I assume you know?"

Amanda nodded as she got to her feet. "Once of my officers has gone to meet them at the airport."

"Really? Stephen should have gone, then with this happening, he had to send our brother-in-law, Terry." She held out her hand to shake. "Thank you for the chat and the tea. It's the best cure, don't you think?" She tucked the printout into her bag as she stood. "I'll do some digging and let you know."

"Thank you. And let's stay positive your mother will be well enough to ask in person again soon."

Eliza smiled, but it was a sad attempt, and failed to reach her eyes. As the women parted company at the lifts, Amanda knew Eliza didn't believe her mother would be having any kind of trip down memory lane ever again.

CHAPTER TWENTY-THREE

Amanda banged her ruler on the edge of the desk. "Right troops, settle down, I'm sure you've all got lots to discuss – I hope you have anyway – but let's keep it nice and orderly, okay?"

The buzz and chatter around the CID office fell to a hush, followed by the scrape and shuffle of chairs as everyone settled behind desks. As well as her team, and Idris Parry, there were half a dozen uniformed officers who had been pulled onto the enquiry to assist with the routine jobs. A sure sign the authorities on the upper floors were eager to see the case solved. Not as eager as she was.

"So, I'm going to go first if that's okay with everyone, as I have a new angle to discuss." Amanda walked to the white board at the front of the room, and tapped the ruler on a blown up shot of Patrick Kavanagh. "If you can turn to page one of the briefing notes, you'll see a detailed report from the forensic anthropology team at Bangor University, headed up by Dr Jenny George. Dr George has done a first-class report on the skeletal remains retrieved from Llyn Maelog, and as a consequence of good old-fashioned detective legwork mixed with a dollop of scientific DNA, we have both identified the person as one Patrick Kavanagh, missing since January 1977, and traced and spoken to his sister, Ruby."

Dara looked up from the report. "Where are you going with this discovery, ma'am?"

"I think there's a link between this death and our two killings. I don't believe it's a coincidence that random bodies turn up in this lake forty odd years apart. I don't buy it. Especially when you read page two of the report and see Ruby Kavanagh confirms her brother was once a gardener at Llyn Maelog Hotel."

A mumble of voices rippled around the room as people digested the information.

"So, you think it's the same offender, then and now?" said Dara. "That means they're either OAPs now or they started their killing spree whilst still in nappies."

A hum of laughter followed the same circuitous route. Amanda raised a hand to curtail the noise.

"Yes, I see that. I'm not sure I do believe it's the same person. But I feel the motive is the same … and that's where we start examining our latest new evidence –"

Amanda broke off as Idris Parry got to his feet. "Can I interject before you move on, DI Gold." He moved to the front and turned to address the crowd. "I agree with DI Gold about the roots of this crime starting with the 1970's disappearance of Patrick Kavanagh. There are clearly a lot of questions still to be answered. But in my opinion this information should be kept within these office walls, and under no circumstances leaked to the media." He gazed around the room as heads nodded, and Amanda looked down at her notes rather than make eye contact herself. "If we are right and the killer or killers knows we're getting close to a motive, and have discovered the original crime, it could have a negative effect on their behaviour. We need them to carry on believing our focus is on McDonald and Chapman. Agreed?"

Content with the positive response, Idris Parry retook his seat. Amanda's heart thumped, there was no way on earth she could tell the DCI she had already given now classified information to Eliza Glenowen. Amanda felt torn. She should be honest and tell her team, but what harm could it do to keep quiet and save herself another pointless showdown with Idris Parry. It was done now. Did she really think Eliza was a serial killer? No, of course she didn't … especially when she'd not even been born at the time of the first murder.

"Gold?"

She looked up. "Sir?"

"I said, when you're ready, please continue."

"Ah, right." She turned to the whiteboard again, and tapped the photograph of Peter McDonald. "So, as I was about to say, motive. Motive and opportunity. We have some exciting new information courtesy of DS Evans …" She paused, noting for the first time, Gethin's empty desk. "Where is Gethin?"

Fletcher shrugged. "He's not turned in yet, ma'am. Kelly reckons he's been cruising the gay hang outs, so we figure he's maybe enjoying himself a bit too much, if you know what I'm saying!"

As if on cue, the uniformed officers, nudged each other and chuckled. Fletch raised both thumbs and winked. Dara and Kelly looked unimpressed, and both had grave expressions.

"Anyone tried to contact him?" said Amanda, checking her watch. "It's gone six o'clock. I'd have expected him back in time for the briefing, whatever he was working on."

"His phone is off, ma'am," said Kelly. "I've tried on and off since I got back from the airport."

"No messages or emails?"

Kelly shook her head. Amanda glanced at Dara who repeated the gesture. An army of ants marched across Amanda's scalp and she shivered. She didn't like it when any of her team acted out of character. In her experience, there was usually a good reason behind it. And as Gethin was by far her most reliable and conscientious member of staff, this didn't get much more out of character.

"Okay, well, we'll discuss that at the end of the meeting."

She hurried through the rest of the briefing, adding notes to the whiteboard about Gethin's witness statement, McDonald's sexual behaviour, Dara's meeting with McDonald's boss, and distributing jobs for the following day, mostly house calls in Rhosneigr for the uniforms and a further look at local gay haunts for Fletch and Dara. She was aware of Idris Parry's eyes on her, burning into the back of her skull, even when her back was turned – and knew she couldn't tell him she'd broken yet another rule by passing on classified information to a potential suspect. Not when he'd come out and publicly backed her for the first time ever. And to be honest, right now, she wanted everyone gone apart from her core team, so they could discuss her missing DS.

The door closed behind the last of the chattering sergeants, and Amanda sighed with relief, pulling a chair in close to Dara's desk, and gestured for Kelly and Fletch to join the group.

"What do we know about Geth? Should we be worried?"

Fletch shook his head and spread his arms wide. "He's like a terrier, ma'am, you know that. He'll have got his teeth into something and lost track of everything else. It wouldn't be the first time, would it?"

"I'm not so sure," said Dara.

"Me neither," said Amanda. "Who spoke to him last?"

"I spoke to him last night," said Kelly. "He wanted to talk through the information about McDonald he'd heard at the Taboo bar. He asked me to brief you, and ensure someone would be in the office to take a statement from Aled Thomas. He said he'd tried to call you too, ma'am."

Amanda looked up, surprised. "Did he? I was at the hospital with Diana Glenowen, and so exhausted I don't even remember checking my phone. Who spoke to Aled Thomas?"

Fletch raised a hand. "Me. Nice enough chap. Left his details if we need to follow up on anything, and signed his name to everything he'd told Gethin about his relationship with McDonald."

"And Gethin said he was going straight to Llyn Maelog Hotel this morning to make some discreet enquiries about Chapman's sexuality in light of the new evidence. Right?"

Kelly nodded. "Yes, and then would check out some of the places Aled Thomas had pointed out to him as meeting places. I think he was hoping he might interview potential witnesses. But he definitely said he'd be back for this afternoon's briefing."

"Dara, can you get onto the hotel, see if he has been there today –"

"Oh!" Kelly put a hand to her mouth. "Sorry to interrupt, ma'am. I remembered something else Gethin said, and it seemed a bit odd at the time …"

"Go on."

Kelly cleared her throat. "He asked me to say sorry to Dara."

Amanda frowned. "What?"

Kelly glanced across to Dara. "He said to apologise for being a twat, and made me promise to tell you he's sorry. Almost like he wanted me to break the ice, but offered no more explanation either. Does it make sense, Dara?"

Dara rubbed the stubble on his chin, and Amanda noted his ear tips were a blazing pink. "Ach, it was something or nowt. He stormed off like a little fool after we'd been out to Rhosneigr talking to the surf dude. I got a bit wound up with his attitude and told him so. He's been a prickly little git with me for a week or so and it came to a head. I've heard nothing from him since, though, and I'm with the boss. It doesn't sit right." He got to his feet. "I'll go and ring the hotel, if that's okay with you, ma'am?"

Amanda nodded, recalling the earlier tension between them.

Dara moved to the furthest desk, checked through the file for the hotel telephone number. He made the call, intermittently speaking, and tapping his fingers together as he was kept on hold. From the body language, Amanda already knew the outcome before Dara slammed down the receiver and strode back across the room. Kelly returned with coffees all round, and Dara pulled out his chair with a grunt.

"Nothing. I spoke to the receptionist, some bloke called Matt Craig, an assistant manager, and that chap, Terry Jones. None of them have seen Gethin at the hotel today. I've left the Jones fella asking around, but I'm not hopeful. Try his mobile again, Kel."

Kelly pressed her phone's Redial button. Everyone held their breath, until she shook her head sadly.

Amanda sipped her coffee. "Okay, let's not start to panic. There could be a hundred and one reasons. He could be ill at home, not able to get word to us. Does he have a land line number?"

Kelly shook her head. "I don't believe so."

"Okay, so Fletch can you get onto IT please. Ask them to put a trace on Gethin's mobile or check for a ping back from the phone's tracker if it's switched off. Let's get that activated with immediate effect." Amanda took a further sip from her coffee. "In the meantime, Dara, let's you and I check out Gethin's home address, in case he's in bed with a bad case of man flu, shall we?"

Dara got to his feet and shook out his jacket. "Sounds a plan, ma'am."

"Kelly, can you text me his address, I know it's off Glynne Road … Seriol Terrace … but I can't recall the number."

"Will do, ma'am," said Kelly, making her way to her desk.

"And you're sure he didn't say anything else last night?"

"No, he rang me as he got into the taxi after leaving Taboo, and when he hung up he'd stopped off at the kebab shop on his way home. I could check there, I guess?" Kelly's eyes were wide. "I've got a really bad feeling about this. What if something happened to him after we spoke, like someone had followed him from the club or something?"

Amanda paused at Kelly's desk, leaned down, and squeezed her shoulder. "Calm and focused, remember? Leave it to me and Dara, we'll be back in no time." She popped into her office, grabbed her coat and bag, and hurried to catch up with Dara, throwing a glance back over her shoulder. "Fletch, update me on the mobile phone soon as possible."

Dara thumped his clenched fist on the front door for the third time as Amanda glanced up and down the quiet, narrow street.

No cars had passed in the five minutes they'd been trying to make themselves heard. A dog barked in repetitive fury, locked up somewhere nearby, and the air brakes of a bus down on the main road hissed to a halt. Dara dropped to a crouch and flicked open the letterbox, letting it shut with a slam.

"Nothing," he said. "Place is in darkness."

Amanda lowered her voice to a whisper. "We need to get in, Dara. What about round the back?"

Dara rubbed his chin, rasp of skin on stubble as he pondered. "I'm sure he said he parked his car round the back. You stay here, ma'am. I'll go and look."

"No way. I'm coming with you. If we've got to break in, I'd rather do it somewhere a little more discreet. If there's access for a car, there must be a back alley between the terraced houses. Come on, let's follow the street to the end and do a left."

Amanda was right. They turned left and left again, circling the high perimeter wall of the end terrace, and found themselves following a narrow driveway that ran along the back of the row, with individual garages on their right. Counting along eight houses, Dara slowed as they reached a double gate, just wide enough to squeeze a car between. The gate was open, muddy tyre tracks through the remaining icy patches. Most of the garden had been turned into a, now empty, concrete car parking space, with a tiny lawn leading onto the back yard.

A silvery light came from the narrow window, which Amanda assumed was the kitchen. The rear door was locked. With a quick glance over his shoulder, Dara used to his elbow to smash the smallest pane next to the handle, slid his hand through the gap and twisted the keys. The door swung inwards in a silent arc. Amanda took a deep breath and followed Dara into the darkness.

The silver light came from the display on the integrated cooker. Dara flicked on the light. The kitchen was clean and orderly. White units, black surfaces, a breakfast bar and one wall of electric appliances at the far end. Amanda noted a bottle of Famous Grouse whisky, half empty, on the nearest worktop. Washing-up was stacked neatly into the drier, breakfast dishes by the look, but there was no sign of recent cooking, no smells or mess. The room was very Gethin.

Dara had moved through the open door into the next room. "Hello! Gethin?"

Amanda followed into the front room, it was spacious and clean, but the air was cold and sterile, lacking the buzz of energy she usually sensed from recent activity. Two black leather sofas, either side of a smoked glass coffee table. One wall was filled with a huge plasma TV, surrounded by an assortment of computer games and consoles, and a modern gas fire designed to look like a log burner.

"Ma'am." Dara pointed to the empty whisky glass and a half-full bottle of mineral water, one at each end of the table.

"Could have had company?" said Amanda.

"An' he took the car, so I'd guess he was the one on water."

"But didn't Kelly say he'd been drinking when he called her? So, why'd he feel the need to sober up?" Amanda went across to the fire and touched it with her fingertips. "Cold. Probably last night then, not today, unless the visitor was a daytime drinker." She moved to the window, peered through the vertical slats of the blind, out into the gloom of Seriol Terrace. "Can you check upstairs, Dara?"

Dara exited through the only remaining door. Amanda listened to the thump of his feet on the stairs, then turned three hundred and sixty degrees in the centre of the room, ensuring she'd missed nothing of importance. She crossed to the small hallway, and inspected the coat stand. Gethin had been wearing a long, hooded, woollen overcoat most of the winter, black in colour, with the toggles. She recalled hearing Fletcher nicknaming Gethin 'Paddington.' And the Paddington coat was missing. She pictured a scene, pale slender fingers, taking his time to methodically fasten each toggle in turn. She prayed she'd see his precise little ways again soon, and she'd hug and curse him at the same time, like she would a runaway son. But on the plus side, nothing here said Gethin had left under duress, and there was no sign of violence. It looked as if he'd left willingly, and drove away, with or without his whisky drinking companion.

Footsteps thumped and Dara reappeared. "Bed's not been slept in, I reckon. Everything's as neat up there as down here. Pile of clean ironing on the top of the stairs, ready to put away. And the bathroom has been scrubbed recent. Not that there's anything to read into that, I've no doubt Gethin was a domestic goddess. He could never stand mess or dirt." Dara coughed. "Can't, I mean … he can't stand mess." He met Amanda's eye and his shoulders slumped. "Jaysus, ma'am. I can't believe we're doing this. What the hell has happened to him?"

"We should contact his parents, see if he's there or been in touch. There could have been a family emergency. Will you give Kelly a call, let her know we're about to leave, ask her to handle it with care. And see if there's an update from Fletch too."

Dara nodded, fishing in his pocket for his mobile, with a hand Amanda noticed had a noticeable tremor. She reached out and touched the back of his wrist. "This row you had. It's not connected, is it? You'd tell me …"

"Christ, no, ma'am. Of course, I would. It was summat or nothing." He swallowed, headed for the kitchen. "I'm regretting it now though, losing my rag, I mean. Wait till I do get my hands on him, the daft wee sod …"

Amanda thought of the last time she'd seen Gethin, pulling on his Paddington coat, and slipping his satchel over his head. His bag. She looked around the room, retracing her steps back out into the hall. No, his bag wasn't here. The rumble of Dara's voice broke through her thoughts and she hurried through to the kitchen.

"Dara, hang on, is that Kelly?"

He nodded.

"Ask her if she can check around Gethin's desk, is his bag

there? You know the satchel thing he used for his laptop. You didn't see it upstairs?" Dara shook his head and repeated the message, waiting, one hand cupped over the mouthpiece. "We're waiting on Fletch, ma'am, he's on the phone to Systems as we speak." He repositioned the phone. "No?" He shook his head. "It's not there, ma'am."

Amanda exhaled, not sure if it was good news or bad. Gethin went nowhere without his bag when he was working, which meant he'd left for work, and most likely the bag was in his car – wherever that was.

"Yes," Dara barked back into the phone. "What they say, Fletch?" He scowled. "Eh, where? Christ where's that?" A pause. "No, never. If I head to Llangefni, get the details texted to the boss's phone, okay? We're leaving now."

Amanda's pulse began to thump and beetles scurried through her intestines. Dara's tone had changed, not for the better. His calmness was rapidly morphing into fear. Amanda could almost smell it on him.

"What?" she said.

"We need to get going, ma'am." He stopped abruptly at the back door. "Damn. Let me ring Kel again, send a glazier out to secure this door. I don't like leaving it, but we have no choice …" Dara was already pressing redial on his mobile.

"Dara!" Amanda tugged his sleeve. "Slow down. Tell me what Fletch said?"

"Yes, course, right. Sorry. The phone is pinging back from some remote spot, woods Fletcher reckons, near Llyn Cefni."

"Where?"

"Exactly. It's a reservoir near Llangefni. Fletch is going to meet us there. Take the Benllech Road out of town, he said, and he'll text us directions. He reckons it's out in the middle of nowhere." He lifted the phone to his ear. "Kelly, we're leaving Gethin's but I've broken a window pane in the back door. Can you call the emergency glass bloke and get a uniform out here to watch the place till it's done? Sorry, gotta dash."

Amanda struggled to keep pace with Dara's long-legged gait as they retraced their steps back along the alleyway, out onto the road, and back into Seriol Terrace. Dara pressed the alarm button and paused at the driver's door, staring over the roof of the BMW as Amanda caught up.

"He's gone off on his own, to one of these gay cruising spots, hasn't he?" His face was sweaty and angry. "The daft eejit. Has he no brains!"

Dara climbed inside and slammed the door, Amanda followed suit. "We don't know what's happened, Dara, no point jumping to conclusions."

"Why else would he be roaming woods on his own, in the dark? Unless he's found himself a new past-time. And why's he turned his phone off? He knows the rules, does he not think we'd be worried, selfish little sod!"

Amanda swallowed down the rising panic, knowing it was out of character for Gethin to break any rules.

"It's his mobile they've traced, Dara. We don't even know he's with his phone. It could have been stolen. Take a few deep breaths, okay, and stay focused. There'll be time for ass kicking later."

Dara managed a wry smile, and turned out on the main road, heading for the A55. "Sorry, ma'am. You're right, of course. But I think the world of the little shite. And I ain't going to let him forget it ever again."

Amanda's fingers curled around the strap of her handbag and she tightened the leather between her hands, as if somehow, subconsciously, she could slow down the speed of the car by tugging on these make-believe reins. It didn't work, of course. Dara kept his foot to the floor, and the narrow road out of the centre of Llangefni flew past the windows in a blur of fractured colours.

"Next left, I think," Amanda said, glancing at the Google Maps image on her phone. "Slow it down a bit, Dara, it looks a tight turn … and you don't want to be scrubbing tuna pasta salad off your carpets for the next week."

Dara released the accelerator a fraction, and the engine tone changed, as a sign post with a brown square announced their arrival. The BMW roared off the road, spitting gravel off the underbody of the vehicle as they sped along a narrow track, which in a hundred or so yards, opened into a car park, enclosed by high fir trees. The outlines of four or five cars were visible between the trees, most in darkness, a couple illuminated by the dull glow of mobile phones.

"Ach, sure it looks like a cruising site. But where is he?"

"Just do another tour of the perimeter, Dara, I thought I saw another track, leading off to the right."

Dara reversed the car, engine squealing, and spun round to face the way they'd entered. He grunted as he saw there was a further car park area away to the right, another half dozen or so cars hidden in the shadows of more regimented rows of pines.

Amanda squinted. "There! Far corner. Look. I'm sure that's Gethin's Vauxhall."

"Yeah, looks it. Check the registration, I remember his ended YOG and he called it Yogi Bear. Daft sod."

As they approached, YOG shone like a beacon from the rear number plate, illuminated by its yellow surround. Dara stopped the car, yanked on the handbrake, and jumped out leaving the engine still running. Amanda caught up, breath jammed in her throat, as he yanked on the driver's door handle. Locked. Amanda walked around the car, pressing her face to the glass, cupping her eyes. The car was empty, nothing in the front or rear, and she could see thorough the tailgate window, the boot area was also empty. Her breathing steadied a notch.

"He's not in there. And the keys aren't in the ignition." She turned as the sound of an engine started up, headlights illuminated the forest floor. "Dara, stop them! No one leaves this car park without speaking to us first."

Dara ran across to the white van and thumped on the

window. Muttered voices followed. She pulled her torch from her pocket, and paced around the car a second time, checking the floor for scuff patterns, or dropped items. Clear. There were, however, a single set of footprints leading from the car, away towards the entrance, where they disappeared into an area of broken tarmac, flooded with semi-frozen potholes. She heard another car engine, and looked up as a red Ford sped towards her. Fletcher had arrived.

He too screeched to a halt and jumped from the car, headlights blazing, and ran towards her. "Anything?"

Amanda shook her head. "He's not here. The car's locked. Do a quick walk through of the area before we start to panic, in case he's gone undercover or having a piss in the woods."

"Will do."

"I'll come with you. I'm not taking any chances. Thirty minutes' maximum search time and then I'm calling Kelly for back-up and SOCO. I'll want every inch of this car park and the surrounding woods going over with a fine-toothed comb." She exhaled, forcing a smile as she saw the downcast expression on Fletch's face. "We'll fine him, don't worry. It's our job."

CHAPTER TWENTY-FOUR

Gethin groaned and rolled over in bed. His head pounded, and for the life of him, he couldn't remember how much alcohol he'd consumed, but it must have been a hell of a night. Dara's face popped into his head. He remembered their petty argument, and moaned aloud. That explained the alcohol. He usually drank to forget, though it rarely, if ever, worked. It left him feeling like this ... like death warmed up, like his liver had liquefied, like he'd never touch another drop of beer in his life again. But he would drink again, of course he would, that was the way his life rolled.

But, oh boy, he seriously couldn't remember the last time he'd felt so rough. He needed to take a sneaky peak at his alarm clock, his inner body clock was telling him it was a work day – but he couldn't risk opening his eyes in case it made him feel worse. It wasn't just his head either. The pain seemed to radiate down through his body, his neck, shoulders, spine ... even his sodding legs throbbed like he'd run a marathon. But his head ... Lord he couldn't describe the pain inside his skull right now.

Okay, deep breaths. He had to do this. He'd count down from ten ... then sit up on the edge of the bed and open his eyes at the same time. Double whammy.

Ten ...

He remembered the quiet Sunday afternoon pint.

Nine ...

Recalled the smell of sweaty, dancing bodies at Taboo.
Eight ...
Clinking bottles with Aled Thomas.
Seven ...
The bumpy taxi ride. Kelly. 'Tell Dara, I'm sorry ...'
Six ...
Dirty kebab burning his tongue. Hot chilli sauce.
Five ...
Famous Grouse. Eliza.
Four ...
Hampton Court Maze. Locked gates.
Three ...
Stephen Glenowen.
Two ...
Oh, good Lord ... Stephen Glenowen.
One ...
Where?

He pushed his body forward, swinging his legs towards the floor, and urged his eyelids upward.

Three things happened.

Instead of the balletic move he'd imagined, his weight swung him sideways and he toppled onto his side, rolled ninety degrees, and ended up virtually face down, suspended like a puppet on broken strings. The second thing was that he no longer had any functioning arms, total numbness below his shoulders and he couldn't feel his hands. Thirdly, his eyes didn't work anymore. He experimented. Open. Close. Open. Nope ...nothing. It made no difference. This couldn't be real, could it? Maybe he was dreaming.

And there was another thing. Fifth? Sixth? He wasn't on a bed. He wasn't on anything. His cheek was pressed hard against something that felt like rough brick. He inhaled a smell like chimneys. With a giant lunge, he kicked out and twisted his body back the way he'd been lying before his dramatic dive, screaming as his feet connected with something solid. Cautious now, mumbling, he inched and shuffled along, until he was in some resemblance of a sitting position, legs crossed, feet tucked beneath him, wallowing in self-pity. His shoulders screamed in agony, not because he'd lost his arms, because they were strapped tightly behind him, something burned hotly into his wrists.

He slumped forward, counting in his head, allowing his brain and body to settle into this new life. He needed to calm himself down and do what he was best at – analyse his predicament. He blinked. He wasn't blind, he wasn't in bed, it was the environment that had changed. Wherever he was, it was cold, dark and he was trussed up like a Christmas turkey. The questions tumbled over themselves, pushing and shoving.

Where was he? How had he got here? Who had brought him here? Why?

"Ma'am!"

Amanda grunted and sat upright. She whimpered as a muscle clicked in her neck, and her spine retorted in a spasm of pain. She'd fallen asleep in the passenger seat of Dara's car, forehead slumped against the side window, her breath casting a misty fog, through which she could see a blurred orange dawn creeping through the branches of fir trees.

"Ma'am!"

The voice was accompanied by a gentle shake this time. Amanda turned to find Kelly leaning across the driver's seat with a steaming cup in her outstretched hand.

"Kelly," Amanda mumbled, wiping her chin for imaginary drool. She accepted the cardboard cup of what smelled like coffee and stretched. "Thank you. What time is it?"

"Almost half eight. The dog team have arrived, they're waiting on instructions."

Amanda nodded, wincing as she took a sip of the milky coffee.

"Sorry," said Kelly, dark eyes peering from beneath long dark curls and a navy bobble hat, "the coffee isn't the best. I stopped at the supermarket in Llangefni and realised my mistake on the first sip. And you know … my first thought was how Gethin would complain like hell …" Her face crumpled and she sniffed.

Amanda swallowed and sat upright. "It's wet and it's warm and it's welcome. Days like today make you reassess your priorities."

Kelly backed out of the car. "Too right. I didn't bother going home last night, no way would I have slept. I've been going over everything he said on the phone, but there was nothing in his voice that rang alarm bells with me. I was more nosy about the tiff with Dara. I wish I knew what happened after we spoke. I know we all do. If anything has happened, I'll never forgive myself … no, that's enough of that." She stopped, one hand on the car door and reached into the inside jacket of her parka. "Oh, I printed this off the internet. It's a map of the reservoir and surrounding area."

Amanda took the folded sheet of paper. "Thank you. Did you go out to Gethin's place and bring some items of clothing?"

"Yes, a dressing gown off the back of the bathroom door and a couple of dirty shirts from the laundry basket." Her voice caught in her throat. "The glazier turned up while I was there, so the place should be secure by now."

"And his parents?"

"His mum spoke to him on Sunday afternoon, he was due at theirs' for dinner but called it off, blaming work. It hadn't concerned them, I got the impression it wasn't the first time. Neither of them have heard from him since."

"They're not panicking, I take it?"

Kelly shrugged and wrinkled her nose. "They're not idiots, ma'am. I'm sure they could hear concern in my voice. I promised I'd get back to them later today."

"No, I'm sure they're not. Let's hope we have something to positive to tell them. God willing."

"Finish your coffee, ma'am. I'll let the handlers know you're on your way."

Amanda took another pull of coffee through the hole in the plastic lid, removed one muddied boot and massaged her foot, straightening the sock which had bunched around her toes. Her calves ached like she'd completed an early morning gym session, when in fact it was down to the hours she'd spend slipping and sliding through frozen mud and blackened brambles, yelling Gethin's name until her throat was raw.

The track behind the car park twisted in and out of trees, a good mile and a half to the far end of the lake, growing increasingly dark and dense the further they ventured into the forest. They'd come across a tumbled down shack, once a bird watcher's hut she thought, as she'd slithered down the reservoir bank to look inside. Empty apart from the remains of a camp fire and discarded rusty lager cars. They saw nothing and no one on their way back to the car park, and once Fletch had dispatched the last of the 'dirty doggers' as he insisted on calling them, the place was silent and deserted. Other than a lone fox that meandered across the track, returning once or twice to investigate, and the distant screech of a bird of prey, the woodland had been at peace.

Amanda wished she could say the same for her brain. Nothing would connect, no matter how hard she tried. And the harder she tried, the less made sense. None of the men questioned at the Llyn Cefni car park had seen the Vauxhall turn up, most had been pretty certain it had already been there when they arrived. Not knowing exactly what time Gethin had vanished – between the ten pm phone call to Kelly and the afternoon briefing at six pm the following day – did nothing to assist the confusion swirling around in her head. But she had come up with a plan in the early hours, issuing orders via phone to Kelly back at the office, and waiting with impatience for first light to arrive. Now, she intended to circumnavigate the whole lake as many times as needed to be sure no clues were missed. It wasn't a thought she would allow herself to dwell on, but if Gethin was here, in any form, the dogs would find him.

She yawned, stretching as she climbed out of the car

and headed to three black Ford Transit vans parked near the entrance. SOCO were still here, working on the area around Gethin's Vauxhall, and out on the road, a recovery truck's diesel engine rumbled, ready to take the car back to the laboratory for a forensic examination. So far, she was relieved to hear no blood had been found ... DNA might however be a different matter.

As she approached, a police handler opened the back door of one of the vans, and four excited dogs – two spaniels and two German Shepherds – leapt from the cage within. They dashed round in excited circles, barking like a pack of Beagles ready to join a Boxing Day hunt. She wished she had a tiny percent of their energy, and said a silent prayer their reward would be a successful conclusion to the search. She opened the map Kelly had supplied, turning it one hundred and eighty degrees, to get her bearings with the road, and gestured for Fletch to join her.

She cleared her throat and tapped the map as he approached. "Just let me check ... we're here, right? This car park to the north east of the lake?"

Fletch nodded. "Yeah, this part is a nature reserve, much of the southern end is a private fishery – you know fly fishing and stuff – with no public access."

Amanda frowned, tilting the map so the weak rays of sun fell onto the paper. "And what's this?" She pointed to a line on the map that seemed to cut the reservoir roughly in half.

"I've been Googling it actually, as I wasn't sure," said Fletch. "It's an old disused railway line built on a low wooden bridge across the lake. Called 'Lein Amlwch' – apparently it used to go from Amlwch Port to nearby Gaerwen and join the main line there, back in the days when the copper mines at Amlwch were open and the town was thriving. Dunno how long it's been closed, but I guess it's still passable on foot." Fletch also tapped another dotted line that led south in the direction of the town of Llangefni. "I do know this is a cycle lane, Lon Las Cefni, I've biked it a few times myself in the past, it follows the river, Afon Cefni, down into the centre of the town."

"So, as well as car parks at the north east and south west corners, we've got those two access points to check out too. And these rivers that feed the reservoir – what's that say …?"

Fletcher lowered his head. "You've got Afon Frogwy coming in from the west, and Afon Erddreiniog from the east. But I don't think either would be used for access, I know for certain the Erddreiniog leads out to some pretty marshy fens. If it were me, I'd suggest we split the dogs into three groups, one to work on either side of the lake, and a third to check out Lon Las and possibly the railway track, depending how overgrown it is when we get there."

"Yes, I agree. Can you and Dara take one each, Kelly and I will double up with the third. If you find anything at all, call me and we'll come to you." She paused and scanned the area. "There were prints leading from Gethin's car, have SOCO come up with anything?"

"Dara was talking to them a few minutes ago, they took photos and an imprint to match patterns, but the steps disappeared into the undergrowth. Trainers though they reckon, size ten."

"A man …"

"Yeah. And once they get the car back to the lab who knows what they'll find."

"No sign of his bag though? Or his laptop?"

"Nothing."

"And SOCO have taken his phone?"

"Yeah. Fingerprinted, bagged and tagged. Battery is dead but it will be ready to analyse when we get back to the office … that's if we've not found him drunk in a ditch and given him the hiding of his life in the meantime."

Fletch's tone was dry but his face was tired and set in stone.

"I would love that to happen," said Amanda, draining her cup. "But something tells me it won't."

Gethin counted to one hundred and twenty in his head, filled his lungs and strained his neck as high as he could, sinews stretching, imagining himself as a tiny defenceless bird in the nest, begging for food.

"Help!"

Right now, he felt every bit as tiny and defenceless himself. As well as a thousand other disconnected emotions setting off spasms like fireworks in his body and brain. He listened, cocking his head to one side. Silence. He started the counting again, somehow he could count and think.

Despite the thick blackness pressing down on him like a blanket, in the past few minutes, half hour, three hours – time was an irrelevance – he'd seen two grey slits of light at the top and bottom of what he hoped was a doorway. The door looked to be halfway up a wall, suspended in mid-air, so Gethin assumed there were steps, but when he'd put his mind to checking out his assumption, he'd realised whatever was binding his wrists behind his back, was also connected via a thick chain to a hook or similar metal attachment in the wall behind him. He couldn't see it, but he could feel it. In effect, he was chained up like a rabid dog.

One hundred and eighteen, one hundred and nineteen, one hundred and twenty ...

"Help!"

Neck strained, muscles strained, ears strained. Silence crackled like fracturing ice. He'd never known silence had a sound, but it did, it creaked and moaned and replied in its own way. He sighed, started the count again.

Yes, it was most definitely daylight. And the dusty corners of his brain were sure the strengthening shafts of light indicated a rising dawn, which meant it must be Monday. Or was it Tuesday? He wasn't sure if he'd slept and couldn't work out if he'd been here two hours or two days – and what use was that to anyone? What kind of a detective was he? The kind who allowed himself to be whacked over the head and carted off to god knows where. Not the best kind.

His mind had started piecing the jigsaw together, and when he'd first come up with the analogy he'd had to physically fight back tears. It was the boss's saying, building the jigsaw, piece by piece, getting the edges in shape. He hoped and prayed with every fibre of his body they were doing that now. Did they even know he was missing? He'd not been at work, so no one would know he was in any kind of danger. As it was, he'd been doing Eliza Glenowen a favour and delivering her home safe and sound. What happened with Stephen Glenowen hadn't been planned, and he certainly hadn't seen it coming … so how could it have any connection with this?

One hundred and nineteen. One hundred and twenty …
"Help!"
He listened, eyes focused on the silvery slits. Silence.

There was a serial killer out there, one who had already disposed of two men – two gay men – in Llyn Maelog. He could be number three.

No, he couldn't go there. Wouldn't go there.

He was a detective for god's sake. It was up to him to solve this. He was a fighter not a quitter. And he was part of one hell of a team of detectives and it was down to him to play his part right now. Think, Evans, engage your brain and think.

He'd been struck on the side of the head, something sticky, blood he assumed, plastered hair strands to his face. After collapsing he'd been brought here. He had to assume it was in his car as he'd been right next to it when he was attacked. So, he could be miles away from Pen Halen and the Bodorgan Estate now. He might not be on Anglesey – or he might be fifty yards down the road. He had no perception of the journey and no memory of anything – or anyone – until he'd woken and found himself here.

Think! Had there been anything said by either Eliza or Stephen to alert him to the danger? No, nothing. Plenty had been said – said and done. He'd found himself in the position where he could have ended up having sex with one or both in the space of a few hours. That was the biggest shock factor of the whole evening – and was it the reason he'd been kidnapped?

One hundred and twenty …

"Help!"

Silence. Now, concentrate on the surroundings. He licked his lips and tasted the air. Other than a dusty ashen taste coating his tongue, the air was cold and damp and sterile. The temperature had risen a little, although it was still freezing, but the increase made him think he was outside. He'd assumed underground, a cellar or similar, but the welcoming signs of daylight had changed his mind. There was nothing else in his dark cell to offer any clues. No sounds or smells. No distant traffic or bleating sheep or squawking pheasants. No saltiness on the breeze or petrol or diesel fumes in the air. He'd tried to slow his heartbeat down at one point, enough to make him extra alert to every sensory perception, but the exercise had yielded no results, simply left him light headed and gasping for oxygen.

So, until Amanda, Kelly, Fletcher – and his stomach clenched as he thought of Dara –

came to rescue him, which they would, he absolutely knew that, he had to sit here, conserve his energy, not think about his aching need for water and keep counting and shouting.

One hundred and twenty …

"Help!"

Amanda studied the mirror and grimaced at the reflection staring back at her. Damp hair pulled back into a tight ponytail, whilst eradicating some of the facial lines, gave her a cold and hard veneer. The lack of make-up, smudged mascara, pasty skin, and grey shadows around her eyes didn't help. She had the look of an old rocker, haggard and hung over, just off stage, minus his face paint. Harsh, no doubt. But in her eyes she looked at least a dozen years older than she was, and right now she felt at least another dozen years older than that.

The hot shower had eased some of the aches, but, as she pulled a fresh polo neck jumper over her head and fastened the waistband of her trousers, she still felt like an old woman who'd fallen down a flight of stairs and bounced off every one of them.

However, she had to leave every trace of pain and lethargy here in the bathroom. The afternoon's briefing would be a circus, she already knew that, and her stomach, despite its emptiness, turned somersaults as she imagined the circus ringmaster – DCI Idris Parry – already taking centre stage. He loved a drama, thrived off the notoriety of a big case, which was only one of the things she disliked about him. But she had to agree, no drama came much bigger than a missing police officer.

The hours out at Llyn Cefni had drawn a blank, neither human nor dog had found a single clue to say Gethin Evans had ever set foot in the car park – so she was willing to conclude from the pointless hours of tramping through frozen undergrowth he probably had not. Which then led to the deduction his car had been dumped, after he'd been taken and left elsewhere. But where? And was he still alive or …

She strode out of the bathroom, checking her watch and noting they had less than an hour until the six pm briefing. Hopefully, the team would have pulled some information together by then. She'd spent the past hour down in the workshops, watching white-suited SOC agents climb in and out of Gethin's Vauxhall, camera's clicking, voices a constant hum. And the first results she had scribbled down in her notebook weren't great, but could have been a whole lot worse.

All three remaining members of her team looked up with faces etched in various stages of exhaustion. Dara looked as if he'd not slept or shaved in a week, while Fletch managed a smile and seemed more alert., despite his washed out, crumpled appearance. Kelly looked drained but focused, her batteries wouldn't run out until this was over, she had an amazing amount of resolve. They wouldn't have thought of food, but she had to, they had a long night ahead and they needed energy. She raised a hand to say she'd be back in five, headed into her office, and rang the canteen, explaining the situation and asking for sandwiches and biscuits to be sent up to CID.

That done, she went back out into the main office and took a seat at Gethin's empty desk, ignoring the tightening in her throat as she did so. She needed to channel him, and there was no better place. If he were here now, he'd be smack bang in the middle of everything, and she wasn't about to leave him out because of his absence.

"Right, we have an hour. I've ordered food, so no arguments, all of you make sure you eat something when it arrives. We have to keep ourselves going." She opened her laptop. "Fletch, you first, what have you found on his mobile?"

"Frustratingly nothing, ma'am. Final calls were as expected. Two from Dara on Sunday morning, one returned. One to his mother around two o'clock. The call received from Alun Wyn Owens as he told Kelly. Then one to Castle Cabs. And the final one to Kelly. That's it."

"How about texts?"

"Nothing on Sunday apart from a random PPI message and an auto alert text about Rugby results. I've checked voicemail too, last one was from his bank asking to arrange a meeting three days earlier, and his mum the previous weekend. His personal email is linked through to the phone, it's not locked, so I've had a browse – nothing of interest – although I got the details of a couple of mates I've put to one side in case. I felt so guilty going through his stuff, I'm sure he'll kick my arse when he finds out."

"He'll understand, Fletch. We're only doing our job. Now we need to find his laptop. Is there any way we can locate those like we did with the mobile?"

Fletch shook his head. "No, it doesn't work the same. There's no phone number to trace. If he's used Google Maps on either of them, that would locate the location, but without having the IP address to hand it's impossible as far as I know. But I will put a call into IT and make sure."

"Damn. So, that's the end of that."

Fletch nodded.

Amanda sighed. "Dara, cheer me up. The men you spoke to out at Llyn Cefni, was there nothing at all of value?"

Dara rubbed his face. "Couldn't get a great deal of sense out of some of them to be honest, not because they were lying, more like they were stoned. Our first impressions might have been wrong, I think a couple of the solo guys in cars were on the prowl for sex, but the young kids told me they were there because of some computer game they play on their phones."

Fletch groaned. "Of course, was it Pokémon Go?"

"Yeah," said Dara. "I got one of them to write it down. I've Googled it since we got back here, not that it makes much sense to me. Seems you collect these Pokémon creatures which pop up here, there and everywhere … and then you have to find gyms at certain locations where you can do battle with your characters to score points and stuff."

Amanda raised her eyebrows. "How the other half live, eh?"

Dara nodded. "Bonkers. There's this alternative reality going on all around us and we're clueless. Apparently that particular car park is a well-known Pokémon gym, which is why it attracts a lot of attention. They're not all after sex."

Amanda rubbed her chin. "Is that relevant, you think?"

"What do you mean, ma'am?" said Kelly.

"Whoever dumped Gethin's car there … is he or she sending us a message?"

"Well, if they are it's lost on me," Dara growled.

"Hmmm. Maybe." Amanda shrugged. "I could well be grasping at straws that don't even exist. Kelly … the kebab shop?"

Kelly cleared her throat. "Yes, they confirm he was there sometime between ten and eleven pm. Alone. He ate in the café and left alone, giving the impression he was heading home. They know Gethin pretty well, said he's a regular customer, and judged him to be in a happy state of mind. I think happy meant slightly drunk, but not falling down smashed."

"Okay, so everything is tying up to what we already know. What's frustrating is there's a black hole in the eighteen-hour period crucial to us. What am I missing? Where else can we look?"

Kelly tapped a biro against her bottom lip. "The only thing keeps coming back to me is Llyn Maelog Hotel. Everything Gethin said on the phone has checked out one hundred percent – except the fact he said he would be going out there first thing the next morning but then didn't go. Why?"

"It's obvious isn't it?" said Dara.

"Not to me."

"Because whoever popped round to drink whisky at his house made damn sure he didn't get to work the next morning."

"But why? It makes no sense."

Fletch cleared his throat. "Three separate people who work at the hotel say he hadn't been there. We have no evidence to show he did either. I'm with Dara ... something happened overnight and he never made the appointment."

Kelly shrugged, but looked unconvinced. "Okay, then don't you think we should go in his place? He felt everything was centred on that hotel. Should we not be thinking it too? I know Geth is our priority, of course, but there's still a murderer out there. What if it's one and the same person?"

Amanda nodded, clicked her mouse to bring the screen to life. "I've been wondering the same. It's not a connection I want to make, but I don't think we can ignore it either. Dara, I'd like you to head out to the hotel first thing in the morning and speak to absolutely every member of staff who was on duty on Monday morning. Make sure nothing has been missed."

"Ma'am." Dara bobbed his head. "What did the lab rats find in Gethin's car?"

"Ah, yes. Not great. No fingerprints at all on the steering wheel or anywhere in the driver's area – it had been wiped and/ or the driver wore gloves. In the boot, there's a tiny stain could be blood, no bigger than the tip of a matchstick, which has gone off for testing. And, also they have recovered wool fibres from the grey nylon carpet in the boot. It's early days obviously, but the first thing sprang to my mind –"

"Gethin's Paddington coat?" asked Fletcher.

Amanda nodded.

"Shite."

"He could have thrown the coat in the boot before now, and carried it around in there …" Fletch trailed off as if realising the emptiness of his words.

Kelly shook her head. "He wouldn't do that. He loved that coat. I've seen him fold it up and lay it across the back seat like a baby. I doubt he'd have lobbed it in the boot, not really Gethin, is it?"

"No," said Amanda. "It's not."

The office fell into an uneasy silence; no doubt everyone could easily picture Gethin's

prone body folded into the small space, blood leaking from an imaginary wound. True, it was too easy to let your mind run away with you, but the longer Gethin remained missing, the more likely the scenario became. Amanda jumped as the door opened, and one of the canteen ladies arrived with a trolley loaded with trays and plates.

"Okay," said Amanda. "Let's get some food inside us. At least we have something to report at the briefing."

"But we're no nearer to finding Gethin, are we?" said Dara. "Another night. I don't think I can sit around eating tuna and cucumber sandwiches while one of me best mates is out there somewhere, maybe freezing to death, and more than likely praying we find him." Dara got to his feet and yanked his jacket from the back of the chair. "You'll not need me at the briefing, ma'am?"

"No, but … where are you going, Dara? We should stick together, I'm not happy with any of us going off alone on anything unauthorised at the moment."

"I'm a big boy an' I've got me phone, ma'am." He tapped his

chest pocket. "I'm going to retrace Gethin's steps on Sunday night, and then I'm going to start searching round these gay cottaging places. Don't worry I'll be out at the hotel at first light …"

"Dara …"

He spun round to face her, his expression drawn and angry. "Please, ma'am. I can't be here making small talk with Idris Parry right now or I'll blow. I've got to keep moving, an' please don't tell me I should go home and get a good night's sleep either, that's an insult, none of us will sleep until we find Gethin. Nor should we, because tables turned, he wouldn't." He broke off and drew a shaky breath.

Amanda shot a quick look at Fletch. She opened her mouth to voice her dissent, then closed it again, and searched Dara's steady gaze before relenting with a nod. "Just take care. For god's sake, no heroics."

"You got it, ma'am."

Fletch pulled himself upright. "Need company, mate?"

Dara studied him for a moment. "Aye. Can do."

CHAPTER TWENTY-FIVE

Gethin's heart jumped and he woke with a start. He'd been drowsing, he recognised the fact, but knew in an instant where he was, and the noise had come from the area of the door. His pulse thumped like a drum, so loud he could hear it in his ears. Adrenaline flooded liquid fear through his bloodstream and he almost wished he'd stayed asleep. He was safe in his dreams. He'd been with Ashley, one of those long summer holiday days of childhood that lasted forever in your memory, walking the high tide mark along the pebbled banks of the Menai Strait as they often had, carrying their fishing gear down to Hangman's Point, for an afternoon of sunbathing and putting the world to rights. Ashley had been inside his head for the past hours, ever since he'd watched the silvery slats of light fade to black, and knew he was going to spend another night in this prison.

He'd stopped counting when it fell dark. Eight hours of yelling at two minute intervals had yielded not one single response, so the chances of anyone answering in the pitch dark was zero. He had to be somewhere remote, probably on private property, no passing traffic or walkers, no nosy tourists, or busy farmers. Part of him missed the counting, the regimented routine he'd developed, but his throat was glad of the respite. His body screamed for water, and his head pounded with a pain he knew came from the onset of dehydration. He tried not to think what would happen next, how his brain would start creating an invisible oasis in the furthest shadows, out of reach of his chain.

He stopped, fully alert now as the noise came again. A double noise. A snap and a scrape. A thud and a scrape. Cool air rushed inwards and he was blinded by the brightest white light he'd ever seen. He clenched his eyes tight shut, corners flooding with tears from the flash of pain. Footsteps approached, thudding down stone steps towards him, and before he could react, something rough was pulled over his head and the light went out.

"Help me!"

Gethin found his voice and thrashed his legs back and forth, not sure what he thought he was achieving, but determined not to stay still and compliant, not to be a victim.

"Who are you? Please, what do you want with me?"

A boot buried itself in his right thigh and pain shot upwards, numbing his limb. Hands clutched his shoulders and dragged him forward. The pressure on his arms relaxed for less than a second as the chain rattled to the floor and was used to secure his wrists behind his back. Another chain tightened around his neck, individual links pinching into soft flesh. Gethin's brain flashed to post-mortem reports of the previous victims, and Dr Sixsmith's theory the same chain had been used both times. He screamed and kicked harder.

"Stop kicking." The voice was a whisper, so close to his ear he could sense warm breath through the hood. "We can do this the easy way or the hard way. It's easier if you walk but if you try anything at all, I can knock you out again and drag you. Understand?"

"Yes, but I don't know –"

A solid whack to the already bloodied side of his head rendered him speechless. Pain spiked and threatened to snatch the last threads of consciousness. He panted, fighting to get oxygen into his lungs, determined to stay alert.

"I'd rather you didn't speak unless you're spoken too," the voice hissed. "I'm not here for a chat."

Gethin forced himself to listen for anything recognisable in the voice. He needed to use all his training as a negotiator to try and make a connection, because that was the only way he could hope to make an escape.

As the chain around his neck yanked him upwards, he gagged and staggered to his feet on legs that had been prone for so long they no longer wanted to hold his weight.

"You're going to walk now." A low whisper. "Then we're going for a ride."

Gethin breathed hard as he managed to stay upright. "Drink. Can I drink?"

"You'll get to drink soon enough. This ain't no picnic. When we get outside, don't try anything. There's no one to hear you. And if you make a noise, I will slit your throat." The chain yanked him forwards like an unruly dog. "Nod if you understand."

Gethin nodded, tiny movements against the choking links.

"Up the steps, six, then outside. Silence. Understand?"

The choker bit into his flesh.

"Nod if you understand."

"Can't ... choking."

"Nod!"

Gethin nodded.

"Move!" Hands shoved hard between his shoulder blades. "Walk."

He closed his eyes and visualised putting one foot in front of the other, how easy it had always been, yet now it took every ounce of concentration. He felt as weak as a new-born lamb, and when his toes scuffed a wall, he stumbled onto his knees, feeling cold stone as he scrambled up the steps one at a time. The chain kept up a constant pressure on his neck. He sensed a breeze ruffle the hood and his throat closed as he was pulled to a halt. Footsteps followed, more thuds and scrapes, then with another shove they were moving forward. The ground felt like water-logged grass, twigs snapping beneath his feet, then it finally hardened out to a gravel path. He inhaled hard, trying to sense anything of the atmosphere through the thick material, but there was an oily smell that seemed ingrained in the fabric.

It was hard to walk and breathe, the hood stole most of the oxygen and his lungs were soon screaming for air.

Gethin staggered. "Can't breathe."

The chain yanked him upwards and he screamed. Another solid whack from a fist connected with his temple and his left ear rang with pain. The voice was a breathy rasp. "I said silence. Remember? Keep walking."

Gethin's feet crunched along the gravel surface. He tried to think how he could engage with his captor. Clearly, conversation wasn't going to be an option, his pain threshold was under threat, much more and he was certain he'd black out again. His lungs were pure torture and the searing sting in his neck burned like hot coals. He had to do something … and fast. He couldn't march onwards like a lost soul heading for the gallows. He wasn't far off delusional, he could sense the boundaries blurring, could feel the press of tears when he imagined a bottle of water. This was where madness started. He coughed and grimaced against the pain scoring his trachea and came to a halt as the chain on his hands tightened, pulling him sideways.

There was a bump and hands guided him forward. "Climb inside."

Gethin took a step backwards, knees shaking. "No, what is it …"

Another solid blow rattled his brain. "Climb inside. It's a car boot, lots of room. Curl up on your side." Hands pushed him. "Now!"

As he felt any opportunity to build up interaction slip away, Gethin shuffled forwards, knees touching a plastic bumper. Carefully, he dropped forward, relieved to feel the chains release their grip as he rolled onto his side. His arms screamed in agony as they twisted in their sockets, but his breathing came easier.

Then the car rocked as the boot slammed shut and the air was still and silent again. Tears stung. He'd been so compliant. It was shameful.

Amanda buried her face in her hands and took deep breaths. Idris Parry's voice echoed around the inside of her skull. He'd taken his role as circus ringmaster even more vociferously than usual, and for once, she had no strength to compete. She didn't care who gave the orders right now, if they were the right orders and it brought Gethin back into the fold.

She opened her eyes, cheeks pressed against her palms, and studied the swirls and lines ingrained into the faux pine surface of Gethin's desk. She wished she could read them, could convince herself there was some secret code here that could explain how they had – in Idris Parry's words – 'lost a senior detective in the middle of a double murder case.' She made a growling noise in the back of her throat, like a tigress warning against interference with her cubs. The DCI was insensitivity personified ... as if they had somehow mislaid Gethin on their travels.

"Ma'am!"

Amanda looked up, Kelly's voice cut through the hum of the office. She was holding her phone aloft.

"I've got Eliza Glenowen on the phone. She says her mother is awake and talking. She said you'd asked to be notified."

Amanda shook her head, brushing the call away with a flick of her hand. Then stopped, thinking ...

"No ... put her through, please, Kelly."

Gethin's phone chirruped and she lifted the receiver. "DI Gold."

"Hello, Detective, Eliza Glenowen here. I said I'd let you know how things turned out with Mother, and it's quite fabulous actually, she's amazed all of the doctors here with her recovery so far."

Amanda released a long drawn out breath, one burden lifted.

"I'm so glad. They brought her out of the induced coma successfully then?"

"Better than that, she reacted as if she'd woken from a sleep that's somehow recharged her batteries." Eliza paused, her phone crackled. "And who knows … maybe it has. She's having a bit of trouble with her speech and one side of her body is affected, but not to the degree the doctors feared. But it's like she has had a new lease of life, and none of the experts can really explain it. She even recognised me … for the first time in weeks."

"Eliza … I can't tell you how pleased I am, truly."

"And there's another reason I called. You asked me when we last met about Harry's boy – do you remember?"

Amanda sat upright. "Of course."

"Well, I'm not sure if I imagined it but I'm sure I heard Mother saying something about Harry or Harold. And muttering about the lady who helped her climb out of the TV. Is that anything to do with you?"

Amanda swallowed hard. "It might well be. Could I come over? Is she up for talking to me?"

"Well, the doctors haven't limited visitors. And I've no idea how long it will last, of course, but at the moment she seems up for talking to anyone who'll listen. If you have any questions, I think now would be a good time to ask them."

"Thank you, really. You've no idea how important this is. I'll be there within the hour. Thank you."

Machines beeped and buzzed as Amanda followed a nurse through the labyrinth of beds in the Intensive Care Unit. She kept her eyes fixed on the heels of the nurse in front, not wanting to see the occupants of the other beds, bodies prone and frail, wired up to machines whose whirs and rasps were keeping brains and lungs functioning. The black shoes stopped and Amanda pulled her gaze upwards, meeting the pale face of Eliza Glenowen. Her mother's bed was in a corner alcove, giving her a degree of privacy, and Amanda was pleased to see Diana was propped upright on her pillows, hands folded on the blanket in front of her. She wasn't asleep, at least her eyes were open, but she seemed distant, her gaze unfocused. With a smile, the nurse left them, and Eliza shuffled across to another seat, leaving hers vacant for Amanda.

"They're talking about moving her tomorrow, out to the High Dependency Unit, I think they need the beds for one thing, but it has to be good news for Mother too."

"Definitely. Can she hear us?"

"I don't know. She seems to come and go. Almost like she's fallen asleep but with her eyes open. It freaked me out to start with." Eliza leaned forward and took one of her mothers' hands between her own. "Mother … can you hear me?"

There was no reaction. Amanda's pulse quickened.

Eliza reached up and shook her mother's shoulder gently, fingers pressing into the peach cotton nightgown. "Mother? You were asking for Amanda, the lady from Plas Coch, remember? She's come to visit."

Diana's body twitched and she turned her head to one side, finally her face came to life and her eyes brightened. It was a gradual process as if the signals were slow or distorted. As she twisted her head on the pillow, Diana's eyes met Amanda's, and she smiled, a half-smile, misshapen by the stroke.

"Hello, Diana." Amanda leaned forward and squeezed a hand as soft as a velvet glove. "You're doing so well. It's lovely to see you again."

Diana gave a tiny nod, grimaced as she swallowed, and lifted one hand towards the beaker of water on the stand beside the bed. Amanda noticed a half bottle of whisky placed discreetly behind a plastic water jug. Eliza retrieved the beaker and held the straw until her mother began to suck, and smiled up at Amanda.

"Another improvement. She's been on an IV line for fluids." Eliza gestured towards the bedside table. "The nurses have turned a blind eye to us bringing in a nip of Mother's favourite tipple in case that's your detective eye having me down as an alcoholic. Although Grouse is my drink of choice too to be fair, blame my father for that one. If it keeps Mother content and reminds her of home it can only be a good thing, and I think the nurses figure if anything is going to kill her it won't be a drop of whisky."

Amanda nodded, desperately wanting to share Eliza's enthusiasm, while inside unsure this poor woman would ever enjoy a glass of whisky again, or be in any state to answer questions about an event that took place almost half a century ago. Wherever the combined ravages of dementia, and now a stroke, had taken Diana's mind, Amanda held no real hope that it would assist her enquiry. And every beep of the medical equipment around her reminded her of the passing of time, of Gethin's disappearance, and how crucial it was to make the right decisions. What if this was a wrong decision, what if it had nothing whatsoever to do with Gethin … or the murders … and she was simply wasting valuable time watching a frail woman cling to life.

Something in her expression must have registered with Eliza. She leaned forward and spoke low into Amanda's ear.

"Wait a while if you can. Once she comes back to us, it's not long before she's rabbiting away again, at least that's been the routine since she woke."

Amanda smiled. "No, no, it's fine. Sorry, I'm grateful for anything she can tell us, I have so much to juggle in my brain right now, I'm as apt to drift away as your mum."

"I can imagine. Since Stephen left, I've been trying to work out what she was talking about. She mentioned a photograph, then something about my father, then I'm sure she was talking about someone called Harry. Next minute she was pushing the blankets away and saying she needed to speak to the woman who helped her climb out of the TV. She became quite agitated – as if she was worried she might forget whatever it was she'd remembered. That's when I called you."

"And I'm very grateful."

"Do you think it's important?"

Amanda paused. "In all honesty, I don't know. I don't have any physical evidence to back up my theory, put it that way. But my instincts tell me the motive for these crimes is hidden in the past. I think your mum knows something that might be relevant. She was certainly at the hotel at the right time." She took a breath. "I'm hopeful. And I'm grateful under the circumstances you're allowing me access to speak to her. It's more important than you can imagine."

Both woman turned as Diana coughed and muttered something inaudible.

Eliza slid the empty cup back onto the side table. "What did you say, Mother?"

"The ... photo ..."

Eliza turned back to Amanda. "She was asking for it earlier, is it the one you showed me?"

Amanda reached into her handbag, passing a copy across.

Eliza held it up in front of her mother's face. "I don't have your glasses here. Can you see? Is this the photograph?"

Diana took her printout with a shaking hand. Her face was hidden from Amanda's view but she spent an age appearing to study the black and white shot of Paddy Kavanagh. Amanda's breathing quickened and she said a silent prayer ... please, please, please ....

A succession of words came from behind the paper, not all of them in any kind of recognisable order.

Eliza tapped the back of mother's hand. "Hey, we're here you know. What are you saying?"

The paper lowered and Diana's face appeared, eyes brimming with unshed tears. "So sad ... it was so sad. I wish ..." She shook her head. "No, I couldn't. Not then."

Eliza shot a glance at Amanda before leaning closer to her mother. "What was so sad? Can you tell us about this young man? Do you want to talk to Amanda about him?"

Diana swallowed. "Paddy."

Amanda's throat tightened. "Yes. It was Paddy."

Eliza gestured they should swap seats, and within moments, Amanda was close enough to hear the woman's breathing, stronger now, even though her face was still twisted in pain or grief ... or regret.

Amanda cleared her throat and tapped the discarded photograph. "Tell me about Paddy, Diana. Tell me what you know."

Diana's chin dropped and for a moment Amanda feared they had lost her again, but she drew in a deep breath and appeared to steel herself to begin.

"Paddy worked in the gardens," she said. "For three or four summers, I forget, we used to take on extra gardeners. He was a lovely boy. Sunny and smiling. Always ready to help. The guests loved him too. Everyone loved him." She paused, rubbed her hands together. "I suppose that was part of the problem."

She spoke in short bursts, with an intake of breath between each, as if the effort robbed her of strength each time. But her voice was strong and focused, and a feeling of relief swept through Amanda. Maybe this wasn't going to be a waste of time.

Amanda inched her chair forwards. "What problem?"

Diana gave a small shudder and continued as if unaware of Amanda's interruption. "A beautiful boy. Oliver reckoned even I was captivated. He was only a teenager though. I was a respectable married woman. I could have fallen for him. I see that, now. No, I saw it then. He was one of those very special human beings that bring a joy and zest to the world."

She stopped, breathed hard, and pointed to the water, the effort clear on her face. Amanda turned to Eliza and raised her eyebrows as her mother took a drink and struggled to settle her breathing. Even though Diana's words were slurred, they were coming across easier to understand with each word, as if once her vocal chords were lubricated she didn't want to stop.

"What was the secret about Paddy?" asked Amanda.

Diana looked down, bony fingers clutched the edge of the

sheets, twisting nervously. She took a deep breath. "Paddy disappeared. I didn't know at first but then the police came. Questions, questions. Last time I saw him he was getting ready to set off fireworks in the hotel garden. Midnight. New Year's Eve 1976." She coughed and Eliza pulled out a handful of tissues from the box and wiped drool from her mother's mouth. "1977 came. But I never saw him again." She swallowed and winced.

"Do you know what happened?"

Diana shook her head. "Of course not."

Amanda frowned. "But you suspected something bad happened to Paddy, didn't you? And you think your husband knew about it?"

Amanda heard a muffled gasp from Eliza but no one spoke for passing minutes.

Diana looked up and nodded slowly. "He wasn't certain. But Oliver had suspicions."

"He wasn't involved in Paddy's disappearance?"

"No, no. But he found out something that troubled him. Troubled him a lot. And he wouldn't talk to me about it. I was only a woman. 'Don't trouble your pretty head,' he'd say. But I did worry. I wondered for a long time."

"Wondered what, Diana? Why didn't Oliver go to the police?"

"Proof, I suppose. He had no proof."

"What proof did he need?" Amanda shook her head. "You're losing me now."

Diana cleared her throat, her eyes were beginning to droop. "Oliver suspected Paddy had been murdered. He never said as much but I knew him. He believed that. But had no proof."

"Okay, I see. But who did he suspect had killed Paddy? And why?"

Diana's eyes were beginning to cloud over and her chin slumped.

"Damn," said Eliza getting to her feet. "I think it's the drugs kicking in again."

Amanda leaned forward and squeezed Diana's hand. "Who did he suspect?"

Diana's thin torso jolted as if a current of electricity had coursed through her body. Her eyes opened and focused on Amanda's face. "Harry, of course."

"Harry? Who's Harry?"

Diana's eyes closed, and with a sigh, she slid back onto her pillows.

Amanda pulsed raced. "Damn it. So near, yet so far. Who is Harry? Or Harry's boy? What did she mean?"

Eliza Glenowen cleared her throat. "Actually, I think I might know."

CHAPTER TWENTY-SIX

Amanda hurried through the twisting hospital corridors, boots squeaking on the polished floor as she half ran, turning left, left, then right, then left, keeping one eye out for the Exit sign as she fumbled in her handbag for her mobile. Her heart pounded and her stomach rolled with constant waves of nausea. She tried hard to force herself to focus, needing to ensure she made the correct decisions in the next few minutes, because one wrong move now could prove disastrous.

With a surge of relief, she saw the rotating glass door in front of her, and pushed herself out into the dark night, inhaling a lungful of icy air, scrolling through her contacts with shaking fingers. She pressed Dara and waited, planning what next to say as her breath exhaled in white plumes around her head like a swarm of bees. But the buzzing noise she knew was in her head, surely her nerves audibly humming. The phone took long seconds, silence pressed against her ear as it attempted to connect, before an automated voice told her the number was temporarily unavailable.

"Shit!"

The word escaped in a yell and she smiled a brief apology to a passing couple heading up the steps into the main entrance. The signal was so patchy in this area; she could tell Dara was out of range rather than his usual trick of having his phone turned off or left in the car.

She searched her contacts for Fletch's name, waiting as the phone rang out once, twice, three times ... and then clicked onto voicemail. She swore, under her breath this time, urging on the recorded message until the phone gave a high beep.

"Fletch. Call me the second you get this message. It's urgent."

Trying not to let frustration boil over inside, she pulled her keys from her pocket and headed for her car. She couldn't afford to waste any more time, if she couldn't contact the guys, she would have to go herself, alone, and hope someone could join her later.

The car park seemed a mile away as she took long strides across the sleek black tarmac, dodging frozen snowy patches, picking her way between glistening streetlights reflecting in melting pools of lying water. There was something in the orange gleam that set a trigger in her brain. Something niggling away at her consciousness but was just out of reach. Come on, Amanda, think! What was it? What had she seen that was troubling her, but hiding in the shadows? Snow? Rain? No. Liquid. Maybe. Golden orange? No. Golden liquid. Light catching golden liquid.

She stopped in her tracks, put her hand to her mouth. The whisky. Of course. Famous Grouse. Oh God, now what should she do? If she was right, she was so close to the truth. She had to go back, had to ask, didn't she? But it didn't make sense, did it?

Aware she was wasting precious time having a pointless internal debate, she turned on her heel and ran back across the car park, slowing as she reached the entrance steps, through the frustratingly slow rotating door again, inching between the bustle of people in the busy reception, and retracing her steps down the corridors. She almost crashed into Eliza Glenowen who was exiting the bathroom outside the ICU department.

"Detective Gold, hello again."

"Eliza, sorry, this is important." Amanda spoke between gasps. "I remembered. Famous Grouse. The whisky, that brand, you said it was your drink of choice."

Eliza nodded. "All I drink other than the odd glass of wine. Why?"

Amanda exhaled. "There was a half empty bottle of Famous Grouse, and a half empty glass, left at my Detective Sergeant's house. Gethin Evans? And it seemed out of context, he wasn't a whisky drinker. I know this seems a bit random, but were you there? At Gethin's house … on Sunday?"

Eliza frowned, colour heightened her cheeks as she studied Amanda's face. "I don't know what that has to do –"

"It has everything to do with everything. Or at least I think so." Amanda reached out and took Eliza's slender wrist. "Please, this is important. It could be life and death important."

"What do you mean?"

"Gethin is missing, Eliza, and I think it's all connected with the case he was working on … with your sacred lake and your family history." She paused for the words to sink in. "Actually, I think you might have been the last person to see him before he disappeared. Believe me, I'm not asking because I'm interested in the love life of my team. I'm asking because you might be the only person who can save his life."

Eliza stiffened beneath Amanda's grip. "You are joking, right?"

Amanda shook her head. "I wish I was. I need to know, Eliza. And I need to know now. I must get moving, but coupled with what you told me about Harry and his family earlier … if you were with Gethin, I have to know." Amanda gulped down the persistent sting of tears. "Please, for God's sake help me, Eliza. Help, Gethin. Please, tell me. Were you with him on Sunday night?"

Eliza met Amanda's gaze and nodded.

The car stopped moving. The rumble of the engine and the vibration beneath Gethin's spine shuddered to a stop at the same time. His heart began to pound and his empty stomach growled. What next? Where were they? And how was this all going to end? So many questions, he could send himself mad trying to find answers to them all. And there was only one person who had the answers, and he wouldn't be revealing anything until he was ready.

Gethin squeezed his eyes tight shut as a door slammed and the car settled on its haunches. He wanted to pray the man forgot about him, left him here and went off on his business. But he wouldn't be so lucky, he knew that, there was a purpose to all this, an end goal. Gethin had the feeling he'd be finding out the conclusion to the story soon. And even as the idea of clawing back his professional skills, thinking of how he'd been trained to negotiate in these situations, he dismissed the plan. He knew he couldn't do it. This wasn't some faceless person whose life or death held no personal stake. It was easy then to remain detached, yet compassionate. Easy then to play the poker game and hope for a winning hand. This was different. This was real. This was his own life on the line.

He flinched as the car boot opened and cold air swirled around him. Hands grabbed the front of his coat and yanked him forward, bouncing his head off something solid. His ears rang and he took big gulps of air through the stifling hood. He had to keep his oxygen up, he had to keep mentally aware. He was no physical match for this guy, he knew that, any hope he had would come from his brain power, not muscle power.

Seconds later, he pitched forward and hit the ground, knees first, with a solid crunch. His hands dragged through freezing wet chippings of some kind, and although he knew it was night time, the air was heavy with animal noises. The screech of a distant owl, the whine of a fox, he was acutely aware in this world of blindness that his surroundings had changed. He breathed through his nose, inhaling hard, taking in the scents around him. The air smelled rich and heavy, laden with a mixture of saltiness and forest decay. His instinct told him the sea was somewhere nearby, but had no sense of sand or sounds of waves. He concentrated hard, hoping to pick up some small familiar detail, but as hands gripped the back of the hood and the chain tightened once more around his neck, dragging him to his feet, he was forced to admit defeat.

"Walk!" The voice was close to his right ear. "Walk till I tell you to stop."

Gethin swallowed, ran his tongue round the inside of his mouth. "Why are you doing this? Please can we talk?"

Something solid whacked him between his shoulder blades and he staggered forward, chain links biting into his throat, as his arms, still pinned behind him, tilted him off balance and he fell back to his knees and howled in pain and frustration. Every inch of his body screamed in agony and the overbearing need for water screeched even louder inside his brain. He couldn't move, he couldn't think. He was ready to quit and once that idea wormed its way into his thoughts, a weight lifted. He didn't have to fight at all. He could surrender.

Hands pulled him upright. "Walk not talk. Do it!"

Gethin shook his head and relaxed his legs, allowing his weight to crumple onto the ground. "No. Please. I need water. I can't do this. Do what you have to do but I'm not going another step."

A boot landed in his midriff, pain like he'd never known exploded air from his lungs and he fell sideways, gasping and writhing.

"Walk!"

Gethin shook his head again. "No. Enough."

A second kick connected with his back, his kidneys vibrated, aching in time with each pant as he fought for breath.

"Walk!"

Gethin took a huge breath and screamed a single word. "No!"

He twisted onto his side and curled himself into a ball, imagining himself as a hedgehog, protecting as much of his body as he could without his arms, steeling himself for the next blow.

But none came.

Seconds passed, Gethin uncurled himself one painful inch at a time, straining his ears for the next assault. When the voice came, it was some distance away, and it sounded sad, almost regretful.

"Why have you made me do this? Why did you have to get involved?"

Gethin sat up slowly, staying silent, wanting the other man to be the one doing the talking.

"It would have been okay, you know. It was over. Everything would have been okay."

Gethin swallowed, keeping his breaths quiet and regular.

"Then *you* came along."

Footsteps approached. Gethin tensed. A hard kick landed on his left thigh.

"You."

Kick.

"You."

Kick.

"You!"

Gethin screamed. "Please! I don't know why you're doing this but I'm not your enemy. Please, stop!"

The blows ceased, Gethin tried to find a less painful position, something hard like a tree root dug into the base of his spine, and his body throbbed where the kicks made contact. He could hear the man gasping for breath, and then with a moan, the heavy breathing was mingled with sobs.

"You've ruined everything!"

Gethin took a deep breath and ignored the pain as he scrambled to his knees, using his trapped arms to balance him from behind.

"Tell me ... tell me what I've done. I'm sorry, whatever it is, I'm s-sorry. We can sort this out. I'm not just saying that. There's another way to sort this out, between us, you and me, no one else need ever know."

The breathing grew quieter, the sobs dwindled away. "Don't talk to me as if I'm stupid. You're a cop. The whole cavalry will be out looking for you. There's only one way this is going to end.

But you need to know this is all your fault, there's no one else to blame, just you. Understand?"

"No. I don't. I don't understand at all. I'm confused and I'm s-scared. I'm begging you with every breath I have left to let me go and I swear to you I'll pretend this never happened." A sob escaped his throat, he swallowed. "Let me live. I beg you. Let me live."

The voice was little more than a whisper. "I can't."

Gethin's resolve crumbed and he began to sob. "Why? Tell me why!"

"You kissed him!"

The roar echoed through the air, like a gunshot, silencing their surroundings.

Gethin stopped crying, heart thumping. "What?"

"Don't deny it."

Gethin sensed movement, the man was stamping back and forth, his feet only inches from Gethin's face.

"I kissed … who?"

"Stephen. I saw you. I saw how he looked at you. How could you!"

The kick took Gethin by surprise, connecting with the side of his skull with the ferocity of a rugby drop kick. His teeth rattled, his neck snapped backwards, and a flash of pain shot along his spine, shooting pins and needles down in his hands. One more of those and he'd be paralysed. He wanted to close his eyes and go to sleep and never wake up, that seemed the only way to be sure this nightmare would end.

"It wasn't like that." He tested his teeth with his tongue, pronouncing his words with care as his brain continued to vibrate. "I was consoling him. Whatever you saw, that's the truth. There's nothing between us. Nothing."

"Yet!"

"I'm not interested in a relationship. You've got this all wrong. I told you so. We can put this right."

"You're lying! You think I can't tell? People have lied to me all my life. My own father lied to me because he was ashamed of me. Smashed my leg to pieces to stop me running away because he was a killer! He killed the person I loved because he couldn't live with the shame of having a gay son. So, I became what he wanted, lived the life he chose for me. I've seen how people use power to control others, and I wasn't going to let Gregory Chapman ruin Stephen's life like my father ruined mine."

"Then let's talk about this. Please. There has to be a way –"
"No!"
"We can." Gethin sobbed. "Please … I understand how you feel. I've faced the same prejudices, fought the same anger. I can help you …"

"What makes you think I need help?" Gethin's head yanked backwards and the words spat into his ear. "You're the one needing help. You think I'm going to go through everything I've done to protect Stephen just to let you stroll in and take him from me. Do you?"

"I don't want to take him anywhere –"

"I have to protect him! Don't you understand? Gregory Chapman was the devil. He got inside Stephen's head. He wanted to take him away. Australia! As if I could let that happen. I'd never let it happen."

"No." Gethin paused, steadied himself. Finally, he knew who it was. It was now or never. "And Peter? Why kill Peter McDonald?"

"Who?"

"The first body we found in Llyn Maelog. That was you too, wasn't it?"

"I was doing my job, protecting Stephen. I saw the way P.J. looked at Stephen one night at the beach. Knees touching as they sat round the fire. Laughing. I couldn't allow that. So, I followed him for weeks, found out he was a dirty pervert, probably a paedophile. I couldn't let a man like that get close to Stephen. Once I got away with it the first time, I knew I could get away with it with Chapman."

"You killed Greg Chapman because Stephen loved him?" Gethin regretted the words the second they passed his lips. "I mean because he loved Stephen …"

Hands grabbed the back of his coat and dragged him along the floor, the chain rattled and snagged beneath his body, choking him. He kicked back and forth, seeking purchase, trying to stop the chain tightening around his neck.

"Stephen doesn't know his own mind." The voice gasped with exertion as Gethin continued to slide along the ground, raking leaves and moss along with him. "That's why I have to protect him. No one will ever take him away from me. No one. Ever."

Gethin screeched as with a yank and a lunge he half flew, half tumbled through the air, and landed with a splash in ice cold water. The shock took his breath away, and, as he struggled for the surface, strong hands gripped either side of his neck, pushing him down, forcing his head backwards so water flooded into his mouth and nose. The chain loosened and the hood filled like a balloon, billowing upwards and over his head. He blinked his eyes against the sting of ice cold water. Above him a blurred outline hovered above the water, while hands encircled his neck, forcing him lower.

He kicked out, treading water, searching for the floor with his feet, trying to push himself upwards, head spinning and lungs already screaming for air. Panic kicked in as his life-long fear of drowning gripped him hard and sent adrenaline flooding through him. He twisted and flipped like an eel, using every ounce of his energy to keep his body afloat. He wished he could free his hands, without them, there was no way he could peel himself away from the other man's grasp. His throat was already closing, the pain coming from the pressure of thumbs into his windpipe sent tears flooding into his eyes.

Gethin blinked and twisted his neck from side to side, surprising himself with the intensity of his fight for life, but the grip was unfaltering, concentrated on the middle of his throat, trapping, he knew, not only his trachea but vital arteries feeding oxygen to his brain. Hadn't he seen enough strangulation postmortems over the years, learned all about broken hyoid bones and oxygen deprivation. Now it was a reality, this combined power of both the hands around his neck, and the underwater pressure, was sending shooting pains through his head as his strength dwindled.

He struggled for another minute or two, no more, before collapsing and drifting downwards, aided by the weight of his water-logged clothing. He was never a strong swimmer, and he'd no strength left now to try. His mind went back to Ashley and he felt a connection. As their lives had run similar pathways, so would their deaths. He liked that, had probably always known. There was a rightness about it. Although he'd spent decades fearing drowning, keeping away from open water as much as possible, in the end life was a circle, everything came back to where it started. He'd wanted to die after Ashley died. He'd wanted to be with his friend more than anything, and now he would, the years of loneliness coming to an end.

He gagged and bubbles swirled around his face, soaring upwards, the roar of a freight train roared inside his head.

Dara ... I'm sorry. I'm so sorry. I know you knew me, saw me, and I punished you for your insight. I wish I could tell you ...

As the hands around his neck released the vice-like hold, he spurted water out of his mouth and threw himself upwards as hard as he could in one desperate lunge. He broke the surface, aware of the night sky littered with millions of stars, guiding him on. He opened his mouth, launching himself forward at the pale face, bent low above the water, still in a crouched position. Baring his teeth, Gethin growled and he took a huge bite out of the man's cheek, tearing and snarling like a rabid hyena at a kill until a bloody chunk of flesh came free.

There was a shriek as the man staggered and fell.

Gethin knew he was signing his death warrant. He accepted it.

As he hit the water with a splash, he slid the flap of skin to one side with his tongue and closed his mouth tight, trapping it in his cheek cavity. A coppery taste filled his mouth and he tried hard not to swallow or spit out the bloody flesh. He relaxed back into the water, feeling the hands reach out for his throat one final time. Thumbs buried into his windpipe. Grey smoke billowed and swirled behind his eyes as the water rocked him back and forth.

He could let go now. He was ready to meet his maker.

And it wasn't too bad. If he ignored the thrumming pain in his head and his chest, it wasn't bad. He could cope. He could say goodbye to everyone …

CHAPTER TWENTY-SEVEN

As Amanda indicated to take the Gaerwen exit off the A55, her mobile buzzed into life. She pressed the Bluetooth button on the steering wheel as she registered Dara's name flashing on the display.

"Dara, thank God!"

"Ma'am? Your message came through on Fletch's phone an' he's driving. What is it?"

"Where are you?"

"Just left the Taboo bar in Bangor. Got chatting to a member of staff who remembers Gethin there on Sunday –"

"No matter now. I need you out at the Bodorgan Estate. I'm on my way but the bloody Satnav is taking me on a wild goose chase. I think I know where Gethin might be."

Dara inhaled with a gasp. "Right. We're on our way. Concentrate on driving for now and fill us in when we get there."

"Will do." Amanda flashed a glance at the map screen and cursed. "Shit. I've took the wrong turn. Listen, I think it might be quicker to take the coast road through Brynsiencyn and Newborough. I've gone A55 and it seems to have taken me miles out of the way."

"Right, I'll tell Fletch." Dara paused. "And ma'am … you wait till we arrive, you hear? Don't get doing anything –"

Amanda pressed her thumb onto the Bluetooth button, disconnecting the call with a beep, and accelerated hard.

The cottage was a Welsh picture postcard scene even in the bleakest midwinter night. Even under little more than the shimmer of a silvery full moon, and one ornamental streetlamp beside the front door, it was clearly a home that had been well loved. White walls, wooden shutters at each window, a sandstone pathway led to a glossy black front door. And tucked away in a small wooded valley in the quietest part of the Bodorgan Estate, Amanda could easily have driven straight past, had she not followed strict directions from Eliza Glenowen.

She banged the brass knocker one last time and exhaled, foggy clouds of hot breath surrounding her as she swallowed down her frustration, and took four steps backwards to stare up at the second-floor windows. The place was clearly empty. No lights inside, no cars parked in the driveway. No sign of life. So, where was he? She'd requested Kelly put a call into the uniformed officers stationed out at Llyn Maelog Hotel ... but he hadn't been seen since lunchtime service according to staff.

Amanda crunched across the gravel surface, following the line of the cottage, around to the rear, where a small, manicured garden nestled against a rocky outcrop. She paused at the rear door, more in hope than expectation, and gave a startled cry as the handle turned and the door swung inwards. She pondered for less than a second, before stepping inside, and easing the door shut behind her.

The kitchen was long and rectangular, moonlight glinted off white enamel and polished chrome. Everything was neat and tidy, no sign of recent disturbance, no cooking smells or dirty dishes. As she made her way from room to room, the house gave off the same sterile feel. Yes, it was a home, but it felt like a home without a soul. Once filled with life and love, maybe, now a cold shell of what it had once been. Upstairs, one bedroom was currently in use, a single bed and small wardrobe showing sign of recent disturbance, a discarded tie, folded clothes and a damp towel. The second room was clearly a marital bedroom, decorated in a 1980s' style, with roses on the wallpaper and matching duvet colour, and fluffy carpet in a wine red colour. The pine dressing table was still covered with jewellery boxes, dusty perfume bottles and make up. It was like walking into a time capsule, undisturbed, perhaps, since the death of his wife?

Amanda stopped at the threshold of the third room, heart pounding in her throat as she heard a noise beneath her feet. The creak of a door hinge. The soft tread of a footstep. Holding her breath, she retraced her steps to the top of the stairs and leaned out into the darkness. Whispered voices. A hurriedly concealed cough.

What to do?

Taking each stair one careful tread at a time, reaching out for a handy walking stick she'd seen resting beneath the coat stand at the bottom of the stairs. Whoever the intruder, it wasn't the owner of the house, who would surely have turned the key in the front door and flicked on the nearest light switch. She was taking no chances.

The muffled voices came from the kitchen. Holding the walking stick out in front of her like a rounders' bat she crossed the hall and threw the door wide.

"Christ alive!"

"Dara?"

"Ma'am!"

Amanda groped for a light switch. "God, you nearly gave me a coronary."

"I'll not say what you nearly did to me, but I'll need to change me pants sooner than planned this week fer sure. An' what in hell's name are you planning to do with that?"

Amanda gave a rueful grin and dropped the stick. "I came prepared."

"I can see that. Prepared for what though is another matter. Did I not tell you to wait till we arrived?"

"And of course that was going to happen. Where's Fletch?"

Dara nodded to a door in the furthest corner of the kitchen, hidden in the shadow of a large American style fridge. "Checking out the cellar. Anything upstairs?"

"Nothing. Place is pristine. Looks more like a hotel than a home. I guess it's a busman's holiday for him. Although the bedroom is a bit of a time capsule …"

Amanda broke off as Fletch reappeared brushing cobwebs from his hair. "Nothing down there apart from dust and old boxes of clothes and junk. Looks like he's a hoarder."

"And no sign of Gethin. What's the story, ma'am, why we here?"

Amanda opened her mouth to speak and stopped as the buzz of her mobile in her jacket pocket seemed to set the whole kitchen on vibrate. She frowned and accepted the call.

"Kelly?"

"Ma'am?" The voice was little more than a whisper. "Ma'am …"

"Yes. What is it, Kelly?"

"I …" Kelly cleared her throat. "I've had a call from PC Roberts, one of the uniforms out at the hotel I spoke to an hour or so ago. A guy's come jogging across to them, a local bloke out walking his dog, said he heard a commotion near Llyn Maelog, out on the far bank over in the trees …"

Kelly trailed off and Amanda glanced at the handset, thinking she'd lost reception.

"Kelly? Yes? What kind of a commotion?"

"A f-fight he said. Two blokes, shouting and splashing. Thing is, ma'am. He reckons there's one of them still out there, floating in the centre of the lake."

"What? Floating … as in … dead? Do we even know?" Amanda saw Dara's eyes widen. "Has no one done anything?"

"Roberts is on his way down there now. I've put in a call for back up too. I didn't know about a dive team? I said I'd call you for instruction and then head to the scene." She paused as if running out of energy. "Ma'am, do you think …?"

Amanda closed her eyes.

Amanda pulled her coat around her more tightly and tried to ignore the throbbing in her toes as the icy cold burrowed through the soft leather of her boots. She squinted and stared out into the darkness of the lake, letting the gentle splash of water, lull her into another place. She was so tired, even the muddy, churned-up surface around her feet looked comfortable enough to sleep on. She wished the divers would hurry up, the waiting was pure torture.

"You okay, ma'am?"

Kelly's voice beside her made her jump.

"I've certainly been better. I'm starting to hate this bloody place."

"I know. This is like a bad nightmare. I keep hoping I'll wake up any minute, preferably at home in bed … and confused."

"I keep thinking what if this eye witness made a mistake? No one else has come forward having seen or heard anything. What if there's nothing out there and we've been standing out here, freezing half to death, for god knows how many hours on a fool's errand."

"He seems reliable and totally certain of what he's seen," said Kelly, trying to stop her teeth chattering. "He's given a full statement to Dara and it's pretty conclusive."

"So, if there is a body … where is it?"

Kelly shrugged. "I put a call into Pathology. Dr Khan is on call … he reckons it has most probably sunk by now, once the gases have expelled and –"

Amanda raised a hand. "I don't think my stomach can cope with the details right now, thanks, Kel."

"You should get another hot drink inside you, ma'am."

"If I take another sip of caffeine, I think I may spontaneously combust." She watched the nearest of the two orange dinghies reach shallow water, do a one eighty degree turn, and make its way back across the lake at the same laboriously slow speed it had maintained for the past three hours. At the farthest bank it's identical sister boat, turned and repeated the exact same process, following the same precise grid pattern. "What's taking them so long?"

Kelly shook her head. "It's a needle in a haystack, isn't it? At least the sun will be up soon, extra light will surely help them –"

Kelly broke off as raised voices carried across the inky water. Torches flashed in the direction of the furthest rescue vessel as the lead diver came to the surface holding one arm aloft.

Amanda exhaled. "Looks like they've found something. Oh, boy, it's times like this I wish I had someone I could pray to. I don't think I can stand this. What if …?" She broke off, unable to continue, unable to say the words in case they became true.

Kelly's voice was thick with emotion. "Don't. Don't say it, ma'am."

As one of the two dinghies headed to shore with half of the dive team, Amanda made her way across to where Dara was standing at the water's edge, watching as the boat cut through the silvery grey water and got closer by the second. He nodded to Amanda, his face set tight and grim, but remained silent. She could tell in the tightness of his posture he was as terrified as she was, but there was no way he was going to show it. As the boat neared, the clearly defined form of a human body bag became visible through the misty darkness. The air fell still and silent as two men in waders jumped out of the dinghy and manoeuvred it onto dry ground, before carefully lifting the body bag and placing it on the grass.

Dara was there first, dropping to one knee, closing his eyes for a moment, in what looked like silent prayer, and then unzipping the upper section.

From behind, Amanda saw his shoulders visibly relax. She held her breath as he turned towards her, a look of pure relief on his face.

"It's the hotel manager. Terence Jones."

When the words Amanda had been waiting for failed to come, she found herself sniffing hard and blinking back tears.

"No sign of life. An' there's a wicked facial wound, looks like he's been slashed or glassed with something." Dara bent lower, unzipped more of the fabric. "He's fully clothed. I can't see any other injuries." He got to his feet, pulling his mobile from his pocket. "I'll ask Dr Khan to head down here."

Amanda released a sigh of relief and shook her head. "I don't understand. I thought I had it cracked. Have we got this totally wrong?"

Kelly appeared at her side. "Don't ask me. I'm as confused as you, ma'am."

"The eye witness said two men, didn't he? So, where's the other man? And was the other man Gethin or what?" She turned her back on the water. "Dara, can I leave you to clear up here? I'm going to talk to the Glenowens. And I want answers this time."

"No! This is a joke, right? Not Terry?"

Stephen Glenowen's eyes were wide and bright with tears as he stood behind his desk, supporting his weight with his hands, as his body seemed to sway like a tree in the breeze. He was pale beneath the usual golden tan, unshaved and casually dressed in jeans a white t-shirt. His handsome face had aged a decade under the weight of the news. In moments, Eliza was at his side, head on his shoulder, one arm wrapped around his waist, offering him wordless support.

Amanda stood her ground, legs shaking, not allowing herself to be distracted by the obvious show of grief. These people, either of them now in her book, could be suspects in a triple murder enquiry. She had to stay focused. She had to discover their secrets – the life of one her team was dependant on the outcome of his interview. She was sure of it.

"I'm really sorry for your loss, sir," Amanda said. "We'll need a positive identification, but one of my officers at the scene recognised Mr Jones. We're certain it's him."

Stephen ran a hand through his hair, before lowering it to cup Eliza's shoulder. "But why? It's like this family is cursed or something. What's going on?"

Amanda shook her head, remained silent.

Stephen exhaled a shuddering breath. "Terry has been like a surrogate father to me for so many years."

Eliza responded, but her words were muffled by lips pressed into her brother's shoulder.

"What?" said Stephen.

Eliza pulled away, looked up with hair plastered across a tear-streaked face. "Not me, Stephen. He may have been like a father to you … but he never really liked me."

Stephen held his sister at arms' length and studied her for several moments, anger and grief etched on his face. "Don't be ridiculous. Terry has been a rock to all of us and to this place. Quite honestly, I don't want to think how we will manage without him."

Eliza pulled away, shaking her head. "No. It wasn't like that. If Mother could tell you she'd back me up."

"What do you mean? Christ, why choose now to speak ill of a dead man?"

Eliza crossed to a chair and dropped into it with a sigh. "Don't be angry. Terry loved you, Stephen. Like a father, or something more, I'm not sure. Sometimes his devotion made me uneasy. But one thing I am sure about is he was jealous of the closeness between us, and he ended up resenting me because of it."

Stephen lowered his head, shaking it from side to side.

"Yes. Ask some of the staff. Ask Glenys Owen, she'll tell you. You were his life, Stephen, it freaked me out a little bit, but it's the truth."

Stephen opened his mouth to speak, then closed it again, and sat down, indicating Amanda and Kelly should do the same.

"We spoke to Mr Jones about his history with the hotel and your family," said Amanda. "We're aware it goes back a long way. You must be devastated by his death, but we do have questions we have to ask. I hope you understand?"

Amanda looked from brother to sister, and both nodded their acknowledgment.

"Your DS by the way …. any news?" said Eliza.

"Not yet."

Stephen looked up. "What's this?"

"Remember … Gethin? He brought me home the other night. He's missing."

If it were possible, even more colour drained from Stephen's face as he studied Amanda. "Really? Is it connected with this nightmare? Gregory. Now Terry." He dropped his head to his hands and spoke through muffled tears. "I can't believe this. It's like everything I touch …"

Amanda cleared her throat. "We seem to be thinking along the same lines, sir. You do seem to be the central focus of this case. Has Mr Jones said anything to you recently, given any indication there was a problem, or he was scared or upset about anything?"

Stephen sniffed and shook his head. "Terry has been a total stalwart through all of this. He's always been that way, and I've known him all my life. Said it was down to a disciplined upbringing … whatever life threw at him he could handle it. Even when Clara died. It was him who held the family together, held everything together, not the other way round."

"His upbringing … his father in particular. Did you know anything about him?"

Stephen shrugged. "Harry Jones? Not really. He worked for us his whole life but he was just a face from my childhood, really. We didn't have any connection with him, did we?" He turned to Eliza who shook her head.

"I didn't like him, always found him a bit scary as a child, with his bushy beard and staring eyes. Clara didn't like him either. There was a massive argument one time, I remember. She said he bullied Terry and always had done."

Amanda flashed a look at Kelly who gave the slightest of nods.

"Was Mr Jones, Terry … was he ever a bully?"

"No!" Stephen looked up. "Never. Maybe Eliza is right. Maybe he did love me, love both of us. I certainly felt more emotion from him than I ever did my real father. I won't have a bad word said about Terry. You've no idea how hard this is ..."

"I do, I promise you. And from what your sister says it was you who had the closest relationship with him. Are you sure you've not noticed anything odd ... any changes in his personality."

"No. If I'm honest Terry wasn't a talker. He was a listener. He was the 'go to' guy. I can't ever imagine him coming to me to talk about his troubles, it was always the other way around. Although ..."

Amanda looked up, aware Kelly had shifted position beside her.

"He made a will recently. Just last week actually. He asked me if I could put it in the hotel safe in the accounts office. Told me I was named as executor and he wanted me to know where it was in case anything ever happened. I presumed he'd been spooked by Gregory and everything ..."

"Is it in the hotel safe?"

"Yes. God. Do you think he had a premonition he was going to die?"

"I'm not sure, sir. But I think in view of the circumstances, we may need to have a look at the will. As it was made recently, it might answer some of our questions. Would that be possible ..?"

Muffled voices outside in the corridor broke into Amanda's train of thought. The door slammed open and Dara staggered into the room, holding onto the door for support. Tears ran down his face as his eyes searched the room, locating and locking onto Amanda's gaze with a look of pure pain.

Kelly gasped.

Amanda slowly rose to her feet as the room spun around her.
"No. Dara. No?"

Dara nodded.

CHAPTER TWENTY-EIGHT

"Why do they say the dead look like marble? They don't, do they? Not at all."

Amanda didn't expect a reply, but felt the need to fill the silence, as if it were her responsibility to ease the pain in the room. And she couldn't. She knew whatever she said, whatever she did ... she could never do that.

Gethin's face was the colour of putty. Eyes closed, lips raised into a gentle smile. He looked naked without his glasses, but totally at peace, as though he'd climbed into bed and fallen in a deep, relaxing sleep. Which he had in a way.

From the neck down, the peacefulness was shattered. Damson-coloured bruises ringed his neck, and from the base of his throat, a crudely stitched Y-shaped incision, joined between his nipples and continued down to his dark patch of hair on his stomach and beyond, hidden beneath a pale grey sheet.

Dr Khan joined them at the other side of the gurney. "I didn't think you'd want to come in person today. It was hard enough for me."

Amanda looked up and met Dara's steady stare. His skin was pale and greasy, stubble thick and unruly. He gazed back at her with sleep-deprived, red-rimmed eyes ... but he was there, at her side. Her rock.

"I didn't think I could either," she whispered. "But I couldn't let him down, could I?"

SACRED LAKE

She swallowed hard as tears flooded. She'd told herself she had no tears left, but each time they proved her wrong.

"It sounded important, doc," said Dara. "I wasn't going to let the boss come in here on her own. Gethin was my pal. I'll be by his side right to the end. It's what he'd expect."

Amanda took a step closer to the gurney, and reached out to brush an unruly curl from Gethin's forehead, as she recalled him doing so many times in life.

"We let you down, my sweet boy. I'm so sorry."

Dara moved closer to her side and gripped her elbow. "No need for that talk, ma'am."

"But it's the truth, Dara. He was on my team. On my watch. We let him take risks and those risks got him killed. I don't know how I can forgive myself." Her voice caught in a sob. "And you know what makes it worse – we can't even close the case and see justice done."

Dr Khan cleared his throat. "That's why I called you. I have something of interest you should see."

Amanda ran the back of her fingers across Gethin's jawline and looked up once her vision had cleared. "What's that?"

"Follow me. I'll show you. I'm pretty sure you can thank DS Evans for getting you the evidence you need."

Amanda returned Dara's questioning frown with a shrug, and followed in the pathologist's footsteps in a daze. In fact, her whole life had felt like one long tunnel of foggy confusion for the past twenty-four hours. Faces, voices, questions. Coming and going in an endless loop. The only light at the end of the awful tunnel was a text from Emily to say she was on the train home, following a call from Kelly. Everywhere she looked, eyes open or eyes closed, on her own in her dark bedroom or in the middle of a busy street … all she saw was Gethin's face. Smiling, cheeky, brave, adorable. The son she'd never had, never deserved, and had gone on to lose.

Kelly had made the trip to tell his parents in person. She had demanded the role, taking the decision out of Amanda's hands, backed by Idris Parry. And she was glad. Deep down, although she regretted what she saw as a dereliction of her duty as a DI, she knew it would have been a step too far for her. This past day, she had been forced to accept she was still human, carried the same emotion and frailties as the rest of the population, and sitting down with Mr and Mrs Evans and explaining the unexplainable – that their only son was dead – might just have pushed her over the edge into a fully-fledged breakdown.

Across at the work bench at the far end of the mortuary, Dr Khan positioned a stool in front of a microscope and zoomed into the object on the slide, displaying it on a computer screen.

"Remember when we recovered the body of Terence Jones from the lake there was a substantial facial injury?"

Amanda nodded.

"It wasn't the cause of death. As I explained he died from a vasoconstriction induced heart attack, most probably as a result of cold shock response from a sudden immersion in the lake. His heart was already weak and the extra work added by hyperventilation and inhalation of water sent his heart into spasm. However, it could have been aided by shock from however he received the facial wound … which was a bite mark."

Amanda frowned and tried to stay focused. "Go on."

"During the post mortem on the … on Gethin … I did a mouth swab and recovered these tiny skin and blood traces from the right cheek cavity." He tapped the computer screen. "I assumed at first they were from his own mouth, a bitten cheek or tongue, but when I tested the blood, it didn't match. Which puzzled me. So, I ran a DNA test on the samples and –"

"It came back as match for Terry Jones?" asked Dara.

Dr Khan nodded.

Amanda frowned, twisting to look back at Gethin's form as if she couldn't pull her eyes away from the reality. "I'm sorry. I don't think I'm getting what you two clearly are."

Dara sighed and gave a sad smile that brought back a hint of life to his tired eyes. "Typical of our Geth. He was being a top copper right to the end. He fought and took a bite out of his attacker. He did it for us, for his team. He wanted to leave us a clue. It might have cost him his life but I reckon he was right proud he'd been a policeman to the end. I'm right, don't you think, Doc?"

Dr Khan nodded. "That's exactly what I think, DS Brennan."

EPILOGUE

Evidence No: ML36/66/17.

LETTER TO STEPHEN GLENOWEN FROM TERENCE JONES LEFT WITH HIS LAST WILL & TESTAMENT.

Stephen,

If you ever get to read this, you will know the truth. Or at least a version of the truth. I left this letter for you because I wanted you to know the real truth, my truth.

I was seventeen years old when I watched my father kill the man I loved and planned to spend the rest of my life with … because he refused to have a gay son.

There. That's a sentence I never imagined I would write.

But that's my truth.

I watched from the bank of Llyn Maelog and did nothing, and that feeling of utter powerlessness has been a shadow across the rest of my life.

I won't go into details, you may well be able to piece together the puzzle, but know that the man I am now began to form that day.

From where I came from, I think I've lived a good life. I can imagine the scorn on your face but I'm not a bad man. Certainly not a mad man. Not like my father.

I am proud of my life. I have worked hard. I have tried to be a good son, good friend, good employee. I have tried to please everyone.

Everyone except myself, that is.

Despite that, believe me when I tell you I loved your dear sister with all my heart. She was my saviour and my strength. And I have tried to support you in a way my own father refused me. I was the one you told first when you came out, even when your own family secretly rebuffed you. I was there for you. And I would have done anything to spare you the pain I suffered.

Did I take it too far? In hindsight, yes. Gregory Chapman became a threat in my life I couldn't cope with. All those feelings of powerlessness came back and consumed me. He was going to take you away. From your home, your life, your family, your business ... and from me. Yes, I admit. It would have broken my heart.

To start with, I planned on scaring him off. Paying him off. I don't know. But then some obsession took hold and before I knew what I was doing, I was planning his death. Imagining how much better all our lives would be. And that's when the madness took hold, or the ghost of my father raised its ugly head. And well ... you know the rest.

I don't know how this will end. I don't know if I can live with what I've done, but I am trying. But know, everything I have done, has been for you, to protect and cherish you, because I love you, Stephen, as if you were my own flesh and blood.

I loved another man once and lost him. I love you and refuse to lose you too.

Hopefully, it will be a happy ending and one day I can be honest with you about how I feel. If not, and it ends with you reading this letter, at least I hope you will understand, even if you will never be able to forgive me.

Have a good life, Stephen.

Forever yours ... Terry x

THE END

Thank you for reading a Triskele Book

If you loved this book and you'd like to help other readers find Triskele Books, please write a short review on the website where you bought the book. Your help in spreading the word is much appreciated and reviews make a huge difference to helping new readers find good books.

Why not try books by other Triskele authors?
Choose a complimentary ebook when you sign up
to our free newsletter at

www.triskelebooks.co.uk/signup

If you are a writer and would like more information on writing and publishing, visit http://www.triskelebooks.blogspot.com and http://www.wordswithjam.co.uk, which are packed with author and industry professional interviews, links to articles on writing, reading, libraries, the publishing industry and indie-publishing.

Connect with us:
Email admin@triskelebooks.co.uk
Twitter @triskelebooks
Facebook www.facebook.com/triskelebooks